"Delicately put together, lik[...]
church at high requiem, wh[...]
together to color the world wit[...] [...] [...] melancholy,
that Irish sadness that never resides far from beauty."
—*Elle*

"Rossi explores the vagaries of fate from one side of the Atlantic
to the other with lush language and superb styling."
—*The Sun* (Baltimore)

"Rich and fascinating . . . Rossi is a subtle writer."
—*Cleveland Plain Dealer*

"Affecting . . . *The Houseguest* is about setting things right."
—*The Washington Post Book World*

"[A] compelling novel."
—*Los Angeles Times*

"A rare accomplishment . . . Remarkable for its
fluidity and grace."
—*Kirkus Reviews* (starred review)

"Wonderful storytelling."
—Elizabeth Berg, author of *Talk Before Sleep*

"Skillful prose and heartrending plot."
—*Publishers Weekly*

"Rossi's writing, as always, is downright beautiful, and the story
itself is moving and skillfully told."
—*Brooklyn Bridge*

AGNES ROSSI is the author of the 1992 story collection, *The Quick*,
a *New York Times* "Notable Book of the Year," and the 1994
novel, *Split Skirt*. She was a finalist for the 1996 *Granta* Best of
Young Novelists Award. Born and raised in New Jersey, Ms.
Rossi lives in Brooklyn with her husband and three children.

AGNES ROSSI

The Houseguest

a novel

A PLUME BOOK

PLUME
Published by the Penguin Group
Penguin Putnam Inc., 375 Hudson Street,
New York, New York 10014, U.S.A.
Penguin Books Ltd, 27 Wrights Lane,
London W8 5TZ, England
Penguin Books Australia Ltd, Ringwood,
Victoria, Australia
Penguin Books Canada Ltd, 10 Alcorn Avenue,
Toronto, Ontario, Canada M4V 3B2
Penguin Books (N.Z.) Ltd, 182–190 Wairau Road,
Auckland 10, New Zealand

Penguin Books Ltd, Registered Offices:
Harmondsworth, Middlesex, England

Published by Plume, a member of Penguin Putnam Inc.
Previously published in a Dutton edition.

First Plume Printing, September 2000
10 9 8 7 6 5 4 3 2 1

 REGISTERED TRADEMARK—MARCA REGISTRADA

The Library of Congress has catalogued the Dutton edition as follows:
Rossi, Agnes.
    The houseguest : a novel / Agnes Rossi.
        p.   cm.
    ISBN 0-525-94365-X (hc.)
        0-452-28197-0 (pbk.)
    1. Irish Americans—New Jersey—Paterson Fiction. 2. Ireland—History—Easter
Rising, 1916—Veterans Fiction. I. Title.
    PS3568.084694H
    813'.54—dc21   99-36122
                                                            CIP

Printed in the United States of America
Original hardcover design by Eve L. Kirch

PUBLISHER'S NOTE
This novel is a work of fiction. Names, characters, places, and incidents either are the
product of the author's imagination or are used fictitiously, and any resemblance to actual
persons, living or dead, business establishments, events, or locales is entirely coincidental.

To Dan, for being a smart and generous host

A NOTE TO THE READER

This novel got its start in the facts of my mother's early life. My mother's mother, Agnes Devlin, after living in America for several years, died of tuberculosis in Ireland in 1932. My mother's father, Edward Devlin, returned to America soon thereafter. My mother was raised by two aunts and attended a convent boarding school in Ireland. These facts shaped my mother's life and so my own. I grew up hearing stories. This story, however, is invented. The characters herein, *all* of them, are figments of my imagination, though some of them are named for and share certain other biographical markers with my relations.

Paterson city motto: *spe et labore*, with hope and hard work.

... the Latin root "spero, sperare" can be read either as "to hope (for good things)" or "to fear (ominous developments)."

—Philip B. Scranton, in *Silk City: Studies on the Paterson Silk Industry 1860–1940*

chapter 1

Shouting. Her father, her uncle. One and then the other. Both. God damn. The hell out. Wrong with you. Out, I said. Out of my bloody house before I. Bastard. The front door opened and closed, opened and closed again. A second door, inside the house, slammed so hard the bed shook. Voices in the street. A car starting, revving. She wanted the noise, the trouble, whatever it was had them shouting and slamming doors and starting cars in the middle of the night, to stop. She wanted to go on sleeping. Stop it, please. God, please. And then, to her surprise and intense relief, quiet. She waited. Was it going to last? She closed her eyes and was burrowing in deep when heavy footsteps started up the stairs. Who? Who's coming?

Aunt Sadie rushed in and pulled the covers back. "Get up and get dressed. Come on. Be quick about it."

No question but that Maura would do as she was told. Would attempt to, anyway. She'd undressed carelessly the night before, though, there having been no one to put her to bed but herself. Other sock? Shoes? "I can't see, I can't find my—"

Sadie turned on the light. "There."

Maura saw Sadie's face over the lamp for an instant, saw tears, red eyes, blotches, and was embarrassed, sorry for Sadie's shame, frightened. Aunt Sadie crying?

"*Will* you come on?"

Sock found and pulled on. Shoes stepped into, never mind the laces. No time. Hurry. Done. Run down the stairs.

"Put your coat on. Button it."

A strange yelping sound from her mother's room. Daddy? Daddy's making that noise? She looked at her mother's door, closed, implacable, at Sadie's face, altered, not itself, then bolted back upstairs.

"Where the hell are you going? Get back here. Don't make me . . ."

Maura pulled the covers off her bed, revealing, down at the bottom, a beaded green evening bag. She grabbed it, put it under her coat, ran down the stairs.

The night air was cold and damp, a shock, a stimulant.

Sadie opened the car door and Maura climbed into the back, settled against the freezing-cold leather for a moment then got on her knees for a look out the rear window. Lights on all over the house, upstairs and down. The front door wide open.

"Bastard," Joseph said.

"To the end," Sadie answered. "Right to the bloody end."

"Not that we're there yet. Not to the end of this mess yet. There's still the question of . . . no more time for discussion, you realize, now Agnes is dead."

Now Agnes is dead. Maura began to wet herself. The warmth was welcome, the letting go. She knew there'd be hell to pay but she couldn't stop once she started. She couldn't stop till she couldn't go anymore. *Now Agnes is dead.*

"He says he's going regardless. Alone. He says he's going alone regardless what happens."

"So you've said."

"I've said, yes, but haven't gotten a response, have I? Might just as well been talking to myself. You've got to make up your mind, Sadie, and soon. What's it going to be?"

Sadie turned and looked out the window.

"You've got room and money enough, God knows."

"And what about you? You and Peg? You'd hardly notice one more with that mob you've already got. A child should be with other children, surely."

"I've made my decision, haven't I? I've told you and him and anybody else wants to know where I stand. It only waits for you. Do we find a place for her with the nuns or will you take her in? That's all that's left to be decided. We're all waiting on you."

Sadie pulled a handkerchief from the sleeve of her coat and blew her nose loudly.

"Very nice. Very eloquent. Hardly qualifies as a response, though."

"You make me sick, that's my response."

The car stopped in front of Sadie's house with an ominous thud. "Might not start again, not easily, anyway," Joseph growled. "Will this goddamn night never end?" He reached into the back and pulled Maura out. "Bloody hell. She's pissed herself. All over my backseat, too. I'll never get the smell out."

Sadie's house was smallish and squat, whitewashed plaster with dark green shutters. It sat farther back from the road than the houses on either side and so seemed reticent, out of step, old-fashioned. There were two wide windows facing the street, one on either side of the front door. Set close to the ground, these windows bestowed a kind of eagerness on the house that was at odds with its overall reserve, making it look like a guest on the fringes of a party who wants to mix but is nervous just the same.

As Sadie, Joseph, and Maura passed single file through the drawing room, Bell came down the stairs like a gentle ghost, a shawl around her shoulders. "Agnes is dead then?"

Sadie stiffened. "Yes, Bell. She's gone."

"A good death, was it?"

"A noisy one," Joseph said. "I never in my life saw a more reluctant passing. And now Edward's carrying on like a bloody madman. Threw us out, closed himself up with the body and a bottle of whiskey."

Bell looked at Maura, whose eyes were fixed on Rex, Sadie's dog, as he sniffed the sodden hem of her coat. "Sadie?" Bell said.

Sadie didn't answer.

"We're taking her, Sadie?"

"You know what the alternative is," Joseph said. "Just say the word and I'll make the arrangements."

"Shut your mouth," Sadie snapped.

"What's it going to be, Sadie?"

"I swear to God you've all taken leave of your senses, you

and him both. All of you. You want an answer, Joseph? Here's an answer. No Devlin's going to be dumped on the nuns as long as I'm living."

"That's a yes then? You'll take her? For good and all?"

"You make me sick."

"That's a yes. You're a stubborn woman, Sarah. Always have been. I'd have thought you'd jump at the chance, considering."

"That's enough now," Bell said. "You must be frozen, the lot of you. I'll put the kettle on."

Joseph didn't wait for the water to boil but headed home to tell his wife the good news. Agnes is dead and the girl is with Sadie and Bell, where she belongs. He'd hoped that if he could get Maura into Sadie's house for the night Sadie wouldn't turn her out again, considering. And I was right, he bragged to Peg. Didn't even take the night. Getting her under the roof was all. Best thing for everybody. Give the two old dolls something to do with their time besides get on each other's nerves.

"She's had an accident," Sadie said, sitting down at the kitchen table, looking, for a moment, mildly concussed. She seemed to recognize the tea things spread out before her but didn't seem to know what to do with them. "Relieved herself all over the backseat of Joseph's precious car. I didn't mind that a bit. Might have done it myself if I'd thought of it. Her clothes are all wet, anyway. She can't sleep in what she's got on."

"Oh," Bell said, looking down at Maura. "Oh. Well. It happens, I suppose. Children. Did you bring anything for her to put on?"

"There wasn't time. You can't imagine the carrying-on over there."

"Right. We must have something a child can wear. If you weren't after me all the time to clean out the closets and such, we'd have old clothes. You never know when you're going to have a need. Do you see now why I don't like to get rid of anything?"

"Will you shut up, Bell? Will you let me have a cup of tea in peace?"

* * *

A couple of hours before the end Agnes had come back to herself and asked for Maura. "My little girl. I want to see my little girl."

Maura was summoned and came down the stairs slowly. Her mother had been ailing for years, tuberculosis, so Maura was accustomed to sickrooms. But this visit, she knew, was not going to be like the others.

"Go on," Sadie said. "You don't want to keep your mum waiting, go on."

Maura approached the bed and all the adults, save Edward, filed out.

Oil shone on Agnes's eyelids and lips. Her face was flushed, her breath ragged. Her eyes sparkled as eyes will when they aren't getting the oxygen they want. She plucked at her nightgown, at the bedding, tapped the mattress and said, "Here's Maura. Here's my sprite, my fairy girl. Come on and sit by me."

Maura looked at her father. He nodded.

Maura sat down. Agnes took her hand and kissed it. "Were you in bed? Did they get you up just now?"

Maura shook her head. "I wasn't. I was upstairs but not in bed."

"Not in bed? Doing what, then, madam?"

Before Maura could answer Agnes started to cough and couldn't stop. Adults—Edward, Sadie—swooped down with handkerchiefs open and tablespoons brimming. Maura got herself out of the way but was noticed before long, and banished. "Upstairs with you, let's go. No sense upsetting her. No sense making this harder on everybody than it has to be. Go on."

chapter 2

"How is he, do you suppose?" Sadie ventured after she and Joseph had driven in silence for a mile or two.

"Passed out, probably, facedown."

Edward was neither. Freshly shaved and wearing his good suit, he opened the door before Sadie knocked.

"You survived then?" Sadie said. "You made it through the night?"

"I did."

Brother and sister looked into each other's eyes. Here was somebody, a sibling, too, who had felt as badly waking up this morning. Somebody else who was managing, barely, to put one foot in front of the other.

Sadie cleared her throat. "I hope that's last night's whiskey I'm smelling and not this morning's," she said.

"Lay off him, will you? Let's all just try to get through this as best we can. Come on, Edward, you and I'll go collect Beecher."

Sadie poured salt and a bit of white vinegar into a basin then added hot water. She looked around for a rag, couldn't find one, had to use a fancy dinner napkin instead. Trust Agnes to have a wicker basket full of good linen but not a single old dish towel.

Eyes stubbornly lowered, Sadie went into the back bedroom and put the basin on the nightstand, pushing aside cod-liver oil, cough syrup, a bottle of whiskey. She opened the window, took a deep breath of damp December air, turned around.

Her knees nearly gave out.

"Mother of God."

She pulled back the sheet and tenderly lifted Agnes's nightgown. Agnes had always been slim. She was emaciated now. Sadie leaned over and kissed the hollow beneath Agnes's breastbone. Coming back to herself and fearing contagion, she uncapped the whiskey, took a swig, gargled then spit in the basin.

"What's a big girl of fourteen want with a baby of six?" people used to ask. Sadie loved to brush Agnes's hair once, bought her ribbons and sweets. Agnes accepted Sadie's offerings as if they were her due. She ran hot and cold, kissing Sadie one minute, abandoning her the next. As the girls got older, Agnes began to prefer her own company to Sadie's. In the middle of a perfectly pleasant afternoon, Agnes would stand up and announce that she was going home and Sadie wasn't to follow. People snickered. A big galoot like Sadie pushed around by a cheeky little thing like that Neligan girl.

The elbow and shoulder joints were stiff. Sadie had a time getting Agnes's nightgown off. The men wouldn't be much longer. She had to hurry.

"Forgive me," she whispered, yanking hard.

When Agnes's father, a widower of nearly eighty, decided to send her to nursing school, Sadie convinced hers to do the same. Sadie wanted to be a nurse about as much as she wanted to fly to the moon, but if Agnes was going away, Sadie was going with her. Agnes seemed to think Sadie's coming along was a grand idea. She oversaw Sadie's packing and talked about the adventures they'd have. They weren't in London a week, though, when Agnes said, "Don't be hanging on me, Sadie. I haven't come all this way to spend my time with you." Shunned and far from home, older than most of the other girls, watching from a distance while Agnes ran around with the more stylish British students and blithely broke the heart of a handsome intern, Sadie was miserable. When her father got sick and she was called home to help care for him, she was secretly glad. Agnes completed the course with honors, returned reluctantly to Omagh, and went to work in the Catholic hospital there.

Edward was home for a last visit before leaving for America when he encountered little Agnes Neligan all grown up. At first Sadie found Edward's attention to Agnes flattering. He was her favorite brother, not as arrogant as the others and smarter, too. His falling for Agnes was testament to Sadie's excellent taste in girls.

When Sadie realized a wedding was in the works, her enthusiasm for the match evaporated. If Agnes insisted on getting married, why didn't she pick a husband who planned to stay in Ireland? Spooked by the intensity of her own jealousy, Sadie willed it underground and vowed to conduct herself with perfect composure in the face of Agnes's betrayal.

She kept her eyes on her knitting or her newspaper when the lovers came through the door. She stopped going to the mass they went to. She developed a sudden, passionate interest in her brother's prospects.

"Agnes Neligan's not sturdy enough to be a good wife," Sadie told Edward the first time she got him alone. "To have babies and all the rest of it, especially in America, a hard life that'll be."

Edward took off his glasses and rubbed his eyes. "You're making a fool of yourself, Sadie. Sulking and staring the way you're doing. Instead of wasting your time—I'm marrying her, Sadie, count on that—why don't you see if you can find yourself a husband?"

"While I've still got half a chance, you mean?"

"I didn't say that. What about Benny Macdonald? Or his brother, the older one, what's his name?"

"I don't want either one of them."

"I know you don't."

"I don't want any husband."

"You might get yourself one just the same."

Sadie felt the sting of salt and vinegar in her chilblains as she submerged the napkin in warm water. She washed Agnes's face, steeling herself as best she could against the grief gathering in the pit of her stomach. Sadie *had* to check the pain. If she didn't, she'd never get through the wake and funeral the way a sister-in-law of the deceased would be expected to. And people would be watching her closely, she knew. How's Sadie doing? How's funny old Sadie holding up?

Edward and Agnes, husband and wife, set off for New York. A year later, while working at Bellevue Hospital, Agnes contracted tuberculosis. "I warned him," Sadie said to Bell when Edward's first letter asking for help with the medical expenses arrived.

Seven years later, with Maura in tow, Edward brought Agnes back to Omagh to die. That's what she'd wanted. "Take me home," she'd said. "Write Sadie and tell her I want to come home." Sadie met the train, determined to keep her wits about her despite sweaty palms and pounding heart. Hadn't she gotten on just fine alone? Hadn't she done very well for herself?

Edward carried Agnes off the train and held her while a porter struggled with the collapsible wheelchair. Sadie approached slowly, telling herself to expect a great change. After all it had been years, her own hair had gone grey, her middle had thickened.

When Agnes left Ireland she was charming to look at. She had clear skin, bright eyes, softly rounded forehead and chin, glossy brown hair. She radiated pleasure in being young and good-looking. When she returned it was as if somebody had taken that vibrancy and burned it up in the hottest fire imaginable. From the ash, then, this new creature had been made. Beautiful, all right, in a particular sense, yes, beautiful. So serious. So still. Chastened. The cheekbones still high, higher, in fact, the chin still graceful, the white skin nearly translucent in the winter sun, the green eyes blazing with fever. But what had animated the whole package before, the pretty vitality, had been replaced by fragility, by weariness.

Sadie wanted, desperately, violently, to shoo Edward and the daughter away. She wanted to put herself, her own bulk and stubborn good health, between Agnes and the world that had ruined her.

This bedding will have to be burned, Sadie thought, washing Agnes's privates. I'll have the place whitewashed inside and out and still won't find a tenant for six months. She looked at the fine underclothes and maroon dress that Edward had set out on a chair. I'd have put her in her green with the cinched waist, she said to herself, and sobbed once, hard. "Get hold now, get hold." Grunting, she lifted Agnes's legs and bottom. Sadie was a big woman, a great walker, an avid gardener. Lifting what remained of Agnes was no strain. The noises Sadie made kept her grief at bay, rooted her more or less in the realm of doing, of tasks, one after the other. Keep moving. Right. Push this, pull here, stretch to reach a button, a garter.

Before long it was done. Agnes was dressed for burial. All but her hair—how dull it had become, how thin. Sadie didn't dare attempt to arrange it. She could barely manage her own. If she tried to do Agnes's, it would come out all wrong and that would be a source of amusement to the others. Imagine Sadie thinking she could do hair, and Agnes's no less. Imagine Sadie thinking she could do Agnes's hair.

"All right then. Give us your hand."

The sound of Joseph's voice came through the open window. Sadie flinched but didn't let go of Agnes's hand until Beecher knocked.

There was a hint of something lewd beneath the undertaker's solemn expression. "Well," he said, eyeing Agnes. "You've done half my work for me, Miss Devlin, and an excellent job, too. All but the hair and this and that. Look at her, will you? She's lovely still. Isn't she, Miss Devlin? Isn't she lovely still? An angel if ever I saw one."

chapter 3

Six days after Agnes was buried Edward, having already gone from Omagh to Dublin, from Dublin to London, from London to Southampton, boarded a Cunard steamer bound for New York. The sky that morning was a brilliant blue, more an American sky than a British one, Edward thought, walking around to the far side of the ship, wanting to put as much distance as he could between himself and his fellow third-class passengers, who were weeping, some of them, and waving handkerchiefs to well-wishers on the dock. Edward had said that sort of good-bye eight years before. (From this very port he and Agnes had sailed, and though they hadn't known a soul down below, they'd waved vigorously along with the rest. Good-bye, England, good-bye!) This time Edward wanted his leaving brusque.

Edward Devlin was not quite six feet tall and narrow-shouldered. He wore wire-rimmed glasses and looked mild-mannered and brainy, the way engineers do. He was thirty-four years old. When he was seventeen and a scholarship student at the National University, he joined the fledgling Irish Republican Army. His time was divided between his studies and his duties as a member of one Debate and Oratory Society under the auspices of which he and other aspiring revolutionaries made hand grenades. On Easter Monday, the first day of the 1916 rebellion, Edward reported to his assigned post at Jacob's Biscuit Factory, where, only an hour into the uprising, he shot and killed a woman, a very tall woman, a bloody amazon, or so she appeared ever after in his mind's eye. She'd been about to hit one of Edward's comrades on the head with a brick. Shot in the chest, she buckled then went straight down like a building expertly imploded.

The British army put a stop to the Easter Rising in short order. "Hang the traitors!" Dubliners shouted as hundreds of defeated rebels were marched through the center of town. One particularly irate old crone hit Edward square in the chest with the contents of her chamber pot. He gagged and spat. "Afraid they'll throw you off the dole?" he shouted over his shoulder while the old lady laughed and pointed him out to her biddy friends.

Leaders of the rebellion, men Edward revered, were executed by firing squad. From his jail cell Edward heard the early-morning volleys three days running. On the fourth night a priest came to hear confessions. "You're to be shot in the morning, Edward Devlin. Write a letter to your mother and I'll see she gets it." At dawn Edward and nine other terrified young men were lined up against a wall in the prison yard. The priest blessed them in Latin and they were blindfolded. The soldiers fired. Edward fell over, sure he was dead. Then he heard jeering and felt gravel in his knees and elbows. The soldiers had fired over the prisoners' heads. Interrogations followed.

Two mock executions later Edward was willing to answer all questions put to him by anyone holding a gun. He told what little he knew, was knocked around some, and released. Without a moment's hesitation, he went back to his engineering courses and his secret meetings. In 1919 he fought in the guerrilla war, ambushing Black and Tans, blowing up ancient castles and modern bridges, going hungry, sleeping in fields and barns and closets. When partition was proposed and the civil war started, Edward, a commandant by then (the IRA used German titles so as to avoid British ones), fought with De Valera and the anti-partition forces, was captured and spent nine months in New Bridge prison, where he was treated far worse by his former comrades than he'd ever been by the Brits. A bayonet at his throat, he was forced to watch while seven of his men were tied in a circle, wrist to wrist, and a live hand grenade was dropped into the center. Edward hardly remembered the explosion. He'd seen dozens by then. What haunted him was the memory of the few seconds just before, each man trying to save himself, the strong yanking the weak over.

When De Valera surrendered, Edward, the youthful enthusiasm pretty well burned out of him, decided that Ireland, such as it was, split in two now and his part, the North, still under British rule, would have to get along without him. Ireland, let it be said, was not a bit sorry to see him go. Diehard nationalists were persona non grata in the Free State. Edward had little choice but to shake off what remained of his rebel identity, pull out his engineering degree, head for America, and see what he could make of himself there.

Home for a last visit, flat broke and ashamed that at twenty-five he was wholly dependent on his father who'd never had any use for rebellions or rebels, Edward sat at the kitchen table one morning staring moodily at the heel of his German army boot, impatient to clear out but, as he was asking for yet another "loan" from his father, feeling a certain obligation to disguise his eagerness to be gone. He looked up and there was Agnes Neligan in her nurse's cap and cape.

"Morning, Edward. Is Sadie about?"

"Haven't seen her," Edward lied. "Cup of tea?"

Edward sailed tourist third cabin, a designation that steamship companies came up with in an attempt to make up for revenues lost when America decided she'd had just about enough of the tired, the poor, the huddled masses. Replacing steerage, tourist third cabin was intended to attract working Americans who had the desire to go abroad but only modest means. Edward had desperately wanted a private cabin, felt entitled to one after all he'd been through, but when, standing in the ticket office in Dublin, he was presented with the difference in price between second class and tourist third, he had no choice but to admit that he couldn't afford solitude. "The cheaper one then, thank you."

As soon as he got on board he went down below to get rid of the one very heavy suitcase he'd been lugging around for days.

The steward who pointed out Edward's cabin said, "Ah, you're in luck." Although 27D contained four bunks, two uppers and two lowers, only one besides Edward's own would be occupied. It was 1934. Far fewer people could afford even tourist third.

Glad, at first, to be away from the crush of fellow passengers and the festivities going on up above, Edward was tempted to stay below until the ship was out at sea. How better to express his disdain for the sloppy emotionality that went with leaving? It took about a minute and a half for 27D to go from cozy to claustrophobic. The ceiling was low. There were rivets along every seam and exposed pipes, two of them red-hot, a third icy-cold and frosted. Despite Cunard's attempts to make the six-by-eight-foot cabin homey, bedspreads monogrammed with large, threadbare *C*'s, a spindly green plant in a pot on the shelf under the tiny sink, 27D was better suited to soldiers of very low rank or prisoners than tourists.

Having crossed several times before, Edward knew he'd have hours and hours to spend in the cabin, if he could stand it, and hours more staring out at nothing but miles of grey ocean. He decided he'd better go up while there was something to see from the deck. As he pulled the door closed, which felt more like shutting a cabinet than it did closing a door, he experienced an inward rustle of curiosity about his cabin mate. I hope he's quiet, Edward thought, willfully reverting to his earlier resentment about having to have a roommate at all. I hope whoever it is doesn't expect much in the way of company from me.

Up on the third-class deck, Edward squinted in the sun as the tugboats moved into position. Getting out of Southampton was tricky, Edward knew from a conversation he'd had with a steward on a previous crossing. There was a shoal, a shallow patch called the Brambles, that made navigating out to the open sea perilous. Knowing about the Brambles made Edward feel superior to his fellow passengers, who obviously didn't have a clue that the way out was going to require every bit of the captain's skill. They were chattering away loudly, shouting, really, so as to be heard over the wind and the rumbling engines. They were laughing and drinking. Three couples were even dancing, which struck Edward as evidence of a particularly desperate good cheer, there amidst the undisguised practicality of the third-class deck, where massive coils of thick rope were in everybody's way, where a giant, very rusty, and obviously important metal ball was chained to the railing, where crates of one kind and another and mountains of steamer trunks took up most of the room without apology.

Edward found a space against a wall and lit a cigarette. So far he'd outrun his grief. First there'd been the wake and the funeral, which required a kind of movement, through time if not over ground. Drink, move over one to make room for, drink, eat what somebody insists must be eaten, eat half of it, anyway, lean in to be kissed, pat back when you're patted, squeeze the hand that's squeezing yours, drink, drink a lot, kneel down, sit, stand, say our father, hail Mary, sing, tromp over wet ground, stand and shiver, throw dirt, listen while other people throw dirt, drink, drink, drink. Then had come the all-consuming task of getting himself from Omagh to the spot where he now stood, an orgy of train schedules, launch times, hire cars, taxis, tips, money changing, go, man, go.

Now he was where he would remain for six days. The beginnings of something unpleasant burbled up in his chest and Edward went on the offensive. Assuming the posture of cynicism, he hoped the captain was not particularly skilled or was drunk or both and wouldn't get past the Brambles, would run the goddamn ship aground, do major damage, send people sliding into the cold, cold English Channel.

Not feeling sufficiently protected by his suicidal/homicidal musing, Edward reminded himself that he'd been had. He'd tried to live a meaningful life, dedicating himself first to his country and then to a woman. Neither pursuit had proved worthy of his devotion. (Was it the nature of that devotion? Edward wondered. Had it been in both instances too great by half? Had his yammering enthusiasm somehow brought about, predicted, ensured, the dissolution of its object?) Didn't matter. Nothing mattered. He was finished. Done. He would never again attempt to live a life based on any sort of ideal. Ideals, he'd come to believe, were the result of attachments. In America, this time around, he'd be a man devoid of attachments. He'd gamble and drink, come and go as he pleased, answer to no one. Maura had been asleep when Edward stopped at Sadie's to settle up. He wouldn't let Bell wake her, refused even a last look at his six-year-old daughter.

At long last the ship began to move. Edward felt and recognized the particular thrill of launching as it penetrated even his determined gloom. Go, he was thinking, faster, come on. There was a distinct surge in the energy of the revelers too. Everybody seemed to know that they, all together, for better or worse, they and no others, were moving away from the safety of shore toward open water. Glasses were refilled, smiles that had grown stiff with cold and waiting loosened, two more couples found their way to the dance floor. Edward scanned the crowd, thinking of the Brambles and wondering if he'd be able to pick out his cabin mate, a single fellow like himself, a lone traveler. That chap over there with the fancy flask and the big ears? The delicate young man bending to tie his shoe? The hardy, hatless bald fellow with the thick mustache?

Edward remained on deck until the ship was out in open water, until the regular lift and fall of the bow was well established, until his dread of six days of enforced idleness returned in force. Suddenly exhausted, he went down below intending to sleep for a couple of hours. He pushed open his cabin door and saw a form huddled beneath a blanket on one of the lower berths.

"Hey, there."

"Hello."

"Seasick already?"

"Dunno."

"Your first time out?"

"Yep. Won't last, will it, do you think?"

"Depends. Some get better in half a day. Others never do."

"Christ."

"Edward Devlin."

"John Mahoney."

Shaking his bunkmate's damp hand, Edward got his first look at the man's face and thought it handsome, and familiar. "Do I know you from somewhere? Have we met before?"

"Don't think so," Mahoney said, turning to the wall.

"Watch out for that pipe by your feet. It's red-hot."

"Right."

"It's a wonder it hasn't started a fire."

Mahoney groaned.

Edward took off his hat, coat, and shoes then climbed onto the berth above the vacant one, thinking he'd give John Mahoney as much privacy as possible. The prospect of sleep, which had been so tantalizingly certain on deck, evaporated. Edward lay on his back, agitated, addled, listening to the occasional moan from down below.

Mahoney never recovered fully though he did surface a couple of times when the sea was as calm as the sea ever got. "I'm better, I think, thank God," he said more than once, only to have the color drain from his face three-quarters of an hour later. "Jesus, it's back."

Edward, though not seasick, never that, a point of pride, just some slight vertigo the first day out, was far from well. He ate very little, though the food in tourist third was decent and ample. He walked around and around the deck to tire himself out so that he might sleep two or three consecutive hours, day or night, he was beyond caring which. In Ireland Agnes had seemed close at hand, though dead. He'd been surrounded by her clothes, her brush and her comb, perfume bottles, sickroom paraphernalia. In the midst of so many of her belongings and busy with the funeral, he'd felt capable of beginning his new life as a man who believed heart and soul in nothing. In his cramped cabin, out at sea, lifting and falling and listening to Mahoney pant and swallow, he wasn't so sure.

All Edward had that bound him to Agnes was his wedding ring, a nearly full bottle of opiate-rich cough syrup, and a photograph of her sitting on a bench in a train station peering down into her open purse. Edward was sure that he'd taken the picture but couldn't for the life of him remember where or when. Were they on the way to the clinic in Switzerland or that place in the Adirondacks? She was wearing a winter coat, so it couldn't be Arizona, so bloody hot there. He took a long swallow of cough syrup, held the photograph at arm's length, and brought it toward himself slowly. Hoping to jog his memory, he turned the picture facedown, let it be for as long as he could stand to, five, ten, fifteen seconds, then snatched it up in a surprise attack.

Nothing.

His recollection of that moment, if he'd ever had one and he felt sure that he must have at some point, was gone. The loss of those few seconds tormented him. Bad enough you can't count on people to hang around. Memories, too, it turns out, can simply vanish. Sleep-deprived, hungry, high on cough syrup, Edward believed that locating the memory of the instant that photograph was taken would anchor him, would give him something small but solid to hold on to.

Then he remembered that he'd turned his back on the whole notion that there was ever anything for anyone to hold on to. He stood up decisively, banged his head on the berth above, was not deterred. He put on his coat and went up to the deck, intending to throw the photograph and his wedding ring into the sea. He couldn't do it, could not convince his fingers to release. He walked the deck weeping over the loss of Agnes and berating himself for weeping.

Practical concerns kept Edward from going round the bend entirely. He was worried about money. All he had in the world was what Sadie had given him for the house in Omagh, which he'd inherited from his father. After Sadie deducted what Edward had borrowed over the years for medical and travel expenses, precious little remained. Edward knew he'd have to find a job in a hurry once he got back to New York. He also knew that, times being what they were, finding work wasn't going to be easy.

Not long after daybreak the third morning out, having slept for an hour and a half, Edward gave himself an assignment. He was to come up with a list of people who might help him find a job once he got to New York. He wasn't, he told himself, without connections, contacts, friends—acquaintances, anyway—

who might at least point him in the right direction, provide a lead or two. He found he couldn't think clearly in the close quarters of 27D, so he headed up to the deck to walk. ("Five laps equal a mile," a fellow walker had said in passing, literally, the day before. At first the words sounded strange to Edward, like something out of a spy novel, what one operative says so as to be recognized by another. After figuring out that what had seemed a nonsense sentence, a string of words chosen at random, was actually a simple statement of fact, Edward tried then and at each subsequent session to keep a tally of the revolutions he completed just so he could say "I walked this many miles today" but he was never able to. His thoughts always wandered, he lost count, he had to start over again at zero.) He'd gone around once and hadn't come up with a single name for his list when he spotted Mahoney sitting on the corner of a bench underneath a steamer rug that had somehow found its way down to third class. Beside Mahoney on the otherwise empty bench was a sandwich, chicken on white bread, with a small bite taken out.

"Hey, there," Edward said, glad to be distracted from his task. "Feeling better?"

Mahoney shook his head slowly, staring out at the water, and then, as if wondering what else was wanted of him, he narrowed his eyes and looked up at Edward.

It was then, in the hazy early-morning light and ceaseless wind, that Edward figured out why Mahoney looked familiar. Years before, when Agnes and Edward had first arrived in New York, they'd become fast friends with a bunch of other young Irish and had all hung around together, drinking and dancing and running around the city till all hours. There was a man, John Fitzgibbon, Fitz he was called, who served as a kind of role model and patron saint to new arrivals. Fitz owned, as Edward recalled, a silk mill in Paterson, New Jersey, and lived out there, too, though he'd gotten his start, made his first real money, in New York. Fitz used to show up now and then at parties and nightclubs and diners, always very late, always alone. The younger people made a big deal of him, paid close attention to his comings and goings. Nearly everybody, it seemed, had a story to tell about a favor Fitzgibbon had done, an intercession. He arranged for loans, hospital beds, places in the police and fire academies, larger apartments when babies came, hack licenses, all manner of things.

Mahoney was about the same height as Fitzgibbon, five eight or nine, had the same compact, well-formed body, the same curly hair, cut short, the same very blue eyes, narrow and wide set, the small perfectly formed nose, the good skin, fine-pored and clear. It was a face that was saved from prettiness by the mischievous, masculine charm that animated it, a face that seemed amused by its own good looks. Fitzgibbon's was, any-way. Whatever normally animated Mahoney's face, if anything did, was eclipsed now by seasickness.

Edward had not paid much attention to Fitz in the old days. Fitz had existed on the periphery of Edward's world. If anything, Edward had been a little put off by the man's self-importance. He was a flashy dresser, Edward remembered, favored bright colors, red vests, yellow ties, silk pocket hand-kerchiefs. Fitz hadn't had anything Edward needed then. He and Agnes had both found work within a couple of weeks of ar-riving. Their combined salaries and their childlessness made them desirable tenants, so they'd had little trouble finding an apartment they liked well enough. Edward had spoken to Fitz only a couple of times after being introduced. Their conversa-tions had been cordial but brief. In fact, Edward remembered, his most substantial link to Fitzgibbon was through Agnes. One New Year's Eve Edward and Agnes had wound up in the back-seat of a car heading out to Fitz's house in New Jersey for a party. Edward and Agnes hadn't been invited, they'd crashed. Edward hadn't spoken to Fitz the whole evening, had been, in truth, a little afraid to, being a gate-crasher, but Agnes had danced with him, slow-danced, straight through a couple of songs. Edward remembered watching their lips move and won-dering what they'd found to talk about so intently. In bed the next morning Edward had asked Agnes what she'd thought of Fitzgibbon. She'd lowered her eyes, the implications of which had made Edward instantly jealous. "Nice enough. A bit of a flirt. A good friend to have, isn't that what people say?"

Yes, Edward thought, staring hard at Mahoney, who appeared to be sleeping, that is what people say. It's what they used to say. Let's hope it's still true. If ever I needed a good friend. Optimism spread through Edward's system like an opiate, soothing his nerves, easing the strain. He didn't ask himself if it made sense to put so much confidence in a man he hardly knew and hadn't seen in years. He luxuriated in the unexpected respite from worry.

Without knowing it exactly, without, anyway, articulating it to himself, Edward was shored up by the route he'd taken to get to Fitz. Under an ambivalent sky, lifting and falling, out at sea on a British liner, wrenched, nearly broke, weary, weary, weary, Edward had happened on a man who could have been the younger brother of the man he needed to remember at exactly the moment he needed to remember him. Show me the way, Edward had been asking without knowing it, and the way had been shown, or so it seemed. There was a chance, however slight, that the universe was not entirely random, that one thing might possibly be connected to another in a world that seemed not just indifferent to the notion of connectedness but actively, hostilely opposed to it.

Paterson. Why the hell not Paterson? I've had more than enough of New York to last me. Fitzgibbon. Fitz. Right.

Mahoney, as if seconding Edward's motion, sat up. Looking even more like Fitzgibbon than Edward originally thought—there it was, that glimmer, that liveliness—Mahoney reached for his chicken sandwich and took a gargantuan bite.

chapter 4

The ship passed Sandy Hook to the west and Sea Gate to the east before inching through the Narrows into New York harbor. Edward was up on deck with everybody else, steeling himself against what he knew was coming: a sharp left turn and then, all at once, ready or not, the massive reality of New York. When the Ahhhh came, when eyes widened and all together hundreds of people said Ahhhhhhhh, Edward grunted. Oh, Agnes had said when their ship made that same turn and New York was there all of a sudden, smack in front of them. Oh, she'd said the way people do when they're all but speechless. Oh. Oh. Will you look at that? Have you ever in your life? She'd wrapped her fingers around Edward's wrist and squeezed and started to cry. Only then had he realized how badly she'd wanted to come, how glad she was to be there. More than their modest wedding, their wedding night, the subsequent nights they'd spent in hotels and then in their second-class cabin, their first shared glimpse of New York—it wasn't a glimpse, it was a gorging, a feast, the way New York might be presented to a person who asked for it as the first of three wishes—marked the beginning of their time together.

Feeling as if he might actually die of the pain, as if his body hurt too much to do anything but give out, Edward was desperate to get off the ship. He endured the condescension of immigration officials, the long lines at customs, the shouts and waves of longshoremen, and headed off, lugging his heavy suitcase past abandoned warehouses, putting one foot in front of the other, wanting only to be out of the city where Agnes had been healthy and his wife.

He wished he were numb, wished his mind was blank but for the desire to be gone. The memory of Agnes's first encounter with New York had opened the floodgates, though. There was the corner where they'd stopped so that Edward could unfold his map and try to get his bearings and where Agnes had drifted away to look in store windows. There a familiar coffee shop. There, oh Jesus, the hotel where they'd stayed the first three weeks. Edward had all he could do to keep moving.

But then something happened that changed everything. The handle of Edward's suitcase snapped off at one end.

There are difficulties and there are difficulties. It's one thing to be moving along a sidewalk in winter all but overwhelmed by grief for a beloved wife recently dead. It's something else entirely to be faced with the prospect of getting a large suitcase without a working handle halfway across town. "Son of a bitch," Edward said. "Jesus goddamn Christ."

Suitcases are designed to be carried one way and one way only, Edward discovered as he experimented with various other nonoptions, each of which seemed workable for about ten paces. Yes, Edward thought, carrying the suitcase out in front of him like a large box until the pain in his lower back could not be ignored. "All right, like this," he said, suitcase on his shoulder the way a waiter carries a tray, fingers splayed beneath it, until the damn thing slid off and narrowly missed a passing child. He wound up dragging the bloody thing along the sidewalk, not caring a whit for the damage he was doing to the underside, half hoping, even, out of spite, that the bottom was being torn to pieces.

Pennsylvania Station. Evening rush. Edward found himself amidst packs of businessmen in suits and ties. He fell in step, got swept along by the current. It was easier dragging the suitcase along the granite floor, so much easier, in fact, that Edward had the distinct and pleasurable sensation that he wasn't moving of his own volition, that he'd surrendered his individual will and was being carried along by the collective will of the crowd.

He caught the first train to Paterson and rented a room in the Alexander Hamilton hotel in the center of town. The Colt Lounge was just around the corner and crowded with lawyers and judges from the county courthouse across the street. They were a lively bunch, good company for a fellow just arrived in a small city where he knows only one man. Edward planned to have a stiff drink or two, treat himself to a steak dinner, go to bed early, and call Fitzgibbon first thing in the morning.

A well-dressed Irishman named Gerry bought Edward's third drink then asked if he was interested in playing a few hands of poker. Edward had played cards to pass the time during his guerrilla days and so he accepted the man's invitation eagerly, hoping to add to his reserve fund, money he'd need to survive if Fitzgibbon had gone bust or didn't remember him or wasn't willing to help.

Six men sat at a table in the back room. When the hand finished, one player got up and Edward took his place. The dealer nodded a terse hello and called the game. Edward knew he'd been asked to play because he looked like somebody who'd sweeten pots but not win many. Determined to keep his wits about him, to miss nothing in case the game was crooked, he accepted a drink when one was offered but only moistened his lips and tongue each time he raised his glass.

After a few unfortunate hands (You're limbering up, Edward told himself, don't get rattled) the cards began coming to him with what could only be described as a kind of grace. Beauties in every hand. One ace dealt, two more picked up. A spade or a diamond when, trusting a hunch, he went out on a limb after a flush. Face cards, twice, on an inside straight. Edward read the other men's faces with preternatural accuracy, knew when they were bluffing and when they'd burn him if he stayed in.

Sixty-seven dollars to the good and beginning to wonder if he'd be rolled on his way back to the hotel, Edward was asked, rather abruptly he thought, to give up his seat by a big fellow with a crescent-shaped scar on his cheek. "We're here every night but Sunday, cuz. See you again, huh?"

The crowd in the bar had changed considerably. The lawyers and judges had been replaced by a meaner bunch, unemployed mill hands and young Italian toughs. There were a couple of women, too, sitting cross-legged at the bar, looking bored and vaguely bad-tempered. Edward's instincts told him to clear out but the new money in his pocket and the exhilaration of winning said otherwise.

He found a stool in the corner and hunkered down with a drink, eyeing the people around him. He tried to strike up a conversation with the bartender, asked if he knew Fitzgibbon, but the man made it clear that he had no interest in talking to a stranger.

An edgy weariness settled over Edward. He could still feel the pitch of the ship in his belly and along the soles of his feet. It was too late to get dinner now and sleep was surely a long way off. He closed his eyes, saw his hotel room, double bed, ruined suitcase, the newspaper he'd bought on the train, and began to drink in earnest.

He'd remember only fragments of what followed. His tipping the bartender extravagantly and still not winning the bastard over. The man with the crescent-shaped scar: "Do yourself a favor, Irish, go home and sleep it off." Going on and on about Agnes to the old man on the next stool, counting the days she'd been dead on his fingers.

Last call, finally.

A blonde smiled at Edward and he smiled back. She nodded and so did he. She came over and whispered in the ear of the old man, who promptly surrendered his seat. Her name was Dora. Her hair was yellow, her eyes close-set, her nose narrow and long. She had a face like a rat's and her manner was rodent-like, too: scavenging, fueled by a minimal and strictly acquisitive intelligence. She stroked Edward's arm and asked if he wanted a date.

"Lovely. That'd be lovely."

Off they went down the street and up and up a narrow staircase. Inside a room that smelled of oil smoke she took off her coat then her dress, bra, and underpants. "Two dollars and you can't sleep here. You go as soon as you finish."

Edward had never paid for sex though he'd fantasized about doing so and would have gladly when he was a student if he'd had the money and the nerve. Tonight, though, the idea struck him as wildly insulting. What he thought he'd been up to was raunchy in a way that sat well with him: alone in a room with a woman and Agnes not dead a month. Nothing matters. But it turned out he wasn't even calling the shots in his own degradation. Suddenly, drunkenly, he was furious. Determined to be the victor in some sphere, any one at all, he wanted to get the better of this ugly woman. What he'd do, he decided, was have his way with her, do it, and then refuse to pay. Grab his coat, be off down the stairs.

"You've got money, haven't you?" Dora said, clutching an afghan to her breasts.

"I do. Course I do."

"Show it to me."

Satisfied, she licked her palm and got down to business.

It didn't go well. It didn't go at all, despite Dora's prolonged if somewhat brusque ministrations.

Edward sat up, put on his glasses, pulled up his trousers, said he was sorry, this had never happened to him before, he hadn't been sleeping, hadn't eaten a decent meal in a week. He took out his wallet, having every intention of paying up now.

"Ten dollars," Dora said. "You took more than your share of time. Any normal man."

Edward hesitated, not because he disagreed, she had worked very hard, but because he hated to be a sucker. About to voice his objection, Edward looked up and saw Dora holding a very large knife.

"Give me all of it then, you're so fucking smart."

Edward knew she'd cut him as soon as look at him. He walked out thirty seconds later minus his watch, his cigarette lighter, and what had remained of his poker winnings.

Please God, he thought when morning came and daylight woke him, let me have dreamed the prostitute with the knife. He felt for his watch. His wrist was perfectly, reproachfully bare. He sat up and shuddered. Robbed by a woman, a whore no less. It doesn't matter, he thought to counter the humiliation washing over him, nothing matters. He rooted through his suitcase for what was left of Agnes's opiated cough syrup.

He woke a second time, hours later, and took a long bath, scrubbing vigorously then soaking mournfully, adding hot water as needed, turning the spigot with his left foot so as not to have to heave himself up. He dried himself tenderly, dressed, then went out and ate a mound of potatoes and eggs, heavily salted. One of Agnes's doctors used to say that salt was the best thing for a hangover.

Hoping that fresh air and exercise would return him to the land of the living, Edward went for a walk through town. The Depression had hit New York hard, but it had decimated Paterson. Half the stores on Main Street were empty. There were packs of men milling around on corners, smoking and silent. And like a bloody idiot, Edward thought, I've come here for a job.

As often happened when he was hungover, nearly everybody he passed on the sidewalk looked familiar to him, a lingering effect of alcohol's way of making strangers seem like friends, perhaps. It was gentle enough, this diffuse sense of familiarity. Edward felt a kinship with all Patersonians. Life is very hard, yes, it doesn't make a bit of sense, but we keep trudging along. Then Edward noticed a blonde who looked like the prostitute trudging his way. He pulled the brim of his hat down and picked up his pace.

Maybe Paterson's too close to New York after all, he thought. Maybe what I ought to do is head for a city I've never set foot in before, Chicago, say. He'd always liked the sound of that word. "Chi-ca-go," he chanted in time with his footsteps. "Chi-ca-go." Even farther west, maybe, Denver, Los Angeles. Then Edward thought of Fitzgibbon, saw the handsome face in his mind's eye, saw it smiling, nearly flirting.

Come through for me, man, Edward thought. "Come through, John Fitzgibbon."

Just saying the name gave Edward a lift.

"Fitz-gib-bon."

"Fitz-gib-bon."

* * *

Lying on his hotel bed not sleeping but not fully awake, Edward watched the light fade. He didn't mind this part of a hangover, his thought patterns loosened, images drifting in and out, the boundary between waking and dreaming blurred. In his mind's eye and then in the gathering darkness, he saw his mother, angry at him for alienating his father. "Stay away from those men, Edward. D'you hear me? Heroes, are they? They'll watch you die then toast you after." He saw the men he'd played cards with at the Colt. He'd shown them, at least. A rube, was he? An easy mark? He saw Dora clutching the afghan to her breasts and Sadie moistening her thumb to count out pound notes. He saw the woman he'd shot so long ago, her knees buckling, going down.

He ached for Agnes, for her body under his in the early morning as it had been so often during their first lusty days in New York. Her hospital shift started at seven. They made love at five or six. Half dressed, white stockings on, hair pinned up, she'd climb back into bed. He closed his eyes and saw the cleft of her ass, the dip of her waist, her tender and changeable nipples.

Without her he felt as if he were flying apart.

He ran his hand over one pillow and down along the sheet, following remembered curves. He kissed the air and winced when images of the night he spent alone with her corpse cut in on warmer memories.

chapter 5

The woman who answered the phone at Fitzgibbon's mill asked Edward's name. He gave it reluctantly, sure he wouldn't be put through. He was surprised then, and a little unnerved, when Fitzgibbon picked up a few seconds later.

"Edward Devlin, I heard you were in town. Giving the boys at the Colt poker lessons the other night, were you?"

The skin on Edward's face tingled unpleasantly as it always did when he feared he was being made fun of. What else did Fitzgibbon know about the other night? Edward still had vestiges of a hangover and was still acutely ashamed about what had and hadn't transpired between himself and the prostitute. "It was a good start to a bad night," Edward said.

"Was it? What happened?"

"Never mind. Nothing I won't recover from."

"I'm sure of that. Listen, I'm in the middle of something just now. Are you free this afternoon, Edward? Come by the mill and say hello to an old friend, will you?"

To kill time and keep his spirits up until his meeting with Fitzgibbon, Edward walked the length of Market Street all the way to the border of East Paterson and back again to the center of town. He passed churches and row houses, a burlesque theater—girlies, the sign said—and half a dozen vacant lots, some dotted with lean-tos made of every conceivable sort of refuse. Through a chain-link fence, he watched two bums open a can with a knife and a rock. Would that be such a bad life, he wondered. Bloody cold for it now. He shoved his hands deep into his coat pockets. What the devil had happened to his gloves?

When Edward and Agnes had lived in New York, a walk down a city street was inspirational. When Agnes didn't have to work on a Sunday they used to put on their best clothes, go to twelve o'clock mass at St. Patrick's, then stroll up Fifth Avenue to Central Park. Edward had dreamed then, in a vague sort of way, of making his fortune as a builder. Plenty of Irish have, he used to tell himself. There's so-and-so, not much older than I am, and what's his name, the brother of that fellow from Belfast, more money than God. Although Edward wasn't actively pursuing financial independence or any other particular ambition—he was much too busy holding down a perfectly ordinary job and running around the city till all hours, getting settled, he called it—he nevertheless imagined a future that included a town house on Park Avenue for Agnes, trips abroad, large automobiles.

Manhattan encouraged such lofty goals. It at least allowed for the possibility of making it big. Why *not* you, the tall buildings and busy streets seemed to ask. Paterson, though, Paterson sighed heavily and said, "Look, you, it's come to this now. Surrender your aspirations or prepare to be disappointed."

Edward was reminded of home. The squat mountains in the distance, the general grubbiness, and something less tangible, too. A stubbornly boisterous spirit of absolute defeat. A lively appreciation for the futility of all human endeavor. "What are you getting yourself in an uproar about?" the fronts of narrow row houses asked. "Won't make a bit of difference what you do. Shut up, will you? Shut up and sit down. Make yourself at home. Because you are, you know. You are home. Drink?"

No wonder so many Irish found their way here, Edward thought.

By a quarter to three Edward had found his way to 36 Mill Street, a large L-shaped building of weathered brick. He stood staring up at a sign to the right of the main entrance. The sign was a curious affair in that it was actually two signs, one lying on top of and partially covering another. The sign on top was a piece of battered plywood. FITZGIBBON DYE WORKS AND INDUS-TRIAL PARK. Brush strokes were visible in the black paint and the letters were far from uniform in size. Whoever made the thing had clearly miscalculated how much space he'd had at his disposal. The ends of the words WORKS and PARK were written in extremely narrow letters that grew taller as they went, as if they hoped to make up in height what they lacked in breadth. Edward sensed the anxiety the sign painter must have felt when he'd seen the right edge of the plywood fast approaching with so many letters yet to go and wondered why the man hadn't taken the time to measure.

The plywood sign lay on top of a stately copper plaque permanently affixed to the brick of the building. A waterfall was engraved at the top. Beneath that were the words Fitzgibbon Silks, or so Edward surmised from the letters that were visible on either side of the plywood. Taking off his glasses and rubbing his eyes, Edward wondered why a man would rename his business and indicate the change by hanging a slapdash piece of work like the plywood sign. Fitzgibbon must have been forced to change his company's name. Most likely he'd gone belly-up as Fitzgibbon Silks and wound up in bankruptcy court, where he'd lost the right to continue operations under the original name.

The plywood sign was aggressively ugly. It seemed intent on being an affront and perhaps it was. Perhaps the circumstances that had forced Fitzgibbon to cover, to partially cover, the older, engraved sign had left him bitter and pugnacious. He may have wanted to show a judge or a couple of lawyers or his impatient creditors that while they had succeeded in putting a good man through the wringer, they hadn't destroyed him completely. Bloodied but not beaten, was he? Intent now on reviving his business, under whatever name, however recklessly, with no regard for keeping up appearances in the community, for being a good neighbor? Of course, Edward thought, I shouldn't be in such a hurry to discount the practical explanation. Fitzgibbon may simply not have had the money for a proper sign, may have had no choice but to use what he had on hand, a piece of plywood and an inch of thickened black paint in the bottom of a can.

Humiliation washed over Edward when he thought of his

intuition, his probably irrational belief that Fitzgibbon would come to his aid. He thought, briefly, of his bunkmate, Mahoney, saw the peaked face in his mind's eye. The resemblance to Fitzgibbon hadn't been all that great, and even if it was, so what? One man's looking like another doesn't mean a thing. Edward felt foolish for having allowed himself to put so much stock in what was clearly wishful thinking. He might just as well have picked a name out of the phone book, an Irish name, and presented himself to Mr. Kelly or Mr. Donahue or Mr. Doyle. Here I am. Help me.

So disheartened was Edward by his own gloomy interpretation of the double sign that he considered turning around and heading down the steep hill back into town. Only his dread of sitting in another bloody coffee shop or wandering around aimlessly some more kept him in place. Edward dearly wanted to have to be somewhere at a particular hour. He had an appointment, damn it, and he was keeping it, for better or worse. Even as he made up his mind to go ahead with his meeting, he wondered at his own peculiar situation. How was it that he who had once been connected to dozens of people by blood or affection or common interests found himself standing outside a mill in Paterson, New Jersey, with no ties to anybody save a man who would no doubt be surprised and amused to learn that one Edward Devlin considered him his last hope? How has this happened? Edward asked, feeling as if he'd dropped down from the sky. The events of the last several weeks, Agnes's death, her burial, his crossing, and the first days and nights in Paterson, seemed a disturbing and disjointed dream.

However flimsy Edward's connection to Fitzgibbon, he couldn't afford to discredit it entirely, much less sever it, because if he did he'd be hurling himself into a void, a vast empty space. To bolster his enthusiasm, to give himself some reason for continuing to believe that Fitzgibbon would save him, Edward recalled the sound of the voice on the other end of the telephone. Fitzgibbon certainly hadn't talked like a man who was barely hanging on. He was glad to hear from me, Edward thought, and eager for us to get together. It was he who picked up the phone so fast, mind, he who invited me to come see him.

Before long Edward had himself more or less convinced that his own reflecting on something as trivial as an unattractive sign-board was evidence that he was coming apart, unraveling.

To Edward's great relief (he might have gone on musing forever), a surly-looking guard in a navy-blue uniform headed his way. Good, let's get this show on the road.

"Afternoon," Edward said, straightening his tie.

"What can I do for you, buddy?"

"I've come to see Mr. Fitzgibbon."

"That so? You got an appointment?"

"I do. Three o'clock."

The guard pulled a small notebook from his shirt pocket. "Name?"

"Edward Devlin."

The notebook was opened, scanned. "Company?"

"Sorry?"

"There's no Devlin on my list. What company you with? Sometimes they put you down by your company name."

"I'm not with a company at present. I'm a friend of Mr. Fitzgibbon's."

The guard stared impassively. "You're not looking for a job, are you? Because I'll save you the trouble. He ain't hiring unless you're a dyer and you don't look like a dyer to me."

Edward blanched and then rallied in response to his own discomfort. "Look, I was invited here by Mr. Fitzgibbon and I'll thank you to inform him that I've arrived. Thank you."

"Hold on," the guard said, sounding suddenly tired and hard-used. "Nobody tells me nothing out here. Let me call inside."

Edward did his best to appear important and offended. The whole situation, being stopped by an officious tough, being treated badly because his name didn't appear where it was supposed to, was familiar though it took Edward a few seconds to figure out why. He'd had several similar experiences as a revolutionary. He'd find his way to some secret location, finally, only to be stopped by some mouthy teenager who'd been told to stand guard, who had never heard of Edward and who hadn't been informed of his coming and who treated him shabbily.

"All right," the guard said. "Go 'head in."

Edward pulled open the heavy wooden door and stepped into a vestibule, where he was immediately reassured by the sound of heavy machinery in operation. Whatever the hell Fitzgibbon Dye Works and Industrial Park was, it was up and running, a going concern. Expecting someone, Fitzgibbon himself, a secretary or clerk, to come and collect him, Edward assumed an expectant posture, shoulders square, chin up, expression composed. Nobody came. Edward took off his coat and draped it over one arm. He took off his hat and ran his fingers through his hair, eyeing the metal door on the far wall. It didn't look like the sort of door a visitor should venture through alone. Just beyond it, clearly, was the loud machinery, the factory floor. Not knowing what else to do, Edward stood stock-still and waited.

The metal door opened a long minute or so later and a young woman leaned in. "Mr. Devlin?"

"Hello."

"Mr. Fitzgibbon's expecting you. Follow me."

Edward did as he was told and soon found himself crossing a cavernous room between long rows of power looms. The floor vibrated under his feet, making the insides of his ears itch. The sway of the looms was so strong that walking between them was like wading across a current. Surveying the walls and ceiling, Edward admired the sturdiness of the building and wondered about its construction. The architect couldn't have known the punishment his building would one day come in for and yet he'd designed a structure that was able to withstand what was probably the equivalent of an earthquake a day.

The young woman moved at a good clip without looking left or right. Edward kept up but managed to take note of something odd. It was clear that the work going on all around him was not a single, unified effort but was instead a collection of small, discrete operations, all performing the same task, weaving cloth on power looms. There were probably half a dozen small shops, separated one from another by chicken wire. Each of these groups consisted of several looms, as many as ten, and two or three very busy workers.

The chicken wire dividers put Edward in mind of the plywood sign out front. Dividers and sign shared a kind of antago-

nism that was the result of their flimsiness. What is here today
may not be here tomorrow, they said. So there. How was it that
a structure that would be standing long after all of its current
occupants were dead and buried had come to house so much
that was so insistently transient?

Edward was grateful when he made it, finally, into a long
hallway, where the roar of the looms let up a bit. The young
woman turned and smiled. "Sorry about that," she said, gesturing toward the mill floor. "If the guard had sent you around to
the side door like he was supposed to. Anyway, this is Mr.
Fitzgibbon's office. Knock and he'll let you in."

Edward said thank you then took a moment to determine
what sort of knock was appropriate. Three firm raps, he decided, and no more until at least a minute had gone by. He'd
count the seconds if he had to.

Edward's knuckles had barely made contact with the door
when it swung open.

"Edward," Fitzgibbon said, extending his hand. "Come on in,
man. Sit down. Sit down and tell me how you've been keeping."

Edward wondered, fleetingly, how an Irishman and a Patersonian came to be so effusive. Concentrate, he scolded himself.
Kiss his ass but good. Fitzgibbon was still handsome, of course.
His blond hair had a good bit of grey in it now, as did his mustache; there were deep creases in the corners of his eyes; the
mischievous gleam that Edward had remembered so distinctly
and half resented seemed tempered by age and experience.
Edward sat in one of the two chairs opposite Fitzgibbon's mammoth desk and told of his recent bereavement as concisely as
he could because he didn't want to seem pathetic and was
afraid he'd lose his composure if he went into any more detail
than was absolutely necessary.

The walls of Fitzgibbon's office were a kind of clapboard,
painted white. A bank of windows ran along the top of one of
them. The glass was textured so that it let in light but not sky.
Small framed pictures were arranged in quaint groupings at
various places on the walls. There was a collection of fashion sketches, women in old-style evening dress, and another
of black-and-white photographs of Paterson vistas, the famous

waterfall, the clock tower above City Hall. There was a simple chandelier, workaday pewter, hanging from the center of the ceiling. A fat dictionary, well thumbed, lay open on a wooden stand.

"Now I'm back," Edward said, drawing his story to an abrupt conclusion when he sensed he was talking too long, "and looking for a job. It's a hell of a time to ask anybody for help finding work, I know, but, well, I'm a civil engineer, and a good one, university trained. I thought, Mr. Fitzgibbon, that you—"

Fitzgibbon held up his left hand and narrowed his blue eyes as if to say there'll be time to talk of practical matters later.

"Call me Fitz, Edward, please. We're not strangers, you and I."

How white his shirt cuffs were, how perfectly pressed, set off by gold cuff links, delicate ovals.

"First let me offer my condolences. Agnes gone. What a shame. So young, God rest her soul. You did the right thing, Edward, taking her back to Ireland in the end. A young person should never be buried far from home."

Edward warmed to Fitz's good opinion, felt it in his joints and between his shoulder blades. Despite his vow to leave the moral universe behind, he wasn't yet beyond the reach of praise, especially when it came from such an appealing source. Edward looked down at the black-and-white tile floor and imagined, all in an instant, a great and good friendship developing between himself and this vital, prosperous man.

The two men sat in silence a moment and then Fitzgibbon rubbed his hands together and commended Edward for coming back to America. "We go on, don't we?" he said, meaning, Edward knew, we Irish. "A young man like yourself. You've suffered a terrible loss to be sure but you'll survive. You'll start over now, you will."

Seeing himself as Fitz seemed to and feeling noble, Edward nodded.

"Come on till I show you around the place," Fitz said, getting to his feet. "Have you ever been inside a dye works?"

"I haven't," Edward said, doing his best to sound enthusiastic but having no desire to return to the noisy room with the chicken wire and the looms.

Outside the office door Fitzgibbon turned right and headed

away from the mill floor. The noise and the shaking of the power looms grew fainter. Edward followed Fitz into a large room that while certainly not what anyone would call well appointed was orderly and pleasing in a workmanlike way. Tall windows, the glass clear and clean, ran the length of all four walls. The light was plentiful and true. Vats of dark liquid, blues and reds and several of the deepest black, were arranged in tidy rows. Somber men in shirtsleeves dipped fat skeins of thread that hung from cross sticks into the vats then moved the sticks back and forth slowly and rhythmically. Watching the men work was pleasant and mildly hypnotic. They moved with care, their expressions intent.

"Gentlemen," Fitzgibbon said when it became clear that several of the dyers had taken note of his presence. Edward smiled at the subtle ways the greeting was acknowledged. One man nodded exactly once, moved his head up and then down. Another raised his eyebrows. A third lifted an index finger.

"This is the only part of the silk business I give a damn about anymore, the dyeing. Labor's all but ruined the rest of it as far as I'm concerned."

A dyer raised his cross sticks and peered at the skein of thread hanging from them. Edward understood then why the light in the room had to be as good as it was. The dyers had to be able to see subtle differences between one shade of wet silk and another.

"There's no water in the world for dyeing like what's in the Passaic River. Soft. You've got to have soft water for dyeing and we've got the best. Three-quarters of the silk dyed in the States is done here because of the water."

"That right?" Edward said, thinking of the sign DYE WORKS AND INDUSTRIAL PARK. So this was the dye works, and the other, the cavern with the frenzied workers and chicken wire, that was the industrial park.

"Do you know what my specialty is, Edward? Do you know what I do better than anybody else?"

Edward shook his head.

"Make black. The purest, the deepest, the richest black in

the business. Right here. There's no end of call for it. Mourning clothes and evening dress, people need black."

"They do, absolutely."

"They want it. They want black. And it's the hardest color to get right, too. Mine's brilliant, the best you're ever going to find. And furthermore it's permanent. My black won't come off on your skin and won't fade to ash in a year's time."

"What's your secret?" Edward asked, intending only to convey a sense of how impressed he was but understanding from the sudden stiffening of Fitz's face that his process for making black was exactly that, a secret.

"Only one person beside me knows that, Edward. My master dyer. I had to bring him and his whole bloody family over from Italy. It was worth it, though. Nobody knows color like this man. No body. I'd take you back to his lab and introduce you but he doesn't like to be disturbed when he's working as hard as he is just now. You know he must be good for me to indulge him the way I do. Come on and I'll walk you out."

Edward was sorry to see the meeting coming to an end so quickly. He didn't think he'd made his case for deserving help finding work nearly strongly enough and, beyond that, the prospect of heading back out into the cold made him grim. His own inner resources were so thoroughly depleted that he wished he could tap into Fitz's, which seemed inexhaustible. What Edward wanted more than anything was to remain in Fitz's company a while longer, to go where Fitz went, see what Fitz saw. It was a strange sort of longing and Edward recognized it as such. More evidence of his general dissolution. Get hold of yourself, he thought. If Fitz says the meeting is over, it's over. The worst thing you could possibly do is overstay your welcome. One more mention of needing a job, a parting shot, when we shake hands.

Fitz escorted Edward out of the building via the side door and into the bright winter sun then stood with his arms crossed. "Lovely day, isn't it?"

"It is," Edward said. Then, determined to make conversation, he added, "So you've got the dye works and you're a mill, too. You're weaving silk here as well?"

"In a manner of speaking."

"You must have forty looms inside."

"Sixty, actually, but they're not mine, not anymore."

"Not yours?"

"You've heard, I'm sure, of the years and years of strikes and things here. Paterson workers are a rebellious lot. Maybe whatever it is in the water that makes the dye . . . anyway, it got so bad it was impossible for a man to stay in business never mind make any money. Until I finally hit on a solution. It was right under my nose all along. If the workers were so bloody unhappy as employees, striking every time I looked at them cross-eyed, let them see how they liked running their own shows. I'm not the boss anymore, at least not of the weavers. The dyers, that's a different story. The dyers still work for me. But the weavers have the great privilege of working for themselves. I sold them the looms, on time. None of them had the money to buy outright, of course. I'm now what's called a converter. I buy raw silk and pay independent contractors to weave it. It's better for everybody. I don't have labor troubles every goddamn week and the weavers have the advantage of working for themselves."

Edward thought of the harried workers he'd seen rushing from loom to loom. He was certain they'd have a much different interpretation of the structural change that had taken place in their work lives. As a younger man, like many Irish nationalists, Edward had had socialist leanings. Not that he'd had much patience for the specifics of economic theory, one hypothesis set on top of another, pronouncements that had never and would never be proved, but he had gone along with the notion that rich people have too much money and poor people too little. Standing outside the red-brick building with the well-dressed John Fitzgibbon, though, Edward didn't give a damn about the plight of the working men and women inside. In fact, Fitz's being an exploiter, an opportunist, a good businessman, made him all the more attractive. A man doesn't make a success of himself by being tender-hearted.

"Anyway," Fitz said, looking at his watch. "I'm sure that's more about the silk business than you ever wanted to know. Good to see you, Edward. Thanks for coming by."

"My pleasure, Fitz. And thank you for the tour. Do you

think, what I mean to say is, have you got any advice for me on the job front just now?"

"Are you a citizen, Edward?"

"I am."

"Good. That'll help. There's a lot of federal money floating around these days. They're going to be building roads and bridges and God knows what everywhere you look. Give me a couple of days. Let's see what I can scare up."

"Right. I'll call you next week then, Monday or Tuesday?"

Fitz looked Edward up and down without making any attempt to disguise what he was doing. Then he smiled his once boyish and now slightly weary smile. "Are you free for dinner tonight by any chance, Edward?"

Edward spent the remainder of the afternoon in Wexler's Men's on Main Street. Buying new clothes was a calculated risk. If a job didn't materialize, he'd be in even worse straits financially, but he was feeling hopeful and believed an investment in his appearance would pay off. In Fitz's office Edward had felt shabby. Because of medical and travel expenses, he hadn't bought any new clothes in years. There were shiny patches on his pant legs, a deep crease in his belt; his lapels didn't lie right anymore.

He bought a handsome grey suit, double-breasted, with wide lapels and padded shoulders, a striped tie, a pair of warm gloves, and half a dozen white handkerchiefs, much to the delight of Mr. Wexler. Not another soul came into the place the two hours Edward was there. Wexler was only too happy to turn up the pants while Edward waited. No other alterations were necessary. "A perfect forty-two regular," Wexler said. "You're a lucky man. You can buy off the rack and it looks custom-made."

Laden with packages, Edward returned to the Alexander Hamilton. Shaving, he paused periodically to peer at himself in the mirror and say, "Come on, come on," not knowing what he meant by it exactly but feeling the need to urge himself on. It was during one of these spurring sessions—he was looking himself in the eye and wondering about Mrs. Fitzgibbon, straining to remember if he'd ever met her—when his grief caught up with him. He sat down hard on the edge of the bed.

The enthusiasm he felt for his new clothes and his dinner engagement was suddenly gone. All he wanted was to lie back, pull the covers up, turn out the light. He didn't think he had the energy even to take off his shoes. As if to make up for the couple of hours' respite from thinking of Agnes, his brain produced a vivid image of the instant of her death, her shoulders jerking strangely forward and her jaw dropping. Edward remembered waiting for the next breath and it not coming. His head had reeled, his consciousness rushed up and outward so that the voices in the room, Sadie's, Joseph's, had seemed to come from a great distance. He'd been afraid he wouldn't feel Agnes's death at the very instant it happened, but he had, he surely had.

How in God's name was he going to get through dinner with the Fitzgibbons? He didn't feel capable of putting two words together, never mind holding up his end of a three-way conversation with people he hardly knew and wanted to impress. He was lying flat on his back, looking up at the ceiling and cursing himself for accepting Fitzgibbon's invitation, when the possibility of not going, of simply not showing up, crept in. He didn't *have* to go, did he? He didn't even have to call and say he wasn't coming. (The prospect of a telephone call unnerved him nearly as much as going to dinner.) He didn't have to do anything he didn't want to anymore. That was the whole point now, wasn't it?

A stern element in Edward's nature piped up then and proceeded to lay out the terms under which he could *not* show up at the Fitzgibbons'. He didn't have to go, that was true, but if he chose that option he'd do so with the understanding that he was burning a bridge. Fitzgibbon wouldn't forgive such a slight and certainly wouldn't lift a finger to help after it, and why should he? Edward remembered the lean-tos on Market Street and told himself that if he didn't keep his engagement with Fitzgibbon, if he chose to indulge himself by spending the evening in bed, he would, in effect, be abandoning all hope of finding a decent job and so had better be prepared to join the ranks of the un- and underemployed. He'd check out of the Alexander Hamilton in the morning and find a room in a boardinghouse. He wondered if he could talk Wexler into taking back the suit and then remembered how chipper Wexler had been when he realized there was an actual customer in his store, one with money to spend. The poor bastard had probably convinced himself that the sale of one suit was evidence of things beginning to turn around.

So unruly were Edward's emotions, so out of whack, that it was his concern for Wexler that got him up. He could not bring himself to disappoint Wexler. He didn't acknowledge as much, told himself instead that he was his father's son, whether he wanted to be or not. He was responsible when push came to shove. He certainly wasn't cut out for opening cans with rocks and things. I wouldn't last a week on the street, he thought.

Up, then. Up and finish dressing. Come on.

He had some trouble tying his new tie but getting it done generated a mild momentum that made putting his jacket on easier. He was all right, he was going, wallet in the back pocket of his trousers, handkerchief in the right front, a quarter, a dime, and two pennies in the left.

The Fitzgibbons lived in Paterson's best neighborhood, its only really good one, an enclave of big houses and landscaped lawns, a couple of streets on a hillside that looked out over the rest of the city. The house was a great big Victorian, a hulking Queen Anne, three stories plus an attic, with arches and gables, a turret on one side, a wraparound porch. It stood, Edward thought, leaning back to take in the whole of the house at once, rather too close to the street. A house its size wanted more of a buildup, a lead-in, than was offered by the short path from sidewalk to wide brownstone steps with brass railings.

He hadn't forgotten that he'd been there once before, though the outside of the house didn't look familiar. He strained to remember details of his earlier visit and they came easily enough, a five-piece band playing too loudly, a crowded dance floor, long tables of lavish food, and candles, lots and lots of candles burning, in the bathroom even, down the long hallways.

Back then he'd never have stood outside looking up. He'd have piled out of the crowded car—they were always piling in and out of cars and restaurant booths and tiny apartment kitchens in those days, pile in, everybody, pile out—and marched right inside.

Which is the way to do things, Edward thought, impatient, again, with his own propensity to drift. A simple dinner with genial people. Get on with it.

He marched up the stairs onto the porch and rang the doorbell. A matronly woman with grey hair and a weathered complexion answered.

"Evening," Edward said.

"Right. Come in, then. They're expecting you."

Edward wiped his feet thoroughly before following the unsmiling housekeeper into the front hall. "Cold out tonight," he said, taking off his hat and coat.

" 'Tis."

"Not that I was out very long. Took a cab from my hotel. Downtown. Where I'm staying at the moment."

The housekeeper had no apparent interest in how Edward had come or from whence.

He'd always been uncomfortable in the presence of Irish help. Several of his and Agnes's acquaintances had had Irish maids years before when times were good. (An affectation, he'd thought even then, a bit much.) He tended to talk too much to prove he wasn't putting on airs but the servants never seemed to appreciate his democratic impulses. Just the opposite. They seemed to waste no time in pegging him as a man who himself had no servants and deserved none. They treated him very badly. He'd hardly gotten in the door before this one turned on him. Why do Irish hire Irish? he wondered. Wouldn't the colored make life simpler all around?

"This way. Come on."

The housekeeper led the way to a large living room. Where the band was, Edward thought, and the dance floor, all the furniture taken out.

"Here he is," Fitzgibbon said, turning, poker in hand, from the fire he'd been tending. "Here's Edward Devlin and right on time, too. Come on in. Sit down and warm yourself. You remember Sylvia, don't you?"

Sylvia Fitzgibbon was considerably younger than her husband, fifteen years at least, Edward guessed. She had dark curly hair, fair skin, brown eyes, a wide smile. He didn't remember her and knew he would have if they'd ever met.

"I'm so glad you could join us," she said, her voice polished and poised. "Sit down, please."

"Here you go. A little something to take the chill off."

Edward's stomach, still not fully recovered from the binge of two nights before, clutched at the smell of whiskey, but he was nervous and glad for a drink just the same.

"Have any trouble finding us? Make your way through the wilds of Paterson all right?"

"Fine. My cab driver knew right where to go. I didn't even have to give an address. Fitzgibbon, I said, and he said Thirty-eighth Street."

"Paterson is a very small place," Sylvia said. "It doesn't take much to be well known here."

She wasn't Irish, Edward was sure. What was she? Italian? No, he didn't think so. Jewish, that's right. He remembered hearing something once about Fitz's having married a rich Jewish girl—department stores or something, wasn't it?—and causing an awful row with her family. Why hadn't he remembered that before?

"What a lovely home you've got."

It was lovely, too. It was certainly sumptuous. Decorated, done, every inch of it done. The walls in the living room were painted a very pale green, the kind of color that changes dramatically in response to changes in light, like certain eye colors. The wood floor was the deepest brown. There were two Persian rugs, the dominant color of both a rosy red.

"Sylvia's doing," Fitz said. "Sylvia did all the decorating herself."

"It's magnificent."

Sylvia acknowledged the compliment with a nod and a faint smile.

Edward had just started on his second drink when the house-keeper appeared.

"Thank you, Bridget," Sylvia said. "Are we ready for dinner?"

In the dining room the wood floors, moldings, and mantel

were light-colored, golden. A smallish round table sat in the center of the room. Edward found he was famished and ate heartily, rib roast, Yorkshire pudding, mashed potatoes, green beans in sweet butter. Warmed by the fires, eased by the excellent whiskey, sated by meat and potatoes and bread, Edward felt better than he had in months. He was congratulating himself on being in town only three days and sharing the table of such pleasant and prosperous people when Sylvia put down her coffee cup and said, "I was so sorry to hear about your wife, Edward. This must be a very difficult time for you."

"It is, yes. Thank you."

"My sister died of TB. So I . . . I know what a terrible disease it is."

Edward was struck by Sylvia's candor. It was unusual for anyone to be so forthright about tuberculosis. Most shied away from calling the disease by its name. TB was a poor person's illness, associated with tenements and bad hygiene and on and on. Actually, Edward was himself somewhat surprised to learn that Sylvia had had a sister with TB. Even though his own experience had proven time and again that plenty of well-off people got it, some small, unthinking part of him still believed that TB was linked to economic status.

"I'm sorry," he said. "Recently, or . . . ?"

"Oh, no. Years ago. When I was seventeen."

"Let's move on to happier subjects, shall we?" Fitzgibbon said. "Tell us, Edward, I'm curious, what do you think of Paterson so far?"

Glad for the change in subject, though feeling some lingering discomfort about the impatience in Fitzgibbon's voice, Edward launched into a description of Paterson that included his sense that the city exuded a deeply contradictory spirit, a lively morbidity, an intensely cynical optimism. He succeeded only in getting all tangled up in his words. His impressions of Paterson eluded even the most determined attempts at articulation now. They seemed vague and sentimental, if not downright incoherent, in the company of the forthright Fitzgibbons. Edward stammered and doubled back on himself, recovering his footing only when he settled for blandly singing Paterson's praises. A fine city, it was. Reminded him of home. Having a bit of a hard time now but what city wasn't?

Thinking he saw the Fitzgibbons exchange a glance (is this guy all right?), Edward was glad when Sylvia suggested they go back to the living room, where they'd be more comfortable. Fitz took his place by the fire. Sylvia sat on one end of the white sofa just opposite, Edward the other. Fitz put a log on the fire, lit a cigar, and told the story of his beginnings in America at Edward's prompting. Fitz had come over from Dublin by himself at fourteen, worked his tail off, saved his money, convinced Sylvia's father to back him in a modest venture. "A mick and a Jew, can you imagine? We were a good team, though. I made a pile of money for old Sam, don't worry."

"And what did he think when you took a liking to his daughter?" Edward asked, knowing from the gossip he'd heard years before that he was probably treading on corns but wanting to draw Sylvia into the conversation.

Fitz removed a bit of tobacco from his tongue. "That was years later. Sylvia was just a little girl when her daddy and I were business partners."

Sylvia sat with legs crossed at the knees and arms folded. She seemed to be admiring or at least inspecting her own left shoe, rotating her foot at the ankle and gazing steadily at it. Edward found himself enjoying the tension in the air. It made him and the Fitzgibbons seem better acquainted than they actually were.

"Did you and ... I'm sorry but I've forgotten your wife's name," Sylvia said.

"Agnes."

"Did you and Agnes have children?"

"One. We had one. A girl."

"Oh ... I'm so sorry, Edward. I had no idea."

"Pardon?"

"Tuberculosis also? I'm so sorry. Please forgive me."

"No. Oh, no. She's alive and well, my daughter. She's back home."

Sylvia cocked her head to one side. "Will you send for her once you get settled?"

"What kind of a question is that, Sylvia? None of our business, is it?"

"She's with my two sisters, her aunts, safe and sound."

"The man's clearly done what he thinks is best."

Fitz got up and began poking at the fire. Nobody spoke for thirty seconds or so and then, when Edward was about to begin praising the dinner all over again, Fitz brought up the troubles. Edward soon found himself the recipient of an impassioned lecture on the evils of partition. Ordinarily he didn't have much use for Irishmen in America with strong opinions on matters they didn't understand, but tonight, determined to indulge his host, he was only too happy to listen and nod his head and say of course, absolutely, right, right again.

It was after midnight and Sylvia had excused herself momentarily when Fitzgibbon said, "Doesn't make any sense, you venturing out in the cold at this hour. Why don't you spend the night, Edward? We've got plenty of room."

When Sylvia returned she took the news that Edward had gone from dinner guest to houseguest in perfect stride. "Good," she said. "I'm going to say good night, though, if nobody minds. Fitz, you'll take Edward to his room and show him where things are?"

"If it's all right, Fitz, I think I'll turn in myself. The good food and the whiskey's gotten the better of me, I'm afraid."

"Not a'tall. A solid night's sleep is what you need. Go on. Sylvia'll take you up. I'll see you in the morning. We can ride downtown together."

Sylvia led the way to a guest room on the second floor. She turned on the light, showed Edward where the bathroom and extra blankets were, then paused in the doorway. "You must be exhausted," she said.

"I am that."

"Let me put your mind at ease about one thing, anyway, if I can. Fitz will find you a job. He likes you. It's been ages since I've seen him in such good spirits. He'll do whatever he has to, he'll find you a job."

Edward nodded, uncomfortable in the role of petitioner. "About my daughter," he said.

"That's none of my business. I'm sorry if I put you on the spot. It's just that Fitz hadn't mentioned you—"

"All the same, I just want you to know that she's well taken care of. I wouldn't want you to think . . . the thing is, my wife wanted her to go to a proper Irish boarding school. When she's a little older, they start them very young, you know."

"How old is she?"

"Six. Six years old."

"If that's what her mother wanted, of course. I really didn't mean to pry. Anyway, good night, Edward. I probably won't see you in the morning if you're going to leave with Fitz. It was a pleasure meeting you. I'm sure I'll see you again."

Edward lay awake considering how easily the lie had come off his tongue. Agnes had never expressed any desire for Maura to go to boarding school. In all the time Agnes was sick she'd voiced concern about what would happen to Maura only once. They were in Arizona and Agnes was bad off, dying, the doctors said. Edward had stepped outside for a smoke, sat down on the steps of the little house they'd rented, and looked up at the lurid southwestern sky.

Inside, unbeknownst to Edward, Maura began to cry.

Agnes, sick as she was, managed to get out of bed and make her way to the baby's room. When Edward came inside he found Agnes sitting on the stairs with Maura on her lap.

"What're you doing out of bed?"

"Shhhh. I only just got her back to sleep."

"You are not supposed to be up."

"Promise me something, Ned."

"Depends."

"Will you or not?"

"What?"

"Promise me that you'll remarry. That you won't try to raise her alone."

chapter 6

Maura woke up in the big bed, looked around, and went slack with disappointment. She'd fallen asleep hoping that when she woke up she'd find herself back home in the apartment in New York City, where she'd lived longer than she'd lived anywhere else. She closed her eyes and summoned images of home, the long tiled hallway where her footsteps had echoed so satisfyingly, the pink ceramic dish of bobby pins beside the bathroom sink, a striped necktie hanging over a doorknob.

"Your father's gone back to America," Aunt Sadie had said one morning several weeks before. "He left after you went to bed last night. He'll write once he's got himself settled."

Rex scratched at the door and Maura got up to let him in.

"Hey, pup."

The dog lay down on the rug while Maura dressed and together they went down to breakfast.

Bell put a bowl of oatmeal and a quart bottle of milk on the table.

"Every bit of it," Sadie said. "No leaving half like you did yesterday. I haven't money to waste on indifferent eaters, Lady Jane."

Maura gazed at the oatmeal, picked up her spoon. One . . . two . . . three mouthfuls swallowed like medicine.

"Do you want to get sick like your mother was?"

"No."

"Then eat."

"I don't want it."

"It's not a question of want, is it? It's a question of you won't have anything till dinner and then we'll see who doesn't want what. Now put on your coat. I've important business to see to this morning."

As Sadie and Maura walked down the street, Maura hung back so that she could look carefully at the faces of people passing without attracting Sadie's attention. There were times, minutes, hours, chunks of afternoons and evenings, when Maura believed that her father had gone back to America. (She imagined him pushing the door to the apartment open, pulling his keys from the lock, taking off his hat and coat, and hanging them in the hall closet by the round table with the black telephone on it.) This morning, however, Maura thought it entirely possible that she might spot her father on the sidewalk in Omagh and so was keeping an eye out, getting a look under as many hat brims as she could. Her nose started to run in the cold morning air and she sniffed.

"Didn't Bell give you a handkerchief? Use it. Listen to me now. Listen to what I'm about to tell you. Don't say a word once we get over there about your mother being sick in the house. Not a word, understand?"

"Yes."

"Say it. Say what I told you."

"I have to be quiet and not say that—"

"Don't say anything and you won't get yourself in trouble."

It was a much better house than the others Sadie owned, including the one she lived in, and now it was hers, free and clear, a substantial addition to her holdings. Edward had tried to talk her into an informal arrangement. "You'll get the rent, Sadie. For all intents and purposes the house will be yours. Never mind about the paperwork. You and I will have an understanding and that'll be that. I'm your brother, for Christ's sake. You can trust me." Sadie had refused to give him one shilling until he consented to make the transfer legal. Putting the key in the door, she reaped the reward for standing her ground. Ownership agreed with her.

Sadie went around opening shades to let in the morning light. She'd been back in the house a dozen times since Agnes's death. The place had been cleaned and whitewashed and Sadie had supervised, indulging her grief when she got a minute to herself, alone in the back bedroom, one hand on her throat. This morning, aside from a purely physical agitation, the most noticeable symptom of which was a tingling high up in her nose, Sadie was aware only of her desire to get the place rented.

Maura had not set foot in the house since she'd left it in the middle of the night weeks before. She made straight for the back bedroom.

Empty. No furniture. No curtains.

Nothing.

She looked in the closet. A row of hooks along the back wall, all of them empty. She spotted the end of a candle in a corner, two inches of smudgy wax and a charred wick. She held it on her open palm a minute then slipped it into her coat pocket.

"What've you got?"

"Nothing."

"Liar. I saw you put something in your pocket. Get over here."

Maura shook her head.

"Give me what you've got."

Maura produced the candle end.

"What d'you want that for?"

"Nothing."

"To light, no doubt, once you get your hands on some matches. Give it."

"I won't light it, I promise. I'm just . . . I just want to keep it."

"Give it to me, I said." Sadie held out her hand and snapped her fingers.

"No."

Maura turned her head at the last possible second so that the heel of Sadie's hand clipped her jaw and ear.

"I'll break your arm I catch you with matches."

In the kitchen Sadie pinched the bridge of her nose, opened the cupboards to make sure they were free of mouse droppings, turned on the tap, looked at her watch. "If they haven't come by a quarter-past we're going home. A person who can't be prompt for an appointment isn't likely to pay his rent on time. Stop sniffling, Maura. You're all right. If you'd do what I tell you to do when I tell you to do it, we'd all be better off. I don't know what your mother and father let you get away with but as long as you're living under my roof you'll do as I say."

A ruddy-faced husband and wife arrived a few minutes later. "Sorry to keep you waiting, Miss Devlin," the man said. "We had a bit of trouble finding the place. Had to stop and ask. Now, let's have a look around."

"Hello," the woman said, cocking her head to one side and smiling at Maura. "What's your name?"

Maura looked at Sadie.

"Go on. Tell the lady your name."

"Maura Devlin."

"My niece. You can have the house as of the first of February. I like to start all my tenants on the first. Keeps things straight, I find."

"We'll take a look upstairs, if you don't mind."

"Go on. Fresh paint up there as well."

When the prospective tenants were out of earshot, Sadie glowered at Maura. "What've you gone deaf-mute all the sudden?"

"You said not to talk."

"I told you not to mention your mother. If somebody asks you your name, for God's sake, you answer. You don't stand there with your fool mouth hanging open."

Sadie took the lease out of her bag and spread it on the counter. She loved the official look of it, the formal language, the straight black lines for signatures.

"All right then. You've seen what there is to see. Will you be taking the house or not?"

"About the rent, Miss Devlin."

"Eight pounds per annum, payable quarterly. Just as was stated in the advertisement."

"We heard something last night."

"Did you? What did you hear?"

"We heard that your brother's wife died of consumption here just last month. It's a terrible disease, isn't it? Contagious as it can be. They say it gets into the walls of a house. We have four children, four girls, and, God willing, a boy on the way."

"The rent is eight pounds as was clearly stated."

"Will you take six, considering?"

Sadie pursed her lips. Agnes, she thought, even from the grave your hand finds its way into my pocket. "Educated people like yourselves. I wouldn't think you'd go in for superstitions and that's all it is, you know. This house has been thoroughly disinfected, top to bottom. I'd live here myself in a minute, with my niece. I'm her guardian now, nobody but me to look after her, poor thing's an orphan, but it's too much house for us, more room than we need."

"Six pounds, Miss Devlin. Otherwise we'll thank you for your time and be on our way."

"You won't find anything else this size for the price."

"We'll take our chances."

"Four children already and your wife expecting, you ought to have a roof over your heads. Six pounds it is then. And see that you pay promptly. Don't make me regret my generosity."

Sadie had been prepared to go to five to get the place rented so she was in good spirits on the way home. She nearly offered to stop and buy Maura a treat but then remembered the wasted oatmeal and the candle end and decided she'd been far too permissive already. I'll probably be burned to a cinder in my bed for my trouble.

In the afternoon Maura went with Bell to the market. The butcher's helper, a homely fellow, a little slow in the head, stuck his tongue out at Maura and called her "Yank."

Maura turned to the door, expecting this Yank person to be coming through it.

"You," the boy said. "You're a Yank, ain't you? You're not Irish. You were born over there in America and that makes you a Yank, sure it does."

Maura was puzzled. At home in America she'd been Irish, she was certain, and nearly everybody else, her mother's doctors, the various people who'd looked after her while her father was at work, most of the other mothers and fathers in the apartment building, had been Yanks. Now here in Ireland, according to this big-headed boy, *she* was a Yank. It didn't occur to her to argue. She assumed it was her responsibility to figure out what was what now, who was who. "Yank," she said, trying the word out and liking its brawny sound. "Yank."

"Please, Maura," Bell said. "Don't say that. It's very vulgar."

Bell planned to unload her charge on Sadie as soon as the marketing was done but when she and Maura got home Sadie was nowhere to be found. No accident, that, Bell thought. "Go into the drawing room then, Maura. Sit like a good girl. Don't touch anything. Just sit and wait for your tea."

Maura wandered around looking at glass figurines, swans and seashells and ballet dancers, then peeked into the kitchen and saw Bell sitting at the table reading a newspaper. Maura crept upstairs to the room where she slept and closed the door after herself as quietly as she could. She kneeled down by the bed and pulled the beaded green evening bag from under it. "Yank, Yank, Yank," she whispered as she took out an empty perfume bottle, her mother's, a thermometer, a gift from a pretty young nurse in Switzerland, a plain white handkerchief that had belonged to her father. She stuck her nose into the empty purse, inhaled deeply, and gave herself over to the memory of a long train ride during which she'd been allowed to sit on her mother's lap and rest her head against the lapel of the red leather jacket her father had insisted her mother put on. Coming back to herself, Maura reached into her pocket, pulled out the candle end, and added it to her collection.

Living under the same roof as Agnes's daughter was proving even harder than Sadie had thought it would be. To acquaintances, to Bell, and to herself most of the time, Sadie pretended it was the inconvenience of caring for a child that rankled. The inconvenience was the least of it. Sadie had been denied Agnes's company, her affection, her passion, but had wound up by default with her work, what should have been her work, the drudgery of raising her child. My lot in life, Sadie thought. My share. Drabness always. For other people the drama, the comings and goings, the adventures, the intrigues. What do I get? The responsibility, the tedium, the expense. Sadie found cold comfort in knowing that she alone had kept Maura out of an orphanage. She suspected that the others, Joseph, Edward, had known all along that she would not be able to stand by and watch while a Devlin was made into a charity case, dumped on the nuns while half a dozen Devlins, including the child's own father, were walking around alive and more or less well. Assured of her right-mindedness, her strong sense of duty, her inability to let an obligation go unmet, her brothers had probably wondered only what had taken her so long. Sadie will do it. Of course she will. What the hell else has Sadie got to do?

Had Agnes been of a similar mind? Sadie wondered. Had Agnes, too, been so sure of Sadie's willingness to take on whatever needed taking on that she hadn't thought it necessary even to ask? It was one thing for Sadie to know that her brothers viewed her as someone who had very little reason, ever, to say no, something else entirely to think that Agnes had. But what other explanation could there possibly be for Agnes's not asking Sadie to take Maura in? There'd been plenty of opportunities, all those hours spent at Agnes's bedside. Why hadn't Agnes asked Sadie to look after her daughter then? Not able to stand the idea that she hadn't merited asking in Agnes's eyes, Sadie convinced herself that Agnes hadn't asked because it had never occurred to her that Edward would abandon their daughter. Agnes had assumed there'd be somebody to take care of Maura—Edward, the child's father—a perfectly sensible assumption.

There was all of what Maura signified about Sadie and then there was Maura herself. She was small for six, and impish, Sadie thought. She had big round eyes, green like her mother's, and slightly bugged as if she were always, always startled. Her hair was cut short, stick straight, blond on its way to brown. She wasn't meek, exactly. There'd been several displays of defiance, mild ones to be sure, refusing to eat what was put in front of her, that bit with the candle end in Edward's house, but these incidents seemed more quirks than acts of rebellion, unconnected to any larger outrage. For the most part Maura seemed intent on staying out of the way. She walked around looking apologetic, as if she knew full well that her presence was a nuisance and understood why. She had no idea, so far as Sadie could see, that she'd been treated very badly. The girl seemed to accept her mother dying and her father running off as her due. Watching through the kitchen window while Maura arranged a pile of twigs in a tidy row, scattered them, lined them up neatly again (even in her play there was grim resignation), seeing her charge down the stairs in mismatched socks after a single warning that if she didn't get a move on they'd be late for mass, Sadie was repulsed. Some adults are drawn to children who remind them of themselves. Others feel an immediate grudge.

And then, to make matters worse—why is there always some stupid incidental thing that draws to itself all the currents and crosscurrents swirling around it?—Rex had taken a shine to Maura. Rex was Sadie's dog and Sadie's alone. She liked him better than she did any other living creature. And now, adding insult to injury and irritation to smoldering rage, the bloody dog had taken a shine to Maura. He followed her from room to room. Sat waiting outside her bedroom door. Put his head on her lap and gazed up at her face seeming, almost, to smile. Right there in Sadie's house, day in and day out, a satiric reenactment of the greatest betrayal of Sadie's life. The daughter of the man who had stolen her love usurping the affections of her dog.

A letter came from America. Would Sadie look into sending Maura away to boarding school? It's what Agnes wanted, Edward wrote, a convent education for her daughter.

"I don't know why we didn't think of it before," Bell said. "Let's do it. Let's send her away."

Sadie was greatly relieved to see that Edward was finally showing some concern for his only child. She'd been mortified by his abdicating his responsibility and her mortification was fundamentally clannish. We're Devlins, she'd wanted to shout, not just at Edward but at Joseph, too, and at Bell, who, Sadie was certain, would have let the child go to the nuns if it had been up to her. We were not brought up to shirk our responsibilities, God damn it, God damn all of you. She'd thought of her parents and the sacrifices they'd made, the long hours they'd worked, to educate their sons, Edward an engineer, Joseph a doctor, to raise the family's standing. She'd been glad that neither her mother nor her father had lived to see Edward do what he'd done. Of course things would have gone very differently if they were here, Sadie thought. They'd have sat Edward down and told him a broken heart was all well and good, life is hard to be sure, disease and death and all the rest of it, but there's no excuse for irresponsible behavior. You will provide for your daughter one way or another. You will. And if Edward had bolted in the dead of night or some bloody thing—that he was capable of such cowardice Sadie had no choice but to admit—they, her mother and father, would have died before they let a Devlin be declared an orphan.

In the weeks leading up to Agnes's death when Edward had made his outrageous intention regarding his daughter known and Joseph had announced that under no circumstances would he take Maura in and Bell had said nothing, *nothing*, Sadie had suffered the pain of having her most basic assumption about who she was, who they all were, called into question. She kept waiting for her brothers and sister to come around, to remember what sort of people they were. When it became clear that the events she was witnessing, the rows, the refusals, were, in fact, conclusive evidence of the kind of people her people actually were, Sadie felt as she imagined a soldier might who thought himself a member of a dedicated if sometimes fractious unit until, marching into battle, he looked over his shoulder and saw his trusted comrades turning tail, scattering.

The disillusionment she experienced regarding Edward was the hardest to take. She'd looked up to him once, had been proud of his various academic achievements, his intelligence, his modesty. He'd been brave and adventurous, too, defying their strict and stubbornly apolitical father, putting his own life at risk countless times, fighting the good fight for independence. How was she to reconcile Edward the rebel, the sacrificer, the disregarder of his own comfort and safety, with this new Edward, Edward the feckless? She began to wonder if the impulse that had gotten him involved with the IRA in the first place wasn't also responsible for his shameful behavior toward his daughter. Hadn't Edward always been inclined to view himself as someone whose life would not be spent in an ordinary fashion but would be writ large? Not enough for Edward to lick his wounds after Agnes's death and take his very ordinary daughter's very ordinary hand and get on with the business of raising her. No, Edward had to go off like a rocket; *his* grief had to be monumental.

His desire to see Maura in boarding school could be taken as a good sign then. He was coming back to earth. Deigning to concern himself with the particulars of raising a child. It would have been a lot easier for Sadie to convince herself of this optimistic interpretation of Edward's request if his letter had included some mention of money. Boarding school was expensive and he bloody well knew it. Sadie suspected he also knew how eager she'd be to pack Maura off and how likely, therefore, to consent to pay the bills herself.

She agreed to do just that, finally, not for Edward, not for Maura, not even for herself. For Agnes. Sadie discovered that Agnes dead wasn't much different than Agnes in America, once the shock of the death itself eased. There were no letters, of course, but there'd never been too many of them. Sadie had tried to be angry. And succeeded for a time. Serves you right, she thought. (Sadie had years of practice conversing with an absent Agnes.) Leave a child behind without making any arrangements for her care and you deserve what you get. If it weren't for me your only daughter would be in an orphanage, remember, scrubbing floors and eating spoiled meat, your precious daughter. Was she precious to you, Agnes? Were you ever able to think of anybody but yourself?

Sadie wasn't able to keep her ire up, though. She talked to Agnes mostly in bed, and there, before long, tenderness overcame anger and Sadie was courting Agnes's good opinion again. You're right, of course. We're not doing much more than keeping Maura alive here. She'll be better off at school. There'll be other girls there, at least, and if nothing else she'll get a decent education. I've got money enough. I can afford it. If this is what you wanted, dearie, why didn't you tell me? All you had to do was ask. I'd have welcomed a confidence, a duty.

When Maura was told that she was to be sent away to school she·screamed bloody murder. She writhed around on the drawing room floor. She punched and kicked and spat.

"Please please let me stay here," she howled.

"Stop it," Sadie shouted, slapping Maura's face and arms and shins. "Stop it right now, you ungrateful thing, half an orphan, you ought to be glad . . ."

Maura lay in a heap on the rug until her sobs subsided. Then she marched upstairs to the room where she slept and pulled her mother's evening bag out from under the bed. The thermometer broke easily enough, one good rap against the headboard and it shattered. The perfume bottle proved much sturdier. After whacking it against one leg of the bed several times to no effect, Maura took the bottle downstairs and out into the street. She crouched in the road, brought the bottle up, intending to smash it with all her might against the pavement. She couldn't bring herself to do it. She lost her nerve. She leaned back on her haunches and let out a scream that brought Sadie and Bell to the window.

"I'll break her goddamn neck. I'll teach her to make a scene in the street, carrying on like I don't know what for everybody in town to—"

Bell stepped between Sadie and the door.

"Get out of my way, you damn fool. I won't have her making a spectacle."

"Let her be. She'll be gone in a few months' time. For God's sake, Sarah, let her be."

Maura wrapped her fingers around Rex's collar.

"Let him go. He doesn't want you holding on to him all the time. Let go of the dog, I said. Now. *Let him go.*"

Maura let go but Rex didn't move. He sat beside Maura's chair and looked up at her in that expectant way dogs will when they seem to be awaiting further instructions.

Sadie went to the drainboard and cut a piece of ham and

lured Rex outside with it. Maura remained at the kitchen table, listening to the clock tick. She wet her index finger, dabbed at some spilled sugar, licked, and imagined a knock at the front door, her mother's voice in the hall. (How bright that voice would sound in the drab house, how unlike the voices usually heard there.) Get her things together, Bell, she's coming with me. I'm better now, as you can see, I'm all better now. Thanks very much for taking care of her. I was ill as you know but the doctor says I'm all better now.

And then would come the rush of leaving, Auntie Bell fussing and Aunt Sadie scolding—but chastened, too, Aunt Sadie cowed, Aunt Sadie obeying Agnes's directives, do as I say, Sadie—and Rex yipping under everybody's feet.

Safe out, Maura would look up at her mother and say, "I knew you would come."

"Of course. Of course you did."

chapter 7

Edward left the Fitzgibbons' house sure that he'd have a job before long. When he didn't hear from Fitz the following day or the one after that, he told himself to be patient. It wasn't like the only thing a man like Fitz had on his mind was finding work for an unemployed Irish engineer.

Still, Edward's money was going fast. He worried about running out constantly and spent a good deal of time coming up with strategies for what he'd do in the event that he found himself broke. If worse came to worst, he'd wire Sadie and ask for a loan. She'd never refused him before but now Agnes was dead, who could say how Sadie would respond? Edward thought about taking the train into Manhattan and seeing if he could hook up with any of the people he used to know. He'd go by some of his old haunts and see if anybody was still around. He very nearly boarded the train one morning but as he was climbing the stairs to the platform, he realized that he was in no shape to revisit the places he and Agnes used to go. He doubted anybody would be left, anyway. That world, the one of seven or eight years ago, seemed to have vanished. He certainly didn't need to spend the day wandering around looking for what didn't exist anymore.

Even when he wasn't actively worrying about money, there was a high-pitched whine in the back of his head that said, Well, isn't this nice, you're sitting on your ass reading the newspaper, having your shoes shined, eating a plate of scrambled eggs, watching a woman in high heels cross the street and meanwhile you're out of work and nearly broke.

He knew that he should move out of the Alexander Hamilton but he didn't want to. There was a pleasant businesslike anonymity about the place that shored him up. The sterile surroundings argued against extremes of emotion. Sitting in his perfectly bland, perfectly comfortable room, he could most of the time believe that he was in transition between one life and another, was moving forward, however haltingly. Besides, if he found cheaper lodging he'd have to call Fitz and let him know of the change so that Fitz would be able to reach him when there was news. Edward hated the idea of ringing Fitz in his well-appointed office and saying, I've moved into such and such boardinghouse, there's a phone in the hallway, let it ring awhile. To do that would be humiliating and, furthermore, it would reveal a lack of confidence in Fitz's ability to do what he said he would do.

Edward never went into or came out of the hotel without at least catching the desk clerk's eye in case there was a message from Fitz. The daytime clerk was snippy and officious. He seemed to find Edward a nuisance. The fellow who took over in the evenings was soft-spoken and amiable. He clearly felt sorry for Edward, had a particular way of frowning when he shook his head no, no messages, nobody's been by asking for you, that made Edward bristle. Five days now and not a word.

Edward decided that he'd better at least start looking for a cheaper place to live. He read the classifieds, asked the waitress in the coffee shop where he had his breakfast if she knew of any rooms for rent, got some idea of what he'd have to pay. Not much, it turned out. There were vacancies all over town. Anybody with an extra bedroom in Paterson, it seemed, was looking to rent it out.

Eventually Edward got tired of just walking by boardinghouses and decided to have a look inside a couple. The rugs were uniformly filthy. The hallways all smelled of cheap food cooking. It was clear that nobody ever sat in the cramped parlors. Boarders slept and possibly ate and got the hell out. Still, Edward was surprised by the distaste he felt. He'd never been particular before. He hadn't had to be. Agnes had been that for both of them. When she was alive he'd thought he'd have been perfectly happy in the most modest of rooms, but as he tromped in and out of various establishments—the landladies all had dirt under their fingernails—he found himself chafing at the thought of taking up residency amidst scratched furniture and yellowed bed linens.

He wondered if his visit to the Fitzgibbons' had spoiled him. Impressions from his dinner there came back to him unbidden while he waited to get word, specific physical memories, dense Persian rugs under his feet, the smell of cut flowers, wood smoke, candles burning, and vistas, views from within, the wide red staircase with its ornate bannister, the dining room table set for three. There was a general sense of plenty about the place that Edward couldn't help comparing to the mean feel of the boardinghouses he inspected. He glanced at lumpy mattresses and thought of the bed in the Fitzgibbons' guest room. He couldn't remember ever sleeping on one as comfortable. Seven hours he'd slept, seven solid hours, a small miracle. Sunlight was streaming in the window when he woke and for several seconds he didn't know where he was or how he'd come to be there. He wasn't distressed, he luxuriated in the blankness. What a relief it had been to be without particulars for those few seconds.

Finally, eight long days after he'd been to the Fitzgibbons' house, Edward returned to the Alexander Hamilton around six o'clock one evening and found Fitz sitting reading a newspaper in the lobby. He wouldn't deliver bad news in person, Edward thought.

"There you are," Fitz said, folding his newspaper carefully.

Too carefully, it seemed to Edward. *He's stalling for time before he tells me he's sorry but . . .* "I was just thinking about you, Fitz, and here you are. How's everything? How's Sylvia?"

"Good. Fine. I've been meaning to stop in and see you but haven't had a spare moment until now. How're you holding up, Edward?"

"Getting a bit restless, to tell you the truth. I can't stand being idle. I'm not cut out for it."

"Course not. A young man like yourself. Let's get ourselves a drink, shall we? Let's go over to the Colt."

Edward had avoided the Colt Lounge since making a fool of himself there his first night in town, but he couldn't very well dictate where he and Fitz would drink. "Sure," he said, noting with no small pleasure that the irritable desk clerk was paying close attention. "I'm so glad to see you, Fitz. I've been wondering—"

"Of course you have. My apologies, Edward. It's just been one thing after another the last couple of days. Come on, we'll talk over a pint."

The bartender gave no indication that he recognized Edward, though Edward recognized him. The place was crowded. Half a dozen men greeted Fitz as he made his way to the end of the bar, where a pair of stools sat empty. Fitz held up two fingers and within seconds two mugs of beer appeared.

"So tell me, Edward, what have you been doing with yourself since I saw you last?"

Come on, man, Edward thought. Have you got anything for me or not? "Nothing much, Fitz. Getting my bearings mostly."

"Right. Give yourself a little time to get adjusted. Things'll come together, you'll see."

"To tell you the truth, Fitz, funds are getting pretty low. I'm going to be in real trouble if I don't find work soon. Have you had a chance to, you know, have you heard of anything?"

"You don't think I'd come to see you if I hadn't?"

Edward felt at once relieved and annoyed. Out with it, he thought. Stop playing games.

"You start on Monday morning," Fitz said, looking into a bowl of peanuts, selecting one. "It's a county-administered project, using federal funds. A traffic circle or some bloody thing. Anyway, it's an engineering slot, from what I gather. I have a name and a number for you, a buddy of mine, decent sort. You call and he'll give you the details."

"Jesus, this is good news." Edward took a long swallow of beer and felt his nerves settle. He had a job, he was saved. "Thank you, Fitz. I won't forget this, I want you to know. I was getting worried, I'll admit, when I didn't hear from you. I was just about to give up my room at the hotel and move into something cheaper. I've spent the last couple of days looking at boardinghouses."

"I had no idea things were so bad, Edward. You should have told me. I'd have gotten back to you quicker. I'd never have let you twist in the wind if I'd known. You looked like you had more than a few dollars in your pocket when you were at the house."

"I'll be all right, I'll be fine now I've got a job."

"Course you will, but, all the same, Jesus, I hate the thought of you in a boardinghouse. They're awful places. I've lived in more than my share. A man like you, a professional. Why don't you get yourself a proper apartment?"

"I haven't got furniture or dishes or anything. For right now I'm better off with just a furnished room, I think. I don't mind, really. It's just a place to sleep, after all."

"Will you excuse me a minute, Edward? I've got to make a phone call."

While Fitz was gone, Edward ordered two more beers and luxuriated in the ease he felt knowing he'd be back at work soon. Flush with good fortune, he looked around at the other patrons, no longer caring if any of them recognized him. He remembered the powerful inclination he'd felt to call Fitz and ask for his help, how sure he'd felt that Fitz would come through. For once, his intuition had been right. He felt lucky, as if the fates had smiled on him, given him a goddamn break for a change. The only other time he'd felt similarly blessed was when Agnes had agreed to marry him. It didn't hurt to think of it now. In the wake of his good fortune even his grief was less burdensome. He remembered sitting on a bench in the center of Omagh waiting for Agnes, having made up his mind that he was going to propose. She'd been late and he'd worried that he'd got the time wrong—they'd said eight o'clock, hadn't they? When she'd appeared in the distance, finally, taking her sweet time, he'd stood up and met her halfway, impatient to say what he had to before he lost his nerve. "Will you marry me, Agnes? Will you come to America?" "Yes," she'd said without a moment's hesitation. "Yes. My answer is yes."

"It's all settled," Fitz said, sliding onto his bar stool. "You're going to stay with Sylvia and I until you get your sea legs. We've got more than enough room at the house and we both—I just called her and she couldn't have been happier—we both insist that you be our guest for as long as you like."

chapter 8

It never occurred to Edward to say no or even to affect polite resistance and say he didn't want to be any trouble or put anybody out. The invitation was so unexpected and so flattering that Edward felt light-headed in its wake. Accepting seemed the easiest, most natural thing in the world and brought a potent sense of relief. All he had to do was go along, give over to the will of another. Move into your house? I'd like that, thank you. He felt as he had in Pennsylvania Station just after he'd gotten off the ship, marching along amidst hundreds of businessmen as they headed home, tapping into their momentum, spared the burden, however briefly, of decision making, of responsibility. He and Fitz finished their beers then went directly back to the hotel, where Fitz waited in the lobby while Edward went upstairs to get his things.

Even alone in his hotel room, where trepidation or at the very least some slight discomfort in the face of Fitz's boundless generosity might have crept in, Edward's confidence didn't falter. His movements were crisp and efficient, if a bit rushed, as he put his clothes, his shaving kit, his toothbrush, and the photograph of Agnes into his suitcase ... oh, that goddamn suitcase. He'd forgotten about the broken handle. Cursing himself for not having had the thing repaired while he'd had so much time on his hands, cringing at the prospect of carrying the wreck out in front of Fitz, he shoved it out into the hall and then stood at the foot of the bed a moment, looking around to see if he'd forgotten anything. His giving the room a fast and final once-over, eyes darting from pillow to night table to writing desk, had more to do with habit than genuine concern. Traveling with Agnes, going from one clinic or sanatorium to another, he used to be responsible for making sure they hadn't left anything behind, a book she was liking and would make a fuss about losing, an inhaler, some insubstantial undergarment, lace and elastic, easily missed among the rumpled sheets.

The instant he realized what he was doing he stopped. Agnes was dead, Edward didn't need to be careful anymore. What the hell did it matter if he left something behind? There was nothing he'd miss except the photograph and he had that. He didn't turn off the light, didn't even close the door after himself.

Riding down in the elevator, he was surprised to discover that catching himself doing something he used to do for Agnes and realizing there was no need any longer didn't sting. Or, rather, it didn't only sting. Beneath the burn there was a curl of exhilaration, of liberation, the sense of being relieved of a duty.

In the lobby Edward nodded at Fitz then went to the desk to settle his bill. The night clerk smiled, tilted his head to one side, and said, "Mr. Fitzgibbon's taken care of it for you."

"I can't let you do that," Edward said, turning to Fitz.

"Call it a loan if you want. You'll pay me back when you get on your feet."

"I'd rather not, Fitz, really. You've done so much already. How much was it?" Edward asked, turning back to the desk clerk, who was watching the proceedings with an amused and indulgent expression, as if he were witnessing newlyweds playing at bickering as they checked in or out.

"Our dinner's getting cold, Edward, and we're keeping this young man from his work. Come on, my car's just outside. What's the matter with your suitcase?"

"Damn handle snapped on the way down."

Fitz frowned and put his index finger up. A bellhop with a small cart appeared. Edward's suitcase was wheeled—was whisked—out to Fitzgibbon's car.

Sylvia wasn't home when Fitz and Edward got there, which

struck Edward as odd since presumably she'd been there half an hour before to get Fitz's phone call.

"Some charity function or other," Fitz said by way of explanation. "Don't ask me what. I can't keep them straight. My wife's become very interested in good works the last couple of years."

"About my hotel bill," Edward said, self-conscious in the presence of talk about charity. "I wish you'd let me pay you for that. You've found me a job, you're putting me up—"

"Twenty-two dollars and forty cents," Fitz said. "If it means that much to you."

Edward's desire to pay his own hotel bill was absolutely sincere, but still he felt let down, embarrassed, by Fitz's sudden willingness to allow it. Edward pulled out his wallet, opened it, and was horrified to see just a ten-dollar bill and two singles. He'd broken a twenty that morning—where had it gone? The rest of his money, his stash, was inside one of his socks at the bottom of his suitcase. "Here's twelve," he said, not wanting to put his wallet away without having anything to show for having pulled it out so emphatically. "The rest is in my suitcase for safekeeping. I'll get it."

Relieved that Fitz made no move to follow him, Edward hurried back out to the front hallway. He'd have hated for Fitz to see the jumble of dirty clothes inside his suitcase. Edward got down on one knee and was looking for the wool sock with the by-now slender roll of bills in its toe when he spotted, off to his right, a pair of sturdy black shoes, two thick ankles, the bottom of a grey dress.

"Hello, Bridget. How are you? Nice to see you again."

"Mr. Devlin."

"Edward, please."

"So you're going to be with us a while, are you?"

"Looks that way, yes. A short while. The Fitzgibbons have been nice enough—"

"The same room as before," Bridget said, putting her hands on her hips. "Leave any clothes you want washed on the chair by the bed. And don't be expecting me to do your business shirts. Those you send out."

"Fine. Good. Thank you, Bridget."

"Hmm!" Bridget said, as if she'd just been told something that surprised but didn't please her. And then she was off.

Edward found the sock, pulled the roll of bills from inside it, and hurried back to the living room, a ten and a single in his hand. Fitz took the money without comment, folded the two bills in half then slipped them into his vest pocket. Edward sat down on the couch in front of the fireplace and found himself wishing that Sylvia would come home. He felt suddenly awkward in Fitz's presence, ill suited to the task of keeping up, of being good company. Fitz's charm, his bluster and bloody high spirits, made Edward feel bumbling by comparison, soft, dreary.

Sylvia didn't get home until just after midnight. By then Edward was undressing for bed, having done, he thought, a reasonably good job of entertaining, and being entertained by, Fitzgibbon. Edward lay back on the extraordinarily comfortable bed in the guest room, his room now, and, listening to the faint hum of distant voices, Sylvia's and Fitzgibbon's, he fell into a deep sleep.

For the next month or so Edward lived a double life. He was a houseguest and a grieving widower. As a houseguest, he was obligated to be reasonably cheerful at the breakfast table and to join his host and hostess for dinner when they asked him to, which didn't happen very often as the Fitzgibbons dined out most nights, together or separately. Left to his own devices, Edward attended to his grief, lay on his bed looking up at the ceiling, hardly moving for minutes at a time, walked the streets feeling disoriented and acutely uncoupled, pining for Agnes. It was an odd combination, houseguesting and grieving, and Edward experienced it as such but, still, he was glad he wasn't alone. As he boarded the bus after work in the evening, he thanked God he wasn't going home to a room in a boarding-house. Even if Bridget was the only one at the Fitzgibbons' when he arrived, and she often was and none too friendly either, there was at least the potential of company.

Which isn't to say that Edward went directly home after work every night. He didn't want to make a pest of himself and,

besides, he didn't care much for sitting alone in the fancy dining room eating what surly Bridget served up, and so he made a
point of having his dinner out more often than not. He ate in
taverns named after their owners, Frank's, Willie's, Pete's, developed a taste for American french fries, sometimes remained
at the bar long after he'd finished eating, drinking beer and half
listening to whatever was on the radio. A few times, feeling un-
comfortably full and wanting something with more kick than
beer, he'd switch to rye and get good and drunk. On those
nights he'd walk home feeling for the first part of the trek a diffuse but potent connection to the city, wreck of a place that it
was, down at the heels, perfect for the man he'd become. It
seemed to embrace him, to accept him anyway, as it fitted and
started all around him, glass breaking in the distance, a woman
shouting drunkenly, the smell of damp cement. He'd sometimes discover that there were tears running down his cheeks,
as if his eyes had gotten started without him, and he'd run
headlong into a bout of missing Agnes. He'd say her name as
he made his way up the hill and before long he'd be talking
whole sentences to her. It's too hard. It's just too hard here
without you.

At least once a week he'd go see a burlesque after dinner.
Never before in his life had he seen such blatant randiness.
Tassels and garter belts and spangly brassieres. Some of the
men in the audience held newspapers unsteadily on their laps
but this struck Edward as crude. He waited until he was back at
the Fitzgibbons' and there in the privacy of the second-floor
bathroom he'd summon the evening's stripper, part by gyrat-
ing part. Most nights the memory of a pair of heavy breasts
or an open mouth was enough to take him where he needed to
go, but sometimes his energy would flag and the only way he
could finish was by summoning Agnes in nurse's cap and white
stockings.

It took Edward a while to admit but he was rather disappointed with the job Fitzgibbon found for him. Hearing so
much talk about federal funds and thousands of people put
to work, he'd hoped to be made part of a team, imagined a

roomful of engineers working on their separate assignments, all part of a larger project. He'd hoped for a sense of good fellowship, much visiting between drafting tables, cordial lunches in a noisy cafeteria. The job he got turned out to be almost completely solitary. He was given a small office in a building that housed the county government and one-quarter of a secretary, Annette, and was told to design a traffic circle on nearby Route 46. It was a project that had been underway, in a manner of speaking, for some time, handed off from one administrator to another, resurrected recently by the flood of federal funds. When Edward took over, it was mired in false starts. Eager to prove himself worthy of Fitzgibbon's intercession, he began his job industriously. He spent days poring over the fat sheaf of blueprints and specs, computations worked out by hand, sheets of carbon paper that belonged in the trash, even a paper napkin with what looked like the beginnings of a budget on it. As he turned the pages over and over again, a sense that the whole mess added up to nothing—*nothing*—crept over him. Finally, head spinning, he put aside what he'd been given and started fresh. It took some doing, some digging around, but he managed to get his hands on the plans from which other traffic circles had been built and he examined them intently. He spent hour after hour making the studies and the calculations, the drawings, the tabulations of materials required, the estimates of cost. He got the use of a county car and made several trips out to the site at various times of day to measure and see the flow of traffic for himself. He was a bit troubled by the fact that nobody, not his supervisor, not his secretary, not any of the other men who walked past his office carrying slide rules and fat file folders, ever asked how things were going or even what he was up to. He was conscientious, though, was at his desk by eight every morning, took only a half-hour for lunch, stayed until the stroke of five. When his plans were in order—they were lovely, really, every figure checked and rechecked, every line in place—he walked them over to his supervisor's office and deposited them with the man's secretary. And then he waited. And waited. Finally he got word that he'd done a very good job except that the overall cost was too high, the volume projections too low, would he mind having another go at it? And so he did. Bigger and cheaper. Bigger yet and cheaper still. Twice more. Less enthusiastically each time. When his third circle was rejected Edward understood that nobody much cared if the bloody thing ever got built. In fact, there seemed to be considerable investment in its remaining forever in the planning stages.

Leaving Ireland, Edward had envisioned himself living all alone in the States and the image had flattered him because it was in keeping with his notion of himself as a lone wolf, a man devoid of sentimental attachments. He had romanticized solitude, hadn't taken into account his own nature, which was fundamentally and finally social. The fact of the matter was that he'd never enjoyed his own company much, not hours and hours of it anyway, but he'd expected, naively, to be a different person in his new life, to be radically altered by the loss of his beloved wife and by the effect on his psyche of the drastic action he'd taken regarding his daughter. What he discovered within two months of moving in with the Fitzgibbons, of course, was that he was more or less the man he'd always been. Faced with the painful reality of his grief and the tedium of hours and hours to fill, he found himself alternately bereft and bored.

One evening, instead of going directly up to his room when he entered the house, Edward took a deep breath and went into the living room instead, a plan of action he'd devised while riding home on the bus. He sat on the white sofa in front of the fireplace, picked up *The Saturday Evening Post*, and began to look through it halfheartedly, the way he had so many times in doctors' waiting rooms. Except for the muffled thuds of Bridget working in the kitchen—*what* was she doing in there?—the house was quiet. Despite his self-consciousness about planting himself in one of the common rooms and waiting to see if either Fitz or Sylvia happened by, Edward found himself comforted by his surroundings. There was a kind of cohesiveness to them. A good deal of thought had gone into the arrangement of the furniture, the color scheme, all of it. Edward thought of Sylvia doing the place, coming up with a general idea and then making the idea manifest, dozens and dozens of decisions made one at a time, and with care. It was really very pleasant sitting there in the early evening, turning the pages of a magazine, looking at the pictures, reading a line or two.

Edward heard the tap-tap of Sylvia's high heels and had some difficulty maintaining his composure. He wondered if she would think it strange that he was sitting in the living room all alone. Would his desire for company be too obvious? Would she feel obliged to entertain him?

"Edward," she said. "I didn't hear you come in."

"I just got home, came in, a few minutes ago."

Edward tried not to call the Fitzgibbons' house "home" because he didn't want to give the impression that he planned to stay on permanently.

"And how are you? Did you have a good day?"

"I can't say that I did."

"No?"

"I know that I ought to be grateful to be working at all, and I am, believe me, I am, but there's not enough for me to do down there, I'm afraid. Time passes slowly."

"I'm sorry to hear that," Sylvia said, sitting down in a chair to Edward's left. "What is it you're doing again? Remind me."

"Supposedly I'm designing a traffic circle, a roundabout, we called them back home. I've done three already, three perfectly good ones, but nobody is too interested in them. I've been told to do another one but I honestly don't think anybody cares one way or the other."

"Par for the course," Sylvia said, shaking her head. "Paterson is famous for bureaucratic sinkholes. Try not to take it personally. Have you talked to Fitz? I'm sure he could find you something less . . . what? . . . tedious."

"No, no. I'm lucky to be working at all. Times being what they are. Forget I mentioned it, will you? Don't tell Fitz I was complaining. I wouldn't want him to think I'm not grateful because I am, I truly am."

"I think he knows that."

"Does he? Good. And how about you, what kind of a day did you have?"

Sylvia leaned back and closed her eyes. "Not much better than yours, I'm afraid."

"What've you been doing?"

"I went to see my father."

"Oh?"

"He doesn't exactly have all his faculties anymore. My mother died seven years ago and my father's aged a lot since then. He doesn't always know where he is. I mean he thinks he does, he's sure he's in his first store or in his mother's house or God knows where. I had to go in today and hire another nurse, that makes four this year. And then I took him for a walk in the park in his wheelchair, which he hates. He can still walk but not any distance. The whole time he was complaining about being in the chair and various things. I did my best to block out his voice and concentrate on feeling the sun on my face. The sun is on my face, I kept thinking. The sun is on my face. Here's Fitz."

"Evening, all," Fitz said, loosening his tie. "Edward, where's your drink? Sylvia, you don't offer a man something to drink after he's put in an honest day's work?"

"Sorry, Edward. I wasn't . . . I guess I assumed you were going out."

"He's not going anywhere. You're having dinner with us tonight, Edward. Time alone is all well and good but enough is enough now. Get us a drink, Sylvia, and tell Bridget we're three for dinner."

"Is that all right with you, Edward?"

"Will you stop being so bloody polite? The man's perfectly comfortable where he is. Anybody can see that. Except he's about to die of thirst."

"We can't have that."

Edward wondered why he had waited so long to make himself available. Here the Fitzgibbons had only been respecting his privacy, or trying to. Well, they could have it, his privacy. A stiff drink and good company had it all over privacy at the end of a long day.

chapter 9

Sylvia was on the telephone in the front hall when Edward came in. She was wearing a strapless black dress with a cluster of silk roses over one breast, and her hair was piled on top of her head. Edward took off his hat and smiled. She turned away.

"Will you not be ridiculous?" she said into the phone. "How can I go without you?" She listened with eyes closed for a moment. "No. No. Because I don't want to, that's why." She hung up without saying good-bye then stood with her back to Edward.

Feeling foolish, there with his hat in his hand, Edward considered turning around and going back out the front door then decided to go up to his room instead and stay there a while, give Sylvia some privacy and a chance to compose herself. At the foot of the stairs he hesitated. How lovely her bare shoulders were. The nape of her neck.

"What's wrong, Sylvia?"

She sighed loudly and shook her head.

"Anything I can do?"

She turned around. There were tears in her eyes. "My hospital charity dinner is tonight. It starts in exactly one hour and Fitz can't come. Some catastrophe or other at the mill. I'm the goddamn president. I can't go alone."

"I'll take you. If you want."

Sylvia wiped her eyes carefully, running her middle finger above and beneath, the way women will when they want to preserve mascara and eye liner. Agnes used to do that a couple of times over the course of an evening out. If there was no mirror available she'd turn to Edward and say, "How are my eyes? Am I smudged?" He had to stop himself from telling Sylvia that her makeup was fine, that it had survived the brief bout of tears.

"Do you want me to go with you?"

Sylvia smiled. "That's very sweet of you, Edward, but I don't want to put you out. It's not your fault that . . . Fitz has known about this dinner for months."

"I'd be glad to take you. I haven't got any plans, God knows. I'd like a night out."

"Would you really? I can't promise you'll have much fun. You know how these things are."

"I have no idea how these things are, actually, but you're in need of an escort and here I am."

"Here you are," Sylvia said, smiling too brightly, the way a person will hard on the heels of being furious.

"Give me a few minutes to shave and change my clothes and we'll be off."

Edward hurried upstairs, glad that he'd just gotten his new suit out of the cleaners. He didn't let the water run long enough to get really hot, didn't lather his face properly, cut himself under the chin. "Damn," he said, and the bleeding started. Handfuls of cold water didn't do a thing. Bits of toilet paper got saturated and then were useless. Edward got a little panicky. He so much wanted to come to Sylvia's rescue tonight and not to need rescuing himself and now here he was with blood running down his neck. What he needed was a styptic pencil. Fitz probably had one in a medicine cabinet upstairs. Edward put his trousers on then stood outside the bathroom for a moment, trying to determine Sylvia's whereabouts. When he didn't hear a sound he decided to take his chances and sneak up to the third floor.

The Fitzgibbons had separate bedrooms, Edward discovered, separate sleeping quarters, anyway. What appeared to be Fitz's room looked as if it had once been a den or study. There was a desk on top of which sat several bottles of men's cologne, a shoehorn, a brush and comb. There was a massive leather chair, black and studded, a dartboard, a print of geese in flight. The study, Edward thought, of a man who does precious little studying. There was, at the far end, a kind of makeshift arrangement, a single bed and an armoire, half a dozen pairs of men's shoes lined up in a neat row.

Doesn't necessarily mean, Edward thought, to stave off the sudden warming in his chest.

Across the hall was the master bedroom. It was large, well appointed, insistently feminine. There were lace curtains on the windows, a floral spread on the bed, a lavender rug, a collection of crystal perfume bottles on the dresser, a silver hand mirror facedown. Captivated, having lost sight of his reason for coming upstairs in the first place, Edward stood in the doorway a moment before venturing in. On the nightstand was a photograph in a silver frame, a teenage Sylvia with her arm around a younger girl—the dead sister?—standing on a beach smiling, squinting into the sun. How healthy she was, Edward thought, holding the picture in his hand, examining it closely, how fit, how strong. The other girl, the sister, had already been sick, that much was clear. The bones in her face were so prominent that the skeleton head beneath the skin, the death's-head, with its swells and hollows, was plainly visible. The eyes—tubercular eyes have too much life in them, Edward thought. The vigor that's fleeing the body stops off, somehow, in the eyes, a parody of vibrancy, too bright, too bright.

"Edward?" Sylvia called. "We should be going."

Edward flew out into the hallway. "I've cut myself shaving and I . . . Have you or Fitz got a styptic pencil?"

"Where are you?"

"I didn't want to bother you. I thought I'd take a look up here. In the bathroom, I mean. Never mind, the bleeding's stopped. I'll be down directly. Never mind."

It took Edward about a minute and a half to finish dressing. As he came down the stairs Sylvia was standing in the front hall gazing up at him.

"Sorry to rush you but I should have been at the hotel an hour ago."

"No, I'm sorry to keep you waiting. I'll drive if you like."

"That's all right. I'll drive. I know the way."

Edward smiled at the sight of Sylvia behind the wheel in her black dress and mink stole. She looked like a woman in a movie poster, a heroine who takes her life into her own hands and dresses really well doing it.

In the hotel lobby she excused herself, she had last-minute details to attend to. "I won't be long. You'll be all right out here?"

"Fine. I'll meet you inside."

"Good. It's the Ambassador Room just over there. See it? We're at the head table."

What a grand place, Edward thought, looking at the several plush couches, the end tables with magazines fanned out on them, the wing chairs. Heading for a corner where he could sit and smoke, he caught sight of himself in a wall mirror and thought he looked rather dashing in his dark suit.

Other guests were arriving, a steady stream of them, couples ranging from early to late middle age mostly, a few genuinely old ones. The women all had the well-fed, well-groomed, well-girdled look of suburban matrons. They seemed glad to be dressed up, grateful for a night out. The men looked vaguely put upon, like they'd rather be home, like they wanted drinks and lots of them.

The Ambassador Room was a cavernous place with ornate chandeliers in two rows along the ceiling. There were dozens of round tables, elaborately set, several forks and spoons and glasses at each place, stiff cloth napkins folded to resemble doves, bright red flowers and tall white candles. People milled around saying hello and looking for their seats, place cards in hand. Edward spotted Sylvia talking to the orchestra leader, gesturing emphatically. He'd get a couple of drinks and join her.

There were bars in each of the four corners, all mobbed. Edward headed for the closest one and stood waiting his turn. The bartender, a young man, tall and thin, seemed, in the interest of efficiency, to have abandoned any notions he might have once had about courteous service. Stone-faced, he pointed at people, they ordered, he made the drinks, stray ice cubes flying, whiskey and mixers sloshing. The woman in front of

Edward spoke very softly when her turn came. "Rye and gin-ger," she whispered. The bartender bristled and pointed at her a second time. She ordered again. "Rye and ginger, please." People glared. A few repeated her order loudly. One man called out his own, deciding, apparently, that this woman had been given the opportunity to shape up and now should have to do without a drink. When Edward's turn came, he leaned in and shouted.

"There you are," Sylvia said. "Is that for me? Good. Thank you."

"Cheers."

"I'll be so glad when this night is over. It's been hell to plan. You would not believe the budget they gave me. Fitz is here in spirit, anyway, for what this whole shebang is costing him."

"The work's done now. You should relax. Enjoy yourself."

"Right. I could at least be a good date. I'll try. Come on and I'll introduce you around."

Sylvia led the way to a long table at the foot of the dance floor. There were chairs along one side only and all but two at the center were taken. She began at one end of the table and worked her way down, introducing Edward to hospital execu-tives and their wives, officers of the charity and their husbands, making excuses for Fitz. It was immediately apparent to Ed-ward how much everybody had been looking forward to spend-ing the evening with Fitz. Their collective disappointment was obvious in the clouding of their eyes and the slackening of their shoulders. "What a shame," one man said as he shook Edward's hand. "I wouldn't have come if I'd known he wasn't. I'd have gotten out of it, too." "Nice to meet you, Mr. Devlin," the wife said, looking positively heartbroken. Edward wasn't put off by the reception he got. In fact, he found it invigorating. He rather liked being introduced to a group of people who were all sorry to see him. No expectations, no pressure. He was an outsider and glad to be one.

The sober-looking hospital president stood all alone in the middle of the dance floor and made a brief speech welcoming the guests, thanking Sylvia and the rest of the committee for their tireless efforts, lamenting Fitz's absence. Just saying Fitz's name seemed to inspire the man. He warmed to his task, put his hand on the microphone, and said, "We have to be sure and have a good time here tonight. We don't want Mrs. Fitzgibbon going home and saying we're a dull bunch."

They're all a little in love with him, Edward thought.

Dinner was served. The first course was fruit cocktail, heavy on the citrus, light on the sweet pears, dotted with maraschino cherries. Sylvia was chatting with the couple to her right so Edward tried to join the conversation to his left, looked at the person speaking, narrowed his eyes as if he was considering what was being said, though, in fact, he could hardly hear over the determined dinner music, smiled when the others did, but had no idea, except in the broadest sense, what they were talking about. Salad followed fruit cocktail and then came beef Stroganoff. Edward decided he'd better pay attention to his dinner. The courses came rapidly one after the other and the dour waitresses had no qualms about removing plates that had barely been touched. Edward thought of Bridget, the Fitzgibbons' sunny housekeeper, and of what a perfect addition she'd make to the hotel staff. He looked around and wondered how the atmosphere at the table would be different if Fitz was sitting in his place. He considered turning to the woman on his left and telling the story of how he'd come to town without a job or a place to live and Fitz, Saint Fitzgibbon, had saved the day but he decided that would be indiscreet, though why exactly he couldn't have said. He wound up just watching the dogged waitresses work.

After the dessert plates had been snatched away, the lights were dimmed. Matches were struck as people took it upon themselves to light the candles in the centerpieces. The orchestra began to play. Sylvia listened intently for a moment then smiled her wide smile. "I really splurged on these guys. What do you think?"

"They're good. They're very good."

"They are, aren't they? Now people better dance."

People did. Within a few minutes a dozen couples were on the floor. Edward was surprised that nobody asked Sylvia to dance. She so clearly wanted to. She sat bobbing her head to the beat and smiling hazily at the dancers. Was she off limits because she was Fitz's wife? Did nobody dare dance with Fitzgibbon's woman? Ridiculous, Edward thought. Still, he couldn't quite bring himself to ask her.

"Dance with me, Edward?" she said.

Sylvia was a natural, Edward discovered. She could move, was both relaxed and lively. Dancing well and easily was something that Edward had always been able to do but had never much valued. The ability seemed to exist in isolation, a vestige, he thought when he thought about it at all, of his pagan ancestry. Within a minute of taking the dance floor with Sylvia, he realized that he'd never liked to dance all that much because Agnes had not been a very good dancer. He'd not really known that before, not said it to himself in so many words. Agnes had wanted to be good, possibly even thought she was, insisted, anyway, that they dance every chance they got, but had absolutely no sense of rhythm and was too concerned about how she looked from one minute to the next to get by on sheer enthusiasm.

And Agnes had been thin even before she got sick, slight, skinny.

Sylvia was substantial. She had broader shoulders, stronger arms, fuller breasts, rounder hips. There was about Sylvia a sumptuousness, a reigning sense of plenty.

One song ran into another. Edward and Sylvia kept on dancing. Edward noticed a couple of people, men mostly, watching over their partners' shoulders and wondered if Fitz would get a detailed report of how well and how long his houseguest had danced with his wife. I hope so, Edward thought, spurred on by the thrilling and jarring experience of having his arms around a woman who was so clearly not Agnes in a large room, dimly lit. He pressed his fingertips into Sylvia's back and she moved closer. He inhaled deeply, smelled a hint of perspiration beneath Sylvia's perfume, and, thinking of the separate sleeping quarters on the third floor, wondered if Sylvia was comparing him to Fitz. Probably not. Fitzgibbon isn't dead, after all, only stuck in that noisy mill of his. Still, Sylvia's angry at him for standing her up so if she's comparing me to him I'm probably coming off pretty well. I hope so. I hope he can't dance. I hope the bastard can't dance.

"Let's get a drink," Sylvia said in his ear. "Take a break and get a drink."

The room was crowded now and people kept streaming in. The new arrivals, most of whom had bought the cheaper ticket, drinks and dancing only, were younger and more casually dressed. Does Sylvia have friends among these people, Edward wondered, or is she always stuck with the older set? She turned and reached backward for Edward's hand so they wouldn't get separated in the crowd.

The mood of the bartender hadn't improved any but Edward managed to get two drinks in short order. He and Sylvia drank them down, genuinely thirsty and eager to get back out on the floor.

The room was darker, the crowd drunker, the musicians thoroughly warmed up and playing harder now. Edward felt all the dreariness of the last months working its way out of his system. The smoky air, the effect of the guzzled whiskey, the fullness of Sylvia in his arms, healthy Sylvia who moved so well, the sound of swing, its exuberance that seemed hard-won, grounded, that was in no way trivial, a kind of wise liveliness, like genuine laughter in the middle of a bad time. Individual instruments piped up and were heard, and seemed, some of them, the clarinet, the saxophone, in their expression of emotion and experience, to be straining to become human voices, to be teetering on the brink, right on the verge, so close, nearly there.

Other men cut in a couple of times. Edward had no choice but to let them. But he never lost sight of Sylvia for a second and went straight back to her after a minute or two with the other man's partner.

In the car on the way home Sylvia talked about what a success the night had been, how people were obviously tired of scrimping and saving and doing without and were finally ready to have some fun again, thank God, because the hard times had hung around long enough now.

Fitz's car was not in the driveway when they pulled in.

Edward saw the information register on Sylvia's face in the shadowy light, a slight stiffening. She put both hands on the wheel and, looking straight ahead, said, "Thanks for filling in tonight, Edward. It would have been so awkward. It would have been awful."

"It's me who should be thanking you. I had a great time."

"Did you really? I'm so glad. I did, too."

Sylvia suggested a nightcap and they took their glasses out to the porch and sat on the steps. The air was cool, the quiet welcome. There was a perfect half-moon. Looking out at the house across the street but acutely aware of Sylvia in his peripheral vision, Edward wished there was some way to broach the subject of Fitzgibbon's absence, earlier and now, without seeming to pry. He didn't want to badmouth Fitzgibbon—the man was at work, after all, and anyway it was bad policy to cast aspersions on one spouse to another—but he did want to let Sylvia know that if she wanted a friend to talk to he was more than willing to listen.

"You didn't grow up here, did you, you grew up in New York?"

"That's right."

"Must have been a big adjustment for you, coming out here."

"It was, I guess, but I didn't think much about it at the time. Newly married and all, you know how it is. New York to Paterson is nothing compared to the moves you've made in your life. Do you miss Ireland, Edward? Do you miss home?"

"I don't really. Though like you say I haven't had much time to think about it. It's been one thing after another for so long."

"Fitz never talks about Ireland, never ever. I mean he talks a lot about being Irish, being Irish is a big part of who he is, but never about growing up in Ireland. I used to ask him, I remember, early on but I stopped at a certain point. At a certain point married people stop asking each other about their pasts, don't they?"

Being assumed to have firsthand knowledge of the behavior of married people made Edward acutely and painfully aware of his current status. He'd been a married person, he was not one any longer. He pressed his thumb, index, middle, and ring fingers, one at a time, into his thigh, counting the months. Four. Four months now Agnes was dead. He looked up at the half-moon and was sorry for having so cavalierly assessed Agnes's worth as a dancing partner. She hadn't been *that* bad, she'd been all right, she'd enjoyed herself, which was the point, wasn't it? Four months. Christ. He thought of the Fitzgibbons' separate bedrooms and got anxious and decided it was high time, really, past time, that he start looking for a place of his own.

chapter 10

Edward walked toward the house and saw that Sylvia was not sitting on the porch as she generally was now that the weather had turned warm. The disappointment he felt unsettled him so much that he began to lecture himself. He had no business expecting her to be there when he got home. He'd better get out of the house tonight, go to the races, get drunk, it didn't matter what.

"Is that you?" she called from upstairs.

Not entirely certain that *you* meant him, Edward hesitated then said, " 'Tis?"

"Good. Come up here and give me a hand, will you?"

Edward climbed the stairs in the direction of her voice. When he reached the landing on the third floor he stopped. "Where are you?"

"In the attic. Come on up."

She wore shorts and a man's shirt tied at the waist. "I can't stand it a minute longer," she said, surveying the chaos of boxes and discarded furniture. "I have to get this mess cleaned up."

Edward thought longingly of his place on the porch and his drink. "It must be a hundred and twenty degrees up here, Sylvia. Can't this wait until the weather breaks?"

"No, it cannot. Will you help me or won't you?"

Edward went off to change out of his suit.

He'd made several trips back to Wexler's in recent weeks, so he had five or six new shirts, several pairs of slacks, and his first pair of sandals, but nothing appropriate for cleaning an attic. He considered asking to borrow something of Fitz's but the prospect of doing that was too much even for Edward. The hell with it, he thought, and put on new clothes.

After prying the tiny window open so they might have at least the illusion of fresh air to breathe, he went to work clearing one part of the floor so that Sylvia could sweep. Where'd she learn to handle a broom so deftly, he wondered. They'd just begun to make some headway when Sylvia crouched beside a battered trunk, opened it, and began pulling out photographs and letters by the handful.

"Here's my father," she said, handing Edward a photograph.

Edward glanced at it, handed it back. Surely Sylvia didn't expect him to dote on her mementos while he was lugging boxes in this godawful heat.

"And here's my sister, Ruth," she said, peering at a small photograph. "Sit down a minute, Edward. Let that stuff go."

Alleluia, Edward thought. We'll be down on the porch in no time.

"Ruth died in 1917. She was only thirteen. I miss her still, I really do. I mean I actively miss her. I wonder what kind of woman she'd be, who she'd have married, if she'd have babies."

"How come you don't? Have babies, I mean."

Sylvia closed the trunk and sat down on top of it. "God only knows. I've been to a slew of doctors. There's nothing wrong so far as they can tell. Keep trying, they say. It'll happen. But it hasn't. And now . . . well . . . it's not going to happen now. Fitz and I don't sleep together anymore."

Edward had never in his life heard a woman talk so plainly about such matters. Her candor thrilled him. "Since when?"

"A while."

"You've had a fight. You'll get things straightened out."

"No. A long while. Nearly a year."

"I'm sorry."

Sylvia nodded.

"You put up a good front. Nobody would ever know you were battling."

"We're not battling. Not the way you mean."

"I had no idea."

"Why would you?"

"I do live in the same house."

"Yeah, well."

"For the life of me I can't understand how he keeps himself from making love to a woman as beautiful as you."

Sylvia stood up and slipped her sister's picture into the pocket of her shorts.

"I've offended you. Forgive me."

"Oh, please. You haven't offended me in the least, Edward. I'm just not used to hearing that kind of thing anymore." She wiped her forehead with the tail of her shirt. "And what about you, Edward? You seem better now, than when you first came to stay with us, I mean. Are you? Is it getting easier?"

Edward looked Sylvia in the eye but could not bring himself to answer.

"Where did you used to go at night? Did you have a woman? Is that what kept you out so late?"

"Hardly. I went to the track or to a girly show. I sat in bars and drank myself blind."

"I used to listen for you. I'd hear you coming up the walk singing or talking to yourself or I don't know what. I wanted to get up and make you a pot of coffee but I didn't want to intrude."

The heat in the attic didn't seem so bad now they were sitting still. It was almost a comfort.

chapter 11

Sylvia always spent the month of August at her family's summerhouse on the Jersey shore. She told Edward that he was welcome to come down with Fitz on the weekends. "It's not much, really, just a plain little house, but it's a nice old town and the beach is pretty. Why don't you join us?"

She left early Monday morning, her car packed with suitcases. Edward and Fitz waved good-bye from the porch, Edward trying to impart his wave with *meaning*, to convey that he at least would miss her. That evening he went to a fight and then to a bar but found he didn't have much of a taste for either. He bought himself a new suitcase, a snappy overnight bag. On Tuesday, Wednesday, and Thursday nights he was in bed by ten o'clock. Waiting for the weekend like a bloody schoolboy, he thought as he turned off the light.

At breakfast on Friday morning Fitz said, "I don't know if I can get away just now."

Edward looked up from the toast he was buttering.

"I'm way behind schedule on a big order as it is. No, I don't see how I can get down to Avalon this weekend. But I hate to keep you here. August is hell in Paterson, isn't it? So bloody hot. There's a train that goes as far as Tom's River, I think. If you take that, Sylvia can pick you up at the station."

Edward knew it was his turn to talk, knew he should say something along the lines of "What a shame, Fitz, we'll miss you," but he didn't feel capable of affecting the necessary breeziness.

"That sound all right to you, Edward?"

"I don't want to put anybody out. Maybe I'd better wait till next weekend and go down with you."

Fitz drained his coffee cup then wiped his mouth with a napkin. "Don't be silly, Edward. Take the train."

"Do you think? All right. I'll do that."

"The station's just east of town. You know where it is, don't you? Good. A ticket'll probably run you two or three dollars, round trip. There's a train every hour, I think, in the summertime. Listen to me, will you? You found your way here from thousands of miles away, I'm sure you can find your way to Avalon."

"I can. Of course I can."

"I'll call Sylvia and let her know. Unless you'd rather?"

"Me? No. I don't even have the number. You call, Fitz. Why don't you call?"

"But I won't know what train you'll be on."

"Don't bother with that. I'll catch a cab from the station."

"It's quite a way, Edward."

"Doesn't matter. I'll jump in a cab."

"Big spender, hey?"

"I don't want to put Sylvia to any trouble."

Fitz paused to straighten his tie. "Sylvia wouldn't mind, I'm sure. She likes to drive, says it relaxes her, though what she has to be tense about I can't imagine."

"I'll jump in a cab. That way I can get there when I get there, you know. I won't have to worry about keeping Sylvia waiting on the other end."

"Have it your way then." Fitz got up and put on his jacket. "Enjoy yourself down there. I'll see you when you get back."

Edward had spent dozens of very long days in his office but none compared to this one. Only his fear that Fitz would find out kept him from jumping on the first train to Avalon. A weekend alone with Sylvia. By the water. In a house that didn't belong to Fitzgibbon.

Three times before the morning was out he put his brand-new valise on his desk, opened it, and rearranged the clothing inside. During the last of these sessions his secretary, Annette, came in and looked shocked, as if instead of a valise he had the makings of a bomb spread out on his desk.

"What's all this, Edward?"

"What's it look like? A suitcase. I'm going away for the weekend."

"To where?"

Americans had this way of asking whatever they wanted to know, straight out, and expecting answers, too. It was either childlike or condescending, Edward could never decide which.

"A friend's house."

"Where?"

"Annette, I'd never ask you, not if I saw ten suitcases stacked up on your desk."

"Sorry. It's a big secret or something?"

"Look, I'm going to lunch now. Back in an hour."

Edward went directly to the train station and bought a ticket on the 5:07 to Tom's River. Then he went into a liquor store and asked the clerk for a bottle of his best champagne. As the clerk was sliding the bottle into a box and the box into a narrow bag, Edward imagined the moment five or six hours hence when he'd knock on Sylvia's door. "Champagne," he heard her saying. "What's the occasion?"

"Your husband is a hundred miles away. That calls for a celebration."

Edward knew he would never say anything so bold when the moment actually arrived, especially since he wasn't at all sure how Sylvia would feel about Fitz's absence. She might be relieved or she might feel snubbed, most likely a combination of the two.

"Enjoy it," the clerk said, handing Edward his bag.

"I intend to," Edward responded too emphatically, still under the sway of seeing himself putting the make on Sylvia.

What else could he bring her ... perfume? He stopped in a drugstore and sampled a couple of bottles but the flowery scents and cheap packaging told him that Sylvia didn't buy her perfume where nail clippers and pocket combs were sold. Candy? He lingered over a display of Whitman Samplers—if she were an ordinary girl, if she were Annette, say, one of these would do nicely but Sylvia might take one look at the pale yellow box and say, "How sweet," then tuck it away in a cupboard or closet and that would be the last Edward saw of his cheap chocolate.

It wasn't even one-thirty when he got back to his desk. Three hours to go. How in the world would he survive them? He toyed with the idea of asking Annette if there was something he could help her do, anything at all. He'd have been grateful for some simple repetitive task into which he could channel his nervous energy. He was afraid, though, that offering his services to Annette might make his own uselessness too obvious and put his job in jeopardy. He took a deep breath, opened his desk drawer, and pulled out a long cardboard tube.

Recently Edward had begun work on a set of plans for a traffic circle that could never be built. He'd worked very hard designing the other three, each an improvement on the one that had gone before. None ever got beyond his supervisor's desk. To pass the time he'd decided to dream up a structure with absolutely no regard for the realities of asphalt, steel, or concrete. Why bother his head about practical matters like traffic flow, cost per square foot, the effects of repeated exposure to freezing and subfreezing temperatures? This circle would exist only in his mind's eye and, to a lesser extent, sadly, on paper.

Edward spread the plans on his drafting table and settled onto his stool, feeling more liberated than ever from the constraints of the physical world by the adrenaline percolating through his system, his body's response to anticipating a weekend alone with Sylvia. Why not a vortex with a hairpin turn at the top? Why the hell not? Three levels, four, five. And a good steep incline, too, for velocity.

He didn't abandon his training completely, mind. He was perfectly happy to abide by the fundamental principles of density, stress, and torque when doing so didn't get in the way of his fancy, but when he had to choose between logic and some imagined element, when he wanted something to exist in a particular way but it couldn't and still conform to the rules as he knew them, he opted for the impossible every time. No vehicle had a prayer of exiting this circle in one piece—unless, Edward thought, tapping slide rule with index finger, touching pencil point to the tip of his tongue, it was very late at night so there were no other cars on the road and the driver was nimble and willing.

Every so often he'd glance at the clock and see that another ten or fifteen minutes had passed. At quarter to five he rolled up his long sheet of drafting paper and slipped it into its cardboard tube. He didn't dare leave these plans out where somebody who knew his way around such things might see them. He had only one goal as he left the building: to get his rear end on the train to Tom's River. So singular was his focus that he didn't notice Fitz's car, didn't hear Fitz blowing the horn.

"Ed-ward. Edward Devlin, for God's sake."

"Fitz! Sorry, man, I didn't see you."

"I guess not. You went right past me, head in the clouds."

"Sorry. Have you changed your mind then? Are you coming after all?"

"I have and I am."

"Good. Right. There you are."

Fitz smiled. "Get in."

Edward felt certain that he'd been compromised badly in those seconds when Fitz had been trying to get his attention on the street. He knew how he must have looked, valise in one hand, paper bag in the other, damn near running toward the train station.

"What's in the bag, Edward?"

"It's nothing. I picked up a bottle on my lunch hour. You and Sylvia never let me contribute—"

"A bottle of what?"

"Wine."

"Wine, is it?"

"For a change. I thought—"

"You're getting very fancy in your old age, Edward. What kind of wine?"

"Champagne, actually."

"Champagne no less. Sylvia loves it. Did you know or was it a lucky guess?"

"Does she? I didn't know. I went into the liquor store and saw it sitting there and figured what the hell."

Feeling like a complete idiot, Edward looked out the window to see if there was anything out there about which he might comment and so change the subject. He'd rarely seen such a nondescript stretch of road.

They'd only gone a mile or two on Route 1 when they hit traffic. Fitz sighed loudly, tapped the steering wheel, fiddled with his rearview mirror. "I hate this bloody road. Sylvia insists on coming down the shore every summer. As far as I'm concerned Avalon can fall into the ocean tomorrow."

Sylvia was in bed by the time Edward and Fitz arrived but she got up and poured them tall glasses of iced tea. Her hair was mussed, her cheeks sunburned, her feet bare. She wore a thin cotton wrapper. The sight of her in the small and very ordinary house pleased Edward. She looked younger, less disappointed and world weary there.

"Edward's brought you champagne," Fitz said.

"Has he? How nice."

Edward compared the way he'd imagined this moment with the muddle of currents and crosscurrents surrounding him now. Mute, nearly dizzy, he handed the bag to Sylvia.

Saturday was spent at the beach. Sylvia was an excellent swimmer. Edward, though he hadn't swum much before, discovered his own taste for it. The water was much warmer than it ever got off the coast of Ireland. It came as something of a revelation that a person could swim in the sea without going blue from the cold. The air was clearer, too, and the sun beat down. Fitz spent most of the day under an umbrella reading the New York papers.

For dinner they had take-out fried chicken and champagne. Edward flinched when he saw the bottle, afraid that Fitz was going to start in again. He didn't, thankfully. When the bottle was empty the threesome sat drowsing on lawn chairs.

"We can go crabbing in the morning," Sylvia said.

"What's that?"

"Crabbing? Edward, you've never been? Wait till you try it."

Fitz yawned loudly and said he planned to sleep until noon.

In the morning Sylvia was all business, pulling rusty wire traps from the shed in the backyard, packing raw chicken on ice, filling a thermos with coffee, and wrapping buttered bread in wax paper. She and Edward headed for her favorite pier. "The best," she said. "Crabs in droves."

It was a simple procedure: bait the trap with a hunk of chicken, ease it into the water, tie the string to a post, wait a minute or two, pull the trap in hand over hand, and see what you had. Blue crabs, two or three at a time if you were lucky. Sylvia was strict about throwing back the ones that were too small. "Let's see," she said when there was a questionable one. She'd peer at it, holding her thumb and index finger the requisite five inches apart. If the crab didn't measure up, she'd toss it back. "See you next year."

Edward knew he was watching Sylvia do something she'd done as a girl. This was summer for her, this pier, these traps, a wooden basket lined with seaweed and slowly filling with blue crabs.

Newspapers were spread on the picnic table in the backyard. A great platter of the day's catch, boiled scarlet by the restaurant down the block, was placed in the middle. Sylvia, Edward, and Fitz went to work, cracking and sucking, secreting out slivers of sweet white meat with their fingers and tongues. It took hours but eventually the newspapers were covered with shell fragments and everybody was sleepy, their lips and tongues and fingertips tender.

On Monday Sylvia talked Edward into hitting tennis balls with her. They walked to the public courts and played alongside a pair of teenage boys whose eyes bulged, Edward noticed, whenever Sylvia bent to retrieve a ball. Edward had never played before and he wasn't much good, but Sylvia, glad for any sort of partner at all, was endlessly encouraging. "You've got a natural swing," she shouted. "You just need practice."

In the evening she emerged from the outdoor shower with her bathing suit in her hand and a bath towel around her. Edward thought he would die of desire. She came downstairs a few minutes later in dungarees and a sweatshirt, pulled a fishing rod and reel out of a closet, and headed down to the beach to go surf fishing. Edward followed her and watched from a distance as she cast gracefully, powerfully, pointlessly, over and over again.

chapter 12

Back in Paterson Sylvia drummed her fingers on the arms of her chair. "Let's get out of here, Edward. Do you want to? Fitz won't be home at all tonight. He's gone to Baltimore to see about new equipment. Let's go out dancing. What do you say?"

"We could do that," Edward said noncommittally, though he was pleased and deeply, too.

"Or . . ."

"What?"

"Do you know what I've always wanted to do?"

Edward held his breath. "What? What have you always wanted to do?"

"I've always wanted to see a burlesque. Take me to that place downtown you used to go to."

Jesus, Edward thought. "I don't know, Sylvia. It's pretty raw."

"So what? I'm curious. If I don't like it, we'll leave."

Imagine a woman wanting to see a strip show and honest enough to admit it. Edward knew he'd end up taking her and he wanted to, badly, but he felt he'd better be cautious, for both their sakes. "What'll Fitz say?"

"We won't tell Fitz."

"Somebody else will."

"Let them."

Twenty minutes later Sylvia posed at the top of the stairs in high heels, a slim-skirted low-cut green dress, and red lipstick.

Tarted up, Edward thought, the way she fancies women who frequent burlesque houses dress. He gaped at her as she vamped her way down the stairs. When she got to the bottom, she spun around like a runway model, punched Edward on the arm, then put on a raincoat and a hat with a wide brim.

The dress was for me, he thought.

The Paterson burlesque house had a cement floor and hard wooden seats. The curtain was a faded, dusty red. The lights dimmed just as Sylvia and Edward were finding their seats. The orchestra, such as it was, began to play. The curtain opened on ten or twelve girls in various states of undress, feathers and spangles and garter belts. They kicked and twirled and sang off-key. There were good-natured catcalls from the audience.

"Still game?" Edward whispered.

Sylvia nodded.

The dancing girls were followed by a comic who told off-color jokes, most of which were about adulterous couplings of one kind and another, husbands coming home unexpectedly in the middle of the day, lovers under beds and in bushes. When the punchlines came, Sylvia laughed loudly. Too loudly, Edward thought, she's keeping her nerve up.

A girl singer was next, good-looking but fully clothed. She sang about lost youth, about going astray, and finished with her back to the audience, her left leg, white and shapely, exposed via a surprise slit in her black gown.

The theater went dark, the audience waited. A single rose-colored spotlight illuminated center stage. Edward watched Sylvia out of the corner of his eye. Her lips were parted and she was leaning slightly forward.

The stripper slipped onstage as if she hadn't intended to perform but was nudged from behind and found herself out there alone, obliged to entertain. Edward saw that she was younger and better-looking than the women he'd seen on previous visits. Then he wasn't sure that he hadn't seen her before. She looked familiar . . . or did she?

"Gentlemen," the announcer said, "I give you Minna."

She had light brown hair and very white skin or so it seemed in the spotlight. She wore a strapless gown, deep red. The skirt consisted of strips of fabric that hung down from her waist in front and behind, leaving the sides of her legs bare from ankle to hip.

Edward's blood surged when he realized why the girl looked familiar. She reminded him of Agnes. It wasn't that she resembled Agnes exactly, at least not in the ordinary sense. It wasn't her eyes—he couldn't see them, anyway, not really—or her forehead or the shape of her face. It was rather something in her overall effect, her personality as conveyed by her physiognomy, the way her head was set on her body, the attitude expressed by the geography of her neck and shoulders.

Edward attended to this observation with one small part of his brain while the rest devoted itself to the far more compelling reality of Sylvia in the next seat. How was she taking things so far? She seemed to be going along in the right spirit but what if she suddenly turned prudish or disdainful? What if she acted as if the sight of a young woman removing her clothes did nothing at all for her? And what if it didn't? Could a woman be got going by watching another woman undress? Edward did not want to be caught being insufficiently ironic. He turned to look at Sylvia. She put her hand on top of his on the armrest and pressed her fingertips against his knuckles.

All hope of irony was lost.

And all the while the stripper was like Agnes.

It wasn't, Edward realized, the way she looked *to* him. It was the way she looked *at* him and the rest of the audience. Just as Agnes would have if by some impossible series of events she'd wound up stripping in a dump in Paterson.

All of this might have changed the course of the evening. It might have rattled Edward so that he couldn't go on going after Sylvia. It might have but it didn't. The connection to Agnes ran through Edward's desire like a fuse.

The stripper walked from one end of the stage to the other, deftly flicking the strips of dark red that hung down from her waist. Her stage persona seemed to be a complete lack of artifice. She didn't sing about wanting love, didn't play a character like some of the others, an amorous widow or Leda being raped by the swan. Minna sauntered back and forth, looking out at the audience with a sort of mild curiosity in her eyes and the set of her face, exposing long, white thighs and offering brief, tantalizing glimpses of nether curves and shadows.

Ordinarily by this point in the show men would be shouting "Give it up" or "Take it off." There were no shouts of that sort, no shouts at all tonight. Were the other men intimidated by this girl's detachment?

One by one strips of red silk were tossed into the orchestra pit until all that remained below Minna's waist were red panties, garter belt, and stockings. She untied something at her neck and the top of her dress fell, revealing a lace brassiere. She ran her fingers along its edges, up and over the swell of her nipples. Facing the audience, she bent at the waist and reached behind her neck as if she were about to unfasten her bra. Seconds passed slowly. Minna shook her head saucily then disappeared behind the curtain.

"Is she done?" Sylvia whispered, her lips brushing Edward's jaw.

Minna was back, bare-breasted. She raised her arms above her head slowly. This, her expression seemed to say, is what you paid your money for. These. Here then. Have your fill. It's nothing to me. She shimmied back and forth across the stage, breasts jiggling. She stood dead center and rotated her hips as if she were writing the letter O with her pelvis.

Edward turned and kissed Sylvia on the mouth. When the lights came on they got up and, holding hands, walked out to the car.

"I don't want to go home, if you don't mind."

"Of course. Of course not. Where to then? Is there someplace we can go?"

"I know where."

It was a kind of clearing at the far end of a parking lot attached to a playing field. The moon was full, the night was clear, Sylvia and Edward made love in the car and sat, unbuttoned and unzipped, generally disheveled, afterward, smiling at what they had done and confessing how long they'd wanted to do it.

chapter 13

Summer ended and Maura found herself sitting beside Sadie on a southbound train. A few miles out of Omagh she realized she hadn't said good-bye to Rex. She felt very badly for a few seconds, wondering if the dog would wait outside her door the following morning, then decided if she'd neglected Rexie it wasn't her fault. There wasn't time for anything with Aunt Sadie giving orders and Auntie Bell fussing.

"Another hour, not even," Sadie said, putting aside her newspaper to look at her watch. "Do you want a ham sandwich? Or an orange? Your Auntie Bell packed some oranges. Do you want one?"

"Yes."

"Which? A sandwich or an orange?"

"An orange."

"Please."

"Please."

Sadie opened a brown paper bag, pulled out an orange, and bit into the peel to start it. "There. And don't make a mess. Put the peel in your pocket till we get off the train."

Glad to get hold of the nice round orange so soon after breakfast, Maura set about peeling it. Sadie unwrapped a ham sandwich and took a large bite.

"Bell's put enough butter on this for two sandwiches. After I told her to go easy. How is it, your orange? Is it sweet or what?"

"It's good."

"The last one you'll have for a while. The nuns won't go in much for treats. But you're not going there to eat, are you? You're going there to learn, to apply yourself to your studies. It's not going to be easy either. If these nuns are anything like the ones who taught me, well, suffice it to say it's not going to be easy. You're going to have to work very hard, pay attention, follow the rules, do exactly as you're told. You won't be able to wander around with your head in the clouds the way you've been doing. Hear me?"

"Yes, ma'am."

Maura had heard the same lecture from Sadie at least a dozen times in the last several weeks so there was no need to listen. There was, though, a great need to appear to be listening.

"You're a very lucky girl, going off to a fancy boarding school. You should be grateful and see to it that I don't come to regret the money I'm spending."

Maura nodded.

Sadie went back to her newspaper.

Maura looked down and saw her reflection in a strip of chrome that ran along the bottom of the window. Agnes used to get a certain expression on her face when she looked in the mirror. She'd open her eyes wide, suck in her cheeks, and look well pleased, a hairbrush or uncapped lipstick in her hand. Maura liked watching Agnes look in the mirror. She liked the doubleness, the two mothers, rearview and front facing. She liked also the particular calm that settled over the room whenever Agnes was happily occupied, which she never was quite so thoroughly as when she was looking in the mirror. Maura leaned close to her own reflection in the strip of chrome, widened her eyes, sucked in her cheeks, traced her lips with her index finger.

"What are you doing?"

Maura looked up. "Nothing."

"You were too, I saw you, admiring your own reflection. That's exactly the kind of nonsense the nuns won't tolerate. Wait and see."

The convent of the sisters of Saint Joseph in Cavan was an enormous place, much bigger than either Sadie or Maura had imagined it would be. The entrance road took them past a couple of tidy gardens, a small lake, a playing field, and four-story brick buildings one after the other. Sadie told the driver to wait and then she and Maura got out of the car.

"Come on," Sadie said, putting a hand on Maura's shoulder. "They're expecting us."

The nun who opened the door was tall and thin. Her head was encased in a stiff, three-sided rectangle of white from which a dark blue veil hung.

"Miss Devlin?"

"Afternoon, Sister. Sadie Devlin, that's right, and this is my niece, Maura, Sister. She's to start today. It's all arranged, all paid for."

"Of course it is. Hello, Maura."

Frightened of the nun, mistaking the wimple for some kind of bandage or medical apparatus, Maura took a step back.

"All right. Say good-bye to your aunt then."

Maura burst into tears. It was the size of the place that scared her most. She thought she'd disappear into it and never be seen or heard from again. "You have to tell him where I am," she sobbed. "Make sure he knows. You have to make sure."

"I've told you a hundred times," Sadie said, smiling at the nun and using a tone of voice Maura hadn't heard before. "Your daddy knows you're off to boarding school. He'll be waiting to hear how you've behaved, too, on your first day. You don't want me to tell him you were carrying on, do you?"

Maura shook her head, hiccuped.

"Your car is waiting, Miss Devlin?" the nun said. "Have a safe trip home."

The massive door opened then closed and Aunt Sadie was gone.

"All right, Maura, pull yourself together. Come on."

Maura sniffed hard, swallowed, licked her lips.

The nun looked at Maura a moment and then said, in Irish, "Come with me."

The strange sounds hung in the air.

Aunt Sadie had warned Maura that all classes and conversation would be conducted in Irish at school. "It's no easy language, believe me. I had to learn it once, a hundred years ago. It takes twenty-seven words to say the simplest thing. Wait and see." Maura hadn't taken Sadie's warnings to heart because she thought what Sadie and Bell and the others in Omagh spoke *was* Irish.

Maura had to hurry to keep up with the nun. She was led into a kind of supply room, where a second nun sized her up in a glance, measured her feet with a metal ruler, then gave her two uniforms, daily and Sunday, three blouses, a pair of shoes, a lace veil for chapel.

Maura followed the tall nun up three flights of stairs, carrying her uniforms in a white cotton sack, glad, in spite of everything, to have gotten so many new things all at once. "Excuse me," she said when she stepped on the hem of Sister's habit. Sister turned around, shook her head, raised her index finger, said some kind of something, and seemed to be waiting for Maura to repeat it. Maura did the best she could in that regard and Sister corrected her pronunciation. Once, twice, three times the phrase passed between them.

When they arrived at their destination, a small room with a narrow bed, a dresser, and a straight-backed chair, Maura was left alone to change into her uniform, which she did as quickly as she could, knowing without ever having been told that one doesn't keep a nun waiting. When Maura emerged, Sister tugged on the hem of her jumper and straightened her collar, talking quietly but emphatically in Irish. Maura had no idea what was being said but liked the tone of Sister's voice. There are clear rules here, it suggested. Follow them and you'll be all right. Maura also liked having her clothes straightened by someone so much taller than herself. She gave over, offered herself up. Fix me. Make me how I'm supposed to be.

Off they went to the refectory, afternoon tea. Sister pointed out Maura's place and then said what Maura could only assume was good-bye and good luck. What a long walk it was from the doorway to the empty chair. Maura was dumbfounded by the sheer number of girls present, hundreds, it seemed, and a lot of them big, fourteen, fifteen, sixteen, ladies to Maura and noisy ones, too.

Maura took her place at a table of newcomers. They were a

glum bunch to be sure, away from home for the first time, their eyes glassy now with terror hours old. If Maura had been put at a table of noisy big girls, she might have been timid and weepy but in the midst of girls nearly as small as she was and sadder by far, she felt all right. She cleared her throat and said, "Pass the milk, please."

A big girl came out of nowhere and, shrieking Irish, pulled a thick leather necklace down over Maura's head.

Girls at surrounding tables pointed and laughed.

Around Maura's neck hung an ugly piece of tarnished metal on a dirty leather shoelace. Looking from it to the hissing crowd and reviewing the last thirty seconds, Maura surmised that the medal was punishment for speaking English. She was right. The nuns had devised a system that saved them the bother of monitoring their charges every minute. There was just one necklace. It circulated from offender to offender. Once a girl had it the only way she could rid herself of it was by catching another girl speaking English.

Maura's misfortune seemed to boost the spirits of a couple of her tablemates. They grinned into their pudding and chatted with each other in Irish. They were, it turned out, native Irish speakers from rural districts who'd been lured to Cavan with scholarships in the hope that they'd help the others, nuns and students, with their accents. These girls understood exactly what had happened and were delighted to learn that a skill they already possessed, and one they'd never been particularly proud of, was so necessary in this fancy place.

The other girls at Maura's table put down their spoons. A couple wept openly. All they knew was that the smallest among them had made a perfectly reasonable request, had asked for the milk for God's sake, and for that had been jumped from behind and taunted by giantesses two and three tables away.

Maura, for her part, once she got past the shock of the attack, knew only that she wanted to be rid of the hateful medal. Waiting, hoping, ready to pounce, she eyed the trembly little girls on either side of her.

chapter 14

While the tub filled, Sylvia rested her elbows on the mantel above the fireplace and looked deep into her own eyes. Affront, fatigue, sadness, and something else, too . . . a glimmer of delight?

She hadn't been attracted to Edward when they first met. What she'd felt was sympathy. He seemed such a lost soul with his wire-rimmed glasses, his recent bereavement, his new suit. She made friendly overtures because she was bored and lonesome, thought they might just as well keep each other company as long as he was going to be living in the house, had no intention, so far as she knew, of beginning an affair. Until that moment up in the stifling attic when the light hit his face in a particular way and he asked why she didn't have children.

Sylvia bent over at the waist and began to brush her hair. She'd brushed her hair this way, doubled over, for as long as she could remember, since early adolescence at least. It was a private pleasure, an opportunity to commune with herself, blood rushing to her brain, the world around her, the room, anyway, the room and its furnishings, temporarily upside down.

Bath oil turned the water a lovely translucent pink. Sylvia's skin would be especially soft later and Edward would say as much, kissing her neck, resting his cheek on her chest, running his hand over the swell of her hip. He seemed to know how badly she needed to hear praise spoken out loud. In bed with Edward Sylvia felt lustier than she ever had before, which was saying quite a lot. As a teenager Sylvia had appreciated her body the way a young athlete should. Swimming, tennis, golf, archery, kissing boys outside dances, sneaking gin, making love in dorm rooms and then climbing out windows and running back through the dark to wherever it was she was supposed to have been all along. The intensity of her response to Edward both pleased and puzzled her. Is it just that I'm older now? Have I come into my own in this department? Of course the fact that I haven't slept with my husband in a year might have something to do with it.

When they were finished, when she and Edward were lounging damp and loosened, Sylvia felt happily far away from the facts of her life, from her husband and her house and the half-dozen or so anxieties, regrets, and grudges she spent so much of her time nursing.

She stepped into water as hot as she could stand, sat down, winced, leaned back. "Ahhhh."

Sylvia first laid eyes on Fitzgibbon in her father's office. Home for Thanksgiving weekend from her freshman year at college, she stopped in unannounced after a morning's shopping. Sam Schultz had no choice but to introduce Fitz to Sylvia, though he clearly didn't want to.

"This is my daughter and this is Mr. Fitzgibbon, who was just leaving."

A good suit and a gorgeous tie, golden yellow as if there'd been saffron in the dye, Italian shoes. Lively blue eyes. Arrogance, a brash and playful confidence, that seemed a challenge, that appealed to Sylvia's competitive nature.

Was it Sylvia's father's reluctance to make the introduction that prompted Fitz to wait outside?

"I've got a car, Miss Schultz. Can I give you a lift home?"

"Home, Mr. Fitzgibbon? How do you know I'm going home?"

For her childhood and much of her adolescence, Sylvia was her father's favorite. Tall, solidly built, red-haired, she took after his side of the family and her appearance pleased him. He liked her outspokenness, too, rewarded it, believing she was like him and preferring her to her younger sister, who was docile and soft-spoken. A family of four, two pairs. Sylvia was Sam's child, Ruth was Lavinia's. Sam radiated pleasure in Sylvia's company. Come on, he'd say, you and I, we'll take a walk by the river. And they'd walk along the East River and Sylvia would feel the absolute ease that comes in the presence of someone who says, who doesn't have to say, You are perfect exactly as you are, you are just right, you.

Everything changed when Ruth got sick. Tuberculosis was an immigrant's disease. Sam asked the doctors if he could have brought it home from the garment district on his hands or in the weave of his clothes. He devoted himself to Ruth in her illness, seemed determined to make up for all the years when he hadn't shunned her exactly but he hadn't loved her easily either.

Sam Schultz must have had a limited amount of paternal affection to give. Either that or he believed Sylvia had gotten more than her share early on and so could be expected to do without entirely after a certain point. Sam turned on Sylvia after Ruth died. He very nearly winced when he looked at her, as if they'd been conspirators in something shameful, as if she'd been the cause of his neglecting Ruth when Ruth was alive. Sylvia was suddenly too loud, too fond of attention. Keep your voice down, Sylvia. Act like a lady. He talked a shrine to Ruth's meekness—she'd been an angel, a gentle soul, a gift from God.

Sylvia had loved Ruth dearly, had wanted to die herself when Ruth got sick, had, in fact, offered herself up to God in Ruth's place. Kill me now, she'd thought, lying flat on the floor by her bed. Leave her alone and take me, go ahead. Why are you doing this? Why'd you make her at all if you were just going to put her through hell? Nobody had any idea how Sylvia suffered. Sam was too busy assigning blame, the water, the doctors, city life, and Lavinia was lost in her own agony, *her* girl, her perfect child, sick and not going to get well. After Ruth died, when by all rights Sylvia should have been mourning the loss of her only sister, her primary other, she was instead engaged in various pointless and pathetic maneuvers to win back her father's affection.

She'd been cautiously hopeful riding up in the elevator to Sam's office that afternoon. It had been a busy weekend, the holiday, family from out of town staying over. She hadn't yet been alone with her father. And she'd been away at school for a couple of months so had had time to convince herself that things between her father and herself were improving, were getting back to normal. She wasn't in his office a full minute, though, before she felt his discomfort and disdain as keenly as she ever had.

"Home, Mr. Fitzgibbon? How do you know I'm going home?"

Fitz took Sylvia out for a wonderfully lavish lunch. It was after three o'clock. Theirs was the only occupied table in the restaurant. Chateaubriand for two, red wine smoother than any Sylvia had tasted before. A long ride along the Hudson at dusk in Fitzgibbon's snazzy car. "I'm going to pull over now." "For what?" "To kiss you. I'd have done it in the restaurant if that bloody waiter had given us a moment's peace. I don't think I've ever wanted to kiss a woman as badly as I want to kiss you just now." They wound up in a hotel in Westchester, where they drank a bottle of champagne in the bar and then, without suitcases or a wedding ring, registered as Mr. and Mrs. John Fitzgibbon. Later, listening to Fitz snore softly, knowing she'd have to wake him soon to take her home, looking around at various articles of clothing, his and hers, strewn about, Sylvia grinned and felt like her old self again.

Before Ruth's illness and death and Sam's rejection, there'd been a kind of grace in her life, Sylvia was sure. What she wanted had come to her. Her ease was akin to her athleticism. She willed herself to move a particular way on the tennis court, she shot an arrow and it hit the bull's-eye or reasonably close, she swam underwater farther than anybody else and felt the sun on her face when she came up for air.

And then she was summoned to the living room in the middle of the day and told to close the door after herself.

"You are not to have anything further to do with him, do you hear me?"

Sylvia was scared, she was also thrilled. She'd got him, got to him. He was in a state and it was her doing. She thought he might actually hit her and kept a safe distance.

"He's too old for you, he's not Jewish, uneducated, the worst kind of Irish fast talker. I won't stand for it."

"He's a businessman, Daddy, same as you."

"Nothing further to do with him. Your mother is ashamed, heartbroken. You've been making a spectacle, our only daughter running around town and without even the courage to tell me yourself until I have to hear about it from strangers. It stops now, right now, today, it's finished."

"He wants to marry me."

"No. No. No. Do you have any idea how hard I've worked to make a better life for you? Do you know how far I've come from where I started? All you have to do now is *not* do anything stupid. Marry a man from your own class, your own age. I didn't work all these years so you could disgrace me. An Irishman. A Catholic. A hustler. I've said what I have to say. Break off all contact now, today, or go upstairs and pack your things and leave this house."

Her old self again.

Only once did she break down. No particular provocation. She lay beside Fitz one night a couple of weeks after the showdown with her father and the magnitude of what she'd done, of what she was about to do, marry against her father's wishes, cut off all ties, throw in her lot with this near stranger or so Fitz seemed at that moment, scared her to death and she was sorry for everything that had happened and wished she were back in her dorm room where she belonged. "I'll understand, you know," Fitz said in a voice without a trace of sleep in it, "I'll understand if you want to change your mind and stay in your daddy's good graces." Sylvia stopped crying. "No," she said, chilled to the bone and less sure of what she was about to do than ever. "Absolutely not. I love you and we're getting married."

She never forgot his willingness to let her go. She told herself that he'd made the offer out of concern for her well-being but didn't believe it. He'd made the offer because he could, because, finally, it didn't matter to him if they got married or they didn't. If she backed out he'd go on with his life very happily, make some more money, marry somebody else, stay in touch even, like an old friend, send her flowers on her birthday, an expensive baby gift when her first child was born.

She went from college girl to businessman's wife in the course of a single winter. When Fitzgibbon was home he was attentive, affectionate, romantic, romancing, but he worked long hours and Sylvia's afternoons and evenings were hard to fill. She tried hanging around with her single friends in Manhattan, half hoping all the while that Fitz would object. He didn't. He encouraged her every time she said she was thinking of calling so-and-so and seeing if she wanted to go to a matinee, have an early dinner. "I'll get you a car and a driver," Fitz would say. "Spend the night. Go on. Do you good."

Before long Sylvia's interest in her old friends waned. She had less and less in common with them, was bored by their talk of boys and clothes and college life. They seemed to look down on her for being married and for living out in New Jersey. The boonies, Syl, how do you stand it? What do you do for fun in *Paterson*? A couple went so far as to convey a subtle contempt for Fitzgibbon—they used a certain mildly ironic inflection when they said his name—that ignited Sylvia's loyalty and made her wish that she was right then having dinner with her husband instead of with a couple of yammering girls. This is my last trip in, Sylvia would think. What's the point anymore? My life's not here any longer. I've outgrown all of this. I'm a married woman now. I should be at home with my husband.

Except that her husband wasn't at home much himself and when he was he often seemed restless, distracted. Sylvia felt as if she were losing her footing, backsliding, as if this new enterprise, this next stage, marriage, wasn't going well, was faltering. She decided to take action, *do* something. She made a concerted effort to become friends with the wives of Fitz's friends. Invited one or two out to lunch. Made a point of remembering names, not just of the women themselves but of their children. Her advances were not received any too warmly. Sylvia had a reputation in Paterson by this time. People thought she was standoffish. They knew about her frequent trips into Manhattan and resented them. Paterson's not good enough for her. She thinks who she is. And the truth of the matter was that Sylvia had looked down on Fitz's friends when she first met them. The strongest rushes of loyalty she'd felt toward Fitzgibbon had come hard on the heels of her amusing her girlfriends with descriptions of her new set. I'd better start having babies, she'd said, so I can join in the conversations about croup and who's a good dentist and who isn't, you have no idea what it's like.

People in Paterson felt sorry for Fitz, thought he'd married an ice princess, and he, Fitzgibbon, such a warm person, so naturally affectionate, what a shame, he deserves better. Fitzgibbon had been a bachelor for so long, a flirt, a source of a bit of excitement. Half the women in his circle secretly believed he was carrying a torch, such was the nature of his attention. Each one thought she was his favorite. Each one had wondered what might have happened between herself and Fitzgibbon if she hadn't been married already. A couple, the lonelier among them, the truly vain, harbored notions about having been the cause of Fitzgibbon's remaining single as long as he had. These ladies wouldn't have welcomed a bride, no matter who she was, but Sylvia didn't help matters with her condescension, her haughty reserve, what looked like reserve, anyway, but was, as often as not, awkwardness, a temporary shortage of social grace born of a heightened awareness that she didn't know the ropes, exactly, didn't speak the language. She was a New York City girl, nineteen years old, socializing with Patersonians and suburbanites in their thirties and forties. Sylvia, so much younger than the other wives and good-looking, too, buxom, curly-haired, impossible to ignore. Sylvia with her New York accent and her nice clothes—I guess they're expensive but they look plain Jane to me. If I had her money I'd dress better than she does, trust me. Sylvia, who'd been to college— For what? To sit in that house? To get her hair done and go shopping? Sylvia with her department-store-owning family— It's not like it's Saks Fifth Avenue, for God's sake, not even like it's Meyer Brothers—was not exactly welcomed with open arms in dear old Paterson.

She shopped, wrote a conciliatory letter to her mother and got a prompt, pallid response, played tennis when she could find a partner, primped, spent hours and hours having facials and manicures, had her hair done three times a week, waited for Fitz to come home. A lot of nights she fell asleep on the sofa, all dressed up, and woke to the smell of cigar smoke and the sounds of Fitz moving around in another room, turning the pages of a newspaper, breaking up kindling to make a fire. She'd lie perfectly still and consider, gingerly, his coming into the house and not wanting or needing to see her.

The desire for a baby came over Sylvia slowly. The wisecracks she'd made to her friends had been a way of preparing the ground, getting ready. She found herself noticing babies when she was out, shyly at first but with increasing boldness, lingering over advertisements, imagining herself pregnant, running her hands over her stomach in the bath, and wondering how she'd feel about a big round belly.

All she had to do was wait. And she didn't mind that, was perfectly happy to let the thing happen in its own time. The anticipation was enough. For a while Sylvia felt as if something good was in the works, something potent and mysterious and life-altering. All she had to do was wait. And then, for a time, with a vestige of her old self-confidence, she believed she was pregnant every single month. Her breasts got bigger, her belly bloated, and then she bled. Next month then. Or the one after. It's just as well, really, she'd think, counting on her fingers. I wouldn't want to be nine months pregnant in August, God knows.

A year came and went. Two. Three. There were doctor visits, a very early miscarriage, the size of a grain of rice, they told her, not a baby, not even close, a short stay in a New York hospital for a scraping.

"I'm sorry, love," Fitz said after he'd sent the private-duty nurse out of the room. "What you need is a couple of weeks away. Your mother's down in Miami, didn't you say? Why don't you join her? Get the train out of Grand Central. She'd love to have you all to herself."

"Leave me alone."

"Avalon then? Take Bridget with you. You always enjoy yourself there."

Humiliated. Furious. All the time sad. Hadn't it been

enough that she'd lost Ruth and her father? Was this what life amounted to? One grief after another. Each harder to bear because of the last.

Waking up from a nap or just drifting off to sleep at night, Sylvia would sometimes see a particular baby in her mind's eye. The baby, a girl, was crying as if she'd been at it a while, all in a lather, blankets bunched and damp around her. This baby wasn't conventionally cute like the babies in advertisements but there was an urgent idiosyncrasy in her face and in her distress. There was intelligence and tenacity in her creaturely glare.

Sylvia's arms would bend at the elbows, her fingers would splay, so powerful was her desire to pick this baby up. It wasn't just any baby. It was *the* baby, the one who hadn't come.

Restless, agitated, Sylvia would go downstairs to the kitchen, the front parlor, the porch, looking for the baby, as if she might simply have mislaid it, as if she would walk into a room and there it would be. She knew that what she was doing was irrational but didn't care. Walking from room to room soothed her, eased her longing. She never let herself go so far as to get in the car or set out on foot, but she wanted to. If she had obeyed her impulses she would have. Self-protection and self-regard and the fear that she was going to pieces kept her home. She didn't want to subject her fantasy baby to the mute and unyielding facts of the real world, railroad crossings and bread trucks and stray cats darting down sewers.

In time Sylvia made an uneasy peace with her childlessness. She still hoped to get pregnant but didn't let herself count the days of her cycle and stopped gazing at babies in department stores. That she and Fitz had relations much less often than they once had seemed, in a paradoxical sort of way, a good thing, a hopeful thing. They'd probably been trying too hard. A more casual attitude, one that let luck and coincidence in, had to be better.

There was a kind of fundamental sturdiness to Sylvia, a base of practicality. This was her life? All right, she'd make the best of it. She would not whine, would not feel sorry for herself. Her own mother's dissolution in the wake of Ruth's death served as a cautionary tale. Sylvia wouldn't dwell on Fitzgibbon's stubborn detachment, the part of himself he kept to himself, the surface warmth and chilly depths. She admired him still for his cunning and his charm, which, she reasoned, was more than a lot of wives could say of their husbands. He may not have been particularly attentive but neither was he unkind. He never begrudged her anything and, as far as she knew, he didn't blame her for their not having children. Here Sylvia had to tread lightly. She didn't dare press, even within herself. What she knew was that Fitz had always acted as if their not having a baby was her sadness. If it pained him he never let on.

All right. Fine. She'd enjoy the money Fitz made—there seemed to be no end of that—and occupy herself as best she could, keep busy. Casting about for something to do with her time, she considered going back to college but had no desire to study anything and admitted to herself that she hadn't liked college much her first pass through. Besides, she knew she'd feel ridiculous, a married woman, nearly twenty-four, surrounded by chattering coeds. She could, she supposed, devote herself to some charity or other, something to do with children, even, in memory of Ruth, volunteer at an orphanage or foundling hospital. Doing so would have made perfect sense but appealed to Sylvia not in the least. She sat in the front parlor after breakfast one morning, watching dust motes in a beam of sunlight, aware of the quiet house all around her and of her own boredom and distress, when it came to her. Of course. She'd decorate the house, do it over top to bottom.

Fitz had bought and furnished the place before he was married. Bridget, who'd been Fitz's cleaning woman in New York, moved her family, her chronically unemployed husband and her sons, to Paterson so that she could become Fitz's housekeeper. It was she who oversaw the first furnishing of the house, buying whatever Fitz told her to buy and taking it upon herself to get what was needed to round the place out. By the time Sylvia arrived with her four trunks, her hatboxes, her college textbooks in a stack tied with twine, the house was more or less done. There were carpets and drapes, couches and chairs, dressers, night tables, pictures on every wall, and, in the entranceway, making the place look like a boardinghouse, an enormous brass coat tree. I should have gotten started on this ages ago, Sylvia thought, getting to her feet that winter morning. I'm the wife. I'm Mrs. Fitzgibbon. I get to do the house.

She began slowly, knowing she had all the time in the world. She spent weeks in the public library on Forty-second Street reading *The Decoration of Houses* and turning the pages of design magazines. Much to her surprise, having never been an early riser, she found she liked getting up at six, putting on what she thought of as serious clothes, wool skirts and flat shoes, and heading across the river so as to be waiting when the library opened its doors. She bought a black-and-white copybook in a drugstore and took heartfelt if chaotic notes, sentences that offered more in the way of inspiration than instruction. She looked around the main reading room and noted how the fine mahogany tables were set off by the pewter lamps. (It was a great comfort to be amidst other people who also had nowhere else they had to be on a weekday morning.) At noon she got a sandwich or a bowl of soup in a cafeteria and knew and enjoyed knowing that she looked like a secretary or clerk on her lunch hour. Before heading back to the library she'd take a walk to reflect on the morning's reading and clear her head for the afternoon session. She loved coming home to Paterson after dark, surfeited on words and images taken in, her head full of visions of how the house would look when it was done.

She started with the master bedroom because it was a manageable space and because it was private. If she was going to make mistakes, and she was, she knew, everybody did, she'd make them up on the third floor, out of sight. Doing the work was a lot harder than preparing to do it had been. What was needed, she discovered after a couple of false starts that were costly in terms of money and confidence, was a kind of quieting, a looking within to get a clear sense of how she wanted the room—that room, with its givens, the aspects of it that could not be changed—to look. What sort of atmosphere was she after? What mood? Once she identified that, she set out to realize it, to make it manifest. That effort, the groping toward the real objects, the paint and paper, the wood, metal, wool, silk, cotton, and glass, that would both inhabit and generate the small world she was making, was all-consuming. Groping, that's exactly what she was doing, feeling her way through antique stores, galleries, upholsterers, fabric and lighting shops.

Though it had been far easier to sit in the library imagining doing the work and gathering practical tips and inspirational dictums, actually doing the work had richer, if less frequent, rewards. Sylvia was engaged in a selection process. Out of all the stuff in the drecky world, all the throw pillows and hassocks and grandfather clocks, she was culling what was necessary, what was right, for the space she was claiming. She had, she quickly discovered, more of her father's intuitive sense of how to combine colors and textures than she'd ever given herself credit for. I come by it honestly, she said to herself more than once when a good decision was easily made. No accident, I suppose, the old man (Sam was always the old man in her head now) doing as well as he did.

The bedroom when it was finally done, and it took a solid year, was as close to Sylvia's original vision as she could get it. She'd made a place, she thought, she imagined, where she and Fitz could retreat from the world. The room was simple, elegant, with a kind of dash that was feminine but not girlish. There wasn't a single thing in it she didn't love.

The rest of the house took another three years. The going was often hard. There were compromises, dozens and dozens of them, but still Sylvia was more or less satisfied with the result. There were corners, anyway, views if one stood just here or just there, that were perfect.

The house was done. Finished. The realization came over Sylvia abruptly. She was at the breakfast table sipping a third cup of coffee and thinking that the moldings and mantel and doors she'd had bleached and restained a lighter shade, a golden brown, might just be too light after all. The room hadn't turned out as she'd imagined it would. It was all right in itself, it wasn't horrible, but it had nothing to say to the rest of the house, was a kind of odd patch, and such an important place, too, the dining room. If she started over with it, started by having the woodwork darkened, she could do much better, she was sure. When she found herself thinking that perhaps the dining room was right and the rest of the house was wrong, she shuddered and something inside her called out a warning. If she didn't stop now, today, if she allowed herself to change so much as the rug under her feet, what had been meaningful work would become the driest compulsion.

Nothing for it, the house was done.

Which cleared the way for good works, charity. She joined several in town. She tried to be useful. She hated every minute of it. Sitting at meetings listening to intelligent and well-meaning people argue about how names should be arranged on letterhead was bad. Having strong opinions about such things and feeling compelled to voice them was worse.

While the redecorating was in full swing, Fitz's attitude toward Sylvia turned patronizingly indulgent. Though he was clearly relieved that Sylvia had found something to occupy herself with, he couldn't seem to help making fun just the same. He treated her as if she was an endearing, indulged simpleton. He teased her more or less continuously. "It's just a lamp, Sylvia, for God's sake," he'd say, grinning. "Hardly a matter of life or death, is it?" What rankled most was the inaccuracy of his perception. His demeanor toward her had so little to do with the person she knew herself to be. She was many things, self-centered, opinionated, sharp-tongued even. But she was not flighty. Or frivolous. She was not silly. Sometimes, though, she lost her footing in the steady stream of trivializing. It was sometimes just easier to go along. To be, for a time, anyway, what she was perceived to be. The fact of the matter is, she'd think to herself in these moments of dissolution, it *is* just a lamp. It is.

About a year before Edward came to town something shifted, something gave way. What had passed for good-natured marital banter ceased. There was a sharp and sudden meanness in the air. In her most self-pitying moments Sylvia blamed Fitz. He'd become impatient with her, snappish, even insulting. He began to question her expenditures and once, in front of Bridget, asked if she'd put on weight. She had, twelve pounds, and had more or less convinced herself that they looked good on her, gave her a certain fullness, twelve pounds in all the right places.

"Are you putting on weight, love?" he'd said, and her cheeks had burned, her throat closed.

When she wasn't feeling sorry for herself, she acknowledged that Fitz wasn't the only one whose attitude had changed. She found herself impatient with his lack of formal education and with his stubborn insistence on playing the poor boy made good. He was getting a bit long in the tooth for all that, wasn't he? He'd been a successful businessman far longer than he'd been poor, for God's sake. What had once seemed charming, his ability to entertain a dinner party single-handedly, was coming to seem more and more like plain old long-windedness. Why did he talk as much as he did? Did he really believe he had so much worth saying?

The marriage breathed its last one evening. Fitz was dressing for a political fund-raiser, the sort of thing Sylvia had long since stopped attending. He'd recently had several suits custom-tailored and stood in front of the mirror in the bedroom admiring one of them.

"Well worth the money, don't you think, love?"

Sylvia looked up from her magazine. "You never call me by my name. Do you know that?"

Fitz cleared his throat. "The jacket especially. See the way it sits on my shoulders?"

Staring not at him but at his reflection, Sylvia said, "You know what you look like?"

"What?" Fitz said, turning to receive what he clearly thought would be a compliment.

"A gangster going to court."

Fitz sniffed hard, adjusted his tie, patted his lapels, turned on his heel, and walked out.

He slept in his study that night and the following.

After waking up alone the third morning, Sylvia moved every stitch of his clothing, every belt and shoe tree, across the hall. Then she went out and bought a pair of wildly expensive lace curtains for what had become her room. She washed and pressed them herself, inhaling the steam that came off the hot cotton and asking herself if she'd ever have the courage to leave him.

She sat up, pulled the rubber stopper out of the drain, let the tub empty halfway, then turned on the cold water full blast. She lay back, savoring the two extremes of temperature on her skin, distinct pockets of one and the other. She got out of the tub, toweled off in front of the fire, rubbed body lotion into her damp skin, took the clips out of her hair, bent over at the waist, and started brushing.

chapter 15

Only an exhausted child or a drunk could have slept through the morning bell. Maura did, dreaming of sitting on an anonymous but hospitable lap eating chocolate ice cream, listening with perfect, peaceful disinterest to an adult conversation, to the sound of the voices not the sense of the words. The ringing bell worked its way into the dream, became an angry voice barking one strange word over and over, a demand, an order that Maura didn't understand so couldn't possibly obey.

"Okay," she said, thinking the voice belonged to Aunt Sadie or to her father or to the tall nun who'd answered the door the day before. "Okay, okay, coming."

Fear gave way to embarrassment when Maura was brought back to full waking consciousness by the sound of her own voice. She looked around her dorm room and put a hand on her racing heart. The girls in the rooms on either side were up and about, were, Maura had to assume, dressing, which meant she'd already fallen behind.

The clothes she'd worn the day before, and the hideous medal, were on the chair by her bed. Rushing made her clumsy. Buttonholes were stiff, her zipper uncooperative and jerky. Her tights went on crooked. They pulled in some places, sagged in others. Yesterday's heels sat blackly, stubbornly, on top of today's ankles.

Maura joined the stream of girls in the hallway, wound up in a long, narrow bathroom, and took her place on line. Most of the other girls, Maura noted, carried small cloth bags from which, once they got to the row of sinks, they withdrew combs and brushes and bars of soap in wax paper. Bell had packed a bag like that for Maura, everything new inside, some things still in their tantalizing drugstore wrappers, but Maura hadn't brought it with her because she hadn't known where she was going. She considered running back to her room but didn't think it wise to give up her place on line.

When her turn came she closed the stall door after herself, peered through a gap at a girl brushing her hair at one of the sinks, and wondered why there were no mirrors. The toilet seat was pleasantly warm and unpleasantly damp. Maura loosened what she generally kept clenched, waited. Nothing. The girls on either side of her were going. One flush, another, and Maura was still perched on the toilet unable to squeeze out a single drop. She wiped herself as if she'd gone, flushed.

At the sink Maura washed her hands and face then reached up to touch her hair. Short as it was, it tended to stick out in all directions just out of bed. She felt one large ridge in front and several significant tufts over her right ear. She did what she could with wet fingers, nearly panting all the while, acutely aware of the weight of the medal on her chest and the stares and smirks it was eliciting.

From the washroom girls stampeded downstairs where two nuns inspected them as they passed. Straight out the door and into the cold morning air they went. Crossing the courtyard, Maura took great care to keep to the middle of the pack. On the chapel stairs girls pulled lace veils from their jumper pockets, snapped them smartly, bobby-pinned them in place. Maura froze. No one had told her she'd need her veil. How the other new girls had known she couldn't imagine. She wondered which was worse, walking into the chapel bareheaded or turning back and telling a nun that she'd forgotten her veil.

"Sister. I'm sorry, Sister. I don't have my veil. Can I—"

"In Irish," the nun said wearily. "In Irish."

Maura said nothing.

"Oh, go on and be quick about it. By the time you get back, well, there's no way round it, you'll have to sit with the orphans."

Maura raced up the several flights of stairs, her crooked tights pulling something awful and making her feel vertiginous, off-kilter. In her room she grabbed her veil then ran back downstairs. Imitating what she'd seen the other girls do on the chapel steps, she gave her veil a snap then put it on and bent to see her reflection in the brass of the doorknob. She opened one bobby pin and then the other against her teeth the way she'd seen Agnes and, more recently, Auntie Bell do.

Compared to the morning light outside, the interior of the chapel was dark. Streaks of bright color shot across Maura's visual field, spots, outlines of the last things she'd seen in the sun, stone stairs, black bannister, right angles of the open doors. Maura took a tentative step into the lively darkness then stopped, not daring to go any farther until she could see. A large hand clamped onto her shoulder and steered her into a pew.

Once her eyes had adjusted Maura saw that she was sitting in the last row of half a dozen rows of girls in grey dresses with dingy white kerchiefs on their heads. No way round it, you'll have to sit with the orphans, the nun had said. Looking from one face to another, from one pair of hands, knees, ankles, scuffed shoes to the next, Maura began to tremble. She ran one hand over the front of her jumper and fingered the edge of her lace veil.

In the row just ahead one orphan girl whispered to another. A nun, older and meaner-looking than the ones sitting up front with the students, reached over and flicked the girl on the temple with her middle finger. *Thwock.*

The rest of the day was a blur of ringing bells, long hallways, nuns pointing at wastebaskets and blackboards, chairs, desks, and crucifixes, saying the Irish words and waiting for the girls to repeat them. Eyes. Hands. Rosary. Finger. Shoe. Shoes. Foot. Feet.

After supper, a silent study period, and evening prayers, the girls were sent upstairs to bed. Maura went happily. All she wanted was to be where nothing was expected of her.

Savoring the privacy and safety of her small room—already it was distinct from the others, already it was *her* room—she took off her jumper and blouse and got free of her twisted tights.

Patches of skin on her upper thighs were chafed and sore. She sat on her bed in just underpants and undershirt, dabbing saliva on the abrasions. The slight sting was welcome, the cool that followed lovely. Maura shuddered and sighed.

A bell rang, the light in the hallway went out. Maura sat in the dark for several seconds then got up, located her nightgown, and put it on.

Down the hall a girl started to cry. An eerie, high-pitched hum as if through closed lips. Maura listened intently, thinking of the other girls in their beds listening, too. A second girl started. Her cry was louder, full-throated, gravelly. And then half a dozen girls were weeping, wanting their mothers and fathers, sisters and brothers, home.

Dry-eyed, Maura rolled toward the cool plaster wall. All day something had been nagging at her. Whenever there'd been a lull, when by some miracle she'd made it to a classroom before her teacher, when she sensed that for whatever reason she was all but invisible to the nun in charge, a potent anxiety had made its presence felt in the pit of her stomach. She hadn't had time to attend to it, had only received its cryptic bulletins: There's something in particular you ought to be worrying about, there's fresh trouble. Now, in bed but not sleepy, with the sobs of a dozen girls in her ears, Maura let the thing that had been threatening to reveal itself all day come.

Orphan. Orphanage.

The girls in the ugly grey dresses in chapel that morning. Her winding up among them. "No way round it, you'll have to sit with the orphans."

The words *orphan* and *orphanage* were inextricably connected in Maura's mind with the weeks her mother lay in the back bedroom of the house in Omagh. At the top of the stairs when she should have been in bed one night, Maura had heard her uncle say those queer words to her father and had gathered that an orphanage was a place she might be going to after her mother died. She'd imagined something along the lines of the sanatorium, where she, her mother, and her father had lived for a time. That place was very nice, an island of ease and stability in Maura's otherwise knockabout existence. There'd been a separate building, a kind of hotel, for the families of patients. Maura and her father had shared a small room with a marble sink in one corner. ("Put your head down and go to sleep now, Maura. It's late. Your mum will be looking for us first thing in the morning. We don't want to keep her waiting, do we? Put your head down, I said. For the love of God, Maura, will you go to sleep?" Yes, she would, actually. She would put her head down and go to sleep, smugly happy the way only a child who has succeeded, at long last, in getting a satisfactory rise out of a parent can be.) The hospital sat on a mountain amidst green lawns and flagstone paths. The nurses were young and pretty. Patients were served six meals a day in the dining hall or on their balconies as they preferred. Agnes had taken all her meals in her room. Maura loved the look of her mother's dinner tray, so private and tidy, dessert waiting patiently beside soup, meat, and bread.

That night at the top of the stairs Maura was baffled by her uncle's anger and her father's silence. Why should the prospect of her father and herself returning to the place with the sinks in the rooms and the dinner trays cause a fight?

The girls who were still crying sounded nearly worn out, ready to give up, give over to sleep. Maura pulled her knees up and took herself to task for being ignorant about the nature of orphans and orphanages. You stupid idiot, there's no green grass, no Mommy, no Dad, no dinner on trays. There's ugly grey dresses and sitting in the back in chapel and hits on the side of your head.

She thought of the lectures she'd only half listened to. Behave yourself. Mind the nuns. Don't waste the bloody fortune it's costing to send you. Be grateful. Do well. Don't make a fool of yourself or of me.

Or else.

Or else what?

With the heels of her hands against her closed eyes, listening to the last holdout, the one girl still crying, Maura saw herself walking between Aunt Sadie and a whiskery old nun into the squat building on the edge of the school grounds into which she'd seen the skinny girls in grey dresses disappear after mass.

* * *

When morning came Maura resolved to rid herself of the ugly medal. It took another three days for her to realize that by wearing the necklace in plain view she was giving the other girls time to switch from English to Irish when they saw her coming. What she needed to do, obviously—I should have thought of it before, why didn't I?—was take the medal off and put it in her pocket.

Finally, on her way from one classroom to another, she turned a corner and happened on two older girls chatting in English. One of them looked up, seemed to recognize Maura as the medal wearer, tapped the other's arm. Maura kept on coming. The big girls grinned at each other and swatted at Maura, saying, "No, no," as they might have to a dog. Maura was not to be stopped. Nothing two girls, however large, however breezily confident, might do could compare to the punishment awaiting Maura if she failed to live up to Aunt Sadie's expectations. The big girls weren't smiling any longer. One pulled Maura's hair, the other pinched her under the arm, hard, harder. Maura seemed not to feel any pain or to feel it only briefly. She managed to get the leather strap over the top of one girl's head. The other girl looked scared and backed off. Maura yanked the necklace down with all her might. "There," she said bravely, recklessly, in English.

Ten chaotic and violent seconds later the necklace was again around Maura's neck, where it remained, against a backdrop of rapidly healing scratches and welts, until another week had gone by and she had the good fortune to cross paths with a timid and absentminded seven-year-old.

chapter 16

"You don't look a'tall well, Mr. Fitzgibbon," Bridget said, putting a platter of lamb chops on the table.

"What? I'm not my usual handsome self then?"

"No, mister, you're not. You're peaked."

"There's a flu going round," Edward volunteered. "Couple of people on my floor were out with it today."

Sylvia took a drink of water to channel the flash of anger she felt into an action, however innocuous, however small. It had been a long day. She'd felt her mood dip several times, waiting while a clerk wrapped a sweater in tissue paper, halfway through a solitary lunch, standing on the porch gazing out at the street. She'd told herself to buck up. Evening would come and she'd be alone with Edward. But if Fitz wasn't feeling well—and he *did* look pale—he might not go out after dinner as he usually did on Thursday nights.

Damn it, Sylvia thought, running her finger through the condensation on her water glass and imagining herself coming clean there and then, saying, God, enough is enough. Fitz, you know perfectly well that Edward and I are having an affair. I don't want to play this game any longer.

She couldn't imagine herself saying those words. Rather, she could *only* imagine herself saying them. In her mind's eye she saw mock disapproval on Bridget's face, gossipy interest, muted glee. All the weight of the real world, the dishes on the table, the drapes on the windows, the smell of mint sauce and mashed potatoes and coffee brewing, precluded Sylvia's taking such a disruptive action. She wondered how people ever got up the nerve to drop bombshells, make scenes. How did they find the strength to buck the inertia of the physical world with its dead-weight insistence on preserving the status quo?

She took another drink of water and considered simply asking Fitz if he was going out, but in her mind the question was tainted by all she'd imagined saying, so she kept silent.

"You'd better stay put tonight, Mr. Fitzgibbon. If you know what's good for you."

"I may just do that, Bridget. I may stay close to home tonight."

After dinner Fitz excused himself and went up to bed.

It was late October now and much too chilly to sit on the porch. Sylvia and Edward drifted into the living room and settled on opposite ends of the couch, she with a magazine, he with a detective novel. They were like a married couple spending a quiet evening at home and might have enjoyed the novelty of that if they both weren't acutely aware of Fitzgibbon up above.

Sylvia thought she heard something and looked up.

"Why don't you go and see how he's keeping?" Edward said.

"Do you think? I don't want to wake him if he's asleep."

"Go on. Maybe he needs an aspirin or something. He wasn't himself. He's got whatever it is going round."

Climbing the stairs, Sylvia had a heightened sense of herself climbing the stairs. She thought perhaps her reluctance to get where she was going was responsible. Like when you were a kid, she thought, and somebody told you to get going, to march, and you had no choice so you went, but you went slowly, you made getting there last.

On the first landing she stopped to listen and thought she heard Fitz breathing. I can't hear that from down here, she thought. It's the wind or the furnace or something. She considered standing where she was for a minute or two then going back downstairs and telling Edward that Fitz was fine, sound asleep, and suggesting they go out for a drive.

The second staircase seemed longer than the first, steeper,

too, though it wasn't, Sylvia knew. Still, the climbing took considerable effort. She felt the strain in her chest and down her thighs.

The door to Fitz's study was partway open, which surprised Sylvia and made her feel unaccountably tender. It didn't occur to her that Fitz might have wanted to keep an ear out for what was going on downstairs, only that he hadn't wanted to shut himself off completely. She leaned into the room and saw, to her great relief, Fitz asleep on top of the covers in just his undershirt and shorts. She took a step in, then another, intending to spread a blanket over him, terrified, all the while, that he'd wake up and catch her in so intimate an act. She pulled a blanket from the closet shelf then held it in her hands, rubbing the border across her lips and watching Fitz sleep, taking in his vulnerability and sweet animal self.

He stirred and Sylvia drew back, petrified. He didn't come fully awake but close enough so that his personality, his waking self, asserted itself in his face. Sylvia spread the blanket over him then hurried out into the hall, where she stood biting down hard on her thumb and wondering what was going to happen. When, exactly, would everything go to pieces?

"He's fine," she told Edward. "Sound asleep. Let's go out for a drive, all right? I suddenly want to just get in the car and drive. It's early yet and I've hardly been out of this house all day."

At breakfast the following morning Fitz was all bluster and watery eyes. "You can't give in to these things. It's mind over matter. The trick is to behave as if you're feeling good. Fool the body into believing it's well."

Sylvia remained at the breakfast table long after Fitz and Edward had gone off to work. Her second cup of coffee tasted bitter and a smear of egg yolk on a plate turned her stomach. She went upstairs intending to shower and dress but lay down on her unmade bed instead.

When Bridget came up to clean hours later, Sylvia was fast asleep.

It was afternoon when Sylvia woke up. She'd dreamed of the

baby girl for the first time in ages. That and the bright light and her not having any idea what time it was or how she'd come to be lying under her bathrobe in just a bra and underwear caused her to lose her bearings. For a moment there was just her free-floating self and the memory of the baby's face, the baby's distress. Sylvia allowed herself a brief indulgence in pure sadness then steered her consciousness toward impatience, not having any desire to sink back into her old babyless funk again.

Great, she thought. I've been sleeping since just after breakfast. Which means I've caught whatever Fitz has.

She didn't mind, not really. It was something of a relief. Being sick would excuse her from the make-work busyness of her day. She pulled the covers up even though she was hot. She'd always liked a fever. The heat made her languid and unguarded, like a drowsy child.

She slept again and woke up sicker. Her joints ached and her throat hurt when she swallowed. She tried to fall back to sleep but couldn't, so she got up, washed her face, brushed her teeth, put on a flannel nightgown and robe. Exhausted, she sat on the edge of the bed a moment before going downstairs.

Propped against a bowl of apples in the kitchen was a note from Bridget, a reminder that she had the evening and the following day off for her twin granddaughters' christening. "I'll be at my son's house if needed," the note said. *If needed* was underlined twice.

All right then, Sylvia would see about dinner herself. Bridget had left a pot of chicken soup on the stove. Easy enough to heat that up and toast some bread. She'd even squeeze some oranges. After lighting the oven, slicing some bread, and carrying a net bag of oranges in from the pantry, she sat down at the table, spent.

Fitz came in, pale and bleary-eyed. "You've got it, too, love?"

Sylvia nodded. Love? Was he back to calling her love?

He looked at her half-prepared supper. "No Bridget?"

"The twins' baptism."

Fitz nodded. Then he squeezed a dozen oranges, made a pot

of tea, toasted the bread Sylvia had cut, and put everything on a tray to carry into the dining room.

Watching him work, Sylvia was surprised and impressed by how well he knew his way around the kitchen. When had he learned where everything was? For those few seconds she saw him not as her husband, or as her adversary, but simply as a man who could get his own dinner if he had to.

"It's a bad one, Fitz, isn't it?"

"It's a mother. Get the door for me, will you?"

Edward came in a few minutes later, wan and dull-eyed.

"Three down," Fitz said.

They ate as much of Bridget's good soup as they could then settled in the back parlor, a smallish room, the dominant color of which was a brownish pink, a terra cotta that was rooted in the glazed tile around the fireplace and that Sylvia had cultivated elsewhere with infinite patience, in the pattern of the wallpaper, the leather of the couch, the continents on a large globe in one corner. Fitz turned on the radio and got some blankets from the cedar closet. There was talk of building a fire but nobody did it. One radio show ran into another while Fitz, Sylvia, and Edward dozed, compared symptoms, made the trek to the kitchen for aspirin and ginger ale. Everybody was in bed by ten.

In the morning they bathed and put on fresh pajamas before reconvening in the back parlor, weak but clean. They drank tea with lemon and honey then ice cream sodas and played a game of spades which Fitz won handily. They took their temperatures. Sylvia's was highest, a hundred and three. She asked Edward to rub her shoulders and moaned softly when he did.

The afternoon paper arrived on the front porch with a loud thud that made everybody jump.

"Thank God," Fitz said, getting to his feet. "The rest of the world is still functioning out there. I was beginning to feel we three were all alone in the universe."

The room was pitch dark when Edward woke up. He couldn't tell how he was situated in space, which way he was facing, where the walls were or the window was. Without a physical context, he floated for several long seconds, unmoored and wanting his bearings, eyes darting in all directions. Then one corner of the mantel, a right angle of pale marble, asserted itself into the void and the rest of the room fell into place around it.

Edward sat up and realized he was alone, which meant he'd been asleep when Sylvia and Fitz went up to bed. He wondered if they'd gone together, if they'd tried to wake him. He imagined them standing over him saying his name. I hope I wasn't snoring or drooling, he thought, running his hand over the leather couch, checking for wet spots.

He knew that he ought to go up to bed but the thought of the climb exhausted him. What harm would there be in his spending the rest of the night on the couch? He looked at the clock on the mantel, strained, but wasn't able to make out the time. It could have been as early as midnight or as late as three or four. Sitting absolutely still, slack-faced, half gone already, he gave himself permission to remain where he was. Maybe the next time he woke he'd have the energy for the climb up to bed.

With his chin nearly on his chest, he was half listening to the hum of night sounds, the furnace firing in the basement, the wind in the trees, and telling himself to go ahead and lie down, when, much to his annoyance, he became aware of a distinct wakefulness setting up shop between his temples. I'll be up the rest of the bloody night, he thought, lying down resolutely, turning onto his side, and facing the back of the couch, burrowing in, something he'd done as a child when he'd had quite enough of the world and wanted to withdraw, retreat, be left alone for a while.

The relief Edward hoped to get by employing his childhood strategy didn't come. As he lay with his forehead snug against the back of the couch, his wakefulness increased. He began to fidget, tensing the muscles in his thighs, biting his lower lip, scratching his scalp. The unwelcome alertness intensified, soured, became a potent anxiety.

It was unlike anything Edward had ever experienced before, a painful blend of guilt and dread that wasn't attached to any external reality, at least not any Edward could identify. It seemed to exist in isolation, a feeling state with a life of its own. Edward took deep breaths to calm himself but the increase in oxygen only made him light-headed, which, in turn, heightened his terror, enlivened it. He wondered if he was about to have a heart attack or a stroke or some other physical calamity. Is this how a person feels just before?

He couldn't be still. He sat up and sniffed and coughed and shuddered. He thought, suddenly, acutely, intently, of Agnes.

The company of a familiar person is a complex business to be sure. There are the obvious elements, those that register on the senses, the look of the person, the sound, the smell. And then there are subtler strains. The presence of an intimate casts a detailed shadow, creates a force field, changes the air in a particular way all around. Sitting alone in the back parlor, Edward didn't see Agnes or hear her or smell her. He felt her. He experienced the specific internal changes he'd undergone in her presence. His consciousness permuted into what it had been when it was receiving signals from hers.

Something told him not to resist, not to question, to be still and let whatever was happening happen. He did nothing—nothing—but luxuriate in Agnes's company, in the sweet relief of reunion. He'd pined so intensely for her once and here she was. The darkness all around was thick with her.

Edward couldn't have said how much time had passed when he first became aware of having to contribute to his sense of Agnes's presence in order to still feel her in the air. He hated to admit that whatever it was that had existed in its own right was fading, so he went on bulking it up with memory, with remembering, for as long as he could. It was no use. She was gone. He had no choice, finally, but to admit that all he was doing was sitting alone remembering Agnes, generating images of her, the shape of her face, the color of her hair, the reflected warmth of one of her good moods.

The sense of Agnes's presence had completely eclipsed the anxiety that preceded it. Edward did not remember the painful dis-ease he'd felt. He was too busy reliving what he'd experienced, wondering at it, feeling himself privileged to have had some kind of contact, however insubstantial, however fleeting, with something other than the physical world, with its relentless order, its weights, and its measures, its one day after another with no going backward no matter what.

Much to Edward's consternation, and in the midst of his celebration, he realized that he was having to talk himself into believing what had happened only minutes before. Even as he was congratulating himself, even as he was thinking, yes, I've had a glimpse of something extraordinary, he was skeptical. Come on, will you? It's late and you're sitting alone in an old house, not your own, and grieving still, still pining. You're sick besides.

Edward stood up as if doing so would allow him both to chase whatever might have remained of his brush with the otherworld and to assert his practical side, to regain his usual perspective. His knees were weak. Putting his palm to his cheek, checking for heat, he thought that perhaps it had all been some sort of fever dream. Agnes had had them often enough. In the throes of one she nearly always thought she had an appointment and insisted on getting dressed, full makeup, stockings, the works. Edward had learned to let her do what she was determined to do. The delusion nearly always lifted before she was half done and then, in a slip and one stocking, she'd come back to herself and be embarrassed and cry because she'd unwittingly put on a show.

Nothing for it but to go up to bed and see if he could be persuaded to sleep by crisp cotton sheets and an excellent mattress. At the foot of the stairs Edward thought of Sylvia in her bed and badly wanted to sneak up to the third floor and slip into her room. He imagined undressing in the dark, climbing in beside her, the fronts of his thighs snug against the backs of hers. Did he dare? With Fitzgibbon just across the hall?

He didn't.

What a night this was turning out to be.

After imagining Sylvia's bed, Edward was repelled by the thought of his own and gave up whatever notions he'd had about falling back to sleep.

What he'd do, he decided, was build a fire. The heat and the light would be soothing. The work of getting a fire going would settle his nerves.

He crumpled sheets of newspaper and tucked them under the grate, put some kindling and a log on top. His shoulders and back ached pleasantly. Two days before Bridget, who liked to get a bit of work out of Edward when she could, had asked him to stack a cord of firewood by the kitchen door. He'd resented being asked to do the chore, and had ruined his only pair of gloves before he was finished, but he was grateful now for the simple physicality of sore muscles.

The match flared loudly in the silence. The fire started easily and Edward was so absorbed, crouching by it, that he nearly jumped out of his skin when Fitz said, "Can't sleep?"

"Fitz! Jesus, you scared me," Edward snapped. He'd banged his knee on a poker and was embarrassed by his fright and his clumsiness.

Fitz chuckled. "You didn't hear me coming down the stairs?"

"No, I didn't," Edward said peevishly, rubbing his injured knee. "I was concentrating on getting my fire— Never mind. What are you doing up?"

"Same as you. I can't sleep."

"This flu has us all turned around."

"It surely does. I'm going to have a snort. Will you join me?"

"Absolutely." Once Edward got over being startled, he assumed his usual attitude toward Fitz, a kind of eager deference. "You sit down and warm yourself," Edward said, wondering if Fitz would take offense at being invited to sit by his own bloody fire. "I'll go after the drinks."

"I was going to make a couple of toddies."

"I'll make them."

"Don't skimp on the whiskey," Fitz said, settling himself on the couch.

In the kitchen Edward poured rye and water and sugar into a pot, lit the burner, rummaged in the pantry for a lemon and squeezed it hard, stirred the mixture with a tablespoon. It was pleasant to be on Bridget's turf without her knowledge, let loose in Bridget's kitchen. The sense of mixing up a concoction was nice, too. Edward looked around, wondering what else he might add to his brew. He spotted a bottle of aspirin on the windowsill, shook four tablets onto his palm, dropped them into the pot, added another heaping teaspoon of sugar to offset the bitterness of the pills. When the mixture came to a rolling boil, Edward poured it into two mugs and carried them to the back parlor.

"This'll set you straight."

Fitz raised his mug, burned his lip, cursed. "Better let them sit a minute."

The two men looked into the fire a while then Fitz said, "It just occurs to me that your wife was here once. At one of our New Year's Eve parties, wasn't it?"

Edward turned and stared. "What made you think of that just now?"

"I don't know," Fitz said, gazing steadily at Edward. "She was, though, wasn't she? Yes. I remember dancing with her."

"We weren't invited, you know. We crashed."

Fitz picked up his mug and blew on it. "You and how many others. We'd invite fifty and a hundred would come, a hundred and fifty some years. Got to be too much after a while. Time was I enjoyed it but it got to be too much. Another obligation. Something else to be gotten through."

Edward was intrigued by Fitz's weary tone. He'd long since given up all hope of getting a glimpse of the real man beneath the bluster. Tonight, though, Fitz didn't seem quite himself. The flu, perhaps, or the lateness of the hour.

Fitz nodded slowly, with eyes glazed. "This'll sound strange to you, Edward, but you were lucky, having the rug pulled out from under you the way it was. You had no choice but to make a fresh start. Circumstances beyond your control and all that."

"I don't follow."

"You wiped the slate clean, didn't you? Got to start all over again. There's a lot of us would jump at the chance."

"My wife died, Fitz. By no stretch of the imagination does that make me lucky."

"You were cut loose, weren't you? As free of attachments and obligations as a twenty-year-old? It's very sad and all, of course, but there is an upside to it, isn't there, Edward?"

"Cut loose? Cut adrift is more like it. Left alone."

"Alone, yes."

"I loved my wife," Edward said. He was not unaware of the preposterousness of his proclaiming his love for his dead wife to the husband he was cuckolding. To offset his own discomfort, to set physical pain against the heebie-jeebies, he stuck his index finger into hot whiskey up to the knuckle and didn't allow himself to wince.

"Nobody said you didn't. Ten years ago, was it, when she was here? The older I get, honest to God, the faster it goes."

Fitz took a long drink of his toddy then talked at length about the silk business and how it had changed, gone to hell, thanks to big labor. Edward had some trouble following Fitz's explanation of the current crisis but it seemed that the family-shop proprietors, the men and women working between the chicken-wire dividers, were attempting to organize and strike against certain of the converters, men like Fitz who contracted with the proprietors to turn raw silk into woven broadcloth. What the independents wanted, so far as Edward was able to determine, was a nickel instead of four cents for every yard of silk they produced.

"Businesses striking against other businesses! Only in Paterson. No other city on the face of the earth would put up with such nonsense."

Lulled by the sound of Fitzgibbon's voice and the heat of the smoldering fire, Edward began to get drowsy. He felt his nervousness and what remained of the anxiety that had tormented him earlier lifting. The whiskey and aspirin together? He'd have to remember that combination next time he couldn't sleep. Fitzgibbon talked on and on and Edward felt obliged to stay awake, felt privileged, even, that Fitz had chosen him to confide in. But his eyelids were heavy and his waking mind was shutting down. To rouse himself he cleared his throat, crossed his legs, turned, and faced Fitzgibbon, who sat hunched over his empty mug in pajamas and bathrobe and resembled, Edward thought, a sleek-headed bird, a vulture or an eagle, with bald patches and battle scars, perhaps, but sinewy, still strong, poised for flight.

* * *

Sylvia came down in the morning and found her husband and her lover asleep in the back parlor. She looked from one to the other, sighed, then went and opened the front door. She stood taking deep breaths of cold air and feeling the morning sun on her face.

By afternoon everyone was stronger. Their temperatures had come down, their appetites returned. Edward volunteered to make the one meal he knew how to make, bacon and eggs. They all drank coffee instead of tea. When Fitz suggested a walk, Sylvia insisted they all dress warmly. She wrapped one of her scarves around Edward's neck.

It was the day before Halloween. The air was chilly, the sun just beginning to fade. There were ears of dried corn on the front doors of some houses, jack-o'-lanterns in several windows, a couple of ghosts made from bedsheets fluttering on a porch railing, a black cat with an arched spine on a mailbox. Houses with children, Sylvia thought, by reflex, with hardly a pang. After two days in the house she was grateful for the playful garishness of the Halloween decorations. The grinning, leering pumpkins and the rest of it added a certain antic charm to the otherwise wistful, Sunday-afternoon landscape. She was glad, too, to plug back into the calendar—October 30, she said to root herself, I have to pick up some candy—after feeling outside time since falling asleep on Friday morning. The cold air invigorated her and she found herself enjoying walking between Fitz and Edward with her hands in her pockets. There may be trouble ahead, she thought, there almost certainly is, but for right now, somehow or other, there's peace. What a strange weekend it's been.

Edward was thinking, dimly, of what had happened the night before, wondering if it was possible that he'd had some sort of contact with Agnes's spirit. Or something, he quickly added, uncomfortable with the whole notion and with the words necessary to articulate it. *Contact, spirit, ghost,* for God's sake. Something tasteless, tacky, low-minded about the whole business, isn't there? His experience the night before hadn't been any of those things and yet the instant he tried to describe it he felt himself dipping into the realm of fortune tellers, séance holders, flakes. He would have liked to believe that fever made him delusional and be done with it. But he couldn't, quite. His memory of Agnes's presence and of himself luxuriating in it was too vivid to be so easily discounted.

He looked out at the Halloween decorations and smiled sadly. There in the softening light of late afternoon it made a kind of sense that the truth of how the dead haunt the living would be as fleeting, as wily, as reluctant to let itself be known as what he'd experienced in Fitzgibbon's back parlor *and* that the way that truth would manifest in the workaday world, in the greyish autumn light when the air smells of burning leaves and the sidewalks are deserted, one way, anyway, that human beings would articulate their awareness of lingering presences, would involve carving sinister gaptoothed smiles into pumpkins and giving candy to children masquerading as ghosts.

It made sense, too, that Paterson would embrace Halloween so vigorously.

They, Fitzgibbon, Sylvia, and Edward, came to a particularly florid half-block, five or six houses in a row, all decorated. Skeletons, spooks, a witch on a broomstick, and then, the topper, a graveyard with cardboard headstones for Jack the Ripper, Dr. Frankenstein, Mr. Hyde, among others.

There seemed to Edward a certain wry wisdom in so unsubtle a response. People you've known and loved, dead. And you, too, of course, one day, this afternoon, tomorrow morning, fifty years from now, dying, dying, dead and gone who knows where. Nobody, that's who knows. No body. I thought I saw. I dreamed about. The strangest feeling whenever I hear that song. Oh, hell, say Patersonians, pass the face paint, break out the bedsheets and brooms.

chapter 17

Under the guise of teaching the orphan girls trades, the nuns got the classrooms cleaned, the gardens tended, the food cooked, the laundry done. Maura couldn't keep from staring when an opportunity presented itself: an orphan on her knees with a can of Brasso and a rag, another pushing a wheelbarrow unsteadily, a third in shoes much too big clomping down a set of stairs that went Maura didn't want to know where.

When orphans were too much with her, when they intruded, when they distracted, when they scared her half out of her wits, Maura would tell herself to wait until nighttime. Then, before the lights went out, when she should have been getting ready for bed, she'd take out her mother's green evening bag and open and close it, open and close it, relishing, savoring, celebrating how well the clasp worked, how reliably the two pieces resisted snapping and then, without fail, with a gentle thud that could be felt but not heard, snapped.

She was secretly proud of her small room with its freshly painted white walls and curtainless window. The dresser had been nicked here and scratched there by previous occupants. Other girls have lived here, Maura thought, lots of them. She was no longer just herself, an American girl in Ireland, motherless, fatherless. She was a Cavan girl now, one of many. There was a dove-grey spread on her bed, a faded but still colorful rag rug on her floor. She dearly loved the pink in it.

She loved her uniform, too, the white cotton blouse, the navy-blue serge jumper, the sturdy black oxfords. Other girls complained bitterly, pining for the clothes they'd left behind, pulling photographs of themselves in home dress from between the pages of their copybooks. Not Maura. She liked getting up in the morning and putting on the clothes she'd taken off the night before. Her blouses came back from the laundry gleaming white and smelling of a hot iron.

The first Saturday of the month was visiting day. After breakfast and two hours out in the fresh air, the girls were sent upstairs to wash their hands and faces and put on their Sunday uniforms. Once they passed inspection they were herded into the refectory, where they were given one sheet of lined paper each and told to write letters home, which nobody did. The nuns didn't press the point so long as some semblance of order was maintained. (It often seemed that what the nuns wanted most was for the girls to leave them alone. Whatever they could do to avoid interaction with their charges they did.) The good white paper was drawn on, folded into fans, torn to bits, and made to imitate falling snow, crumpled into balls and batted from table to table. Every so often one of the refectory double doors opened and a nun appeared. She clapped her hands, waited for quiet, called out a name. That girl got up and proceeded to the visitors' parlor, where her guest or guests awaited.

If boarding-school life had taught Maura anything thus far it was that events could be trusted to happen when they were supposed to happen. On bath days there were baths, on test days tests, on Fridays fish, on Sundays mass. It followed, then, that on visiting day there would be visitors. Every time the nun appeared and clapped, Maura sat up straight in her chair, mouth dry, palms damp. Only after several hours had crept past and the double doors were pulled open and girls began to file out did Maura understand that not every girl would be visited.

chapter 18

Edward woke feeling clearheaded and ambitious. His body's defenses had gotten the better of the virus, finally, and perhaps had done some kind of general sweeping up as well. For the first time in a long time Edward felt inclined and equipped to take a good look at how he was living. He sat on the side of the bed, put on his glasses, ran his fingers through his hair, looked out the window. The sky was a dull grey and the wind was blowing. The threat of rain in no way diminished Edward's mood. He was determined to get his life in order, to suss out what needed to be done and do it.

He stood up and put on his bathrobe as if doing so was a necessary first step. He tied the sash crisply, authoritatively, gave it a good firm tug . . . and was waylaid by a kind of internal surge, a moment of exhilaration. What *was* that in the back parlor two nights before?

Wanting to put the main event into context, sneak up on it, catch it unawares in the hope that it would better reveal itself, he set out to describe what had happened in straight chronological order. He started by recalling himself sitting alone on the leather couch. The house had been still all around, right. And there'd been that awful uneasiness, the fear he'd been about to have a heart attack or stroke. What was all that? Insufficient blood supply to the brain or something? Would a doctor listen to a description and say, Yes, it's fairly common for a patient who's experiencing such and such to report . . .

Even so, Edward thought, reminding himself that he wasn't trying to determine the source of the experience but to recall and describe the sensations themselves as precisely as he could. What had happened to him? What exactly? All right, Agnes had come into his mind suddenly, out of the blue. Out of the black, he thought. Out of the quiet and the dark and that miserable agitation she'd come and a delicious ripple had run through him, something like what he used to feel when he and Agnes were together after having been separated for a time, if, say, she'd gone off by herself to a clinic or he couldn't get to the hospital for several days because he had to work or couldn't find anybody to watch Maura.

The sound of Fitzgibbon coming down the stairs brought Edward back to himself. (He'd been living in the house long enough to know instantly when he heard footsteps whose they were.) So Fitz had gotten up early, too, and decided to get a jump on the day. Sure, he was a businessman. He had plenty to do on a Monday morning, especially after feeling so poorly on Friday. In light of Fitzgibbon's industry, Edward was annoyed at himself for standing around in his bathrobe musing when he'd set out to examine his life in a systematic fashion. Concentrate. Stay focused on the task at hand. He looked at the clock on his night table. Not quite six. Fitz really was getting an early start. Edward wished that he had a desk full of work waiting for him, letters to write, checks to cut, calls to make. His desk, he knew, would be just as he'd left it on Friday, empty but for a book of crossword puzzles inside a manila folder.

Inspired by Fitz's example, his own lack of anything to do in his office notwithstanding, Edward decided he'd dress for work while he took stock of his situation. He picked up his shaving kit and headed for the bathroom at the end of the hall. Even though he'd lived in the Fitzgibbon house for the better part of a year, he still kept his toothbrush and razor in his bedroom like a proper guest.

Sylvia, he thought, looking himself straight in the eye and lathering up with his shaving brush, the obvious place to start is with Sylvia. I'm sleeping with and probably love another man's wife. I'm in love with her, he thought, smiling, seeing Sylvia walking between him and Fitz the day before. How strong she'd looked, how fully herself, and, strangely, given the circumstances, how happy. The scarf she'd insisted he wear smelled of her perfume and since he couldn't take hold of her hand or stop in the middle of the street and kiss her, he'd made do with hunkering down into the coil of cashmere and inhaling deeply. I wouldn't have thought it possible so soon after Agnes but there it is. I'm in love.

All right. So that's been established. Now what are you going to do about it? You can't very well go on the way you have been forever. Gingerly, Edward considered asking Sylvia to leave Fitzgibbon. What were the chances she'd do it? Except for the time in the attic months back when she'd confided that she and Fitz didn't sleep together anymore, Sylvia didn't talk about her marriage. Until recently, until this very moment, in fact, Edward had been grateful for what he thought of as Sylvia's discretion. He hadn't wanted to be the repository of her complaints, her bitterness, believing that if he were to become her confidant in this regard he'd seem less manly to her. Also, Sylvia's silence served as a model, set a tone. By not talking about Fitzgibbon, she relieved Edward of the obligation to talk about his own rather touchy situation, that of being both a lover and a recent widower. Feeling extravagantly nasty for a moment, Edward hoped that once he broached the subject of Fitzgibbon, Sylvia would warm to the task of disparaging him and would reveal all sorts of personal and humiliating information, that Fitz was impotent, that he didn't have nearly as much money as he led people to believe, that—the back door slammed, announcing Bridget's arrival—he'd once been romantically involved with mean old Bridget, which was why he put up with her glowering about the place the way she did.

Try to stay in the real world, will you please? What are the chances Sylvia will leave her husband? Edward reminded himself of the Fitzgibbons' sleeping arrangements. Separate bedrooms had to be taken as a good sign but they were certainly not conclusive evidence that Sylvia no longer loved Fitz and would leave him. Husbands and wives struck all sorts of bargains out of desperation, resignation, stubbornness. And when there was money involved who could say what kind of strange and strained configurations were possible?

In the wake of the suggestion that Sylvia might not be willing to leave her husband, Edward, needing a boost, told himself he'd better be bloody certain about his feelings for her before he dared ask her to do such a thing. Did he love Sylvia, really, or had they just been thrown together by circumstances? If he'd never moved into the Fitzgibbon house, if, say, he'd come to Paterson, reestablished his tie to Fitzgibbon and via that come into contact with Sylvia socially, even come for dinner that one time but never again, would he have been attracted to Sylvia, would he even have noticed her particularly? Yes. And yes again. Edward remembered Sylvia pausing in the doorway of the guest room his first night in the house. "You must be exhausted," she'd said. Something had been established between them in that moment. Sylvia had shed her hostess demeanor and, in response, Edward stopped working so hard at being a congenial guest. They'd had to get away from Fitzgibbon, of course. You must be exhausted. I am that. Nobody could admit to being exhausted in front of Fitz. His relentless good cheer, his glad-handing, didn't allow for the possibility of exhaustion.

After they'd returned from their walk the night before, after Fitzgibbon had excused himself and gone up to bed, Edward and Sylvia went into the kitchen and made roast beef sandwiches and ate them in front of the fire in the back parlor. They talked about inconsequential things, the superiority of seeded rye, Sylvia's fondness for mayonnaise, Edward's for butter, the pleasures of a long walk in cold air. Then they closed the door and made love on the clay-colored couch.

Edward needed no more convincing. He loved Sylvia and wanted to marry her. What he needed to do was tell her how he felt, propose, in a manner of speaking. No sooner did he voice this intention to himself than he imagined Sylvia refusing him. I'm so sorry, Edward. I never had any intention of. I thought you understood that. It's probably best if we stop.

And then he'd have lost her. The dread he felt brought home in a way his earlier reflections hadn't just how badly he wanted to hang on to Sylvia no matter what. How had it happened that he'd become so attached to a woman so soon after losing Agnes? If somebody had told him when he was leaving Ireland that he'd be in love before the year was out, he'd have said such a thing was beyond the realm of possibilities. It simply could not happen. It had happened. He was vulnerable again. The ground could give way under his feet and he'd find himself scrambling to recover his balance again, to make a new life for himself, again.

Had Sylvia replaced Agnes in his affections? No, he didn't think so. His response to whatever that was in Fitzgibbon's back parlor proved his love for Agnes survived.

And if Agnes were here? If I had to choose?

The question gave Edward vertigo. To steady himself he cast about for his initial resolve, his determination to get his life in order. It hadn't evaporated completely. He could still feel its presence, what remained of it, hovering.

Agnes or Sylvia?

No point in choosing. No sense. Agnes is dead and Sylvia isn't.

Sorry to put it that way, my love, but it's true.

As dangerous as the place Edward's thoughts had led him seemed, he didn't want to leave it behind, didn't want to move on. Thinking of Agnes and Sylvia at the same time, as a pair, a couple of sorts, two women with something in common, namely himself, was flattering, tantalizing, titillating. Back in the bedroom now, standing by the window in shorts, undershirt, and black socks, Edward wondered what Sylvia and Agnes would think of each other.

Agnes would be nervous in Sylvia's presence. She'd be eager to please, to seem sophisticated, to make it known that she, too, understood about good clothes and the like. She'd talk too much, Edward thought, hearing her voice in his head more clearly than he had since she'd been dead, not words but the quality of her voice when she was excited, the pitch and the pace. She'd wanted so much to seem confident, in the know, when they first got to New York, hated being a newcomer, had worked hard to distinguish herself from the other Irish nurses at Bellevue. Occasionally her nerve would falter and she wouldn't be able to hide her intimidation. She'd gotten the bum's rush in a fancy Fifth Avenue store one afternoon, a place she had no business being. The snooty saleswoman made it abundantly clear that she had no time for working people, Irish especially. Agnes's fingers were trembling when she handed back a pair of gloves she'd so bravely asked to see.

Her hands, Agnes's hands. She had to keep her nails short and wash often with antiseptic soap and hot water. The hands themselves were elegant, white and long-fingered, but they were nurse's hands, hands that emptied emesis basins and changed sheets and shaved bellies. It was a delicious combination of effects, Edward thought, slim fingers a little chapped around the knuckles, a nick here or there, a needle stick. He used to get aroused watching her make a cup of tea.

Sylvia had hands that rarely washed a dish or swept a floor, hands that were themselves much tended to. The skin was smooth, the nails always polished. The color of that polish, Edward had determined, changed about every four days. What was red when he left in the morning might be pale pink when he returned at night. Getting manicures was one of the things Sylvia did during the day, one of the several regular appointments she kept. Edward was amazed, and charmed, by the attention Sylvia lavished on herself. It seemed so extravagant, so indulgently feminine. And yet, for all of that, Sylvia's hands didn't appear particularly delicate. They looked capable. There was about them a latent strength, a sense that they could have done considerably more than they'd been called upon to do.

It occurred to Edward that Agnes's hands were better suited to the life Sylvia's hands had led, and vice versa. By virtue of architecture, design, the arrangement of bone, tendon, muscle, and skin, Agnes's hands were built for leisure. And Sylvia's hands, minus the nail polish and rings, would have done very nicely for a nurse.

Jesus, if he didn't get a move on he'd be late for work, and that after being up since the crack of dawn. Dressing as quickly as he could, Edward told himself that the morning's reflections hadn't been a total waste. He'd made up his mind to declare himself to Sylvia, right? He had, hadn't he? And suppose she refused him? What if she said she'd never leave Fitzgibbon? All right, well, maybe he'd be better off biding his time, keeping his eyes and ears open but not pressing the point, not yet, anyway.

Pausing on the landing, a rush of impatience with his own tentativeness coursing through him, Edward cast around for something he could do, some kind of action he could take. And then it hit him. He could move out of Fitzgibbon's house, get a place of his own. It wasn't much. It was something, a small step toward getting his life in order.

At the breakfast table, after making sure that Bridget was out of earshot—she seemed especially cranky this morning—Edward leaned in and said, "You know, Sylvia, I think I'd better start looking for a place to live, an apartment, I mean."

"I was thinking the very same thing," Sylvia said. "This weekend was too strange, even for us."

chapter 19

On subsequent visiting days Maura knew her name wouldn't be called and didn't much mind. She rather liked being able to do as she pleased for the better part of a Saturday, unstructured time being in short supply at Cavan. More often than not Maura did schoolwork, but of her own choosing and at her own pace. She daydreamed, filled whole sheets of paper with a woman's profile that another girl taught her to draw, played hangman if anybody asked her to, eavesdropped on the conversations of older girls.

Imagine her surprise, then, when an hour into a pleasantly dull, pleasantly slack visiting day, Sister Mary Louis called, "Maura Devlin." Oblivious, Maura went on tracing the outline of her hand on lined paper. The girl next to her elbowed her hard.

"Me?"

"You, Maura. Go."

In a contradictory value system typical of those generated by packs of unhappy children, the prevailing attitude in the refectory on visiting days was that it was better *not* to be visited, much better to be allowed to remain in the relatively lawless zone of the unvisited than to be summoned to the visitors' parlor to sit in the presence of authority figures of one kind and another, mothers and fathers and nuns. At the same time every girl whose name was called was envied as she stood and made her way to the front of the room. (Deserter!) Someone wanted to see her. Someone had made a special trip. Someone had crossed the boundary into the world of boarding school to let her know the larger world was still functioning out there and that her place in it was being held. She was missed. And then, too—the value systems of children nearly always including something of actual value, hard currency of one kind or another, nobody more materialistic than a child—the ones who weren't called resented the ones who were because everybody knew that visitors generally brought candy.

Maura was too startled to pay attention to the response of her peers. She waded through the hostility, holding fast to the sheet of white paper on which she'd been tracing her hand.

It is probably impossible for anyone older than eight or nine to comprehend the intensity of the anticipation Maura felt as she followed Sister down the hall to the visitors' parlor. Maura was all eagerness, all longing, all desire. Pure. Unadulterated, in a narrowly literal sense, un-adulterated, without the mixed feelings, the ambivalence, the self-consciousness that accompany encroaching adulthood. Heart, mind, body, and soul Maura believed that her father had come. He's here, she said to herself with every step. He's here, he's here, he's here.

"Bell and I have come all this way just to see how you're keeping," Sadie said.

Maura could only gape at her misfortune. Aunt Sadie and Auntie Bell planted on opposite ends of a sofa, ankles crossed, large black handbags on their laps.

"What's the matter with you, Maura? Come on."

Sadie's voice was louder than the voices of the other adults in the room. All around mothers and fathers sat with daughters, talking quietly. Maura was jarred from one sort of grief to another. She wasn't thinking about her father any longer, the blow she'd so recently received absorbed or repelled, shunted off, anyway, to be remembered and nursed later or not at all. She was wholly engaged now in the embarrassment of Sadie's too-loud voice. And her appearance. Sadie looked old, old-fashioned, unkempt. She wore a hat that had long since lost its original shape. Her grey hair stuck out from under it in all directions.

Bell, though neatly dressed, looked just as old and nearly as out of place.

Maura rushed toward her aunts to quiet them, to get them, somehow, to conduct themselves properly, certain that she was being stared at by girls with parents, mothers and fathers of more or less appropriate ages—how young they all seemed—more or less appropriately dressed, lipstick on some of the women, lace collars, earrings. If it had been within Maura's power to make her aunts disappear, not just from the visitors' parlor but from the face of the earth, to send them hurtling into the blackest of voids, she'd have done it without a moment's hesitation.

"What've you got there?"

Maura handed Sadie the paper to shut her up.

"What's this?" Sadie snapped, eyeing the partial outline of Maura's left hand. "Not exactly what I'm sending you to school for, is it? Is this what you've got to show for all the time and money and trouble?"

"I didn't mean to . . . didn't . . . it's just something," Maura stammered, caught now between her humiliation and her fear of Aunt Sadie.

"I brought candy," Bell said, opening her bag. "Now where did I put it?"

That night Maura was in bed before lights out. She fell instantly to sleep and dreamed that Agnes was still alive, still sick, and that she, Maura, had run off. She rode on trains and in the backseat of strange cars trying to find her way back. She climbed staircases she hadn't noticed before, one inside the New York apartment, where she hadn't known there were any, another that took her up from what she'd thought was the top floor of Sadie's house.

By nightfall the next day she was thinking mostly of Edward. Worrying about his physical well-being, suddenly, his safety. She was afraid that he'd gotten sick like Agnes and might die, might be somewhere right now dying. Looking out the window of her room, she imagined him lying in bed taking sips of water from a cup somebody held to his lips. Who? Who was there to hold the cup for Edward? She didn't for the moment believe what she'd been told, that he'd gone back to America. Adults said whatever it suited their purposes to say. The undertaker's wife had kneeled down and said that Agnes wasn't dead, she was just sleeping very, very soundly. But Maura had seen her mother's body as still as a steamer trunk, she'd heard all the people crying. She knew that her mother had been put into a long box then buried in a rectangular hole in the ground. If Agnes was only sleeping, what did anybody expect her to do when she woke up?

chapter 20

Edward thought he saw Sylvia flinch when he told her what he could afford to spend on rent, and that after he named a figure twice his weekly salary. She went on then to veto the notion of a furnished place. "You'll wind up with somebody else's cast-offs. I've got a ton of furniture up in the attic. Leave this to me. Tomorrow's the first? Perfect timing. I'll have you all moved in by the end of the week."

Edward felt cared for, looked after. He got a taste of what it might be like to be married to a woman who could take things in hand, get things done.

Sylvia went straight out to look for an apartment. There was certainly nothing unseemly about her offering a helping hand to her houseguest. All the real estate agents in town were acquaintances of Sylvia's and probably assumed she'd enjoy the business of looking, comparing prices, square footage, amenities. Besides, everybody knew how much time Sylvia had on her hands. She lingered over lunch in restaurants, sat for hours on that front porch of hers. At any rate if the real estate agents wondered about Sylvia's taking the lead in Edward's apartment search, they didn't let on. What they thought about her insistence that Edward was very particular about his privacy, that he didn't want to be on a busy street or in a building with a lot of other people coming and going at all hours, who can say?

"He's a very quiet man," Sylvia said, looking this or that

realtor dead in the eye. "He wants something out of the way. What have you got on the west side?"

When Edward got home from work Sylvia sent him straight over to inspect, approve, and pay for the apartment she'd found. "And remember I'm having the whole place painted. Just look at the rooms themselves."

The apartment was on the top floor of a six-story building. "Nobody stomping around above you," the super said. "It's better like that." The rooms were large and the light was good. The double window in the living room looked out at a more or less undisturbed stretch of Garret Mountain. Edward asked to be left alone for a moment, wanting to get the feel of the place before he made up his mind. There was something poignant about the empty rooms, the rectangles and ovals of brighter paint where pictures had once hung, the not unpleasant smell of floor wax and something less easily identifiable, too, what remained of the previous tenant's personal scent. Edward walked from room to room wondering what was going to happen in each. Under what circumstances and in what company would he move out of this set of rooms?

Fitz smiled when Edward told him he'd found an apartment at the dinner table the following evening. Edward had all he could do not to look at Sylvia in the wake of that smile. How did she understand it? What did she take it to mean? He very nearly asked her later when they were alone but since he didn't see how he could without risking a discussion of where he stood, where they stood, in relation to Fitzgibbon, he kept silent.

"You'll need to buy a new bed, a mattress and box spring, I mean. And a couple sets of sheets, some towels. Have everything sent to the apartment and I'll let the super know it's all coming."

Edward went shopping on his lunch hour. Much to his surprise he enjoyed himself once he got started, once a certain momentum was established. He'd never set up house before. Agnes had seen to the furnishing of their first apartment and every place they'd lived after that had been makeshift, temporary. Having money to spend and time to shop seemed a great luxury. The white ones with the blue stripe, I think. The smaller of the two, please. Half a dozen should do it, thank you. He bought everything Sylvia had told him to buy and more. A kitchen clock. A teakettle. A broom and a dustpan.

The night before he was to move in, Edward packed his suitcase and tidied up his room and the second-floor bathroom the way a guest who had stayed for a night or a weekend might. He was eager to be gone, couldn't imagine why he'd waited as long as he had to get his own place. He cited his grief and his attraction to Sylvia. One had engendered passivity, the other made him reluctant to put any distance between himself and the woman he was trying to seduce. (He liked the sound of that, liked thinking of himself as a seducer.) Reasons enough, he guessed, he supposed. But, still, ten months! He'd come for dinner and stayed nearly a year.

Even before it was officially ended, Edward's time in the Fitzgibbon house seemed a strange idyll, an odd patch. Despite the explanations he'd come up with he didn't really know, couldn't remember, couldn't access, what he'd been thinking when he allowed himself to stay as long as he had. Then he remembered how broke he'd been when he first got to Paterson. Didn't have the money to get my own place right off, did I? He thought of the boardinghouses he'd walked through and told himself that nobody in his right mind would have passed up the chance to live with the Fitzgibbons rent free. This explanation satisfied him better than the others had. Nothing like a defense based on budgetary considerations, dollars and cents, to make a questionable course of action seem reasonable, even prudent. Edward put the box containing his wedding ring and his photograph of Agnes on top of his clothes and zipped up his suitcase.

Fitzgibbon had left already when Edward came down in the morning. Thank God, Edward thought, not having been able to imagine how he'd have said good-bye and thank you under the circumstances, telling himself he'd send a bottle of good scotch and a note in a day or two but knowing he wouldn't. Sylvia had a luncheon she couldn't get out of and so Edward headed off by himself.

He put the key in the lock of his new apartment, opened the

door, walked into the living room, smiled. What a good job Sylvia had done. There was a large, inviting sofa, a couple of upholstered chairs, coffee and end tables, a bookshelf, all artfully arranged. The furniture wasn't new but it was in good condition—all this had been in Fitzgibbon's attic? Edward spent a couple of very pleasant hours setting up his bed, unpacking his clothes, arranging the dishes in his kitchen cabinets, looking out his windows.

The love affair came into its own outside the constraints and constructs of the house. Gone was the squelched, sneaky, slightly vertiginous feeling that had been titillating at first but had become restrictive, inhibiting, tiresome. With nice big chunks of private time and a place to go that was newer, even, than their romance, not expecting Fitz, not listening for Bridget, Sylvia and Edward were at long last able to do as they pleased.

They had dinner out most nights, though never in Paterson. Fair Lawn, Ridgewood, Ho-Ho-Kus, they ventured farther and farther afield, feeling like tourists, day-trippers. They didn't eat much. They asked for the check when their food came and carried leftovers home in small, fragrant brown-paper bags.

Home, in a manner of speaking. The apartment was like a playhouse in an attic or a basement where you're *not supposed to be*—it's dangerous, the floorboards, the pipes, the furnace, stay out of there, do you hear me? Like a shed on somebody else's property, a house under construction, an abandoned building, No Trespassing the sign says in block letters, a ruin, a wilderness where any degree of domesticity achieved seems a triumph of ingenuity and industry, a cheese sandwich split between ten-year-olds, the white bread goes grey from grubby fingers but nobody minds, a couple of scotch-and-waters, a cardboard carton of fettuccine Alfredo, a pot of coffee and guess what I've got in my coat pocket, I nearly forgot, half-and-half! Hardly a day passed that one or the other of them didn't pick up something that was needed, salt and pepper shakers, a second ashtray, a butter dish, a set of candlesticks.

They were not husband and wife so there was none of the

gravity of permanence, the undertow of till death do us part. Nor were they sweethearts, exactly. Not in the we'll-get-engaged-when-I-graduate, my-parents-are-dying-to-meet-you sort of way. Not one thing or the other. Betwixt and between. Doing not what they ought to have done but what they wanted to do. And having a grand time. Having fun.

One evening Sylvia suggested they have dinner in Manhattan and Edward, game, welcoming the prospect of widening horizons and thinking he'd enjoy a drive over the beautiful George Washington Bridge, said Sure, absolutely, lead on. Sylvia took him to Germantown, the neighborhood she'd grown up in, and pointed out the apartment building where her family had lived and the school she'd attended. Neither was as fancy as Edward had imagined they'd be and he was relieved. Germantown seemed to be inhabited by a prosperous middle class, people with money in the bank, no doubt, but money that had been earned not inherited. The restaurant Sylvia had planned to go to wasn't there any longer. In its place was a beauty parlor. "Not very appetizing, is it?" Sylvia said, peering through the plate glass. "Suppose we just walk around a while."

Though the night was cold they walked for nearly an hour, arm in arm, a luxury, a treat. They wound up in a delicatessen eating corned-beef sandwiches, drinking coffee, and watching people pass on the sidewalk. When they finished Edward said he'd like to drive home if Sylvia didn't mind, said he wanted to see how it felt to drive over the bridge. They hardly said a word in the car but the silence was companionable. They seemed to be in similar states of mind, sober, sated, completely at ease.

"Do you like the city?" Sylvia asked when they got back to the apartment and were sitting side by side on the couch.

"New York? I liked it better when I was younger, I think. All seems a bit much to me now."

"You lived there for a time, didn't you?"

"I did, yes, a short while."

"Where?"

"Twenty-first Street, on the east side. Murray Hill, isn't that what they call it?"

"Mmm. How long? How long were you there?"

"Couple of years. Not even."

"When you first got to New York? When you and Agnes were first married?"

Edward started at the sound of Agnes's name. "Right." He got up, went into the kitchen, and returned with a bottle of brandy Sylvia had brought over the night before.

"Does it bother you, my bringing up Agnes?"

"It doesn't bother me, exactly. It took me by surprise, though."

Edward busied himself pouring the brandy, seemed intent on getting exactly the same amount in each of the two glasses.

Sylvia picked up a throw pillow and held it on her lap. "Because you never mention her, and if you don't want to talk about this just say so, but I'm curious. What was she like?"

Edward handed Sylvia a glass then took a drink from his own. His reluctance to discuss Agnes had more to do with a sense that he was heading into dangerous waters than it did with grief or tenderness. He was afraid that whatever he said would be wrong, would disappoint Sylvia, would get him into trouble somehow. He didn't entirely trust Sylvia's manner, her gentle tone, the tentative look in her eyes. He was sure that she wanted him to say something in particular, and he'd have gladly obliged if he'd known what that was. He'd have said anything, really, any version of the truth. How does one describe a previous love to a current one? Having no idea what Sylvia hoped to hear, Edward was loath to find out via trial and error. Still he knew that not answering at all would be as bad as the worst of whatever he might say.

"Agnes was a nurse," he began. Saying her name gave him confidence. She was after all just a person who had once been alive and no longer was. She was a simple fact of history. "She grew up in the same town I did but we didn't have much to do with each other until— She was a friend of my eldest sister, Sadie, a pet, you know, big girl, little girl, that sort of thing. Anyway, we were married in Ireland then came straight over here. She got sick working at Bellevue. You know Bellevue, don't you?"

"The hospital? Of course. Go on."

"TB. Right. There were ups and downs. But you know how it goes. Because of your sister, I mean. She'd get better for a while, then worse again. She died on December the eighth."

Sylvia put her hand on Edward's cheek. "It must have been so hard."

"It was, yes. It was awful. But I don't want you to think— I mean, all of that's behind me now. It's over and done with, isn't it? Part of the past."

"Edward?"

"What?" he said brusquely.

"Have you got a picture of her?"

"Oh, come on."

"No, really. Do you have one or not?"

"I do. Yes. One."

"Would you mind? Can I see it?"

"Why do you want to?"

"Because I'm curious. Because you were married to this woman and I'd like to know something about her. God, do you think I'm going to fly into a jealous rage or something? You had a life before we got together. We both did. You know all about mine. I'd like to have some idea about yours."

Edward stood up and went into the bedroom.

"She was very pretty," Sylvia said, holding Agnes's photograph in both hands, thumbs against the bottom edge.

Edward flushed with pride. He liked Sylvia's knowing he'd been married to a pretty woman.

"She looks like the sort of person who generally got her way. Was she?"

"How can you tell that?"

"I don't know. It's there around her mouth and chin. So it's true?"

"That she got her way more often than not? Yes, I guess that's fair to say."

Sylvia nodded, still gazing at Agnes and smiling faintly. "Here," she said after a moment. "I'm glad I've seen her. Now I have a face to go with the name."

Edward took the picture back into the bedroom and looked

at it hard for a couple of seconds—how static the image, how slight, really—before putting it back where he'd gotten it. He sat beside Sylvia on the couch and kissed her. And kissed her again. They touched each other with a seriousness of purpose, each, it seemed, intent on reassuring the other. It's all right. It's you now. It's you and me now.

It was nearly five o'clock when Sylvia got up and began to dress. Ordinarily she hated having to leave, hated the leaving itself, putting on the night before's clothes that smelled of cigarette smoke and stale perfume and heading out into the cold, but tonight she didn't mind. She looked forward to the privacy and the fresh air, to driving her car and hearing herself think.

The streets were deserted but for an occasional drunk shuffling along and a couple of milk trucks making their rounds. Garbage cans overflowed onto sidewalks. The row houses along Broadway, minus people on the front stoops, looked especially weary. The sky was a murky shade of grey, not yet dawn, no longer night. The uneven light suited Paterson but didn't flatter her.

Sylvia was thinking of Agnes, who was a real woman to her now, a woman in a knee-length fur coat with a broad tuxedo collar, a woman with her handbag on her lap. She'd been sick for a long while by the time that picture was taken, Sylvia was sure. Her eyes were cast down but if they'd been looking at the camera, at Edward taking the picture, Sylvia thought with a twinge, they'd have been hollow and manic like Ruth's eyes at the end.

Stopped at a red light though there wasn't another car in sight, Sylvia squirmed in her seat. Even now, all these years later, she could not be still in the presence of the memory of how her little sister had suffered. Where does it hurt, baby girl? Tell me where. Ruth would shake her head and go on whimpering. Belladonna made her violent. Mild-mannered Ruthie, ordinarily a model patient, would growl, curse—who would have thought she even knew those words?—bite. Morphine and she'd sleep nearly all the time and wake up talking. ". . . the tickets? Because you can't get on the train without the tickets. The doctor said I have to be there by ten or I'll miss breakfast and if I miss breakfast I won't get better. Tell him to hurry, Syl.

Tell the man to hurry or we'll miss the train. Have you got the tickets?"

Sylvia pulled into the driveway slowly, taking note of a figure in a window across the street and a light on next door. She closed the car door gently, went around back and in through the kitchen. She wasn't in bed thirty seconds when she heard Fitz's bathwater running.

chapter 21

Maura believed there was a chance Edward would come. He might. He could take the same train she'd taken, the same hire car. He could knock on the front door like Aunt Sadie had done and when the tall nun answered he would say, "Morning, Sister. I'm Maura Devlin's dad and I've come to collect her. Get her things together, will you? She'll be coming back to New York with me. Tell her I'm here, will you please?" And when she was summoned she'd direct Edward to go and sit in the visitors' parlor—and he would do as she said, whatever she wanted he would do, this pliable dad, this smiling, well-behaved one. The other girls would admire him, young and dashing and handsome in a clean white shirt and striped tie, nothing like a disheveled old lady with a black handbag, Edward, every bit a father, her father, her man come to claim her.

Visiting days came and went. She grew impatient but couldn't stand to think ill of him. Could not tolerate the presence of disparaging thoughts. When she couldn't keep the faith any longer—he's not coming, he's never coming—and recriminations began to take shape in her mind, she got agitated. Her thoughts became disjointed, skittish. He could come if he wanted to . . . you're too late, I'll tell him . . . go away . . . Monday's assignment not half done and visiting day nearly over. I'll get in trouble if I don't finish. What's the matter with me? What's the matter with me now?

* * *

The chattering girls got quiet when the nun entered the classroom. Sister walked up the center aisle briskly, put her books on her desk, looked out at the class a moment. A girl in the last row whispered to her neighbor. Maura bristled. Shut up, she thought, taking careful note of the downward movement of Sister's eyebrows, the slight frown. Sister rapped on her desk with a pencil.

"Now that Miss Connelly and Miss Brennan have finished their private conversation, perhaps we can begin today's lesson," the nun said in Irish.

Maura understood what had been said and was grateful. It was coming, Irish was coming. She'd been afraid it never would, thought she'd always be straining to understand, picking out words here and there, repeating phrases to herself in bed at night and on her way from one classroom to another.

"All right then. Much better. Take out last night's assignment and pass it up, please."

Maura opened her copybook and looked over her paper. When she'd finished it the night before, she was certain she'd done a good job. Now she wasn't so sure. Her handwriting looked sloppy and she'd put the wrong ending on a verb in the second sentence. Reluctantly, she passed her paper to the girl in front.

"Who will begin reading this morning?"

Several hands went up, including Maura's.

"Maura Devlin. And see that you don't mumble, Maura. I want to hear every syllable."

Maura got to her feet intending to read flawlessly to make up for the shoddiness of the homework assignment she'd just handed in, to redeem herself. It was getting so that nearly every minute contained the possibility of making up for the deficiencies of the one that had gone before. Hours were charged with a kind of alternating current, disappointing, trying to make amends, disappointing again. Maura began to read and was distracted by the sound of her own voice. She stumbled over a word, got rattled, lost her place and was several long seconds finding it again. She read the remaining sentences rapidly to make up for the delay.

"That was fine, Maura. Come on, who's next?"

* * *

The curriculum was demanding. Success—survival—was not assured. Maura had to devote herself body and soul to her task, had to approach every assignment, every examination, recitation, theme, column of figures, bit of memorization with urgent determination. Not for Maura the automatic attention granted other girls, the ones with mothers and fathers. If Maura was to get any attention at all, and attention was the only route to approval—people had to notice her before they could admire her—she had to earn it.

She lived inside a flurry of competitiveness, hard mental work, writer's cramp, insomnia (she worried), and the occasional singling out for praise by one nun or another that made all the effort and anxiety seem beside the point, not entirely real. Her experience wasn't what mattered. What mattered, what signified, was the response of other people.

When she thought of her mother and father at all, when she spied the green evening bag at the back of her dresser drawer, she felt vaguely remorseful. She thought that she ought to feel sadder than she did . . . but there were verbs to conjugate, Irish, French, German, there were poems to memorize, handwriting to practice (hers was so sloppy), whole chapters to read. She still hated when her name was called on visiting days, still wished Aunt Sadie would take the time to make herself presentable, but the humiliation she felt upon entering the visitors' parlor was something she didn't dwell on. It would be over soon enough and then she could get back to whatever contest she was engaged in at the moment, whatever means she'd seized on that day to prove herself worthy, to secure her right to exist.

chapter 22

Sylvia sat in the waiting room nearly hyperventilating. She smoothed the fabric of her skirt, crossed and uncrossed her legs. She was sure she'd done a thoroughly unconvincing job of giving the receptionist a fake name, her maiden name, the married form of it to boot, Mrs. Schultz. Her voice hadn't actually wavered but neither had she been able to meet the receptionist's gaze.

"He'll see you now, Mrs. Schultz," the receptionist said without any indication that she'd given a thought to what Sylvia's name was or wasn't.

Sylvia made a point of pausing for a second after standing up, a technique she'd learned long ago in finishing school that was supposed to make a person appear composed. Don't immediately lurch off. Stand a second, collect yourself, then go. She walked past the desk slowly. Pretend you're Mrs. Schultz. Sylvia could not follow her own directive, nor was she stronger for hearing it. To Sylvia, Mrs. Schultz had and always would refer to her mother, a woman who would have sooner died than consult a divorce lawyer about the legal consequences of adultery.

"Afternoon, Mrs. . . . Schultz," the lawyer said, scanning a yellow pad. "Have a seat."

Because going to a Paterson lawyer was out of the question, Sylvia had called an old girlfriend she knew was divorced and asked for a recommendation. "I know who you want. He's got the manners of a dockworker, he'll charge you an arm and a leg, but he knows his stuff and he'll keep his mouth shut."

"What can I do for you today?" the lawyer said.

"I need some information. I'm going to be very frank to save us both time."

"Good. Can't help you if I don't know the facts."

"The situation is this. My husband and I have been estranged for some time and I've become involved with another man. What I want to know from you is how I'm likely to fare if there's a divorce."

"You say estranged. Does that mean you haven't been living together?"

"No. Yes. Yes, we do live together."

"Uh-huh. Does your husband know about your boyfriend?"

"Probably."

"Has he got proof? Eyewitnesses, pictures, letters, anything he could bring before a judge?"

"I don't know."

"What do you think, Mrs. Schultz?"

"He could have. It's possible."

The lawyer frowned and rocked his head from side to side as if in time to music only he could hear. "How about him, your husband, any chance he's fooling around, too?"

This was even worse than Sylvia had imagined it would be. She considered ending the interview, getting up and walking out, but if she did that she'd have undergone considerable humiliation and still not have found out what she needed to know.

"No, he's not, not as far as I know."

"You'll want to find out for sure. That could make all the difference. Is there much money involved? What are we talking about here?"

"My husband owns a profitable business. Investments of various kinds, two houses, several cars, antiques, things of that sort." Why am I telling a little worm like you so much? Sylvia continued to herself. You obviously make a good living. How about putting on a clean shirt in the morning?

"Children?"

"No."

"Too bad."

"Can you tell me where I stand, please?"

"Does your husband drink to excess?"

"No."

"Beat you?"

"No."

"Make unreasonable demands of any sort in the bedroom?"

"No."

"Well, then. If your husband decides to sue you for divorce on the grounds of adultery and you're not able to make a counter charge, you won't get much. Judges don't look too kindly on women who, well, you understand what I'm getting at. Especially when there are no children involved. From what you've told me I have to say that you'll be at your husband's mercy."

Sylvia badly needed a moment to compose herself but had to make do with passing her gloves from hand to hand. "Thank you. You've been very helpful."

"I wish I had better news to report but the law in this state is harsh when—"

"Good afternoon."

"I'll be happy to represent you if—"

"Thank you."

"Pay the receptionist on the way out, will you?"

Sylvia lay with her head on Edward's chest listening to rain on the roof and telling herself it was time to get up and get dressed. Earlier, Edward had stepped out for a pack of cigarettes and Sylvia had gone into the bedroom intending to change the sheets until she spotted the photograph of Agnes lying on the dresser. She'd held it under the light and taken a good long look. Rabbit dyed to look like mink, she'd thought. An inexpensive coat, the fur of a young woman who wants to be able to say she owns a fur coat. Beneath the coat a sweater and beneath the sweater a dark velvet dress that, while Agnes was seated, reached all the way to her ankles. How well Sylvia remembered the invalid's way of dressing—There's a draft, Ruthie, put on a sweater, tie a scarf around your neck. Agnes was seated at an angle, knees held primly together, right foot

peeking out from under the folds of her dress, elaborate shoe—
God, was it satin?—with a three-inch heel. Sylvia counted five
thin straps running over the top of Agnes's foot. The fancy shoe
was not set flat on the ground but was tilted prettily, flirtatiously.

And on her face the hint of a suppressed smile, the telltale
expression of someone who knows her picture is being taken
but is pretending she doesn't. And so the prim knees and showing off the shoes. They must have been new, Sylvia thought.
She must have loved them.

"Edward?"

"Mmmm."

"I have to go soon. I'll call you tomorrow, all right?"

Edward sat up and groped for his glasses. "What time is it?"

"Not quite two."

"I hate this, Sylvia. I wish you could stay."

"I do, too. Hear the rain?"

"Do it then. Stay with me tonight."

"I'd love to, believe me, but I can't."

"I don't see why not. It's not as if he doesn't know where you
are."

Sylvia got up and began to dress. When she was finished, except for her shoes, which she didn't put on till she was ready to
walk out the door out of deference to the people down below,
she sat on the bed and crossed her arms.

"I went to see a divorce lawyer today."

"What?"

"Mmmm. It was awful. Humiliating. But I had to find out
where I stand."

"And what did he say?"

"That if Fitz and I divorce I won't get much. I'm the guilty
party. I've violated the marriage contract, committed adultery."

"I want to marry you, you know that, don't you?"

Sylvia closed her eyes for a moment and smiled. "Well, I'm
glad to hear it. I want to marry you, too, but it's not as simple as
that."

"It is. It's exactly that simple. Go home and pack your things
and walk out the door. Done. Let the divorce happen however
it happens. When it's all over we'll get married."

"I don't have any money of my own, you know. My father cut me off without a cent when I got married. I'm not a kid, Edward. I can't just go charging out the door without a thought in my head about how I'm going to live."

"I'll take care of you. I've got a job, haven't I?"

"You may not have one if I leave Fitz."

"What, he'll have me blacklisted or something? Let him. Let him do whatever he's going to do. You and I will manage. Have some faith, will you? I did very well for myself for a long time without Fitzgibbon's help and I'll do so again. I'll be a good husband, wait and see."

"I'm thirty-six years old, Edward. I've been married since I was nineteen. I can't simply pack a bag and walk out the door. I could be charged with abandonment along with everything else."

"This doesn't have anything to do with legalities or money, does it? You don't want to leave him. In spite of everything. You want to go on being married to him. If Fitz and I divorce, you said. *If* I leave him."

"Don't bully me, Edward. I have to do this in my own time."

"Good. Fine. But understand that I'm not going to wait forever."

"It's not going to be forever. Didn't I just say that I went to see a lawyer today? What more proof do you need?"

"Stay here tonight. Take off your clothes right now and get back in this bed."

"I can't do that."

"You bloody well could if you wanted to."

Sylvia got up, walked over to the dresser, and turned to face Edward. "If we're going to talk about getting married, there's something I have to ask you. I've wanted to for a long time but the last time I tried ... it seems a sore subject so I've left it alone. But I can't marry you without knowing."

"Knowing what?"

"About your daughter's situation."

"My daughter? What's she got to do with it?"

"Do you have any intention of bringing her over here at some point?"

Edward got up and put on his trousers. "My daughter is with my two sisters, as I've told you. Very well cared for. Properly looked after. She's started boarding school already, in fact. And will be there until she's sixteen or seventeen, a long time from now."

"I'm getting a bad feeling. You never mention her. Do you write? The only letters you get are from your sister."

"How do you know?"

"Who do you think got the mail at the house every day?"

"Those letters from my sister contain very thorough accounts of my daughter. She's just a little girl, too young to write herself."

"Why are you getting so angry? I'm entitled to ask these questions before I marry you."

"You're a lot better at asking questions than answering them. Tell me now, are you going to leave your husband or aren't you?"

"I am, yes. In my own time. Not recklessly, not foolishly."

"Your own time, how long is that?"

"I don't know."

"Six months? A year? Five years?"

"Stop it."

"Oh, go on. Go. And don't come back until you're ready to give me some answers."

Sylvia's eyebrows shot up but she said not another word. She walked out of the bedroom, located her shoes, hat, coat, and purse, spotted Edward's umbrella on the kitchen counter, decided she was entitled to it, and took it.

Edward tried to fall back to sleep but was too angry. He got up, drank more brandy than should ever be drunk in one sitting, smoked too many cigarettes, fell asleep finally just as it was beginning to get light.

chapter 23

Wretched. The only word to describe how Edward felt. He was anxious and ashamed and remorseful. He was queasy and dehydrated and his armpits stunk. The odor was tangy and unfamiliar. He didn't even smell like himself.

He lay perfectly still and tried to will the telephone to ring. He considered calling Sylvia but knowing the household routines as well as he did, he knew that Bridget would answer. (He heard the housekeeper's voice, affronted, who dares to ring at this hour?) What excuse could he give for calling so early? Unless, he thought, Sylvia is feeling as poorly as I am this morning and is staying near the phone, hoping it will ring. If she was feeling half as bad as I am, she'd have called me by now.

Time to get up. Time to go to work. Edward thought about calling in sick but the prospect of unstructured time terrified him. The void. Who knew what sort of demons might come sniffing around? He'd be kept from going all to pieces by the earthly stolidity of the bus, the elevator, his desk and chair and wastebasket.

The instant he turned the bathwater on he thought he heard the phone ring and ran stark naked into the living room. He waited longer than he should have, toes clenching and unclenching against the carpet, telling himself the phone might still be between rings.

Come on, get ready for work.

The project, the proposed traffic circle, had been resurrected by a recent influx of federal money. Thankfully, Edward had done what Sylvia advised, kept a set of plans at the ready, and one day the call had come. "Your plans, Edward. We want to see your plans." There were bids to be got, paperwork to be filed, numbers to be gone over, adjusted, and gone over again. Edward was never so grateful to be occupied. Concentrating on the figures in front of him, the tame and reliable numbers, black on white, kept the lunatic edge of his distress at bay. There were, though, several incoming calls. Edward's heart was in his throat each time he picked up.

Never her. It was never her.

At lunch he went out for a grilled cheese sandwich and several cups of double-bag tea. Standing in line to pay his bill, feeling small and very sad, he made up his mind that he'd do whatever he had to do to convince Sylvia to leave Fitzgibbon. Everything he'd ever cared about. Everyone. He was not going to add Sylvia to his list of defeats.

He *was not*.

He returned to his apartment after work and knew that what he saw there, the dirty glasses, the unmade bed, the awful stillness, might be what he was going to come home to from now on. Alone again. Jesus.

Sylvia was determined not to call Edward until she knew what she wanted to say. She'd get out of Paterson so as not to be tempted, go down to the shore for a few days, down to the house at the shore.

"I'll call Matthews," Fitz said when Sylvia told him her plan. "Have him clean the place up, turn the furnace on, ice up the refrigerator."

Sylvia didn't trust her own impressions entirely but it seemed to her that Fitz sympathized with her state of mind.

"Why don't I get a driver to take you down? It looks like snow."

"No. I'll drive myself. But—"

"What?"

"No, nothing. Thanks."

"You're welcome," Fitz said, averting his eyes.

Sylvia packed only comfortable clothes, her oldest sweaters and roomiest slacks. When she opened the car door she saw that Fitz had put a kind of makeshift emergency kit on the passenger seat. An ice scraper, several empty flour sacks, a small bag of rock salt, a flashlight. She thought about stopping at the mill on her way out of town to thank him, just that, to say a simple thank you, but she knew, however good her intentions, once she got there the air between herself and Fitz would be strained, the conversation halting. She did drive by the mill, though, in a private gesture of thanks and was struck by the sight of the brick buildings, how old-fashioned they seemed, how distinctly nineteenth century, on the verge of becoming picturesque. It had been five years, she realized, at least five, since she'd been down there.

She'd just gotten onto Route 1 when the snow started in earnest and made driving tricky. Sylvia didn't mind. She was glad. Having to concentrate on the road prevented her from thinking about Edward. And it was an enormous relief to be fully occupied for a change, to be in charge, to put her good reflexes, her excellent hand-eye coordination, to use. She didn't have to think a thing—move left here, slow down—to make it happen and so the car felt like an extension of herself. She skidded a couple of times but was never in any real danger. She kept her foot off the brake and both gloved hands on the wheel and did fine.

The house in Avalon was a small Cape Cod, white, two stories, with a steep gabled roof. A narrow road ran between it and the beach. The view of the ocean was unobstructed and would remain so because Sylvia's maternal grandfather had had the foresight to buy the plot of land directly across half a century before.

All her life she'd loved pulling into the driveway of the small house. She knew the gentle thud of her car leaving the pavement and the crunch of gravel under her tires. She could see several lights burning inside and a faint curl of black smoke coming from the narrow chimney. What remained of Matthews's footprints were visible heading away from the front door. He'd been and gone, good. Sylvia didn't want to see anybody, didn't want to have to keep up her end of even a brief conversation. She especially didn't want to have to explain why she'd come down in the dead of winter all by herself.

She put her suitcase down on a kitchen chair, took off her gloves, unbuttoned her coat, remembered being eight or nine and rushing upstairs the moment she got inside to reclaim her room and change into her bathing suit while her mother bustled around supervising the unpacking. She felt unencumbered, as if she were sloughing off the burdens of adulthood, her estrangement from her father, her marriage, her affair, all of it.

She opened the refrigerator and saw that Matthews had bought some groceries. Had Fitz told him to? A bottle of milk, a loaf of bread, coffee, butter, eggs, orange juice. Good. She wouldn't have to go back out until the snow stopped.

The tap sputtered violently when Sylvia turned it on, ran brownish for a while, cleared. Letting the water run, she opened several cabinets and surveyed their contents, took out the coffee-pot, one plate, one glass, one cup, and one saucer. She opened a drawer and pulled out a knife, a fork, and a cloth napkin, which she sniffed and thought smelled all right. Under the sink she found a bottle of dish soap. She washed her dishes, her knife and her fork, her place setting for one.

Suddenly thirsty, she drank two glasses of tap water then put a pot of coffee on. She opened the door to the pantry and found cans of various kinds, baked beans, beets, sardines, tuna fish. No telling how old any of them were. Sylvia remembered reading in a women's magazine once that cans were all right so long as the tops didn't bulge. These seemed fine. She chose the sardines because they came with their own opener. By the time she'd lit the oven and put two slices of bread to toast on the rack, the coffee was ready.

She thoroughly enjoyed the oily fish, bones and all, and the piping-hot coffee. When she was finished eating, she licked her fingers then washed her dishes and set them on the rack to dry. Upstairs she put sheets on the bed and then barely had the energy to take off her shoes, in spite of the several cups of coffee she'd drunk or, perhaps, because of them. Coffee in the afternoon sometimes made her unaccountably sleepy. She got into bed in her dress, the hem still damp from the walk to the house through the snow. She'd hardly slept the night before. The drive down had been taxing. Sylvia slept the kind of sleep insomniacs lust after. She was dead to the world for several hours.

The room was dark when she woke but she wasn't disoriented, didn't need a minute to remember where she was or how she'd got there. She rolled over and commended herself for getting in the car and making the trek down, for putting a hundred miles between herself and Paterson. No place on earth I'd rather be than where I am, she thought.

She sat up, stretched, made animal sounds she never would have if she hadn't been absolutely alone. At the open window she took deep breaths of cold, wet, salty air. She unbuttoned her dress, pulled it over her head. In just her slip, she leaned out the window. The snow had stopped as far as she could tell, though there was still a good bit of it blowing around. She took off her girdle and stockings, put on a bathrobe.

On her way downstairs she realized that the house was really warm now, too warm. Matthews must have turned the heat way up to take the chill off. For a moment Sylvia wasn't sure where the thermostat was or even if there was one at all. She so rarely spent time in Avalon in the winter and, besides, attending to the temperature wasn't the sort of thing she had much part in generally. She felt as if she was caught between the two houses, unsure what was where in either of them. Was there a thermostat in the front hall or was that the Paterson house? The instant she spotted the dial it was familiar for itself and for its location, just to the right of the light switch in the living room. She set it to sixty-five and heard the furnace go off. Satisfying, that. Touch something here and something in the basement shuts down.

She found her watch just where she'd left it, on the ledge above the kitchen sink. Ten after eight, too late for a walk, much too early for bed. All right, she'd unpack, settle in. The silence was beginning to ring in her ears. No small feat, getting the big Westinghouse radio up the stairs but she managed. She unpacked to the sound of pop music and her own intermittent humming.

She'd told Fitz she'd probably stay two or three days but

now she thought she might want to try for a whole week. Never before in her life, never, had Sylvia set out to spend so much time alone. She came down to the shore every August by herself, of course, but Fitz joined her most weekends and this year Edward had come, too. There were neighbors with whom she was friendly, people she'd known all her life, many of them, like her, children who had grown up and taken over their parents' summerhouses. They came over for drinks, invited her for dinner. The town itself was different in August. It was all but deserted now. Driving in, Sylvia had been struck by how many of the stores were closed. It wasn't a surprise, exactly. She'd have guessed they would be, if she'd thought about it, but she hadn't. Some even had plywood nailed across their front windows against the winter winds and the ever-present threat of hurricanes.

"Yes, Bridget, hello, Edward Devlin calling. Is Mrs. Fitzgibbon in?"

"She's not."

"Not. Right. All right then. How are you these days, Bridget? How are you keeping?"

Sylvia slept until ten o'clock the following morning, despite the long nap she'd taken the day before. She put on a pot of coffee, made a mental note to pick up some half-and-half, sat down at the kitchen table in the quiet of fresh snow outside and the bright midmorning sun. On the table was a cloth made of a rubbery fabric. What's it called, Sylvia thought. Oilcloth, right. It felt gritty under her elbows and smelled faintly of yesterday's sardines. "If Morrison's is open I'll pick up a new tablecloth."

She scrambled three eggs, very soft, and ate them standing by the window looking out at the snow. After running cold water into the frying pan, she went upstairs and took a quick bath. She opened her makeup bag, looked at herself in the mirror, frowned. No sense bothering with all that down here. She rubbed cold cream into her skin, tied her hair back with a scarf.

Shored up by sleep, scrambled eggs, and a whole pot of coffee (the cups were small, she'd lost count), Sylvia headed out intending to walk on the street a while and then, when she began to tire, to come home along the ocean. The houses she passed, the stretches of road she covered, were at once deeply familiar and strange now in winter. Wearing trousers and a heavy plaid jacket that might have belonged, for all Sylvia knew, to Matthews, she was unrecognizable. Her summer friends wouldn't have known her. When a pickup truck passed and the driver, an old man, raised his hand soberly, Sylvia liked thinking he wasn't waving at Sylvia Fitzgibbon, or even at Sylvia Schultz, but only at a fellow year-rounder, somebody else in for the long haul.

She began, after a while, to feel the tug of duty, thought she ought to at least attempt to sort out what she'd come down to Avalon to sort out. What did she want and what should she do in the service of getting it? When trying to make decisions, Sylvia found it helpful to describe the situation to herself as she might to a neutral third party. She just about had her predicament framed in her mind—I'm this, Edward is that, Fitz is the other—when she passed an ice cream stand, a shack, really, closed up tight for the winter. The place had been there as long as Sylvia could remember, was owned by an old lady. She hadn't always been old, Sylvia realized. When I was a girl she couldn't have been more than, what, fifty, which seemed really old to me then. We've been moving through it together, the old lady and I. I wonder what she does in the winter. Sylvia peered at the shack intently, hoping she wouldn't see any signs of occupancy. I'd hate to think of her in there warming her hands at a kerosene heater. She works so hard summers. I hope she's down in Miami sunning herself and counting her money. Once Sylvia allowed her thoughts to take a detour, to wonder about the old lady's whereabouts and wish her warmth and wealth, she wasn't able to get them back on the track of dutiful reflections about herself and her husband and her lover. The truth is she didn't even try.

Morrison's was open. It was a kind of all-purpose store, called itself a department store though it bore little resemblance to Macy's in Manhattan or Meyer Brothers in Paterson.

Morrison's was the kind of place where Sylvia might conceivably find a tablecloth *and* a pint of half-and-half. She hoped that the owners took off for the winter, that whoever was behind the counter wouldn't know her so that she could wander the narrow aisles undisturbed. She had the whole day to fill, after all, and she sometimes liked drifting around amidst the stock a store like that kept, cheap souvenirs (Greetings from the Jersey Shore), scouring pads and feather dusters, clothes that were just far enough out of fashion as to seem truly tasteless.

"Sylvia Schultz, is that you? What are you doing down here now?"

There was something put on in the proprietor's tone, a vaguely theatrical quality to her smile, that led Sylvia to believe that Doris behind the counter had been informed of her presence by Matthews and was feigning surprise. Locals seemed to need to conspire against summer residents.

"How are you, Doris?"

"Nothing wrong at the house, I hope?"

"Not a thing. You don't by any chance have any tablecloths, do you?"

"Table . . . cloths," Doris said, as if she'd never heard the two words used in conjunction before and found the combination intriguing. She bit her lip and seemed to be reviewing her vast and irrational inventory. "You know, I think I do. Hold on a minute now. Where did I see them?"

Doris dragged an ancient wooden ladder from one corner and headed down the center aisle. She opened the ladder, tested its sturdiness, climbed halfway up and pulled a cardboard box off a shelf. "Yep. Here they are. I knew I had some."

At home Sylvia wouldn't have given the tablecloths a second look but here at the shore, inside Morrison's, she found them quite nice. There were half a dozen or so in a range of solid colors. Sylvia selected a vibrant blue, unfolded it, thought the size seemed about right. "I'll take this one. And a pint of half-and-half, please."

"That I don't have. Don't stock it in the wintertime anymore. It doesn't sell. I wind up pouring it down the sink."

"All right then. How much for the tablecloth?"

"A dollar ninety-eight. Would you like me to order some cream for you? I can have it day after tomorrow."

"Yes. Do that, please."

Standing on the sidewalk in front of the store, Sylvia opened her jacket and tucked the tablecloth into her pants so that she wouldn't have to carry it in her hands while she walked. She made it only a couple of blocks past Morrison's before she felt the first twinges of fatigue and decided to head back. Stepping onto the sand, she saw her house in the distance. It looked small but sturdy, well made. Whatever happens, she thought, I can always come here and live. She considered the thousands of women in circumstances like hers, in troubled marriages, with or without lovers, facing divorce. She was better off than most. What would any one of those women have given for what she had, what she was looking at right now, a house that was hers and hers alone?

Sylvia said a silent thank you to her father and then took herself to task when she remembered that he'd had nothing whatsoever to do with her inheriting the house. It had been left to her by her mother. Sylvia remembered seeing the words in print. *And to my daughter Sylvia I leave the house and property at 1811 Ocean Boulevard.* Thank you, Mother . . . Mom . . . Ma, Sylvia thought, unsure for a moment what she, as an adult, had called her mother. She looked up at the house and thought of a time when her mother, her sister, and herself spent several days, a week, at the house waiting for her father to arrive. I'll see you when I see you, he'd said when he put them on the train. Ordinarily they knew exactly when to expect him but this time, for reasons Sylvia had long since forgotten, he wasn't able to say when he'd be down. As the waiting wore on, Sylvia, her mother, and her sister went into a state of suspended animation. They couldn't seem to get on with the business of being at the shore until Sam was there. Nobody said as much, of course, but they all were distracted. They bickered among themselves and told each other to wait until Daddy, until your father gets here. They all perked up whenever a car slowed going past the house. "What a shame," Sylvia said, "that we didn't make the most of the time to ourselves so that when the great Sam finally arrived (only Sylvia had lived to see him become a difficult and not always rational old man) he was the outsider who had to find his way back in."

She walked straight to the water's edge and stood firm when freezing-cold foam covered her boots to the ankles. She could hardly bear the thought that of those three women, her mother, her sister, herself, only she survived.

She hurried back to the house, arrived winded by the effort of rushing across sand. She pulled her tablecloth out of her pants, put it down on an inside step, got out her rod and reel, and traded her wool jacket for a rain slicker with a hood. She found a bucket under the kitchen sink, not that she expected to catch anything. She didn't even bother about bait. Let the fish find its way onto the hook if it was so inclined.

"Bridget, it's Edward Devlin again. Is she there?"

"No."

"Is she expected?"

"She lives here, doesn't she?"

"At any particular time, I mean. Has she gone away or something?"

"That's none of your concern, where she's gone."

"You don't have to get snippy, Bridget. I am a friend of the family's and—"

"Some friend you are."

"She has, hasn't she? She's gone away?"

Sylvia spread her new cloth over the kitchen table. It was lovely, really, the deepest blue, a bit longer than it needed to be, maybe, but better too long than too short. She stirred the tomato soup heating on the stove, set her place at the table, poured hot soup from pot to bowl, sat down, sighed contentedly, picked up her spoon.

The next day she was on the beach fishing again when she sensed that she was being watched. She turned and saw Edward standing some distance away with his hands in the pockets of his overcoat.

"You came," she said when she was close enough to be heard.

There were apologies and deep kisses. The roar of the ocean. Salt spray in the air. Sand underfoot.

"I didn't know where you were. I thought I'd go out of my mind."

"Marry me."

"You marry me."

"I will. Yes. As soon as I can. The answer is yes."

They spent three perfect days together. Sylvia felt as if they were claiming the house, urging it onward, introducing it to the next phase of its long and varied life.

chapter 24

Fitzgibbon holed up in his office until he thought everybody else had gone home. When he walked onto the mill floor, though, he discovered a couple of stragglers.

"Good night, Mr. Fitzgibbon," one man said. He'd been an employee of Fitzgibbon Silks in the old days.

"Good night, Al. Get home safe." Go, Fitz thought, come on, get out. You never worked so late when you were on my payroll.

"See you tomorrow, Mr. Fitzgibbon."

"Bright and early, Lucy. Bright and early."

The last to leave, the master dyer, the best paid of Fitzgibbon's remaining employees, a handsome young Italian with an honest face and a sharp crease in his trousers, said, "You are staying behind again, Fitz. How come is that?"

Fitzgibbon raised his eyebrows, said nothing. The dyer stood with his hands at his sides for a moment and then busied himself wrapping his scarf around his neck and buttoning his overcoat. In what seemed an attempt to recover his dignity, he turned in the doorway. "I am leaving the new black on my bench. Is beautiful. Perfect. I think you can charge whatever you want."

"Good man."

Finally alone, Fitzgibbon walked up and down between the long rows of power looms enjoying the ponderous stillness of the giant machines at rest. Ordinarily he didn't allow smoking on the mill floor because of the risk of fire and because he didn't want the stink of smoke in the silk. He'd been spending so much time at the mill after hours, though, that he'd relaxed his policy on smoking, at least insofar as it applied to himself. These days Fitzgibbon needed the company of a good cigar.

Fitzgibbon had never been what anybody would call a solitary man. He didn't require time alone to hear himself think. He was not contemplative. He did not reflect. He hunkered down and when it was time to stop hunkering down he acted.

Eager to see the new black but anticipating disappointment and wanting to put it off, he made his way back to the dye works and, once there, over to a long, narrow table on top of which sat a large wooden hamper. He upended the hamper, dumping hundreds of skeins of red silk thread onto the work-table, and turned on the white light overhead. Rolling a skein under the palm of one hand, Fitz detected inconstancy in the color. The red faltered when it should have held fast. Fitz thought of the buyer, a persnickety little fruit who would undoubtedly object to the quality of the dye job but who could be counted on to be too far behind schedule himself to refuse delivery. OKTBS, Fitz wrote on a ticket, which he then secured to the hamper with a piece of wire. OKTBS, okay to be shipped. Nearly every lot was okay to be shipped these days.

When it was time to stop hunkering down he acted. How did he know when it was time? How had he ever known? He was nine years old the first time he stayed out all night. Nine. He stole a coin off a neighbor's table, bought bread and milk that he didn't want to share with the other members of his family. He took his booty behind an abandoned building, ate and drank, fell asleep. When he woke it was night and there was a full moon and he was proud of the theft and of managing to keep its proceeds to himself. He went inside the ransacked building and fell back to sleep on a pile of newspapers. When he went home the following morning he discovered that his absence had been noted but not much minded. He was his mother's oldest son, oldest child, and by far her smartest. His going out, his staying out, was viewed as something men did when they were of a mind to. Staying out became something he did.

He did not make up his mind to leave home any more than a bird makes up its mind to fly south. His migration was a response to deprivation and idleness. He heard talk of passage on board big ships, of work in distant cities, the only place for a young man, the only hope. He was fearless, literally without fear. In time he found his way to Liverpool, asked anybody who might know how to get on one of the big ships, located somebody who did, finally, and drove the man in charge of hiring half out of his mind with asking.

"It's no free ride, boy, I don't care what you've heard. It's shoveling coal into a blazing-hot furnace alongside men twice your age, strong men, bloody animals more like."

"I can do it."

"Stokers. Do you know what that is? Men with shovels. Your mum know where you are? I'll bet not. She's in a state somewhere, no doubt, your mum. Burn your face and your chest and your hands and go down the next day to work in the heat with fresh burns. You're tough as all that, are you?"

"I'll do it."

"You again? Like horse shit, you are. You're too young and too small. I'll get my head handed to me for hiring a punk like you. It's a man's job, I'm trying to tell you, boy. Not even. A brute's. If they could teach apes to do it we'd all be better off. You know who it is? You know who you're so eager to work alongside of? Convicts and all manner of bad ones, that's who."

"Jesus, God, but you are a pain in the ass. There's no quitting halfway neither. Think you're clever? Think you can sign on then quit once you're out and cross for free? The foreman'll set the others on you. They'll brain you with their shovels and enjoy themselves doing it. A bit of exercise, a change in the routine, that's what murdering the likes of you will be. Toss your body in the fire after and nobody'll miss you. Is that what you want?"

"How much then?"

"How much what?"

"To take me."

"Hah! You want to bribe me now?"

"I want to go."

"To America. You and every other stray on the street. Get a job, anything, save your money, go steerage."

"That'll take too long, won't it? I'm already sixteen."

"Well, you don't look it."

"I am. I'm sixteen."

"Tuesday week and don't say I didn't warn you. When you're out there and miserable, don't say I didn't warn you. Tuesday week. Berth 11. You know where that is? Give them that's asking this card and see if I don't lose my job for this."

It was torture. He survived it. It was torture and he survived it. Coal dust and ashes sticking to the sweat of seared skin. Crying one way and another, whimpering and weeping and sometimes full-out lowing that couldn't be heard over the din of shovels ringing. The black gang, the stokers. Four hours at a time of the hardest work imaginable, lift a too-heavy shovel and pitch its contents forward, lift and heave, in temperatures far higher than the human body was designed to endure even at rest. Thirst unlike any he'd known before, thirst that made him feel he was a second or two from losing his mind to it, from dying, screaming along with the others, water, water, fucking give me water. And no choice, none, but to continue. To stop was to die. They, the brutal giants on either side, would kill him the instant he stopped, the second the shovel dropped from his fingers, the others would stove his head in for him, burn his body up in the hated fire. He kept lifting, kept heaving. Lifting and heaving. The hair on his knuckles and forearms burned away, vanished. His eyelashes and eyebrows. He slept on straw and learned to scramble as fast as anybody for the contents of the black pan, the leavings of the first-class dinner, slabs of red meat and whole potatoes darkened with grease and other things, green, orange, pale pink, that he couldn't identify but that tasted like heaven.

Days passed as days will no matter how hard until finally he heard stokers say they were getting close, would be coming into port soon now. He had no papers and surmised that he'd have to slip away once land was within reach. He looked around to identify which man to ask for guidance, chose carefully, and, as it turned out, well. "You made it, boy. I never thought you would but you did and that says something for you. All right, here's what you do."

Fitz did exactly as he was told, jumped ship and found his way, finally, to a slimy metal ladder and on it, half drowned, nearly frozen, sick from swallowing Hudson River water, he climbed up and into America. It was 1900.

OKTBS, he wrote on a ticket without bothering to examine the contents of the hamper. Get it out and get paid for it, the sooner the better. Fitzgibbon checked his watch. The new black could wait a bit longer. He walked down the corridor to his office, sat at his desk, opened a drawer, and pulled out a pad of lined paper. He opened a manila folder containing corre-spondence his secretary deemed worthy of his attention, wrote a note on the first piece, scanned the next. Yes . . . all right, he'd answer this one himself. "Dear _____," he wrote. His secre-tary would fill in the blank when she typed the letter up.

Fitzgibbon's handwriting was boyishly sloppy but perfectly legible. He'd always been a little ashamed of it, had meant to acquire a different sort of hand altogether, had, in fact, set out to change it a couple of times when he was younger. He'd wanted to make it more manly, sharper, but always forgot his in-tention after a day or two and went back to writing the way that came naturally. His signature, though, had nothing in common with the rest of his handwriting. His signature was stubbornly illegible. It clearly belonged to a busy and important man. There was a large *J*-shaped mark at the start and then a more or less horizontal line with a loop at the far end. An even larger and distinctly recognizable *F* followed. The rest was a vigorous zigzag that looked like the markings made by a seismograph during a significant quake.

Fitzgibbon had not always signed his name this way. His sig-nature had once been more or less in keeping with the rest of his writing. When he was twenty-six or so and newly in a posi-tion to be signing things, banknotes, paychecks, leases, he noticed that the other men required to sign these various docu-ments all had signatures. They didn't merely write their names when the time came, they executed their signatures. So Fitz sat himself down at his brand-new desk and spent the better part of an afternoon coming up with his own. For a brief time it included a flourish underneath, a horizontal, lazy sort of *S* with two short vertical lines crossing it, but, seeing amusement in a business partner's eyes—in Sylvia's father's eyes, in fact—Fitz understood that his flourish was having an effect exactly the opposite of the one he was after, so he gave it up.

One letter done, a second, a third. Fitz tore the three sheets from the pad and neatly clipped each to the letter it answered. Then he checked his watch again. Now he'd go look at the black. The laboratory was situated at the end of another long hall. Laboratory. The use of that word to describe the brick-walled, hard-used room where the master dyer worked beneath a print of the Blessed Virgin had always amused Fitz. The small room was dominated by a wooden hutch, scarred and stained and spattered, with open shelves containing rows of glass bottles with cork stoppers. At about waist level there was a thick slab of rose-colored marble, a work space on top of which sat beakers and Bunsen burners and lengths of glass tubing. Fitz pulled a string that turned on the overhead light and looked around for his new black.

All master dyers had their idiosyncrasies. This one always put his finished samples into brown-paper sacks. No particular reason so far as Fitz could tell, except that, for the dyer, dropping the loosely coiled skeins into the bag somehow marked the end of a job. Dyers were oddballs, every last one. They worked fifteen, twenty hours at a stretch when they felt like it and then not at all for days at a time. They talked to themselves, picked fights with underlings, were easily offended. Many times, venturing into the laboratory to see how one job or another was progressing, Fitz had been put off by the stink of body odor and wondered how a man who was hardly moving, who was only pouring a bit of this into that and stirring, could sweat so much.

"Mmmmm," Fitz said as he emptied the contents of the paper bag onto marble. "Yes. Yes. Yes." Here it was, the black he'd been after for thirty years, the black that had haunted every moment like this one before this one, the black that had never been achieved except in his mind's eye, until now. It was gorgeous, deep and softly lustrous, complex but in such a way that the eye luxuriated in the total effect without being distracted by any awareness of discrete elements. Fitz squeezed one of the two skeins in his fist then held it up to the white light. Done. A simple objective: the perfect black. Done. And just in time, too. A man could walk away with nothing but the formula for this black in his pocket and be set.

Fitzgibbon's reverie was interrupted by a buzzer going off in the distance. He put one skein of black thread into his jacket pocket, returned the other to its paper sack, straightened his tie and his cuffs, brushed off his lapels, then went to answer the door.

"Fitz, good, I was beginning to wonder if I'd got the time wrong."

"We said nine o'clock, didn't we, Martin? And nine o'clock it is. Come on back."

Fitz led the way to his office, settled himself in his chair, motioned for his visitor to take one of the two chairs opposite. The man, a mild-looking fellow in late middle age with thinning grey hair, skittish eyes, and a thin neck, sat down, hoisted his substantial briefcase onto his knees, and opened it.

"What've you got for me?" Fitz said, leaning back.

"You'll be pleased, I think. The whole thing may be simpler than I originally thought, not that these matters are ever really simple, of course, but—"

"Short and sweet now, Martin. I don't want a lesson in the law. I just want to know where I stand."

"Of course. In a nutshell then. If you and Mrs. Fitzgibbon divorce here in New Jersey, you'll have to charge her with adultery, name Devlin as the corespondent, and a court, a judge, in other words, will determine the distribution of assets."

Fitzgibbon sniffed hard. "There's more, I hope. You said I'd be pleased. I'm not yet, I'll tell you that."

"There's more. The state of Nevada has what's called divorce by mutual consent."

"Nevada," Fitz said, as if trying the word out, seeing how it felt in his mouth. "And how would my assets be distributed in Nevada?"

"That would be up to you. What I mean to say is that mutual consent means the parties have come to an agreement before the case goes before a judge. Mrs. Fitzgibbon has considerable incentive, because of the circumstances, to settle. Not only would a litigated divorce be extremely difficult for all parties, the loss of privacy, et cetera, but she's not likely to fare well when all's said and done. She is, after all, the one at fault."

Fitz looked past Wilkins to a group of framed photographs, various views of Paterson, on the far wall. He loathed being the injured party before this mild-mannered man who until now had served as a legal advisor in matters such as real estate closings and the preparation of leases. If there'd been any other way for Fitz to get out with his fortune intact, he'd have taken it. For a brief time, a day or two, he'd considered running, cashing out whatever he could and disappearing. The idea had appealed to him enormously but his fundamentally practical nature prevented him from following through. He had every intention of starting a new business wherever he wound up. There was talk of another war in Europe. Wars were money machines if a man knew how to position himself beforehand. The price of silk had tripled between 1914 and 1919. Since he would be in business, Sylvia would have little difficulty finding him and once she did she'd be able to charge him with desertion.

"I do want to warn you about something, Fitz, concerning the settlement you offer. I want to advise you to be reasonable, I won't even say generous, Fitz, only reasonable. If what you offer is too modest, you may wind up doing yourself more harm than good. Mrs. Fitzgibbon may decide that she might as well put you through the hardship of divorcing here because she couldn't possibly do any worse, do you follow?"

Fitz shifted his gaze from the far wall to the lawyer's face for one second, an action that clearly rebuked Wilkins for suggesting there was anything in what he'd said that anyone with half a brain would have difficulty following.

Wilkins fiddled with the latch on his briefcase. "Which brings me to another point I must bring to your attention."

Fitz waited.

"It's of a sensitive nature."

"Come on, Martin, out with it."

"There's no chance that Mrs. Fitzgibbon will make a counter charge, is there? What I mean to say is that this plan is based on the assumption that Mrs. Fitzgibbon is at fault. If it should turn out that she has—"

"Have I got a woman, is that what you're asking?"

"Not exactly, no. I'm asking if Mrs. Fitzgibbon has any reason to believe or, more to the point, has any proof that you've got a woman."

"She has neither."

"Fine. Good. I'll leave it to you then to determine what sort of settlement you'd like to offer. Once you make up your mind about—"

"Do I have to go to Nevada?"

"You do, yes. It's a long way, I know, but compared to what you'd have to go through to get a divorce here—"

"And Sylvia? Does she have to go, too?"

"No. It's my understanding that we can manage with a sworn statement."

Fitz nodded. "Anything else I should know?"

"Just this." Wilkins removed a piece of paper from his briefcase and put it on Fitzgibbon's desk. "I've taken the liberty of preparing this dummy document, the first of dozens of real ones like it that will be required should Mrs. Fitzgibbon refuse to consent to the no-fault divorce, if she forces you to sue on the grounds of adultery. I thought seeing the thing in black and white, seeing Devlin named as the corespondent, might convince her to reconsider."

Fitzgibbon eyed the document. He was glad of its existence, was, in fact, impressed by Wilkins's thinking to draw it up, liked knowing that they had a weapon of last resort should one be needed. That said, he felt a strong revulsion for the thing as it lay before him, the look of the word *adultery* in black and white with antiquated language all around. According to this document he was a cuckold. His wife had taken up with another man.

"... adulterous relationship in violation of the marriage contract ..."

Fitz looked beyond Wilkins again, to a fat dictionary on a stand, and imagined an alternate course of events. He saw himself going home and confronting Sylvia about her lover and then doing whatever was necessary to win her back. It was a moment of the densest imaginings, the playing out of an alternate future in an instant. Fitzgibbon pictured himself opening the front door to his house, charging up the stairs to Sylvia's room, swearing he loved her, needed her, he'd kill her if she went near Devlin again, kill them both. He believed he'd be victorious—there was almost nothing Fitzgibbon considered doing that he imagined himself unable to do. He could get her back if he wanted to.

And then what?

After he'd made this grand effort, reversed the course of history, then what? The fantasy of the first battle, the retaking of Sylvia, had come easily. But he could not imagine going on from there. He could not imagine spending the rest of his life with Sylvia. Which decides it, he thought, once and for all. When you cannot imagine living out the rest of your life, you know what you need to do, you go.

"I want you at the house tomorrow night when I lay this whole thing out."

Wilkins's shoulders dropped. "I don't see how my presence will serve your ends. If Sylvia ... if Mrs. Fitzgibbon feels she's being humiliated in front of, well, I am an acquaintance, after all, she's much less likely to cooperate."

"I want you there."

"I'd rather not be."

"Fine. I'll find another lawyer."

Wilkins gathered his papers and put them back in his briefcase. He stood up, put on his coat. "All right, Fitz. What time?"

After Wilkins left, Fitzgibbon sat at his desk for a long while, bouncing the fingertips of one hand against the fingertips of the other. "Ah, well," he said after a time. "Well, well."

Fitzgibbon had not set out to steer his wife into another man's bed. He had not at any point consciously devised a scheme. When he first heard that Edward was in town (and he'd heard the full story, of course, knife-wielding prostitute and all) what he felt was a rush of excitement, a quickening interest. In his mind's eye he'd seen the bookish, pigeon-chested young man with the glasses and the pretty wife. He remembered dancing with her in his own living room. She was slight, spare, and not much of a dancer, as he recalled. He'd had to coax her to keep up, had to lead as a dance teacher might. Later in the evening, antsy, wanting to have a better time at his own party than he was having, he followed the wife upstairs and pretended to be surprised when he ran into her outside the bathroom. "There was a line downstairs," she said, like a schoolgirl who's been discovered where she ought not to be. And then, coming back to herself, her grown self who was accustomed to having men make allowances, she opened her eyes wide, suppressed a smile, or wanted to seem to be suppressing a smile, said, "I hope you don't mind." Fitz had been only too happy to go along, to be the man making allowances. "Mind? Of course not, love. No one as pretty as you should ever have to wait in line for anything, least of all the john." The last was intended to be just slightly off-color, to introduce the not entirely polite into the conversation. He gave her a tour of the second floor and kept his hand on her waist, which made concentrating on his impromptu and completely nonsensical descriptions of various antiques pleasantly difficult. "Now this piece here is French, I believe, Louis the fifteenth or sixteenth or one of them, very rare, anyway, very, very rare." She laughed to let him know she didn't believe him for a minute. He paused in the doorway of the guest room and kissed her because she was so pretty laughing, because there was music coming through the floorboards, because their respective spouses were down below.

When his secretary said an Edward Devlin was on the line, Fitz smiled and reached for the phone, forgoing his usual practice of letting callers wait, letting them ripen. "Edward Devlin,

I heard you were in town. Giving the boys at the Colt poker lessons the other night, were you?"

Two more lawyers came to the mill that night. One of them brought with him a young man who was obviously very much enamored of the idea of attending a business meeting so late inside the mostly dark and cavernous building. Fitzgibbon was repulsed by the young man's jocularity, his callowness, the sense he exuded that he was putting one over, making a very good deal. Still, when all the papers had been signed and witnessed, Fitz offered the young man his hand. "Best of luck to you, son. If you do half as well as I've done here . . ." Fitz fell silent, not having any idea, suddenly, how to finish his sentence. The young man's smile stiffened and the beginnings of buyer's remorse crept into his face.

It was nearly midnight before Fitzgibbon was again alone in his office. He knew that he ought to go home and get some sleep but he was antsy. He wasn't ready to leave just yet. He was about to go back out to the mill floor to smoke a last cigar when he stopped, took off his jacket, his vest, and his white shirt, hung them on hangers he kept on the back of his office door. He went to a utility closet, got out a push broom, took that out to the mill floor, and began to sweep.

Fitz hadn't swept a floor since he'd gotten his first promotion in a garment factory thirty years before. The aisles between the machines were long and allowed for vigorous strokes. The floor was dirty, the work satisfying. What do I pay the janitor for? Fitz asked himself. Then he smiled. He didn't pay anybody anymore. The mill belonged to the young man with the phony smile.

While Fitz was sweeping the floor, he thought only about sweeping the floor, was aware only of the feel of the broom in his hands, the sound of its bristles against the worn wooden planks. When a spot needed going over he went over and over it until it was as clean as he could get it. His eyes scanned for stray bobbins and when he spotted one he stooped to pick it up, put it in his pocket, went back to sweeping. He swept. Fitz swept. Because the floor needed sweeping. Because he needed to sweep the floor.

He did not think of Sylvia or what he was going to present to her at seven o'clock the next evening. He did not reflect on their seventeen-year marriage, did not wonder about its essential nature or the causes of its dissolution, didn't indict Sylvia, tear her down, nor did he go the opposite route and reminisce about the early days, their courtship, et cetera. He did not summon the memory of the first time he'd laid eyes on Sylvia, a little girl, ten or eleven, with her two hands inside a muff that hung from a string around her neck. She was coming out of Schrafts with her mother and little sister and he was going in, alone. They didn't know him but he recognized the mother right off and was charmed, cheered, by the sight of the two girls with their rabbit-fur muffs and their wool coats, red with black piping. It was seeing them, the mother and two daughters, that put the idea of getting married one day into his head, of having a wife and children out and about around town while he was off working, making money, stoking the fire.

The skin between his thumb and index finger began to hurt. How genteel I've gotten, he thought. Gentleman's hands. He kept on sweeping because there was floor yet to be swept and because he was constitutionally unable to leave a job half done.

He was in love with Sylvia when he married her, which is to say that he wanted her in his bed and under his roof. She was the woman he'd been waiting for without knowing he was waiting for any woman. Good-looking, he wanted that. He loved the deep red of her hair, the white skin, the swells and hollows. The sound of her voice. The way she walked into rooms, slowly, head up. He'd never been more vibrantly alive than when he was snatching her out of her college-girl life and carrying her off to Paterson.

He did not ask himself when his feelings began to change. There'd been that incident, the moment that begged to be pointed to as *the* moment. She'd made that crack about his looking like a gangster just when he was thinking he looked like old money in his custom-made suit. When he got home from the function he'd attended that evening, he didn't want to sleep in the same room with her. He spent the night in his study and felt deliciously liberated, unencumbered, alone. He'd dreamed he was driving a car down a long, long stretch of highway and the sense of being in motion was a salve to the part of him that ached with boredom, that was withering in the face of the tedium of his life, and so, the next night, hoping for more of the same, he slept in his study again. When he came home from work the following evening and found all his clothes in his new room, he closed the door, sat down, and was glad.

Still sweeping, he did not ask himself if things would have been different if Sylvia had had a child. Wasn't curious. Didn't wonder. When all that was going on, all that being several years of doctor visits, hospital stays, tears, sulks, days when she refused to get out of bed, refused even to bathe, Fitz had felt helpless. Impotent. Powerless. Paralyzed. And worse, even, beside the point. He didn't have a burning desire for children himself. If one had come along, he'd have provided for it lavishly and happily, been a fond daddy, gotten down on all fours and carried it on his back because that was what fond daddies did. But he didn't need one. He'd never have spent a day in bed over the lack of one certainly. What he did need, though, was not to have the problem *not* having a child created, the big sad problem that took up residence in his formerly happy home, the gloom he was not able to dispel.

"Ne-va-da," he said, a push of the broom for each syllable. "Ne-va-da."

That Devlin had one, a child, and had all but abandoned her, *had* occurred to Fitz and did again now. The fact of the girl's existence had always been strangely pleasing. Now, sweeping, he thought that the businessman in him had understood right from the very start that the girl would prove a significant factor in what was bound to happen. The best deals, he knew, were those that offered all parties what they wanted most. Never before had he been part of an arrangement that so nimbly met the needs of all concerned. He got permission, even the right, to go, to get the hell out of Paterson with most of his hard-earned money in his pocket. Devlin got a wife to take the place of the one who'd died. (Men like Devlin needed wives. They hardly existed without them. They hardly existed *with* them, for Christ's sake.) Sylvia got a child to raise. There wasn't any doubt in Fitz's mind that Sylvia would have the child. He smiled ruefully, first husband to second, to think of how completely futile whatever resistance Devlin might offer would be. Try to get between Sylvia and that child.

He stopped sweeping and rested the broom against his chest. Acutely, even exquisitely aware of the smell of damp dust, the gentle pressure of the broom handle against his breastbone, the feel of the wood floor under his feet, he marveled at the elegant workings of the arrangement and fervently wished he'd been its architect but knew that he hadn't been. He swept the several piles of dirt into one big pile, found a piece of cardboard to use as a dustpan, swept the dirt onto it, moved the cardboard back, and swept again and so on until all that remained was a straight line of dust so fine it wouldn't have been visible to the naked eye if not for whatever was in it that caught the light and reflected it back.

chapter 25

She found Agnes, finally, in a room she didn't recognize, couldn't place, a big room, vast, grand, with a domed ceiling and polished floor. "I was looking for you," Maura said in her own defense, to explain having been absent so long. "And here I am," Agnes answered, shifting in her chair slightly, making several subtle physical adjustments simultaneously that, taken all together, signaled she was ready for Maura to climb onto her lap.

Knees into thighs, a clumsy pivot, bum grazing belly. And there it was, in the peculiar language of dreams, every bit of color, every prop, every sound, shot through with a single feeling state. There it was. What Maura had lost, had been pining for, had for the moment recovered. The proprietary demeanor of a mother, of one's own mother. The sense one got of being looked after, tended to, taken into account, checked. A certain authoritative stillness nearby. The primary other to whom one is related. The seemingly stable, seemingly static already formed self against which the outline of one's fledgling self is delineated. I am a girl and you are a lady. I am small and you are big. I am your business in a way and to a degree I am nobody else's. I want to sit with you.

The morning bell sounded and Maura cried out in her sleep. The first seconds after she opened her eyes were the worst she'd ever known. She lay mute and motionless, despairing, listening to girls rising on either side.

chapter 26

Sylvia stood at the foot of the stairs and listened. If Bridget was in the house she could be counted on to be washing or sweeping or chopping or banging cabinet doors or, at the very least, humming loudly. The house was quiet but for the sound of a passing car. Sylvia ventured into the kitchen to get her own coffee and orange juice.

The kitchen was large, nearly square, spacious. The walls were painted a pale yellow, which set off the tawny brown of the floor, doors, and moldings and softened the black of the enormous cast-iron stove. Two wide windows let in morning light. A year or so after the major redecorating was finished, during a time when the house had seemed suddenly dark, much too dark, Sylvia had had the windows enlarged despite considerable opposition from Bridget, who could not for the life of her understand why a perfectly good kitchen, *her* perfectly good kitchen, was to be given over to chaos, plaster dust, and workmen with muddy boots, in the service of letting in something as insubstantial as light. "What's the blasted electricity for?" Bridget had wanted to know.

Though Sylvia spent precious little time there, she was very fond of the kitchen. Compared to the rest of the house, it was spare. The lack of ornament was a relief. Everything had a purpose in the kitchen, every enamel bowl, every canister, pitcher, grinder, and knife.

Sylvia poured a glass of orange juice, drank it down, poured

another. Waiting for her coffee to brew, she spotted a note leaning against a wire crate of empty milk bottles. Assuming the
note was from Bridget and would say where she'd gone and
when she'd be back, Sylvia walked toward it, one hand out.
Then she recognized Fitz's handwriting and froze.

"Please be here at seven o'clock tonight. Martin Wilkins is
coming over."

The note was unsigned, which made it seem especially ominous and jarring. Not wanting to be alone with this new devel-
opment for even a minute, Sylvia went directly to the phone in
the front hall. Edward was out at the job site. His secretary had
no idea when he'd be back. Sylvia left word for him to call her
the moment he got in then hung up angrily and read the note
again. Fear collided with an almost violent impatience to find
out what was in store. Seven o'clock? She'd be damned if she
was going to wait until seven o'clock. "All right," she said. "All
right now, think."

She'd call Martin Wilkins, of course. Not that he'd be forth-
coming but still she'd learn something from how he dodged her
questions. Wilkins was not in his office according to his clerk.
Nor was he home according to his wife, who sounded genuinely
surprised to get a call for her husband at eleven o'clock on a
weekday morning. Which means he's probably in his office refusing to take my call, Sylvia thought. She considered going
downtown and demanding that Wilkins speak to her, making a
scene if necessary. The composure she'd affected while talking
to the clerk and to Mrs. Wilkins, together with the time it had
taken to find the numbers and place the calls, had worked to
dissipate the shock and unhinged outrage she'd felt in the first
moments after finding the note. She knew that she wouldn't be
able to barge into Wilkins's office and demand answers without
a sure supply of righteous indignation.

Really, she thought, sitting down on the stairs, it's not as if
I'm a happily married woman who wakes up one morning to
find a note from her husband saying he's arranged a meeting
with a lawyer. It doesn't make much sense for me to be running
around demanding to know what this is about. I know what this
is about. For a moment Sylvia felt a grudging admiration for

Fitzgibbon. Somebody was going to force the situation to its crisis and the somebody wasn't her.

The phone rang.

As is often the case when there's any sort of interval between when an urgent message is left and when it's responded to, the situation was no longer quite what it had been.

"Sylvia, what's going on?"

"Hi."

"Hi? Annette said there was an emergency."

"Mmm. There is. Fitz is going to divorce me, I think."

Sylvia told Edward about the note and what she understood it to mean. He, with only a faint tremor in his voice, said he'd be by her side at seven o'clock.

"I don't know. I appreciate the offer . . . but I'd rather hear what Fitz has to say by myself."

After promising to join Edward at the apartment when the meeting was over, Sylvia hung up the phone and went into the kitchen to pour herself a cup of coffee. Leaning against the marble-topped table under the windows, with the sun warming her back and shoulders, she told herself that what she ought to do now was find a lawyer. Adding a bit more cream to her coffee, stirring, putting the spoon in her mouth, she imagined what the girlfriend who had recommended the man with the dirty cuffs and collar would say. Don't kid yourself, honey. Divorce is war. This is no time to be softhearted. Go out and find yourself a barracuda.

Straining to be practical, to act in accordance with the hard-won wisdom she imagined her friend and by extension all womankind voicing, Sylvia considered calling the lawyer she'd been to see and asking him to recommend someone. Her instincts and her gut-level familiarity with the particular truth of her situation told her to hold off. Fitzgibbon hadn't gone out and hired a divorce lawyer. Martin Wilkins is coming over, the note said. Mild-mannered Martin Wilkins who worked out of a tiny office and spent most of his time drawing up wills and leases. If she were to get a lawyer now the evening's meeting might be called off. Wasn't that the first thing divorce lawyers did, forbid direct communication between spouses? If the meeting took place at all it would undoubtedly turn contentious, might even become a battle royal. And then Sylvia would never know how it might have gone if she hadn't rushed to hire a lawyer.

Fitzgibbon was not a stingy man, she knew. He lived to generate money, not to hoard it. Neither was he cruel. Certainly he could be ruthless in the service of an objective, but what objective would ruthlessness serve here?

For a moment Sylvia faltered, nearly giving in to the temptation to believe that Fitzgibbon might actually be outraged. It would have been so easy in that moment to delude herself, to flatter and protect herself by pretending that her husband was wounded by her infidelity and would be out for revenge. With great difficulty, shuddering, Sylvia managed not to lie to herself. She knew and had known that Fitzgibbon was at least as eager to be rid of her as she was to be rid of him. They'd both been looking for a way out. And then along had come Edward. Fitzgibbon would be about the business of extricating himself now. He would want the legal dissolution of the marriage to proceed as smoothly and as quickly as possible. He'd do what he could to keep the blood loss to a minimum.

Sylvia poured herself a second cup of coffee and took it out to the porch. Her reputation around town was pretty well shot. Being seen out of doors in her pink pajamas would hardly merit mention in view of her other crimes. She sat on the railing and smiled unsteadily, tapping one foot and taking deep breaths.

At the stroke of seven Sylvia stood at her bedroom window as Fitzgibbon and Wilkins, their separate cars a small convoy, pulled into the driveway. She met the two men at the door, took their hats and coats, led the way into the front parlor, and sat down. Wilkins fitted and started his way through a kind of opening statement. Determined to keep her wits about her, to be ready at any moment to call a halt to the proceedings if it became clear that she'd erred in not hiring a lawyer, Sylvia was intent on understanding exactly what Fitzgibbon had in mind, no easy task given Wilkins's obvious agitation and his long-windedness. He seemed to swing back and forth between implying a threat by alluding to adultery—he never used that word but talked of Fitzgibbon as the petitioner, the aggrieved party, the one who had grounds on which to sue for divorce—and campaigning for the dissolution of the marriage contract on the basis of fundamental incompatibility. Fitzgibbon didn't make Sylvia's task of ferreting out exactly what was being proposed any easier. He was antsy. While Wilkins talked, Fitz got up, removed the screen from in front of the fireplace, nudged the cold logs with a poker, cleared his throat. He's nervous, Sylvia thought. Good. He ought to be. Finally, when Wilkins had talked himself out, when he'd wound down—he'd clearly expected to be interrupted and when he wasn't he had no choice but to burn through the store of defensive energy he'd brought to his argument—a sheet of paper containing the specific terms of the proposed property settlement was thrust into Sylvia's lap. She held on to the paper with both hands and read. She was surprised and relieved to see that she'd get the Paterson house and its contents free and clear. Her car, too, she was very glad of that though she knew, strictly speaking, the car wasn't worth all that much. She was disappointed, though, by the size of the onetime cash payment she'd receive in return for signing away all present and future claims to alimony. She felt insulted, hurt, until her head cleared and she realized that of course Fitzgibbon would start low so as to wind up about where he wanted to be.

She let him wait a bit, smiling inwardly at the sound of him tending his imaginary fire.

"Well," she said, looking up. Then she cleared her throat, looked down at the paper again, sighed.

Seeming to prepare himself to get down to business, Fitzgibbon returned the poker to its stand and faced Sylvia, his hands in his trouser pockets.

"This seems all right," Sylvia said, "except for the cash payment. It's not much, is it?"

"Thirty then," Fitzgibbon said. "Thirty thousand dollars. This house is worth at least that much, don't forget, when you add in the furniture and all the rest of it."

Sylvia felt something like affection born of the knowledge that she'd been right. Fitzgibbon was not a stingy man. The furniture on the first floor alone was worth thirty thousand easily. Had he forgotten that or had he never known? A stingy man would have remembered the price of the pair of brass chandeliers, the Persian rugs, the pump organ.

"Fifty," she said.

When Fitzgibbon frowned and turned his head to one side, Sylvia sensed that his response, his seeming affronted by the counter offer, was one he'd used many times before in other business negotiations. She said nothing. She waited.

"Forty," he said finally.

"Fifty."

"All right. Fifty. Done."

Struck dumb during the bargaining, Wilkins appeared thoroughly confounded. He'd come in steeled for battle, had several contingency plans in place, one of which involved summoning the police in case the boyfriend showed up and the thing came to blows. But this? What was *this*? He'd seen more heat in traffic court. "All right," he said in a tone that suggested he'd had a hand in the successful completion of a long and arduous negotiation, "now that that's settled . . ." His disorientation was such that he seemed to have no choice but to proceed as he'd imagined himself proceeding. "Now that we've determined a distribution of the marital assets that is acceptable to both parties . . ." His voice trailed off. He opened his briefcase and began pulling out papers.

Preliminary agreements were produced, amended, initialed, signed. A schedule for filing was determined. Wilkins asked if there were any questions. There were none. He asked and answered a few of his own then told Sylvia several times that he'd be available to answer any questions that came to her over the course of the coming days, weeks, what had she.

And then Sylvia and Fitzgibbon were alone.

"That's it then," Fitz said. "Bridget will come by in the next couple of days to pack my clothes."

"Come by? You mean she's quit?"

"Ah, right. I meant to tell you. Retired. She's decided to retire. I tried to convince her to stay but at her age I guess—"

"No. That's fine. I'd have let her go anyway."

Sylvia folded her arms across her chest to steady herself. She wasn't enjoying the strain of this final good-bye but she was grateful for the presence of the strain. The real nature of what survived between herself and Fitzgibbon was revealed. Undisguised. Unmitigated. They were through with each other, done. The last bit of business had been concluded during the settlement negotiation and now all that remained was this, the leaving. It was hard, sad and awkward and grim, exactly as it ought to be.

Fitz leaned in, put one hand on Sylvia's shoulder, kissed her forehead.

His lips were dry, his mustache scratchy. She loathed him for attempting to deny the difficulty of the moment, for wanting to put an overlay of false sentiment on top of a hard truth. She didn't pull back because doing so would have answered a gesture intended to discount feeling with feeling. It's done, she said to herself.

She listened to his footsteps on the porch stairs, his car starting and backing out.

It's done. It's done. It's done.

She'd promised Edward she'd meet him at the apartment but hadn't known how tired she'd be, how disinclined to leave the house. He answered the phone on the first ring and she was comforted by his readiness.

"It's done."

"Is it? And you're coming?"

"I don't think so. I'm exhausted. All I want to do is go to bed."

"I'll come there then. He's gone?"

"He's gone."

"I'll come there."

"No. I . . . Edward, I need a night to myself if you don't mind. I'm wiped out. I'm going straight up to bed. I love you and I'll call you first thing in the morning."

She tried to exalt in her newfound sole ownership of the house but couldn't quite. It didn't seem real yet, any of it. Mine, she said, running her fingers along the banister on the way upstairs. Mine, turning on the light in her room. She took off her shoes, dress, slip, stockings, girdle, and bra, sat down on the bed in just her underpants. She spread her fingers, examined her palms, noticed that the veins on the backs of her hands were more prominent than they used to be. She wondered how she'd come to be thirty-six years old, childless, and now, soon, divorced. She took off her wedding and engagement rings, put them on her night table, thinking she'd find a permanent resting place for them in the morning, rubbed the skin on her ring finger.

Sleep was kind. It came quickly. Giving over, Sylvia was reassured by the pull toward rest and reprieve. That pull, by virtue of its assumption of a need for renewal, was hopeful, forward-looking. It said that the sleeper had to be ready for what would be waiting for her when she woke, what was coming next. Because something surely was. Coming. Next.

Fitzgibbon had planned to get at least halfway across Pennsylvania before stopping for the night. He thought he'd be raring to go, to drive and keep on driving in celebration of his newly recovered freedom. While he was planning the long road trip, his marriage had already seemed a discrete interval in his life, with a beginning and an end, and less real, less authentic than what had come before it and what would come after. Saying good-bye to Sylvia, though, feeling her steel herself against his kiss, walking out of the house for the last time, getting into his car and backing out of the driveway, he felt a kind of generalized disappointment. He couldn't have said what he was disappointed about exactly, but he knew something was wanting. He told himself that he ought to be pleased. The settlement couldn't have gone any better. Had it gone too well? Would a good wrangle about money have supplied what was missing?

After a while Fitzgibbon had to acknowledge that he was not in fact heading out at all but was engaged instead in an activity that was wholly unfamiliar to him. He was driving around. Fitzgibbon was driving around when he should have been driving out. One part of his consciousness attended to practical matters, turning left, turning right, then left again, the feel of the steering wheel in his hands—a bit more play there than he liked, mechanical trouble ahead?—the reassuring responsiveness of the engine to increases in downward pressure on the gas pedal that confirmed the correctness of the decision not to buy a new car for the trip—he'd have had to break a new car in and there was no time for that—but to have his two-year-old car tuned up, checked out, readied for the long ride cross-country. With the part of himself he knew best busy evaluating engine responses and executing turns, the part of himself he didn't have much truck with was free to seek out what it was intent on finding.

McBride Avenue onto Ellison Street. Ellison to Main. Up and down Main, twice, three times, in search of a familiar face. Fitzgibbon wanted to see at least one person he knew before leaving Paterson for good and all. He didn't care who. In fact, he half hoped he'd see somebody he hardly knew, somebody from the farthest reaches of the periphery. He had no desire to stop and talk to anyone, no intention, certainly, of saying good-bye. There, the stupid kid who managed time and again to get past the guard at the mill gate to stand and hit a tennis ball against the far side of the building. Good-bye, stupid kid. And there, waiting for the bus, the lady with the nice ankles from the tax collector's office. Good-bye, ankles.

Main to Broadway and right on Church. Fitzgibbon smiled at his own calling out of street names, a habit Patersonians fell into, a response to the sparsity of street signs. Newcomers and visitors had a terrible time finding their way around. Sylvia, when she first arrived, had found the whole business wildly irritating. She hated having to walk up to strangers and say, "Excuse me," pointing down at the spot on which she stood, "is this Market Street?" I just don't understand, she said to Fitz and, later, to his friends and associates. Why in the world don't you just put up some damn signs so people will know where they are? Today I was standing on what I was sure was Straight Street when a man came up to me, very well dressed, obviously not from around here, obviously fed up. He asked me what street we were on. I had to say I didn't know because all of a sudden I didn't. I wasn't sure, I mean, and I didn't want to add to this fellow's troubles.

In time, though, Sylvia had come around. In time she'd been naturalized. You knew the names of the streets in Paterson not by reading signs but by knowing the names of the streets in Paterson. And too bad about you if you didn't. Figure it out. Ask somebody. No street signs was an inside joke. Kept outsiders off-balance, made them stand out. So thoroughly assimilated did Sylvia become that she smiled along with the natives when a newly elected councilman took it upon himself to put an end to the city's willful refusal to let itself be known. A picture ran on the front page of the *Paterson News*: politician, ladder, block-lettered sign, big smile. Some of the new signs lasted as long as a week. Everybody assumed vandals stole the street signs to sell the aluminum for scrap. Fitzgibbon wondered, driving past what remained of one, a decapitated pole leaning leftward in unspectacular defeat, if it wasn't the city herself that took down the signs. I will not be made easy to find one's way around in. Send me another bureaucrat with a budget. His signs'll wind up with the others, down in the pit where I keep the street signs.

Enough of this now. Enough driving around. Time for me to be going. A long trip ahead. Might just as well drive straight through the night now. Won't stop till I get a chunk of Ohio behind me. A last look, then, and I'll be off.

At the top of a hill, Fitz put the car in neutral, pulled the hand brake, and looked out over the whole of the city, all eight square miles. There was St. John's, there the library, there the clock tower over City Hall. On Fitzgibbon's first visit to Paterson as a prospective buyer, he'd been ushered around by the chamber of commerce president, a dour little man whose demeanor was at odds with his boosterish message. The c. of c. president, himself a business owner ("I make a living, more or less, most years") had described City Hall as majestic, had boasted, if a person speaking in a monotone can ever be said to be boasting, that the building was an exact replica of the City Hall in Lyon, France, ". . . our sister city in the manufacture of silk and so on." Fitzgibbon had hired a couple of French dyers early on, arrogant bastards they were, too. He'd take a wop anytime. Wops didn't think quite so well of themselves and so were easier to manage. No French dyer had ever come close to the new black, Black 31, it had been christened. Fitz slipped his hand under his coat, jacket, and vest to reach into his shirt pocket, where the formula for the new black was spelled out on a sheet of notepaper. Black 31. Rumblings overseas. Mourning clothes. Evening wear. Cheap and docile labor in southeastern Pennsylvania.

He opened the glove compartment and pulled out a flashlight and the map on which his secretary had traced the route he was to take cross-country. Pennsylvania, Ohio, Indiana, Illinois, Missouri, Kansas, Colorado, Utah, and then, at long last, Nevada. A long way, Jesus, a long way to go. America, the genuine article, the heartland, Protestant America. The East Coast wasn't America, not really. Too many foreigners, too crowded, too Catholic, too old, too old worldy. But Indiana? Illinois? Missouri, for God's sake? You're talking America now, son. Fitz desired the strangeness of what lay ahead—Kansas! Utah!—the unfamiliar terrain, climate, accents.

He had no trouble imagining himself moving through one state after another. What he couldn't imagine, what stopped his imagination dead in its tracks, was what awaited him at the end of the long crossing: six weeks of idleness in a hotel while he fulfilled Nevada's residency requirement. Whenever he tried to envision it, he faltered and was left to combat the stubborn blankness with halfhearted notions about taking a much-deserved rest, a vacation. He resorted to using phrases straight out of the hotel brochure. He'd relax by the pool, enjoy the breathtaking sunsets from the balcony of his room, try his luck in the casino. Six weeks of that? He'd go out of his bloody mind.

He put the map on the passenger seat and rubbed his eyes. He'd done it now, hung around so long he'd got sleepy. A ten-minute nap, he thought. And then I'll be off.

He opened his eyes to broad daylight and a painful cramp in his neck. He was sweating and thirsty. The car's heater had been going full blast all night, a wonder he hadn't suffocated. Cursing himself for wasting time, Fitzgibbon rolled the window down. Six weeks without work. Inconceivable. Unthinkable.

Thanking God for the going, he put the car in gear and he went.

Sylvia woke briefly just then, blinked, thought she heard Bridget downstairs then remembered that Bridget had quit. An intruder? Oh, God. "Hello?" she called out. Footsteps on the stairs. "Who's there?"

"It's me. Only me. I still have my key. I couldn't wait to see you."

"Edward, you scared me."

"Don't be scared. I couldn't wait."

chapter 27

Edward and Sylvia were married on May the first in Avalon.
A judge Sylvia had known all her life performed the ceremony. (He hadn't always been a judge. Over a long succession
of summers he'd gone from a fat little boy who cried if anybody
looked at him cross-eyed to a gaping, strangely silent ten-year-
old to a smug adolescent to a hardworking law student to the
youngest district attorney in New Jersey history.) Sylvia had
toyed with the notion of a real wedding, flowers, music, a menu,
but that sort of thing required guests. Who could she invite?
Have the wedding in Paterson and ask the half-dozen or so people she genuinely liked and had always meant to get to know
better? No, a wedding in Paterson would be a cause celebre.
Even the most generous-minded among the possible attendees
would be more curiosity seeker than guest. Her old school
friends, the most dogged of whom still sent the occasional post-
card or birth announcement? Hardly. Sobered by the realization
that there wasn't a single soul she wanted in attendance at her
wedding, Sylvia longed for her sister. Ruth should be there.
Keeping Sylvia company beforehand, hugging her after. No
guests then. Just the young judge and his wife, who, though she
knew Fitzgibbon fairly well from previous summers and had
met Edward as the Fitzgibbons' houseguest just the summer
before, brought a kind of good-natured aplomb to the proceedings, even insisted on coming over in the morning to help
Sylvia dress, arrived with a bakery box of Danish and some-

thing borrowed, a pair of pearl earrings. Sylvia felt a little silly at first, was sure she'd rather be alone with her thoughts, but wound up enjoying the neighbor woman's company. What bride can't use a bit of help with her hair?

Several weeks before the wedding, at Sylvia's insistence, Edward was introduced to Sam Schultz. No man looks forward to meeting his intended's father. ("Hello, I've come for your daughter.") Edward was no different. He dreaded going. From what Sylvia said the old man was irascible. And sure to be dead-set against divorce and remarriage by virtue of his advanced age if nothing else. Not to mention that he probably hated the Irish on account of Fitzgibbon. Edward was wildly nervous riding up in the open-cage elevator that groaned and shuddered before coming to a stop a full six inches higher than it should have. This can't be a good omen, Edward thought, stepping down and out. The door to the apartment opened onto a long hallway that reeked of Vick's Vapo-Rub. "We're here," Sylvia called out too eagerly. "Dad?" A uniformed nurse, Irish, met them half-way. "You're in luck," she whispered. "He's having a good day. Not ornery. Clear as a bell."

"What's doing?" said the old man.

Sam Schultz was without question the smallest old man Edward had ever seen, the smallest adult of any sort but for the occasional bona fide dwarf or midget passed on the street. Sam was *tiny*. Ensconced in a giant upholstered chair, smiling tooth-lessly. How the hell had this little person produced Sylvia? The mother must have been a bloody amazon. Charmed by the sight of this miniature man in suit and tie—Sam looked fey the way little boys dressed up for first communions or funerals do—Edward relaxed. Who could look at the little fellow and not smile?

It soon became apparent that Sam believed Fitzgibbon was dead. Sylvia described the wedding plans: "You remember Gabe Hoffman, Dad, the boy who lived next door to us at the shore?" Sam shrugged and looked into the middle distance as if to say maybe I remember and maybe I don't. In general, though, he seemed to be foursquare in favor of Sylvia's remarry-ing. "Shame about Fitzgibbon, though," he said more than once, grinning, adjusting his lap robe. "Wheeled and dealed himself right into an early grave. Doesn't surprise me a bit. I always knew he would. A man like that." The nurse gave Sylvia a knowing look and mouthed the words, "Let him be."

Descending in the elevator, Edward said, "Did you tell him Fitzgibbon was dead?"

"Absolutely not. I told him he'd gone out west. How he got dead from that I don't know."

"You didn't correct him, though, I noticed."

"Why should I? He's old and senile. You caught him on a good day. You have no idea how difficult he can be. If it makes him happy to think Fitz is dead, let him."

Then, in the car: "Was he always so small?"

"What do you mean?"

"Your father. Surprised me. I expected, well, I mean you're tall. Was he, when he was younger, a small man?"

"I don't know, he was average height, I guess."

So Sylvia was not aware that her father had either been very short right along or had shrunk dramatically in old age. Or both. Most likely both. His little black shoes had barely cleared the seat cushion. She's a good daughter, Edward thought, feeling at once protective and proud of Sylvia. In all her difficulties with her father it had never registered that whatever else the old man was he was also damn near a midget.

"Do you, Sylvia, take this man, Edward, to be your lawfully wedded husband?" the judge said. There was champagne, smoked salmon, scrambled eggs in a chafing dish, fresh asparagus. There was much fussing with a camera. There was a kiss, a real kiss, not at the appointed place in the ceremony (that kiss, predictably, was dry-mouthed, a peck that went on far longer than a peck ever should), but later, when Sylvia and Edward were sitting side by side on a bench in the backyard. "I got it!" the judge's wife said. And she had. A pale pink envelope was slipped under the door several days later. "Look!" Sylvia said. "Is this the best wedding picture ever taken, ever?"

Edward could only get two weeks off so he and Sylvia honeymooned in Avalon. The happiest two weeks of Edward's life. He was continuously aware, to varying degrees, of his good fortune, sitting across from Sylvia at the kitchen table, making love to her at night (ah, the plenty), listening, drowsily, from the living room couch, glasses and newspaper on his chest, while she put groceries away in the kitchen.

Not only did he feel love for her, he also felt loved by her. He was reassured and deeply flattered by how apparent her happiness was. Embodied. Lived. Finding expression in a certain smartness of movement, a jazziness, Edward called it. An extra tap on a cabinet door after closing it. A playful flourish pouring tea. An especially vigorous rubdown with a clean towel after a hot shower. For the first time in his life Edward believed he was making a woman happy.

Even the weather cooperated. There was an early warm spell that encouraged walking on the beach without jackets in the afternoon. Sylvia, sleeveless and barefoot, shirttails fluttering, against a backdrop of sand and sea and blue sky. Then came a storm that lasted a day and a night. Rain beat down on the roof, making the house deliciously cozy, inspiring gratitude for the simple fact of shelter.

They ventured out a couple of times, as other summer residents came down and opened their houses. All around windows were being pried open, wicker furniture was finding its way out of sheds, walks were being hosed down, stones raked, sand swept off porches. Come by for a drink. Six o'clock. Six-thirty. A cookout. Dessert and coffee. Sylvia put on lipstick and perfume, Edward a tie, and off they went. Fitzgibbon had never liked the shore and had always made his impatience plain. "How long can you sit looking out at the horizon, for Christ's sake?" He'd not been popular with the summer crowd. Edward was more to their liking. Still, these forays were obligations to be gotten through. Sylvia and Edward were aware, separately, simultaneously, of being obliged to compose themselves, tone things down, keep their hands to themselves, which they managed to do with varying degrees of success. The envy of other husbands and wives was palpable. At one point, thinking herself unobserved, Sylvia took Edward's face in her two hands and kissed him on the nose, mouth, chin. A teenage daughter of the host and hostess stared with unabashed enthusiasm, rubbing the end of her ponytail back and forth across her upper lip. You're right to stare, miss, Edward thought. This is it. This is what it looks like. Remember it. Don't settle for less.

chapter 28

The ice chamber in the refrigerator was emptied and drained, the bed stripped, the sheets washed, dried in the sun, folded, and wrapped in wax paper so they wouldn't be musty when next they were needed. Sylvia was proud of herself for remembering this domestic detail from her distant past, for resurrecting the image of a large woman with bare arms tearing long sheets of wax paper off the roll and handily protecting the family linen from the damp sea air. Housekeeping was much on Sylvia's mind. She wasn't exactly sure how she was going to manage at home without Bridget but was certain that the services of a full-time housekeeper would be out of reach now. Maybe somebody can come around a couple of times a week and do . . . whatever needs to be done, Sylvia thought.

The shades were pulled against the summer sun. The car was packed. When the house was locked up tight, when it was properly prepared for the period of dormancy awaiting it, the duration of which was not specified by either Sylvia or Edward—would she return for the month of August as she always had, would Edward join her there on weekends like Fitz used to?—the newlyweds went to a local hotel for a breakfast that was supposed to be celebratory but was experienced instead as a detour, a delay, shot through with dread of the long and probably nerve-racking ride back to Paterson.

Waiting to nose between one car and another, Edward wondered if Route 1 was actually, as its name suggested, the first highway in America to be assigned a number. (He imagined a committee consisting of an exasperated and badly paid civil engineer, several managers of one kind and another, a couple of long-winded politicians. All in favor, all opposed. Motion carried. We begin at the beginning, we call it Route 1.) Just how long ago was that? With its dozens and dozens of stoplights, its choke points, its grim-faced farmers on yellow tractors who refused to yield the entire length of long, incredibly long no-passing zones, Route 1 was itself creeping toward obsolescence. Once the freeways were built, and they would be before too much longer, high and wide, monuments to fast and easy passage between one place and another, piddling little four-lane jobbers like Route 1 would be abandoned by all but local traffic. Serves you right, Edward thought, addressing the road beneath him. Riding on Route 1 required forbearance beyond the human capacity for forbearance, it seemed to Edward just then. He badly wanted to get back to Paterson before dark. He hoped daylight would help orient him, ease the strangeness of what was bound to be a strange homecoming.

In spite of the obstacles Route 1 put in their way, Sylvia and Edward made reasonably good time and pulled into the driveway just after five. But for the stale air, which had a distinct element of cigar smoke in it, the house seemed welcoming enough. Sylvia went from room to room turning on lights and opening windows, feeling a fresh appreciation for the good work she'd done decorating the place. Colors seemed especially vivid, patterns smart, textures rich, combinations graceful. She was able to see the overall effect of each of the rooms and remembered struggling to achieve those various effects, get them right. After two weeks at the shore, where all the rooms were painted white and the furniture was haphazard and hard-used, she was glad for the complexity and formality of her year-round residence.

And to think she might have lost it in the divorce. At a certain point, early on, she'd all but assumed she would. She remembered walking on the sand in Avalon during her solo retreat there and thinking herself lucky to have the shore house, thinking she could always live there if worse came to worst. She really had been ready to give this place up, hadn't she? God, what a colossal mistake that would've been. She straightened a picture on the wall, patted a throw pillow, moved a candlestick a quarter of an inch to the right on the mantel above the fireplace the way a mother will straighten her child's collar, finger-comb his bangs, pull a loose thread, after hearing that another child, a classmate, a neighbor, a stranger, another mother's child, has taken ill or been injured.

Once the car was unpacked Edward took a ride into town to pick up groceries. Marveling at the male of the species—having just come in the door after a long drive a man won't mind, he truly won't mind, getting right back in the car and going out for bread and milk—Sylvia went upstairs to shower. She took her time dressing then went from room to room looking for Edward. She found him, finally, sitting on the porch steps with a cup of tea and a cigarette.

"Nice bath?"

"Shower, actually. But yes. Very nice. That ride always wears me out."

"Hungry?"

"Not really. You?"

"I can wait. Come and sit by me."

Sylvia sat next to Edward on the stair. He took her hand and kissed it.

"Are you all right?"

"Mmmm," she said. "Just a little bleary, I guess. So much has happened so quickly, hasn't it? Every once in a while I find I have to stop and catch my breath."

"You're not sorry, are you?"

"No, not sorry. Just a bit cowed or something."

"We belong together, Sylvia. I'm surer of that than I've ever been of anything in my life."

Sylvia looked into Edward's eyes a moment then put her head on his shoulder.

"Is it being back in this house that's got you rattled? We don't have to stay here, you know. We could sell this place and—"

"No. This is my house, ours, I mean. I want us to live in this house."

"Right. You're right. I got some ham and a loaf of Italian bread. I'll make sandwiches."

"Good. Would you bring me a ginger ale, too? There's some in the pantry to the right of—"

"I know where it is."

"Right. Of course you do."

chapter 29

Sylvia got up soon after Edward did, toasted what was left of the Italian bread, made a pot of coffee. The atmosphere at the breakfast table was a bit strained as Edward and Sylvia self-consciously, very nearly bashfully, sidled toward their respective roles, husband and wife, and set about establishing what would surely become their morning routine. Both felt awkward and the awkwardness was disappointing. Both had expected, both wanted, to feel at ease.

"What time do you—"

"I'll be home—sorry, what'd you say?"

"No. That. What time?"

"I'll leave the office at five-thirty and be home directly. Unless you'd rather meet me downtown for—"

"No, no. Let's have dinner at home our first night."

"Right. Dinner at home then. Good."

Sylvia walked Edward to the door, straightened his tie, and saw him off, feeling a bit foolish standing and waving but doing it anyway, standing and waving. She closed the door, looked around the foyer, said, "Well."

She put the breakfast dishes in the sink, poured herself a third cup of coffee, and leaned against the marble-topped table in the kitchen. All right, she thought, jittery from too much coffee and from the unexpected strain at the breakfast table, what now? What needs to be done? First off I'd better find somebody to help with the housework. Though the house had seemed clean enough in the dusky light of the previous evening, this morning the neglect of the last several months was apparent. Tabletops and mantels were dusty, rugs dull. There were employment agencies that supplied domestics, Sylvia knew. She considered calling one but the prospect of hiring a complete stranger and giving her the run of the house didn't appeal. Sylvia gazed out the back window and imagined serving spoons and candlesticks being spirited off.

She put her coffee on the drainboard and went into the foyer, took her address book out of the drawer by the telephone, flipped through it. Betty McBride, a good place to start. Betty was someone Sylvia had always meant to get to know better. The wife of a prominent man from a prominent Paterson family, Betty had always struck Sylvia as smart and capable. In fact, Sylvia remembered, hadn't there been a couple of invitations from Betty years back, lunches, card games, that Sylvia had declined for one reason or another? Running her index finger over Betty's name, getting her nerve up, Sylvia wondered if Betty would snub her now out of loyalty to Fitzgibbon or in defense of the sanctity of marriage. However Betty reacted, she'd surely prove a bellwether. As Betty went so would go the other women in town.

The McBrides' housekeeper, whom Sylvia knew and who knew Sylvia, answered the phone.

"Mrs. McBride, please."

"Who's calling?"

"It's Sylvia Devlin, Alice."

After a brief pause the housekeeper said, "Just a minute, please."

Sylvia sat down on the bottom step and put the telephone on her lap.

"Sylvia?"

"Yes, Betty. It's me. Hi."

"It's Devlin now, Sylvia Devlin?"

Sylvia had sent a wedding announcement to the *Paterson News*. Betty couldn't possibly have missed it. "That's right. Edward and I were married a few weeks ago."

"I see. Well. Congratulations."

"Thank you. Listen, Betty, I'm calling because I need to find someone to come in once or twice a week and do some housework. I'm wondering if you know of anybody, or if Alice might."

"So you plan to stay on?"

"Stay on? In Paterson, you mean? Yes. Edward works for the county, you know, and, anyway, yes, Betty, we're staying."

Betty cleared her throat gently. "You shouldn't have any problem finding someone, not these days. Why don't you put an ad in the paper or post a notice in the market?"

"I'd rather get a recommendation, you know how it is."

"I can't think of anybody off the top of my head, Sylvia, but I'll mention it to Alice and call you back, all right?"

"Thanks, Betty. I'd appreciate that."

"You're welcome. And, Sylvia . . ."

"Yes?"

"Best wishes, really. I hope that you and Edward will be very happy together."

"Thank you, Betty. Thanks a lot."

Sylvia hadn't expected to be so relieved. She felt exhilarated by Betty's good wishes. So Patersonians' loyalty to Fitzgibbon hadn't survived his slipping out of town, his leaving without saying good-bye. Was it just that, Sylvia wondered, on her way upstairs to take a bath, or had she heard something else in Betty's voice? Maybe Betty and the others had come to the conclusion that Fitzgibbon was not wholly the victim of what had transpired under his roof. There'd be comfort in that realization for some of them. Believing that Fitzgibbon had collaborated in what had taken place, that he'd masterminded it even, would allow people to go on thinking of him as a sharpy. Sylvia imagined the end of her marriage becoming a story a certain kind of Patersonian would tell to illustrate Fitzgibbon's cunning. *He was married to this Jewish girl, see, but he didn't love her anymore if he ever had so what he did was . . .* Some people would go that route. And with good reason, Sylvia thought. There's some truth in that version of things.

But she wasn't convinced that an indictment of Fitzgibbon had prompted Betty's generosity. Something kinder, weightier,

more mysterious, had prompted Betty to yield. Pausing on the
landing between the second and third floors, Sylvia allowed
herself to believe that what she'd heard in Betty's voice was a
compassion rooted in some kind of primordial female solidarity,
an inclination to empathize with one's own kind born out of
firsthand, daily experience. I am a daughter, a sister, a wife.
Whatever happened to you I can imagine happening to me.
Whatever you did I can imagine doing.

After soaking in a hot tub for a while, Sylvia unscrewed the
lid from a jar. With her middle finger she dabbed pinkish cream
on forehead, cheeks, and chin. According to the jar's label, the
cream contained fine volcanic ash, which, if massaged into the
skin for sixty to ninety seconds, would reveal a younger and
more beautiful Sylvia to herself and to the world. Volcanic ash,
my foot, thought Sylvia as her fingertips made their way in dili-
gent circles from the bridge of her nose down to her nostrils. I
wonder what's in it really. Table salt? The grit that's on sandpa-
per? The jar, purchased during a spiteful but finally unsatisfy-
ing spending spree a year or so before, had cost eleven dollars at
the cosmetics counter in Lord & Taylor. *Eleven dollars.* A third
of Edward's weekly salary. I won't be buying any more of this
for a while, Sylvia thought with some regret.

After rinsing thoroughly—the abrasive, whatever it was,
found its way under her fingernails and onto her scalp—Sylvia
stepped out of the tub and toweled off. In the bedroom she put
on a pair of slacks and a white button-down shirt then tied a
peacock-blue scarf in her hair. "Now," she said on her way
downstairs, "what am I going to do about dinner?"

In the kitchen were several cookbooks on a shelf by the
stove. Sylvia had purchased them years before when she
thought she might teach herself to make decent meals on Bridget's day off, before she'd been made to understand that Bridget didn't want her messing around in the kitchen, day off or
no. "I can never find anything after you've been in here. Anyway, Mr. Fitzgibbon likes simple food. I'll make a stew or a pot
of soup and you can heat it up. Be simpler for everybody that
way." Sylvia smiled, thinking of the scorn Bridget had had for
the cookbooks. To Bridget's way of thinking, no self-respecting

woman would have any use for such things. You either learned to cook while you were growing up or you left it to people who had.

The *Fannie Farmer* was massive but cheerfully so in its red-and-white-gingham cover. Wanting plenty of room, Sylvia sat down at the dining room table with *Fannie*, a pad of paper and a pencil, and set out to find a recipe that didn't sound too complicated and prepare a shopping list. After considering two or three entries in the chapter on main courses, she lost sight of her objective and began turning the pages in much the same spirit as she might have walked through a museum or a gallery. Isn't that lovely . . . God, much too elaborate . . . What a gorgeous red there. Even more than the most pleasing drawing or photograph, Sylvia liked the quality of the pages themselves. The paper was thick and had a pleasant heft against the pads of her fingers.

She was admiring an ear of corn and noting how the presence of so much white in the yellow kernels played against the faded green of the husk when she felt a sudden warmth and wetness between her legs. Bathwater, she thought. My period's not due for another week. Unless with the excitement of the wedding and all my cycle's off. Maybe I've got the dates wrong. In the powder room she saw blood on her underpants and felt a pang when she thought of all the times she'd hoped for bathwater and found blood. All right. No big thing. She'd go upstairs for a pad and a belt.

She had every intention of returning to her task of planning dinner but took one look into the dining room where the fat cookbook lay facedown on the table and then, some minutes later, found herself wandering from room to room wishing, vaguely, that the phone would ring or the morning mail would come. She picked up a magazine, scanned the cover, put it down. She ran her index finger across the top of an end table. She wrote her name, her new name, in the dust.

God, the place really needed a good cleaning. She could do it herself, she supposed, could vacuum and dust the front parlor and the dining room at least, could mop the kitchen floor, which had felt gritty under her bare feet. Cleaning would be a way, certainly, of burning off the nervous energy she suddenly had.

Now was as good a time as any to acquaint herself with the sup-plies Bridget had kept in the back closet.

Sylvia had to yank with all her might to get the door open. Several brooms, a dust mop, a pair of yellow rubber gloves hanging limply, dejectedly, over the side of a tin bucket, a gal-lon of bleach, a can of scouring powder, silver polish, lemon oil, white vinegar, a string bag of rags, mostly, it seemed, Fitzgib-bon's undershirts torn to pieces. (You think you've removed every trace of a person from a house, who would ever think of the rag bag?) Against the back wall was a vacuum cleaner that looked new though it wasn't. Bridget had despised it, had started violently the only time Sylvia had seen her switch it on, was convinced that all it did was scatter dirt that would only re-settle and then have to be swept up with a broom or caught on the end of a damp mop the way it should have been in the first place.

Disheartened and reluctant to disturb the closet's grim order, Sylvia closed the door. "No," she said. "No, no." With the vague intention of walking around the farmer's market to see if anything suggested itself for dinner—too soon for tomatoes, about right for strawberries?—Sylvia put on some lipstick and a sweater, grabbed her wallet and car keys, headed out.

She felt much better behind the wheel, was glad to see other people and be seen by them. She looked, halfheartedly, for a parking space near the farmer's market but didn't find one, not one that she liked, not one that made pulling in an imperative, so she kept going, her mind blank but for a wordless apprecia-tion of her own driving skills, her dexterity and good reflexes.

She found herself so far east that not to go into Manhattan seemed wasteful or pointlessly contrary. On her way over the bridge she came up with a reason for going. She'd spend a cou-ple of hours browsing in her favorite fabric store, see if anything caught her eye.

The night before Sylvia had woken up at three a.m. and moved closer to Edward, who was sleeping with his back toward her. She put an arm and a thigh over him, pressed her nose into a hollow in his spine. Luxuriating in the smell of his warm skin, she marveled at the monumental changes that had taken place in her life. How lucky she was to have been given, to have secured for herself, a second act, a next phase. Her first marriage was finally over. She hadn't realized until she was out of it just how bad it had been, how embittering. She quoted a line from the divorce papers: *a fundamental failure of the marriage necessitating its legal dissolution.* Yes, she thought, that's exactly right. The marriage fails and then, after the fact, the legal contract between the parties is canceled. If Edward hadn't come to town, she wondered, would I have stayed? And for how long? For how much longer? She couldn't say for certain but she fervently hoped that she'd have gotten out, wanted to believe that at some point she'd have realized that whatever minimal connection once existed between herself and Fitzgibbon had dissolved and that continuing to live together in the wake of that dissolution was stupid and spiteful.

Edward had stirred, rolled onto his stomach, settled back into sleep. With him Sylvia had found warmth and welcome, interest, need, desire. It came as a revelation after so many years with Fitzgibbon that such a state of affairs could exist between a man and a woman. She wondered at the chain of events that had brought Edward to her. It scared her to think how easily they might have missed each other entirely. Had he not come back to America. Had he chosen to settle in New York. Had Fitzgibbon not invited him to stay. For that matter, had Agnes not died. Had Agnes never gotten sick in the first place.

Running her fingers lightly up and down the length of Edward's arm, thanking God, chance, fate, happenstance, Sylvia gazed up at the ceiling. Her eyes lit on the thin strip of blue molding that ran along the top of all four walls. The bedroom had been truculent, she remembered, had refused to come together despite the gorgeous French bed, circa 1800, that she'd seen first in her mind's eye and only later, much later, leaning dejectedly against the back wall of an antique shop (barn) in rural Pennsylvania, the convent lace curtains, the two slipper chairs covered in heavy-weave silk, until she'd painted that thin strip of molding a clear, vibrant blue, a blue that had no obvious connection to the muted colors all around it but managed,

anyway, to heighten and unify them just as Sylvia had suspected, had *known*, it would.

She decided to make some changes in the house in honor of
her new marriage, to honor it. Nothing drastic, of course, there
wasn't money for anything major, but she could certainly re-
arrange the furniture in the front parlor, store a couple of pieces,
hang some new drapes, have the sofa reupholstered, find exactly the right spot for the wedding photo.

A perfectly good reason to go into New York, she thought
coming off the bridge. A bright color for the sofa? Gauzy curtains for the bedroom? She couldn't wait to park the car, feeling
that until she did and was out on the sidewalk she hadn't fully
arrived. She recognized the parking attendant from years before
and would have liked to ask him how he was, how he'd been,
but didn't, of course, since it was clear he didn't recognize
her. Exiting the garage, walking up the steep incline to the
street, she realized that she was underdressed. Had she known
where she was going when she left the house, she'd never have
worn pants or flat shoes. She'd have done her hair properly,
powdered her face, put on perfume. For the first couple of
blocks she felt conspicuous and sloppy without girdle or hose,
hat or gloves, but her discomfort gradually lessened. Seeing
censure in the eyes of a pair of matrons, she felt young and
rebellious, risqué.

Approaching the intersection of Sixth Avenue and Twenty-
third Street, Sylvia spotted a woman who looked familiar. Waiting for the light to change, gazing at the woman's face, Sylvia
was taken by the elegance of its architecture, the broad, clear
forehead, prominent cheekbones, long jawline, strong but softly
rounded chin. I know her, I think. Who is she? The woman
was smartly dressed. She wore a tomato-red suit, a close-fitting
blazer that flared exuberantly beneath a nipped waist, a narrow
skirt. Somebody's sister or cousin, somebody's neighbor? Should
I stop her? And say what? Don't I know you? Haven't we met
somewhere before?

The light changed and the woman got halfway across the
street but then stopped abruptly, causing a minor upset as people behind her veered left and right. She looked down at the

thin black belt around her waist, saw that the buckle had drifted off center, set it right.

Something about the woman's coming to a dead halt without any regard for the people behind her combined with the precise angle of her head as she slid the silver belt buckle back to center allowed Sylvia to put her finger on the source of the woman's familiarity. It was Agnes. In the photograph. The woman looked like Agnes.

A second or two later Sylvia was staring at the back of the woman's head. And then she was following, moving rapidly in flat shoes, dodging pedestrians, never losing sight of the upswept hair, the narrow shoulders, but not able to gain any ground either.

The woman stopped at a newsstand and appeared to be reading the headlines. A high-pitched buzz sounded in Sylvia's ears. Did she have the nerve, really? If she got the opportunity would she approach? I'll ask if she's related, if she could possibly be. Excuse me, I'll say, this may seem like a strange question but by any chance are you related to . . . I wish I knew her maiden name.

The woman put down a coin, picked up a newspaper, folded it in half, and, turning, held it aloft to hail a cab. Sylvia watched, at once relieved and disappointed, as the woman in the red suit got into the backseat of the taxi. In her own legs, down her own thighs, Sylvia felt the awkwardness, the particular strain, of climbing into a car in a narrow skirt. She stared until the taxicab was out of sight, imagining, not seeing but pretending she was seeing, the woman staring back at her through the rear window.

chapter 30

She went straight up to the bedroom and opened drawers in Edward's armoire until she found a smallish wooden box. She carried that over to the bed with two hands as if it was heavy or fragile. Right on top and facing up, the photograph of Agnes.

Sylvia looked hard at the face and knew that she would never know if the woman she'd seen looked as much like Agnes as she thought. One face supplanted the other. If Sylvia had had a slightly different face in her mind's eye as she walked back to the car, drove home, climbed the stairs, it was gone now. Sylvia gazed at Agnes and imagined her stopping abruptly in the middle of Twenty-third Street to slide her silver belt buckle back to center.

Already the memory had taken on the texture of a dream. Driving home, Sylvia had recounted the precise details of the experience to herself the way she did dreams she wanted to remember. And, as in a dream, the context seemed important. *I was walking down Sixth Avenue and people were giving me dirty looks because I wasn't properly dressed. At first I was uncomfortable but then I didn't mind so much. I liked it, in fact. I was glad to be in pants and flat shoes without a hat or gloves. The sidewalk was crowded, I hated having to walk so slowly.*

I looked up and there she was.

It took me a few seconds to place her, Sylvia thought, sitting on the bed with the photograph between thumb and index finger. It took her stopping and looking down. And then I knew. It was this face, or very close to it. This sort of face. This bearing, too. I think. Hard to say now.

Sylvia squeezed her eyes shut in an attempt to clear her head.

Silly to make such a fuss. Thousands of people on the streets of New York. A certain number of them are going to resemble any given person. The possibilities for the human face are not endless, not in terms of broad strokes anyway. This is not a common face, yours, not one I'm likely to see coming and going certainly, but it's not one of a kind either. There are lots of pretty women in the world, on the streets of New York especially with all the actresses and models walking around.

"Every woman with pale skin and good bones is going to look a little like you."

Sylvia put the photograph aside and looked to see what else was in the box. Edward's passport and several letters from his sister. Not much, was it? That a man could have lived as eventfully as Edward had and have so little in the way of mementos confounded Sylvia. Was this all he thought worth keeping? Why wasn't there, at least, one photograph of his daughter? Why wasn't there a birth certificate? Sylvia would have liked that especially, an official document that said on such and such a date this child was born to these parents in this place. Nothing. Sylvia opened Edward's passport then noticed something underneath it. A ring. A wedding ring.

"Oh," she said.

Gingerly she placed the gold ring on her palm and held it at eye level to see if it was inscribed. It wasn't. It was well worn, though, the edges softened, the surface scratched. For a moment she was jealous. Edward's having the ring at all seemed disloyal, a slight; it stung. But then her sense of fairness overcame her resentment—she had another ring, too, after all—and she felt guilty for intruding where she ought not to be, for going through Edward's things without his knowledge or permission. She'd been so eager for another look at the photograph that she hadn't given a thought to whether or not, strictly speaking, she was entitled to one.

Edward would be home any minute. It wouldn't do to have

him come in and find the contents of the box strewn all over the bed. A person ought to be able to keep at least as much as would fit inside so small a receptacle to himself. Sylvia put the ring in first, feeling a kind of affection for the younger Edward and his invalid bride, then the letters from Sadie, and finally the photograph just as she'd found it, face up.

Opening the door of the armoire, Sylvia smelled cedar and looked at Edward's couple of suits, his several shirts, his ties, his two pairs of shoes arranged neatly inside. It came as no surprise that Edward's wardrobe was modest. Sylvia knew every crease, every button. In fact, right from the start she'd found Edward's lack of interest in sartorial matters charming. His disregard seemed an aspect of his masculinity, of his character even, and at a certain point had served to make Fitzgibbon's preening seem proof positive of his fundamental superficiality. But now, after examining the contents of the box and holding the wedding ring on the flat of her hand, looking at Edward's clothing, what there was of it, made Sylvia's heart ache. She thought of all Edward had been through in his life, all the losing battles he'd fought, all the moving around, all the leaving. He'd had to travel light, hadn't he?

chapter 31

All she knew about Agnes, really, aside from that she'd been married to Edward (a lot to have in common, Sylvia thought, a husband, but not particularly telling about who Agnes was), that she'd had a daughter who was now stashed in a convent school in the north of Ireland—this information, too, suggested an area of common ground: Agnes's dying and leaving a young child behind and Sylvia's not being able to produce a child in the first place, failures of the body both—that she'd died of TB, like Ruth, was that she'd been a nurse and had worked at Bellevue.

So it was to Bellevue that Sylvia went, in search of what exactly she couldn't have said, something concrete, perhaps, the chance to be somewhere Agnes had been (Sylvia didn't know, had never known, that Agnes had come to the house uninvited that one time, December 31, 1927), to place her in a context, connect her to a physical reality, to walk hallways she'd walked.

Not at all comfortable with her intention to go, thinking it probably silly, sentimental, even morbid, Sylvia sandwiched the visit to Bellevue between sensible, defensible errands. She was going into the city to order new drapes for the living room and to drop off the wedding photo to be framed. In between she'd stop by Bellevue—I'm curious, she told herself, that's all—and have a look around.

It had a kind of Gothic charm, Bellevue did, with its buildings of sooty red brick set back from the street, its tall, narrow windows with yellowed shades, its wrought-iron gate with the word *Bellevue* worked in sturdy black filigree along the rounded arch at the top. Standing on the sidewalk looking up at *Bellevue* spelled out in black metal, Sylvia remembered that the word had been part of her and her friends' slang vocabulary at school. They didn't know anything about the hospital, really, but its name they had used as a synonym for insane asylum, nut house. They used to say that hated teachers and morose, unpopular girls ought to be locked up there. When Sylvia and her friends got a little older and craziness took on a certain jazzy cachet, they used to threaten to check themselves in when their parents gave them grief or boys disappointed them. During the hard and chaotic months after Ruth's death, Sylvia had secretly feared that Bellevue or someplace like it was where she belonged.

The security guard, a New York City policeman with a gun, nightstick, and handcuffs, Sylvia noted, caught her eye and nodded respectfully as if he knew her or thought he should. Sylvia nodded back crisply, the way she imagined a hospital administrator might. She'd dressed carefully that morning, telling herself that although she'd enjoyed being underdressed on her last foray into Manhattan, once was enough for that sort of thing and, furthermore, if she was properly dressed she'd be less likely to arouse suspicion at Bellevue. She wore a navy-blue suit that was vaguely nautical, white piping on collar and cuffs, a new hat, a silk blouse, neutral stockings, black pumps, white gloves, and red lipstick called American Beauty like the rose.

She couldn't maintain her businesslike stride once inside the lobby. Doctors in white coats or wrinkled surgical garb went in and out, many of them talking loudly so as to be heard over the general din and gesticulating emphatically, all of them moving at a good clip. Steady streams of people in uniforms, white, grey, pale pink, flowed in both directions. Foreigners of every description—Sylvia heard Italian and Spanish and Yiddish and Chinese—were milling around, carrying unhappy babies and rumpled paper bags, leaning against walls from which pale green paint was peeling, sitting on scarred wooden benches and on the floor. Fifteen or twenty bums, old drunks, youngish drug addicts, a sprinkling of lunatics, were doing their part, snoring with mouths wide open, muttering, staring glassy-eyed, shouting at fate or at adversaries only they could see.

Sylvia felt conspicuous and vulnerable, as if any second one of the yellers or somebody with a fresh bandage on his head or, worse, somebody in need of a bandage—one fellow was holding a piece of newspaper hard against the crown of his head—would spot her, sense her fear, and pounce. She considered turning around and heading back out to the street, where, perhaps, she could gaze at Bellevue from the outside and in that way get some sense of Agnes. In the time it took Sylvia to imagine abandoning her mission, her anxiety eased. She realized that nobody, not the drunks, not the foreigners, and certainly not any of the uniforms, was paying the least bit of attention to her. She was embarrassed about how carefully she'd chosen her clothing that morning. As if anybody in this place gives a hoot how I'm dressed.

She noticed an entrance to a hallway on the far side of the lobby. A destination, a direction, good. Making her way down the dimly lit corridor that seemed to lead away from the heart of Bellevue and into the periphery, the hinterlands, Sylvia wondered why Agnes had worked at this hospital and not one of the better ones uptown. Was this the only job she could get or was she altruistic? Did she believe herself called to minister to the poor and the despised? Did she like working here? Sylvia could imagine herself liking it. There'd be no question, anyway, but that one's services were desperately needed. A couple of nurses passed and Sylvia took careful note of their uniforms, striped dresses, white aprons, old-fashioned puckered caps with ribbons. Was that the uniform Agnes had worn? Most likely. If it had been changed in the last five or ten years it would no doubt have been updated, made to look specifically modern, utilitarian, antiseptic. How fetching she must have looked, Sylvia thought, watching a young nurse with an upturned nose go by. How delighted Edward must have been at the sight of her.

It was retrospective jealousy and so, of course, was not rational. Sylvia believed that she and Edward had come together not in spite of their difficult pasts so much as because of them. An essential element of their love was the surprise of it, the good news. They'd stopped believing in romantic love, in any kind of love for that matter, and had to be convinced, were still being convinced day by day, night by night, of the possibility of it. She knew all that and yet . . . Believed all that and yet . . . The thought that Agnes had been Edward's first love made Sylvia's stomach hurt. She remembered how lonely she'd been as a young wife, the hours and hours she'd spent waiting for Fitz to come home, his demeanor toward her when he finally had. She thought of her own body at nineteen, twenty, twenty-one, as good as it was ever going to be, pretty damn good. Breasts firm, belly only faintly rounded, rear end, when, naked, she looked over her shoulder at her reflection in the mirror, a sight to see. She wished that she'd had a full-fledged love affair then. Wished she'd spent long afternoons with a young man who adored her and couldn't get enough.

Nipples tingling beneath suit jacket, blouse, and bra, Sylvia cleared her throat and squared her shoulders. What brought all that on? Agnes, she said to herself. I'm supposed to be thinking about Agnes, not mourning my own twenty-year-old breasts or the love affairs I didn't have. This is where Agnes worked. She walked down this hallway, might have brushed the tips of her fingers against this very wall.

Sylvia considered stopping a nurse, one of the older ones, and asking if she'd known an Agnes Devlin but the prospect of flagging down any of the capable-looking women striding past on rubber soles was daunting. Here were women working on the frontlines, women solidly and busily engaged in the realm of the physical, women whose duties centered around the flow of bodily fluids, the removal of stitches, rubbing alcohol, iodine, people being born and people dying. These women had no time for nostalgia, no time for hesitant questioners and halting questions. Even if I had the nerve, Sylvia thought, and if by some miracle I happened on a nurse who knew Agnes, what would my second question be, Can you tell me what was she like? Embarrassed, Sylvia couldn't bring herself to look at the faces of the next several nurses she passed.

The hallway ended and Sylvia found herself in a second,

smaller lobby, where there was a rather grand staircase—dingy the way everything at Bellevue was dingy but grand by design, sweeping, wider at bottom than top. A small sign on the wall pointed the way to the Catholic chapel.

Sylvia went because she knew she'd be able to sit for as long as she wanted there. She'd been on her feet since early that morning, in heels, and her arches were beginning to ache. Climbing the stairs, she told herself that it was very likely Agnes had spent some time at least in the chapel, considering she was Irish Catholic and devout enough to want her daughter sent to a convent boarding school.

The chapel was modest, a smallish square room, dimly lit, close and damp, windowless. There were no more than a dozen pews leading up to a simple altar on which a clean white cloth had been draped. Behind the altar hung a small metal crucifix, spare, understated, no more than a foot tall and something of a relief to Sylvia, who'd been taken aback and vaguely embarrassed by the enormous crucifixes that dominated the Catholic churches she'd been to for weddings and funerals. This Christ was so slight, so unassuming, you had to look carefully to pick him out. Now where is . . . right, there he is. On either side of the altar were banks of short candles. The few that were lit flickered inside red glass cylinders. In the second row an old lady knelt, fingering a rosary and whispering rapidly. Something in her demeanor—it was businesslike, she was getting her praying done—suggested to Sylvia that, perhaps, the old doll lived in the neighborhood and came to Bellevue often, every day even, to pray for the general good of anonymous patients and their families. Toward the back a middle-aged man who looked as if he hadn't been home to sleep, shave, or change his clothes in several days sat with arms extended on either side, looking up at the altar imploringly. Sylvia imagined him keeping a vigil by the bedside of a desperately sick wife or child until somebody, a kindly nurse, a concerned relative, convinced him to go home and get some sleep. He'd agreed to go, finally. This was as far as he'd gotten.

Sylvia felt like an interloper. First, she was a Jew, not a Catholic, and though her parents were German Jews and far

from religious (her family had gone to an American Reform syn-
agogue on major holidays: men and women sat together; services were conducted in English without prayer shawls or
skullcaps), Sylvia still considered herself Jewish, at least when
she was making her way up the aisle of a Catholic chapel she
did. Second, she had not come from anybody's bedside. Nobody she loved was sick or dying. She half hoped the others,
the old lady, the unshaven man, were mistaking her for a dis-
traught mother or wife. She went so far as to affect an expression of loving forbearance and then, appalled by her own
disingenuousness, slid into a pew, took a deep breath, fixed her
eyes on a flickering candle.

It was so good to sit down, to be out of the rush and tumble
of the lobby, to be relieved of the need to appear to know
where she was going. The air that had seemed damp and cloying when she first came in felt cool and soothing now. Rarely
had Sylvia been so inclined to stay put.

Yes, of course Agnes would have come here. How could she
not have? Nurses work irregular schedules, Sylvia thought, and
Catholics are forever running to church, not just on Sundays but
on holy days, saints' days, all of that. Agnes must have taken advantage of so convenient a means of fulfilling her obligation. It's
possible, too, that she'd come in search of peace and quiet, stillness, reprieve. Maybe she used to come here to sit and collect
her thoughts for a few minutes before her shift started or to begin to recover after it was done.

Agnes had worked at Bellevue, Edward had said, until she
got sick. So she'd had her first symptoms here, the cough that
wouldn't go away, the sudden high fevers, the sweats. Sinusitis,
Ruth's first doctor had said. Bedrest, aspirin, plenty of hot liq-
uids. Then had come new doctors with different diagnoses.
Bronchitis. Pleurisy. Asthma. And all the while Ruth only got
sicker. Sylvia had felt grossly healthy by comparison. She used
to slouch in Ruth's presence, try to make herself smaller. She
quaked to think how hard it must have been to be sick the way
Ruth had been even at the start, feverish, achey, tired all the
time, breathless, and to have been a nurse here. Had Agnes
tried to hide her illness? Had she been reluctant to admit what

she had to suspect? Did she try to convince herself that she was tired because she'd been out late the night before, because she'd had too much to drink, because she'd been working too hard? And the cough? (Lying in her bed listening to Ruth cough in the next room, Sylvia used to alternate between impatience and fright. Shut up, Ruthie. Please, please shut up.) How had Agnes explained the cough? A bit of a cold in my chest. Still haven't shaken it entirely. It's the damp, all this rain we've been having. Went out without my umbrella. But all the while she must have known. She was a nurse, after all. She had to at least suspect.

Sylvia closed her eyes and wondered if it was here in the chapel that Agnes let herself be afraid. She wouldn't have to put on an act here, wouldn't have to try to appear healthy. Was it here that she first said the word *tuberculosis* to herself? Did she wonder how long she'd be able to go on acting as if nothing was wrong? Did she come here to pray for deliverance?

The quiet, the pinkish light, the sound of the old woman saying the rosary, even the restless movements of the unshaven man—he sucked his teeth, crossed and uncrossed his legs, sniffed—were conducive to Sylvia's imaginings. She began to believe the version of Agnes's life she was herself concocting, sensed authority running all through it. She felt what it must have been like to be newly married, a certain disorientation goes with that, Sylvia knew, no matter how happy the union, a certain loss of bearings, to be *so* far from home, to be not well, to suspect, to fear that one is facing a serious illness, a major disruption (pain, frailty, complicated and time-consuming attempts at cure) in a life so recently and majorly disrupted by marriage and emigration, to be footsore and weary at the end of a long shift and running late and due home, to be summoning the energy for the trek while sitting in the half-light listening to an old woman chant for the general good.

"Nice shot," the framer said, holding the photograph at arm's length, drawing it near.

Sylvia smiled, pleased, a little embarrassed. She and Edward were actually kissing in the picture, after all, and she didn't know this grizzled old man from Adam. "My husband and me on our wedding day," she said. The words sounded peculiar, oddly formal, like a declaration. Under the sway still of her meditation in the hospital chapel, she considered how much history was packed into a sentence so seemingly straightforward and simple. Our wedding day.

"Very nice. Let's talk about matting."

Sylvia checked the clock on the night table. Not quite three-thirty. She lay back, listened to Edward snore softly and was soothed by the sounds, the whistling inhale, the silence, the deep sighing exhale. There was so much of Edward in those sounds, Edward unguarded, Edward at rest. His snore was as particular to him as his speaking voice or his laugh.

Sylvia turned her pillow over, adjusted sheet and blanket, settled in. She was tired, limbs heavy, eyes dry, but still she couldn't sleep. Let it go, she said to herself as she always did when she had trouble sleeping. Let it go. *It* referred to the waking world, whatever was happening in the here and now that was preying on her mind. Let it go, she said, not knowing what *it* was exactly, not wanting to know, exactly. Let. It. Go. She could not. It remained. It was too much with her. Admitting defeat—it had won—Sylvia got out of bed.

She sat on the white sofa in the living room, knees pulled to her chest, bare feet on the cushion. She was going to have the sofa reupholstered and so didn't care if she smudged it. Before long she was up and looking for someplace else to sit, tried one of the chairs on the other side of the room but didn't last there either. She went into the kitchen, put a kettle on, then wandered into the dining room, where the cookbook still lay facedown on the table.

She was drawn into the back parlor by the smallness of it, thought maybe she wouldn't feel so antsy there, and by its subtle unfamiliarity. She hadn't spent much time there in recent years. As things between herself and Fitzgibbon had worsened there'd been a divvying up of rooms. The back parlor had been his. He'd read his mail and smoked his late-night cigars there.

She'd forgotten how nice the wallpaper was, Bradbury & Bradbury, a rich terra cotta.

She pulled her robe closed and wondered if a fire would be worth the bother. Was there kindling in the box? Newspaper? She'd never built a fire before though she'd watched Fitz build hundreds. She assembled the necessary components, newspaper, kindling, log, matches, and had no trouble laying the thing. No wonder they call it building, she thought. It really is that, making a structure that will burn. The match flared loudly in the predawn quiet and Sylvia was pleased with herself, touching match to newspaper here, and here, and here. Would the kindling catch? And the log? It seemed about to. Yes. Going. The fire was lit.

Not wanting to return to the couch, which had been chilly under her legs and was too far from the modest blaze, Sylvia went to the cedar closet, pulled out a blanket, and spread it on the rug in front of the fire. No sooner had she gotten comfortable, leaning back on straight arms, than she remembered the kettle and jumped up to get it. She made a cup of tea, added cream, took several sips, added more cream, then went back to her place in front of the fire.

She drank the tea quickly, greedily, the fingers of her left hand wrapped around the cup for warmth. Then she lay down on her side and felt the heat of the fire on her forehead, nose, and knees. She pulled part of the blanket over herself, fell instantly to sleep, and was back on Sixth Avenue chasing the woman in the tomato-red suit. This time, dreaming, there was no doubt but that it was urgent, an emergency, a matter of life or death, that she catch up. The ambivalence, the self-consciousness and self-doubt that Sylvia had felt when she was awake and following the woman in the red suit had been replaced by the potent single-mindedness that's so common in dreams and so rare in waking life. Sylvia *had* to catch up. The whole point of the dream was that she catch up. So she did. She reached out and touched the sleeve of the woman's jacket. (The next day, several times, she'd remember the feel of silk under her fingers.) The woman stopped, turned around slowly, and looked Sylvia full in the face.

It wasn't Agnes at all. It was Ruth. Ruthie, all grown up. Her face, anyway, her child's face attached to the body of a grown woman.

"You're still alive, Ruthie, all this time, how can that be?"

I'm not. *I'm* not.

"I don't understand."

A blue streak. Words tumbling out of her. No pauses. No periods. Something about a doctor, a book, a place in the Adirondacks. Sylvia listened the way she used to, patiently, knowing that's all they really want, to be listened to.

chapter 32

There were three letters in all. The first had been sent to the Alexander Hamilton, the second and third to the house. Sylvia arranged the letters in chronological order by postmarks then read them.

They were brief, their tone scolding. Sadie hoped Edward had pulled himself together. "You were in a state when you left, God knows." Was he working? Not drinking overmuch? Not feeling sorry for himself? "You've found a place to live temporarily? Friends taking you in is better than living in a hotel, I suppose, but you really ought to be settled in your own place by now." Sadie complained of financial difficulties—"America's not the only place people are struggling"—and of the strain of providing for a child when she had all she could do to meet her other obligations. "That said, I am in complete agreement with you. Boarding school is best, under the circumstances. I have all I can do keeping up with my tenants and Bell isn't much use to anybody. I'll make some inquiries but I want you to bear in mind that boarding school is not going to be cheap. There'll be fees, uniforms to buy, travel expenses, and so on. She's your daughter, not mine. Grief is all well and good. Bereavement is to be expected. But the fact remains you've got a daughter to provide for and I'll thank you not to forget it."

Sylvia folded the letters with care, put them back in their envelopes, put the wooden box back in the drawer, closed the doors of the armoire, went downstairs to start dinner.

Steak, baked potatoes, a green salad. She was glad to be occupied, to have tasks that needed doing. Light this, salt that, wash under running water, pierce with the tines of a fork to allow steam to escape, slice, drain, tear into pieces.

She heard Edward come in but kept on with what she was doing, slicing a tomato. Edward came up behind her, nuzzled her neck. She turned around, took his face in her two hands, kissed him on the lips several times.

He made the drinks while she set the table. Tipsy, she put the steaks under the broiler, waited exactly five minutes by the clock, turned them over. "To tell if a sirloin is done," *Fannie* said, "touch it at the thickest point with the tip of your index finger. If it feels like your cheek, it's rare. Like the tip of your nose, it's medium. Like your forehead, well done." Sylvia touched the meat, her cheek, the meat again, her cheek again. Close enough, she thought. I guess they're done.

"And you say you can't cook. This looks lovely."

"Anybody can broil a steak."

"I couldn't."

"Sure you could. You just read the directions in the cookbook. There's a whole section on basics."

"Delicious."

"Not too rare?"

"Perfect. You wouldn't want to spoil meat as good as this by overcooking. Cuts like butter."

Edward talked about a problem he was having at work. Construction of the traffic circle was underway and he was battling a contractor. Sylvia played the part of the attentive wife. "Really?" she said. "Of course not . . . I don't blame you . . . No."

After dinner she suggested they sit on the porch.

"Good," Edward said. "I'll make some coffee and be out directly."

"There's blueberry pie, too."

"You made a pie?"

"God, no. I bought one. In a bakery. It's in a box on the kitchen table."

"Right."

Sylvia sat on the edge of one of the wicker chairs, turning her wedding ring around on her finger and looking out at the street.

Coffee poured and pie served, Edward sat on the love seat and motioned for Sylvia to join him, which she did. They ate and drank without talking for a minute or two and then Sylvia said, "I read Sadie's letters today."

"You what?"

"I read your letters from Sadie."

"Went into my things, you mean?"

"I didn't set out to. I was straightening up and . . . the point is—"

"The point is you were snooping. You had no right to read those letters."

"Granted. I didn't. I had no right. But I did it anyway. And I want to talk. I have to talk to you about—"

"If you had asked to see them I would have gladly—"

"I don't think so. I don't think you would have."

"I've got nothing to hide."

"Edward, please. You told me that your two sisters were glad to have Maura, that they doted on her. That's not the way it is at all, is it?"

"It *is*. That's exactly the way it is. They are glad to have her. Sadie would never let on. She's a gruff old bird but, believe me, she's . . . They're taking very good care of . . . I'm telling you."

"Tell me this, Edward. Do you support her? Do you send money? Because—"

"I will not sit here and be interrogated like a criminal. I did what I thought was best. For her, I mean. What I thought was best for her."

"All right," Sylvia said, standing up then sitting back down again. "All right then. Fine. But your circumstances have changed. Ours have. Please, Edward, go over there and get her. Bring her back here. We'll raise her, you and I. We're settled. We can do it easily. I'd love to have her here, I really would."

"No."

Sylvia took a deep breath, closed her eyes. "Why not?"

Edward stared at the ground between his feet.

"I have to know why not."

Edward sniffed hard.

"How can you live with yourself? She's your daughter, for God's sake. Imagine what she's been through. Her mother dies after a long illness and her father takes off, disappears. She's left in the care of a cantankerous old woman who doesn't want her. Can you imagine how terrifying that is? Can you imagine how much she misses you? Do you have any idea what you've done?"

"It was an awful time. You weren't there, you don't . . . I did what I thought was best."

"Is that what you tell yourself? Is that how you let yourself off the hook? She's a child, Edward, for God's sake. She's done nothing wrong, not to you, not to anybody."

"I didn't say she had. I said that—"

"—you did what you thought was best. Right. Did you, *do* you think it best not to provide for her? Is that still what you think is best?"

Edward said nothing.

"Send for her, please. Please. Edward, I'm begging you."

"No. I can't."

"You can't. And you can't say why not. You're a good man, Edward. I believe that you are. And yet you . . . It doesn't make sense. I don't know how you can go on day after day knowing . . . What would Agnes say if she knew? Do you ever ask yourself that? Because I do. I ask myself. What would Agnes say if she knew you'd run out on her daughter?"

Looking puzzled, disoriented, looking as if he might be sick, Edward stood up and patted his pockets distractedly then turned and walked down the porch stairs.

"Where are you going?"

He didn't answer.

"Don't leave. Edward, please. Please don't leave."

It was the downward slope of the pavement under his feet that got him moving and confirmed for him that yes, he wanted to get away and quickly, too. He was humiliated, angry, bewildered. At the same time, separately, some small part of him was glad to be out in the open air, glad to be moving through it, a free agent, however temporarily, moving fast, faster, away from wife and home and hearth.

He got into town and stopped at a newsstand, bought a pack of cigarettes, and smoked three, one right after the other, walking around and around City Hall. "Not this," he said half a dozen times. "Not bloody this. Not now."

Paterson was closing up shop for the night. Awnings were being rolled up, security gates opened over plate glass, padlocks snapped. Most of the cars were heading out. Soon, Edward knew, only the movie theater and burlesque house and bars would be open. Good, he thought. Suits me fine. All I need now, a bar.

A couple of old men sat at one end, glasses of still beer in front of them. The bartender was middle-aged, balding, fleshyfaced. Edward ordered a shot and a beer and drank them down. His hands were trembling. He wondered if the bartender mistook him for a drunk.

Happened on those letters, my ass. Went looking for them. Went looking for trouble and found some. Women can't ever leave well enough alone. Not happy unless they're miserable.

Then, with a vividness that made his stomach lurch, he remembered the disrespectful tone of Sadie's letters and was mortified to think of Sylvia reading them. Sadie's turned mean in her old age, Sadie is a battle-ax, Sadie talks to everybody that way, he'd tell Sylvia ... except how could that Sadie be the same one he claimed was doting on the little girl he'd left in her care? Christ.

He asked for another shot, drank it, felt a familiar and welcome loosening, felt himself beginning to rise above, or retreat from, the particulars of his own situation. Who was he after all but a man in a bar who'd just had a run-in with his wife? Across the country, all over the world, men by the thousands were drinking in bars after run-ins with their wives. Newlyweds, especially. The first year or two of marriage are bound to be tough going, everybody knows that. Just as he'd gotten a foothold in his tipsy, philosophical detachment, his memory served up an image of his brother with arms crossed and head tilted, Joseph being reasonable. "You don't want her. None of us is in any position. The point is there are places, and not necessarily awful ones, facilities, I mean. Arrangements can be made, you say the word."

"The point is I didn't say the word," Edward said to the empty stool next to him, to his brother, to Sylvia. I didn't have to. She didn't wind up in any facility. She's with family. I did what I thought was best. For her. I did what I did for Maura's own good.

He so rarely said her name, even to himself.

It's a girl, the nurse said, and he knew her name would be Maura. Agnes had picked out two, Maura and Liam, Irish names, for Edward's sake, in the hope of winning him over, Irish names in honor of his youthful politics.

It was a difficult birth. Agnes had labored for three days, starting and stopping. No sooner would the doctor say it was over, false alarm, take her home, see you in a day or two, than the pains would start again. Edward slept when he slept at all in a chair in the hospital waiting room. She'd been weak going into it, hollows beneath her eyes, yellow like a healing bruise, coughing, much coughing, relentless merciless inefficient coughing without the use of her stomach muscles that had splayed to make room for her belly. It's a girl, the nurse said by way of waking Edward up. Ashamed to have been caught napping when he'd been driving the staff crazy for days, demanding to speak to the doctor when the doctor was nowhere to be found, sneaking food in, most of which he'd eaten himself, insisting on detailed updates, he'd leapt out of his chair and groped for his glasses, which, the snippy nurse delighted in pointing out, were right there on the end of his nose.

"Another beer, please."

Agnes's doctor, a specialist, *the* man in New York for TB, had been furious when he discovered she was pregnant. He'd turned and glared at Edward as if to say, This is your doing, is it? Your contribution to the situation? All you could think of to do?

Agnes had come so far by then. She would never be cured, they'd been told, but might enjoy a long, a very long remission.

("You watch, she'll outlive us both," the specialist said, and Edward heard a note of compassion, an awareness of the kind of suffering the sick inflict on those who take care of them.) Rest, they were told, a diet rich in meat and eggs and milk, fresh air, peace and quiet.

And they were warned, in no uncertain terms. They were taken into the doctor's office and warned. They were seated in front of the doctor's desk and warned. "Nothing accelerates the course of this illness like pregnancy," said the doctor in the almost singsongy rhythm, all significant words stressed, that authority figures use when delivering warnings they've delivered countless times before. (How many times do I have to tell you, a tired mother or a weary prison guard asks.) A frank discussion followed. Various options, abstinence, of course, being the safest. Condoms and keeping careful track of dates a second and more realistic choice for a young couple such as yourselves. You're human after all. You can't be expected to. It's better in the long run, we've found, to start from the assumption that you are going to continue having relations than to set yourselves a task that ... Anyway, you understand what I'm saying, yes? Condoms and the calendar. Agnes claimed to understand the whole business of dates, safe times, risky ones, so Edward left the recordkeeping to her. He wore the rubbers, though. He made sure he always had a good supply and used one every time, every single time, even when Agnes said it was safe and he needn't bother he ignored the mischievous glint in her eye—he couldn't begin to imagine what inspired that, didn't want to know, didn't want, certainly, to be to any degree similarly inspired—and insisted. And he bought the best ones, too, the most expensive, in the hope they'd be less likely to leak or tear. Every time he made his preference known at the drugstore counter he felt responsible, he felt prudent, he felt he was taking good care.

It wasn't enough. It didn't work. The missed period, the swollen breasts, the nausea, Agnes's certainty even before the blood test came back. I'm a nurse, aren't I? I'm still a nurse, don't forget. Besides which it's my body and I know what I know.

In spite of Agnes's terror—she didn't want to be pregnant,

she wanted to get better—and his own, some small pitiless part of Edward was proud of impregnating his wife. His maleness, his husbandly purpose, had triumphed over all attempts to frustrate it. So shaken was Edward by a dim and fleeting awareness of this brutish response, a caveman's, he thought, a monarch's, that he poured all his energy into making it clear that so far as he was concerned the pregnancy was an affliction.

They were dazed. For so long Agnes's condition, the ups and downs, the different protocols and her responses to them, had been their focus. And now this process they'd been specifically warned against was underway, was gathering steam, was making its presence known in increasingly obvious ways as the days passed, and all they could do was brace themselves for the toll it would take.

And then Agnes wasn't sick to her stomach anymore. She began to feel the baby move inside her and got excited and grew optimistic (she had, Edward thought, looking into his beer, the entrenched optimism of the beautiful: having been welcomed by the world every single day of her life, she couldn't help but anticipate good outcomes, special privileges, reprieves), she tried to convince Edward that everything would work out in the end. I'll have the baby and go back on my regimen directly. We'll hire a nurse. I can do this, Ned. I know I can do this. Edward was careful not to seem to share her enthusiasm, though he did—how could he not?—for fear she'd think he was less concerned about her welfare than he'd been previously. He went on acting as if the pregnancy was a setback, a hardship, a blow. He made a show of resenting it, of wanting to get it over and done with. And so Agnes had chosen Irish names to draw him in, to win him over.

It's a girl, the nurse said, and his heart leapt.

It wasn't all right, of course. Nothing worked out all right in the end. Agnes never regained the ground she lost. Agnes never recovered.

I did what I did because I'd been burned not once but twice, Edward thought, opting for making declarations over remembering the truth of his experience. I fought for my country. I fought for my wife. I lost both battles, I lost every bloody battle, and both wars while I was at it. I lost and lost and lost. How many times can a man be expected to pick himself up, dust himself off, and carry on?

This argument did not provide Edward the refuge it once had. The notion that he'd become a permanently disappointed man, a man incapable of attachment in the wake of the loss of his beloved, didn't make much sense now that he'd so recently entered into the mother of all sentimental attachments, marriage. He'd intended to live that other life, that solitary, embittered one, he truly had. When he left Ireland he had every intention of drifting, drinking, doing as he damn well pleased. He'd meant to become the sort of person who could not possibly raise a child. He hadn't gone looking for Sylvia, or for any woman for that matter. He'd found her, though, looking or not, and he wasn't sorry, but her existence, the way he felt about her, the way he felt *with* her, the life they'd so recently started together, rendered the cynical drifter defense of limited use to him now.

All right. Why then? Why couldn't he send for Maura?

Edward looked up and saw the bartender looking at him. The man's demeanor, his expression, suggested that he was about to initiate a conversation and Edward was relieved, and flattered. Nothing he'd like more just now than a friendly back and forth over the bar. The other mess, Sylvia's ambush, Maura's fate, the ghost of Agnes hovering over everything, the entirety of his life as he'd lived it up till now, all that could wait. Here was a bartender who might like to talk good-naturedly about nothing for a while.

"How's things?" Edward said, sounding to his own ears American, and pleasantly so. He was American now, or very nearly. The past was over and done with. He was an American man with an American wife. He and the missus were childless. "How's everything?"

The bartender nodded, frowned, shrugged one shoulder, American for not bad, all right. "You're Sylvia Fitzgibbon's new husband, aren't you?"

"I am." Edward liked being recognized, liked the sense he

got of his stature, his potential stature anyway, in Paterson. "And it's Sylvia Devlin now, if you don't mind."

"Devlin, right. I knew the name, couldn't think of it."

The bartender refilled Edward's beer glass, set it down, knocked on the bar.

On the house, Edward thought, nice fellow. Edward was about to ask the nice fellow if he owned the place or was he an employee looking one day to buy a place of his own when the nice fellow said, "So you're the man who stole Fitzgibbon's woman, huh?"

"I wouldn't say that exactly," Edward said in a tone of voice that suggested he would have said that, exactly, if he'd had the nerve and didn't mind the other man's saying it one bit.

The bartender sucked his teeth, nodded. "Between you and me—what's your first name?"

"Edward. And yours?"

"Between you and me, Ed, I always thought it was just a matter of time. Not for nothing, right, best of luck to you both, but I always knew Fitzgibbon was looking the other way."

"Did you?" Edward said and regretted saying. He knew the conversation had taken an ugly turn, knew even that it was about to get uglier still, but didn't know how to defend himself, wasn't quite sure what he ought to have been defending himself against.

"Sure. Sure I did. I'm not one to gossip, right, live and let live is what I say, but if it wasn't you it would have been somebody else. Sylvia was looking, if you ask me. Sylvia was open for business. Best of luck to you both, don't get me wrong."

Feeling unhinged, sorry there clearly wasn't going to be the interlude of idle conversation he'd hoped for, ashamed for having wanted such an interlude so badly, feeling that everywhere he turned he encountered fresh insult, new injury, Edward felt himself begin to cry. He cleared his throat violently, hoping he sounded as if he were reining in rage, not fending off tears.

"That's my wife you're talking about," he said in as menacing a tone as he could manage. "And I'll thank you to keep a civil tongue in your head."

The last bit was something Edward's mother used to say

whenever his language got the least bit salty. He hadn't heard
the expression in twenty years, hadn't ever said it himself as far
as he knew, had no idea from whence it had come, feared it was
some sort of pathetic crying out for his mama. "Outside," he
said, "right now, you and me."

The bartender looked surprised then bemused. "You want to
go outside with me, Ed?"

The old men were watching. The old men were mildly
interested.

"Damn right I do. Nobody talks about my wife that way and
gets away with it."

"Ah, keep your shorts on. I didn't mean no disrespect. I was
just saying—"

"I heard what you said and I'll be outside waiting to give you
my answer."

How long, Edward had no choice but to ask himself after a
few minutes had passed, was he obligated to stand on the sidewalk and wait? Did he want the bartender to come out, really?
He knew that he should want him to, but did he? He knew,
furthermore, that since it was becoming clearer by the second
that the bartender wasn't coming, he ought to be enraged. Another man would burst back in and start swinging, breaking bottles, something. (There'd been a baseball bat behind the bar
and it looked as if it had been put to hard use.) Still another sort
of man would be able somehow to go back in and make light of
what had happened, would manage to recover his dignity by
saying something wildly clever—but what? What?—after pulling open the door and sidling up to the bar. Edward was, he
knew, neither the hothead nor the charmer. He was instead a
man who was perfectly equipped to stand on the sidewalk with
his arms crossed, with his hands in his pockets, with his hands
hanging limply at his sides, waiting for an opponent he knew
wasn't coming. He was a man who would sooner or later—Now?
Not yet—have to put one foot in front of the other—Now?—
and walk away. Which he did. One foot in front of the other.

Jesus. Je-sus Christ. Is there no satisfaction? No seeing a
thing through to its inevitable, what should be but somehow

never quite is its inevitable end? Inevitability seemed to operate only to a point and then things got wild and woolly, or rather things got slack and slow, indifferent as to whether they manifested or not, random. What was bound to happen generally didn't.

Edward wanted another drink. The inebriating effects of alcohol, *there* was something that could be relied on. He wanted a small flat bottle, a pint. A liquor store materialized in the distance, a yellow awning with black lettering, package goods. Edward wasn't able, quite, to trust the neutrality of the place. It looked innocuous enough but after what had happened in the corner bar, Edward was leery. What challenge awaited him under the yellow awning? What test of his mettle? Get hold of yourself. The man insulted your wife. You were ready and willing to fight him. *He* refused, thought Edward, who was about the business then of putting together a version of what had happened that was palatable, easier to digest. It's an ordinary liquor store, for God's sake. Go in and buy yourself a pint bottle.

It was and he did. The woman behind the counter—she was fifty if she was a day and wore her jet-black hair in two thick braids, a little jarring, those braids, but only mildly so—took Edward's money and thanked him and in no way threatened his dignity.

A long swallow, the familiar burn. Top screwed down with the palm of his hand.

Edward turned down a side street. Not the sort of neighborhood one should stroll through after dark, he thought. The child is too great a reminder of the mother, he thought. I loved Agnes more than life itself. Don't want to happen on a vagrant's camp or a pack of hoodlums drinking. I'd have gladly died in her place. So easy for somebody to come out of the shadows and knock me on the head, grab my wallet. Can't live every day with a walking, talking memento of the greatest loss of my life. Wishing he were reckless, wishing he were out on a tear, chastising himself for *not* being too occupied with thoughts of Agnes to concern himself with his own safety, Edward straightened up, scanned the terrain, and moved to the middle of the street to put as much distance as he could between himself and the darkened buildings and the alleys that ran between them.

He'd gone five or six blocks when he heard what he identified after a moment as the roar of the falls. The Great Falls people were always going on about. He'd been in Paterson well over a year and had yet to lay eyes on the famous falls. It would do him good, he decided, given how he was feeling, what he was facing, to stand before something colossal, the raw power of nature and all, something awesome. The rush and the roar and the spray and all the rest of it—cliffs, froth, what have you— might soothe him, might settle him down. Might even guide him toward the kind of reckoning he was after.

He could smell them, he thought, could smell river water, anyway. He kept on, he turned left, he turned right, he advanced, he backtracked. The roar of the falls grew louder, then fainter, then louder again. He knew the falls were in the general vicinity of Fitzgibbon's mill, and so was he now. At least he thought he was. That's it over there, isn't it? They all look the same. If I could just find the river, any part of the river, I could follow it in one direction and then the other.

Was any of it true? Was his grief over Agnes at the heart of his refusal to change his mind about Maura?

He took a drink from his pint bottle—he didn't really have a taste for the whiskey, wanted to but didn't—then conjured several of his most affecting memories, the first time he'd laid eyes on Agnes all grown up in nurse's cap and navy-blue cape, her clear-eyed response to his marriage proposal, her anguish in the face of her final prognosis—"Six weeks, maybe less"—and then, not getting quite the jolt he was after, not feeling devastated enough, he relived the moment of her death and the night he'd spent alone with her corpse. He'd seen her dead as if for the first time every time he dared look. The shock of the stillness. The fright. The profound absence of what had animated that flesh only minutes and then hours before. Life: Gone. Personality: Gone. Agnes: Gone. He'd slept beside her on the narrow bed.

He'd completely lost his bearings by now. He had only the vaguest sense of what territory he'd covered, thought there was a good chance he'd wandered off course and was farther than ever from the falls. You'd think there'd be a bloody sign. Anywhere else with a waterfall would understand that people are going to be coming to have a look. I'll bet there are signs galore in Niagara. His impatience with Paterson transmuted in an instant into fresh anger at Sylvia. She had no right to bring Agnes into it.

Sylvia had no right bringing Agnes in.

Agnes was dead. And it wasn't even as if Sylvia had known her alive. Agnes was nothing to Sylvia but a name, a face in a photograph. None of Sylvia's business what Agnes thought about—

Agnes doesn't think. Agnes is dead.

If she weren't?

Oh, for God's sake, if Agnes weren't dead there'd be nothing to talk about. If Agnes weren't dead I wouldn't have done what I—

If she were somewhere, if she is somewhere, dead but still thinking, still having opinions, what then?

Where the hell are the falls?

What then?

I've walked so bloody far. I don't want to give up without finding—

What would Agnes say if she knew?

Aside from the time in Arizona when she asked him to promise he'd remarry—he couldn't bear to hold the image of her lurching down the hall toward the squalling baby in his mind's eye for more than a second or two—Agnes had not told him what she wanted to happen to Maura. He had to remind himself that he'd made the whole business of boarding school up to ward off Sylvia's disapproval the night they'd met. Hadn't wasted any time, had she, had Sylvia? His first night in the house, questions about Maura.

Six weeks, maybe less, the doctor had admitted when Agnes pressed. For two solid days she wept, suffered terrible bouts of agitation, railed against her many doctors, against America, against the conditions at Bellevue. She refused to go to sleep for fear she wouldn't wake up. ("I'll be right here. I won't let go of your hand.") She broke things, a teacup, an ashtray. In a terrifying display of lunatic strength, she tore open her pillow and shook all the feathers out. They got into everything, everything. (For days after, thinking he'd got them all, Edward found more, and still more, between the mattress and the headboard, in the toe of his shoe.) She stood by the window. She threatened to jump. "If you love me, you'll let me. If you really love me, you'll give me a push." She pointed out passersby who deserved to die so much more than she did. "That one, for example, that miserable old bat. Look at her. Never done a thing in her life for anybody, you can tell. Him with the short trousers and greasy hair. What all's he got to live for? I'm thirty-two years old. I don't want to die." Fed up, exhausted, wanting to smash something himself, Edward called the doctor, who was too busy to come but sent a resident with a hypodermic needle. Agnes slept for nine hours. Edward checked her breathing a hundred times. Edward whimpered. Edward wept. Not now, please, God. Not this way. Not now. Not yet.

When Agnes woke she was meek.

"Hey."

"Hello, you."

"How long was I sleeping?"

"A good while, all night."

Edward didn't mention the resident, the injection. He took her hand and she told him she wanted to go back to Ireland. "Wire Sadie. Tell her I want to come home."

For the time it took to arrange passage and close up the apartment, Edward believed Agnes had made peace with her fate. He was amazed, and deeply moved, couldn't imagine how she'd gone from hysteria to acceptance in the course of nine hours of oblivion, wondered what dreams she could possibly have had. Her own mother beckoning? Jesus Christ all in white? In private punchy moments he asked himself what had been in that earnest resident's syringe. What *was* that stuff? The antidote for the human condition, a colorless liquid that allows one to face one's own death calmly. However painful it was to see Agnes bearing up, and it was painful, she was achingly, hauntingly beautiful, gaunt, gentle and temperate in her resignation, Edward knew that her peace, whatever its source, would make the trip home easier and he was grateful for that. They'd been out at sea a day or two and were sitting on deck chairs while Maura played with an older child, a boy, in the middle distance, when Agnes began talking about setting up house in Omagh, how glad she'd be to be home again. She'd had enough of New York, she said, enough of America. Before the day was out she'd begun half a dozen sentences with "And then when I'm better."

Edward abandoned his search for the falls. His not being able to locate what he knew had to be enormous, a focal point, a center of sorts, the very reason Paterson had come into existence, its natural heart, seemed emblematic of his profound ineffectiveness. Thwarted, as usual. Unable to do what he set out to do. He was convinced that his meditation, his soul searching, his fearless inquiry into his own heart and mind, would have been more fruitful, more satisfying, would have rung truer and therefore have painted him in a better light somehow if it had had as backdrop the grandeur of the Great Falls.

Nothing for it but to head home.

And how should he conduct himself once he got there? Should he be conciliatory or hostile? Wait to see how Sylvia seemed and respond in kind? That's if she was still awake. If she'd gone to bed already should he join her there, slip in beside her contritely or sleep on the couch in the back parlor or, Jesus God, in the guest room, his old second-floor digs?

Imagining Sylvia sleeping alone in their double bed prompted Edward to consider giving in, saying Yes, all right, let's bring Maura over. I'll write Sadie in the morning. How easy it would be to set things right, how little it would take to announce his decision, to say he was willing to give Sylvia what she wanted, a child. Did she have any idea, really, what she was letting herself in for? Was she so caught up in her own desire to have a child and in the vision of herself as rescuer that her disillusionment when it came would prove disastrous for everybody involved? Would he, attempting to solve a problem, create a worse one? He saw Sylvia's face that day in the attic when, on the spur of the moment, without thinking, he'd asked her why she didn't have children. God only knows, she'd said, something like that. Her expression, rattled, vulnerable, let him know he'd stumbled on a great sorrow. She told him she'd been to doctors. She told him that she and Fitzgibbon weren't sleeping together anymore. She let him in. What had existed between them until that moment, a kind of flirtatious potential consisting of each one's heightened awareness of the other and a good measure of caginess, deepened just then and their falling in love became a foregone conclusion.

Sylvia alone in their bed. The memory of her face that day in the attic—so hot up there, tiny beads of sweat above her upper lip, the hair at her temples darkened—elicited a rush of love and pity. He had it in his power to mitigate her sadness. Even if it turned out badly, if all the clichés about stepmothers and stepdaughters proved true, the experience of raising a child had to ease the pain of wanting but not being able to have one. Give in. Give over. Go home and make the announcement. Bask in her approval and her gratitude.

He could not do it. And he thought he knew why.

He ticked off the reasons to himself, rehearsing the explanation he'd give Sylvia. I was burned not once but twice. I was young and idealistic. My country. My first love. The child is too great a reminder of the mother. Grudge, unfair to be sure, not something I'm proud of, but there just the same. Nothing accelerates the course of this illness like pregnancy, that's what the doctor said, Sylvia, do you understand? She wanted an explanation. She'd get one. She'd get several. She could take her pick.

Edward started the long walk home. Why had he let himself wander so far? A mile, easily, probably more. And most of it uphill. The sense that he hadn't quite gotten at what he'd set out to get at, or rather that what he'd gotten at didn't quite satisfy, nagged, made Edward irritable, fidgety. He took a sip of whiskey—was it a bad bottle? a bad batch?—and was about to run through his reasons for doing what he'd done yet again . . . but couldn't bear to. They were beginning to bore him in their particulars and he was going to have to go through the lot one more time, soon, for Sylvia. He attempted to assuage his rest-lessness by congratulating himself, stubbornly, grimly, for hav-ing had the courage to face the truth of why he'd abandoned his daughter.

He hadn't done any such thing, of course. He'd faced *some* truths, yes, all right, but not *the* truth. He hadn't searched his soul so much as he'd taken a guided tour of it. His grief for Agnes was real. His grief for Agnes had not caused him to do what he'd done to Maura.

The truth wasn't dramatic. Or subtle. The truth wasn't what often passes for literary. It was simple, solid, workaday. As rooted in the real world as a missing spindle on a porch railing. A bicycle jack-knifed on a sidewalk. Laundry left on the line overnight. Edward abandoned Maura because he didn't want the work of raising her.

He knew it too well, the work.

For six years he'd taken care of a sick wife and a young child. And was expected to earn a living all the while, too. Was ex-pected, anyway, by Sadie and by the world at large, to attempt to earn a living. Had a whole passel of jobs, part-time, tempo-rary, overtime, leave of absence, full-time, fill in, how's your typing, Mr. Devlin, ever work on one of these, Ed? Yes, yes, there were nurses and baby-sitters, the odd generous neighbor, a relation or two, friends who found their friendships sorely tested—Can the baby stay through the weekend, do you think?—but when all was said and done it was Edward and Ed-ward alone who was responsible.

Edward who did the work.

He'd lived inside a vortex of demands, exhaustion, guilt, worry, mania, coffee, cigarettes, hopeful prognoses, dire ones, claustrophobia, tedium, rage, love, and resentment. There were sponge baths, alcohol rubs, prams, collapsible wheelchairs, soiled sheets and dirty diapers, ointments, broths to be heated, peas to be mashed between the tines of a fork, nails to be clipped, shoes buckled, chest plasters prepared, applied, removed, dis-carded, made over again. Edward didn't stop moving from the time he opened his eyes in the morning, if it was true morning and not three-thirty a.m. or some such time when either invalid or infant cried out, literally, for his attention. How many times did he rush to the crib or bedside only to find the occupant sound asleep, which meant it was the other one wanting him and off he'd go. Wring this, fold that, lift, level, shake, smooth, soothe, put on, take off, rock, burp, squeeze, fill, refill, heat, cool, empty.

Imperatives all.

When it got to be too much, when he felt he could not respond to one more demand, could not *do* one more thing, which toward the end, the last couple of years, happened about ten times a day, he'd stop what he was doing (he was always, always doing), close his eyes, and use every bit of energy he had left to suppress a scream. Enough, he'd have screamed if he let himself scream. E-nough. Finished. Over. Done. I can't take another minute, I want my life back, I get to live, too, I give up, I'm going, I'm gone. But at whom could he shout? His beloved wife, who was suffering, who was dying? His tiny daughter, who seemed to grow more and more leery of the world around her, who looked permanently spooked? (His doing, he knew. Despite all his efforts, the one was dying and the other one could hardly be said to be thriving. He was failing on all fronts. It was business as usual in Edward-land.) Truth be told he often gave in to the impulse to shout when he was alone with the baby. What did she know? Whom could she tell? She had no basis for comparison, had no idea how babies are supposed to be talked to. Qu-iet, he'd bellow. Be quiet, at the top of his lungs, heedless for the moment of his neighbors, embarrassed later in the hallway or on the elevator. *Lie down this minute. I'll give you something to cry about.* Never when Agnes was home. He never let Agnes hear him shout. *Go to sleep, God damn you. L-i-i-i-e down.*

He'd wanted to get free, to be free.

He wanted to sleep for a week. He wanted to concern himself with himself. Wanted to be able, mother of God, to hear himself think. To spend the money he earned on himself. Sleep late when he felt like it. Play cards all night if the opportunity arose. Get up and walk out the door when he took a notion. Himself. He himself.

When it became clear that Agnes was dying, really dying this time, he'd seen a way out and he'd taken it, though he hadn't admitted that to himself at the time and didn't now.

Too bad.

The setting was so apt.

The setting was perfect.

A Paterson side street at eleven-thirty p.m. Barely half the streetlights working. The other half taken out by vandals or by time. No moon. Here was a place where the real reason for doing something could be told.

I saw a way out and I took it.

Now we're getting somewhere, Paterson would have said. *Now* you're talking.

Don't come around Paterson with your fancy explanations. After the loss of my beloved, you say, haltingly, as if you're holding back tears, and perhaps you are. Perhaps your performance is so convincing you half buy it yourself. You are moved.

You may be. Paterson isn't. Paterson rolls her eyes.

I know it isn't fair but some part of me blamed the child, you try, watching now for some sign of sympathy.

Paterson snorts. Instructs one of her legion of bartenders to be mean to you, to take a shot at your wife. Extinguishes half her streetlights. Covers her moon. Puts rusted bicycles in your path.

Give Paterson an interpretation of events that purports to condemn but actually exonerates? She has no choice but to withhold her falls. She knows that standing before a seventy-seven-foot-high waterfall isn't likely to draw a confession out of a man like Edward. Or, rather, standing before a seventy-seven-foot-high waterfall is too likely to draw a confession for a crime he hasn't committed from a man like Edward. A crime of passion. Edward's crime was not a crime of passion. It was a crime of exhaustion. And the coverup of that crime of exhaustion. It was the ordinary failure of an ordinary man. Burdened, tired, selfish, tired, more or less well-meaning so long as the sacrifices required aren't too great, tired, ashamed, haunted, tired. Tired. Free.

chapter 33

Sylvia stared at the ceiling and listened to Edward's recitation. They were lying in bed. He'd joined her there when
he came in and after several minutes of painful silence he
started testifying in his own defense. His voice was flat. There
were no breaks, no pauses. Sylvia listened and made small
sounds of commiseration and understanding. She commiser-
ated, she did not understand. At a certain point she realized,
she *knew*, that she'd have to accept Edward's abandoning his
daughter or lose him. She closed her eyes. When he began to
repeat himself, when in his droning voice he started over at the
beginning, she put her hand on his thigh and said, "I understand now. I won't mention her again, I swear."

In the morning she did her best to behave normally to let
Edward know that her retreat was genuine. It was clear that he
was working hard, too, making conversation, letting it be known
that he wanted nothing more than that they put what had happened behind them and get back to the business of being newlyweds. They couldn't quite meet each other's eyes, though.
Nerves were raw, vision bleary. They hadn't slept more than a
couple of hours. Edward was hungover and Sylvia was wondering if it was too late to cancel the ten o'clock interview she'd
scheduled with an applicant for the housekeeping job.

They tried. Husband and wife both tried. Sylvia went ahead
with her plans to spruce up the house and Edward praised her
efforts lavishly. The wedding picture in its silver frame was

placed at the center of the mantelpiece in the front parlor. ("Good there. Perfect." "I thought so.") Sylvia met Edward for lunch downtown a couple of times and they both got a boost, short-lived but welcome, from going public at long last, making their couplehood official. They ate dinner at home most nights. After a brief hiatus, four nights of lying side by side but not touching, they began having sex more frequently than they had before and at least as passionately. Each was a little strange to the other in the wake of what had happened, what had been revealed. This strangeness, begging to be overcome, made physical contact necessary and enticing.

Despite their best efforts, a pall spread over the house, a persistent and pervasive sadness. Attempts to dislodge it only added to the strain. Sylvia was dreaming of the squalling baby again and feeling burdened and guilty when she woke beside Edward afterward.

But her mind was made up. Edward's behavior toward his daughter was none of her business. People have pasts. Edward had his reasons for doing what he'd done. Who was she to judge?

She found herself crying at odd times during the day, in her car especially. She could hardly turn the key without getting weepy. She wished that her sister was alive, nothing less than that, nothing more subtle. "You'd be thirty-two now and I'd call you up and say how are things with you, honey, can you get away for a couple of days, do you want to go to the other house with me?" The other house, what she and Ruth had called the shore house as little girls. There'd been one house and there'd been the other.

A few times, much to her dismay, Sylvia found herself wondering about Fitzgibbon. How was he doing? Had he settled yet? Where? It seemed so strange that she might, that she very likely would, go the rest of her life without ever laying eyes on him again. She'd heard talk for years about the superior business climate in southeastern Pennsylvania. Had he settled there already, already started a new business? She didn't think so. She had a hunch that instead he'd wound up back in New York, back where he'd started. She imagined him living in a swank apartment and spending his evenings with various women, each of whom thought she had the inside track. In a year or two, perhaps, she thought in an attempt to discount the importance of wondering about Fitzgibbon in the first place, if Wilkins knew where he was, she'd drop him a note, wish him well.

She had absolutely no inclination toward Agnes, no desire to look at the photograph. She didn't think about Agnes at all, in fact, except insofar as she realized she wasn't thinking about Agnes. A good sign, she thought. Looking back on her response to seeing the stranger who resembled Agnes on the street and on the visit to Bellevue, Sylvia wasn't sure what she'd been about in either case. She couldn't remember what had prompted her to behave as she had, had no access in her current frame of mind to the urgency she'd felt only weeks before.

She was ashamed of herself for attacking Edward the way she had, thought she'd handled the whole matter very badly. Perhaps if she'd waited a couple of months, given him time to settle into being married again, if she hadn't admitted to reading Sadie's letters but instead had simply told Edward, gently, gently, that she'd welcome his daughter if he should ever decide to bring her over and left it at that, things would have turned out differently. Nothing good had come of the approach she had taken, of that she was sure. She hadn't been able to persuade Edward to do the right thing. All she'd done was force him to dig his heels in, hunker down in his opposition, formulate that turgid, terrifying argument in his own defense. It was impossible to imagine him changing his mind now. And the godawful gloom? How long would it last? How long until the funk lifted?

Edward was certain that his own low spirits were a response to Sylvia's. He'd feel better if he could get her to come around. He doubled and redoubled his efforts to be a good husband. Made a point of being animated when he came in at night. Brought her small presents, a new hairbrush, bath oil, a subscription to *House Beautiful*. When Sylvia's mood didn't improve, when Edward found himself confronting her pained and preoccupied expression, dull eyes, and pursed lips, resentment began to percolate.

He hated knowing that he'd disappointed her, that her opinion of him was not what it had once been.

Finding that sitting on the porch in the evenings was less and less tolerable, the Devlins began taking walks after dinner. The dearth of conversation was less noticeable, less troubling, when they were walking. And there was comfort in being if not arm in arm then at least side by side, taking in the same vistas, such as they were (ah, Paterson), in heading, for better or worse, in the same direction.

chapter 34

It was a perfectly ordinary evening. Sadie and Bell sat in the drawing room reading a newspaper and knitting respectively.

"Will you have something?"

"For my shoulder. Bad again with the damp. Just a tipple."

"Do you good."

Sadie had discovered that a nip before bed made for more vivid dreams. If it also meant waking at four a.m. with nerves and a headache, so be it.

After a time Bell started in sighing, which meant she would be going to bed soon. (Why can't she just go, Sadie thought. Why the same fuss every bloody night?) Having finished her drink and her sighing ("Ah, well. Well, well.") Bell put her knitting down, looked around, said, "That's it for me, I'm afraid. I'm off to bed."

"Right."

"Don't sit up too late, will you?"

"When I'm ready, I'll go."

"You don't have to get ornery. I just . . . it's been a long day."

"Good night, Bell."

When Sadie was sure that Bell was out of earshot, she poured herself another drink, coughing to cover the glug-glug of the whiskey just in case. One more, taken quickly for maximum effect, and off she went.

Sadie fell right to sleep and found herself immediately in Agnes's presence. They were girls again. Rather the context was that of their girlhood, the texture, the tone, but Agnes looked as she had at the end, gaunt and pale and nightgowned. And Sadie was herself as she knew herself to be now, heavy-limbed, big-bosomed. Agnes's manner, though, her demeanor, was playful, was charming. She was as she'd been at her best, her very best. She was a delight. And, even better, she seemed delighted to be with Sadie. Sadie looked at Agnes and Agnes smiled prettily and with that smile wasn't sick anymore, was young again, fresh-faced, pink-skinned, clear-eyed, glossy-haired, fourteen, fifteen, *young*. Sadie offered Agnes a sweet, a chocolate wrapped in red paper, and felt the candy leave her hand. And then—miracle!—Agnes pulled something from the folds of her nightgown, something for Sadie, something she wanted Sadie to have.

"What's that?"

"For you." Agnes's voice was young, too, was her girl's voice, her voice before Edward, before America, before TB, before disappointment and regret. "For you, Sadie."

"Give it to me then. Give it." Sadie tried but couldn't get hold of whatever it was, something real, something much desired. Her fingers closed around nothing, around air. Her hand had never felt so empty.

"Take it, Sadie."

"I'm trying to. I can't. . . . I'm trying to take it."

"There."

What was it? As is often the case in dreams, it was the lack, the longing, the grasping that mattered. It was a candy or a locket or a bleeding heart. It was what have you. It was in Sadie's hand.

"Come with me now. Will you?"

"Anywhere. I'll go anywhere with you."

Sadie put one foot and then the other on the floor. She stood and walked toward Agnes and, still dreaming, watched herself walking toward Agnes.

She was on her way down the stairs when Rex, wet nose on her ankle, muscular doggy bulk between her shins, got in the way. She lost her footing. Trying frantically, clumsily, to disentangle herself, she missed the second step altogether and came down too hard on the edge of the third, bumped down the fourth, fifth, and sixth, right shoulder smashing along the spokes of the banister. She heard Rex howl as she lost the battle to right herself, to stop herself falling. Her jaw hit a hard edge and she heard, against a backdrop of frantic barking, a loud crack like wood splitting and felt a sickening sensation, electricity loosed at the base of her skull, a shower of sparks, a short-circuiting.

chapter 35

Sylvia looked up when she heard the creak of the hinge on the metal plate that covered the mail slot. She went into the front hall and bent to pick up a magazine and several envelopes, wondering for the umpteenth time why she'd never bothered to get one of those wire baskets, a mail catcher. There was something unpleasant about scooping mail off the floor. She hoped as always to find something unexpected, something personal and diverting, among the bills and advertisements. When she came across the letter from Ireland she assumed it was from Sadie until she noticed that the handwriting, though feminine, was unfamiliar. It was daintier than Sadie's, less vigorous. Must be the other sister, Sylvia thought, what's her name? Funny she'd write now after all this time.

Sylvia put the mail on the table in the front hall for Edward, just as she'd always done for Fitzgibbon. She rather liked identifying common threads like this one. She'd always put the mail on the front table for Fitzgibbon to review when he came in and now she did the same for Edward. Edward would stand, exactly as Fitz used to, flipping through whatever there was to be flipped through, wearing a suit and tie and a distracted expression, a man—any man—in transit between his work and home lives. That this very minor domestic ritual had survived the dissolution of one marriage and the making of another pleased Sylvia, allowed her to believe that marriage had an inherent structure. The high drama, the disruption of her affair, divorce, and remarriage fell away and what remained was a simple but satisfying household routine: a wife putting mail in a particular place for her husband to find when he came in at night.

Sylvia was about to head into the kitchen to have a word with Mary, the young woman she'd hired to come in three afternoons a week, when the Irish letter caught her eye and she picked it up for another look. The handwriting was definitely not Sadie's. Sylvia had an uncannily good memory for handwriting. If she happened to get a card or letter from a friend she hadn't heard from in years, she always knew the identity of the writer instantly. Looking now at the hand that was so clearly not Sadie's, Sylvia felt a twinge of misgiving and hoped the letter wouldn't upset the delicate balance that had been established between herself and Edward in recent days. They seemed to have gotten through the worst of the aftermath of the battle over Maura. While the atmosphere in the house was not what it had been before, it was at least improving. The sadness persisted, no getting around that, no pretending otherwise, but it was not as potent as it had been. There were distinct breaks in it now. After an especially long walk one evening a week or so earlier, Sylvia and Edward had gone straight to bed and slept until ten the following morning. They woke to a steady rain and decided, the weather being what it was, that they might just as well stay in bed. Hot coffee, bread and butter, damp newspapers. Pajamas off and back on again. A long nap. Hot showers. A drive way out into the country through the pouring rain. Edward's head on Sylvia's shoulder on the way back.

It's probably nothing, Sylvia thought, rubbing the tip of her index finger over Edward's name on the envelope then heading into the kitchen.

"Afternoon, Mrs. Devlin. I know the stairs need a good sweeping and I'm going to get to them as soon as I wipe these counters. Anything I can't stand it's crumbs and mess on the counter."

Sylvia heard the gentle rebuke in Mary's words—breakfast dishes had been left on the counter amidst coffee-cup rings and smears of butter—and didn't mind it a bit, welcomed it, in fact, was glad there was another woman in the house, a woman with a round face and intelligent eyes who genuinely cared about the condition of the countertops and not only noticed that the stairs needed sweeping but would actually sweep them as well. Sylvia had hired Mary because of her outspoken manner, even though in other respects Mary hadn't been a particularly sensible choice. She was twenty, married a year, childless. She'd never done domestic work before and was doing it now only because her husband had been laid off. Sylvia knew that in all likelihood Mary wouldn't last a year. Her husband would go back to work or she'd get pregnant or both. But Sylvia had had considerations other than the purely practical in mind when she'd made her selection. Mary had vitality. She was animated and direct, exactly the sort of person we need around here just now, Sylvia had thought. "When can you start?" she'd asked five minutes into the interview.

"That's fine, Mary. Good. And, listen, don't use Comet in my bathtub upstairs, all right? It's too gritty. And would you change the sheets in the master bedroom?" Sylvia heard the front door open, heard Edward come in. "Hello," he called. "Anybody home?"

"There's Mr. Devlin," Mary said. "He's home early today, huh?"

"He is," Sylvia said, smiling. She liked this girl, this observant and forthright girl, liked the sound of Edward's hello, too. He *was* home early, which meant he'd ducked out of the office, seen an opportunity to spend some time with her and taken it. We can go for a drive, she thought, have dinner out, maybe see a movie.

When Sylvia got to the front hall she found Edward reading the Irish letter and looking stricken.

"What's the matter?" Sylvia said, gripped by a fear that something had happened to Maura, something awful and irreversible. "Edward, what's wrong?"

"It's Sadie."

"What?"

"She's fallen down the stairs."

"Oh, no. Is she all right?"

"She's dead. Broke her neck. In the middle of the night. She was dead by the time Bell got to her."

"Oh, my God. Edward. I'm sorry."

Edward handed Sylvia the letter then took off up the stairs.

Sylvia was trembling. The death of a sister, Edward's sister, anybody's sister, panicked her, made her feel she was in the presence of great and enduring loss, calamity. Fallen down the stairs? People fall down stairs and twist ankles, Sylvia thought, bruise shins. A broken neck, for God's sake?

Keeping an ear out for Edward, wondering if she should go after him or give him his privacy, Sylvia sat down on the stairs and read Bell's letter. The first paragraph contained the news of Sadie's death, the dates of the fall and the funeral. She's buried already, Sylvia thought. How sad for Edward, how unsettling. Why hadn't Bell sent a telegram? They're a cold bunch, aren't they?

The second paragraph drove all thoughts of Sadie out of Sylvia's mind. "You ought not to have left Maura with us in the first place," Bell had written. "Sadie and I were in no position to raise a child. Now I'm alone I won't even consider it. You will undoubtedly think this harsh, and perhaps it is, but understand that if you don't agree to take your daughter in, send for her, come and collect her, she will be placed in an orphanage as soon as I find one willing to take her. I've already begun to make inquiries. This is not a bluff, Edward. Write or wire me and let me know what you intend to do. If I don't hear from you in a month's time I will proceed exactly as I've described."

Sylvia looked up to find Mary drying her hands on a dish towel.

"Bad news?"

"Not entirely, no."

Mary nodded matter-of-factly. It seemed to come as no surprise to her that in the ordinary course of events a letter might bring news that sends one member of a household running and leaves another looking cautiously hopeful.

chapter 36

Edward was waiting for his bus home, having slogged his way through the day's work, dazedly adding a page or two to the final report on the traffic circle. It was finished. The traffic circle on Route 46 was up and running. On the first day of its operation Edward had taken Sylvia for a ride around it, and around it, and around it. They'd been cut off once—"Watch, Edward, *watch!*"—had cut other drivers off twice. "What an ingenious design," Sylvia had said gamely, consolingly, over the din of blaring horns.

Since receiving Bell's letter a couple of days before, Edward hadn't slept much. Sadie was his older sister. She'd been a part of his world, a small part to be sure and one that had shrunk over time but a part all the same, for as long as he'd been aware that he was himself and the world was itself. But what he was feeling at the crowded bus stop, what he'd been feeling during the hours he couldn't sleep, wasn't bereavement. It was regret.

Sadie had been a character, a caricature, a piece of work, a pip. Her orneriness, avarice, eccentricities made for amusing anecdotes. Though most people, Edward included, were afraid of Sadie face-to-face—tough old bird, sergeant-major—behind her back they made jokes. Edward had recalled and regretted and couldn't stop regretting how Sadie had been teased about her brief stay at nursing school in London, her one foray out of Omagh—Sadie a nurse, Sarie Gamp sober, God help us, had been Edward's contribution to the evening's entertainment—

and how she'd taken it all as if it was her due. Looking into the face of a grey-haired woman at the bus stop, Edward remembered Sadie's hands trembling when, finished unpacking, she'd closed her valise and slid it under her bed. She was, he thought, after a quick and familiar computation, his own age plus six, forty-two when she died. How could that be? She'd seemed fifty-two at least. Even sixty.

He'd never once imagined her dying, he realized. Death seemed an inappropriate end to Sadie's life. Out of proportion. Entirely too serious. Too dramatic. Too grand. If all there'd been to Sadie was what he and the others had thought, Sadie shouldn't have *died*. She should have gone off to the grocery store or the post office and mysteriously, or, rather, not mysteriously but matter-of-factly, amusingly, anecdotally, disassembled somewhere along the way. Trailed off. Wandered away from this life, her life, such as it was, such as it had appeared to be, somewhere between the bank and the butcher shop.

Except that wasn't what had happened. Except that she'd been alone on the staircase in the middle of the night. Oh, Sadie. Oh, Sarah. Stumbling. Losing your footing.

I'm sorry, Sadie. Sorry that I never bothered to get to know you better. Because I liked you. I did. Or always meant to. Always sensed the presence of something whole and compelling, the beams and girders of your true self, beneath the bluster and self-parody. In some vague and irrational way, some fundamentally lazy way, I assumed I'd get around to knowing you sooner or later. One of these days.

A bus appeared in the distance and Edward leaned forward and squinted. It wasn't his.

He hadn't lost sight of the fact that he had a decision to make, a decision to announce, anyway. It wasn't just thoughts of Sadie that had been keeping him up at night.

Another bus, his. He climbed on board, found a seat, rested his forehead against the cool window glass.

A subway train at night when Maura was a year and a half or two and overtired, fussy. Settle down, baby girl, shhhh, shhhh. Embarrassed in front of the other riders. Acutely aware of their displeasure. Patience going. Patience gone. Fantasizing about putting his hand over the baby's mouth to stop her crying. And then, sweet Jesus, she'd given over, given in. "Legs around, head down," he told her as was his custom, as was their custom. (He'd forgotten they'd had customs but they had, of course, dozens of them.) She put her legs around his waist and her head on his shoulder and fell asleep. That train could have run on forever. He could have sat holding the sweet sodden weight of his baby girl sleeping forever.

She'd been left with the elderly couple across the hall for the weekend. We'd be glad to have her, the old lady said, how much trouble can one little girl be? The apartment smelled of mothballs and, faintly, of urine. The old lady confessed that when her husband got up to go to the bathroom at night he sometimes got confused, lost his bearings, had more than once relieved himself in a corner. Dropping Maura off on Friday afternoon, mad at her because she'd been snarly all morning, detecting the unmistakable tang of urine, Edward had quipped to himself that the odor ought not to bother Maura much since until so recently she'd been incontinent herself. (Medical terminology had worked its way into his vocabulary by then.) On Monday afternoon he found the old people glassy-eyed and silent, standing on either side of Maura against the wall opposite the elevator. One little girl, it had turned out, could be mountains of trouble. "I was waiting for you," Maura said, bolting, making a run for it, for him, arms outstretched. "Hours," the old lady said. "She's had us out here for hours."

She couldn't have been more than a few months old, small enough still to be carried in his arms while he picked up a couple of cans of condensed milk, went to the post office and the bank. A beautiful day in early summer, warm, windy. She'd pushed against him, arched her back, looked up at the blue sky and the green leaves, grinned for the first time in her life. Even he, harried, sleep-deprived on the heels of another bad night (both baby and mother had been up more than they'd been down), had not been able to ignore the rapture on her face as she saw what there was to be seen. There you go, he said, and kept saying because it had seemed all he had to offer as a father—I can recommend blue skies and white clouds without reservation, warm days in early summer are not to be missed. See, Maura, he'd said. There you go, there you go, there you go.

Edward got off the bus at his corner and headed up the hill toward home. He found Sylvia sitting in the front parlor.

"Shall we send for her then?"

Sylvia put her hand on her heart. "I was so afraid."

"Well, you needn't have been. I never had any intention of letting her . . . I've made the arrangements. Everything's taken care of," he said, pulling something from his breast pocket. "This came today."

It was a receipt from a steamship company for the sale of a one-way ticket for an unescorted minor between Southampton and New York. Said ticket had been sent by certified mail to the address in Northern Ireland as per the customer's instructions.

chapter 37

Sylvia stood in the doorway of the second-floor guest room with arms crossed and eyes narrowed, trying to decide what would stay and what had to go. Despite the graceful arrangement of the furniture, the clear morning light, the taupes and tans and whites, the bits of black here and there for definition and contrast, the room felt dreary, uninhabited, close, all but airless in the way of rooms that rarely get used.

She took the curtains down, rods and all, and draped them over the banister in the hallway, where they would remain until they could be handed off to the only dry cleaner in town who could be trusted with silk. She rolled up the rug, tied it with an old scarf, hoisted it over one shoulder, and carried it up to the attic. She put the candlesticks, the half-dozen books, the clock, the several vases, and the two-hundred-year-old cup and saucer that had always seemed too fussy by half into a cardboard box. She pulled the bedspread off and took it downstairs to be washed so that it would be clean when it went into the cedar closet.

She stood in the center of the room, arms crossed again, eyes narrowed, then went upstairs to put on pants and flat shoes and to tie back her hair.

She pulled the mattress and box spring out of the frame and dragged them one at a time down the hall. Straining, heaving, sweating, swearing, she managed to get every piece of furniture out so that by noon the room was empty but for the overhead light fixture and the wallpaper.

Which was next to go. An hour and a half in the hardware store. A how-to book. Drop cloths. A bucket and a sponge. A putty knife. Masking tape. She went home and spread the drop cloths and laid out her tools for an early start the following morning. She read and reread "Stripping and Scraping Old Paper." When she woke up the muscles in her shoulders hurt so badly she thought she might have done some real damage moving all that furniture by herself, might have pulled or even torn something, but three aspirin and a scalding-hot shower loosened her up.

The wallpaper was stubborn, tenacious. It didn't seem to want to come down. A day and a half of soaking and scraping. One room. One focus. One world. Sponge into water and out again. Blade over plaster. Wet wallpaper tearing. Her own footsteps and throat clearings. The sound of herself swallowing coffee while she looked out over the rim of the cup at what she'd accomplished and all that was left to do.

There were several trips back to the hardware store, where she felt wild-eyed, where the voices of other customers and clerks sounded peculiar, bright and loud, where the vast array of merchandise for sale, bins of nails, fat books of wallpaper samples, an entire wall of paintbrushes and rollers, made her anxious, so many choices, so many decisions to make. She bought a second putty knife when the first seemed too inclined to nick the plaster beneath. A bigger sponge. And then a garden sprayer. Diluted ethyl alcohol works better than plain water, the clerk said. What? You're taking wallpaper down, aren't you? Ethyl alcohol works better than plain water. Now you tell me? Anything else I should know? The telephone number of a professional, probably. Very funny. How much do I owe you? You want to start a tab, Mrs. Fitzgibbon? It's Devlin, Mrs. Devlin, and yes, go ahead, start a tab.

Another whole day scrubbing the bare walls with buckets of hot water into which increasing amounts of Lestoil were poured, a judicious couple of capfuls at first, a third of a bottle toward the end. Less toil my foot, Sylvia thought, eyes burning and tearing. The solution found its way inside her rubber gloves and stung the places she'd nicked during the scraping.

Paint won't adhere to plaster unless it's good and dry, the clerk warned. Wait a day or two. Rush this step and you'll be sorry. And set up a fan in there while you're at it.

Determined to be patient, to wait as long as it took, Sylvia pulled a heavy box from her closet shelf. Her color wheel, her sample books, notes and sketchpads, lists, business cards, swatches, dozens and dozens of paint chips. She sat against one wall in the empty guest room, favorite pencil in hand. I'm eight years old, she said to herself. My mother is dead and I've been shunted around the last couple of years. Now I've come here to this big house and they tell me this is my room. She wondered, briefly, how she would appear to a frightened eight-year-old. Big? Deep-voiced? Would she look like a rival, an interloper, a disappointment? She missed the emptying out, the stripping and scrubbing. Emptying a room and then making it emptier still, taking it all the way back to bare walls is easy compared to this, she thought. What sort of room would I want?

Not coming up with much in the way of an answer, thinking she really didn't know the first thing about eight-year-olds, finding it impossible to believe that she'd ever been one herself— eight?—she went downstairs to get another cup of coffee and wound up chatting with Mary, knowing all the while that pad and pencil were waiting and that she ought to be getting back to them. "It's a lot of work, no? Why don't you hire somebody? My husband's brother paints and hangs wallpaper. You want me to call him?"

She sketched tentatively at first, then confidently, then tentatively again. She erased a lot. She turned the page and started over. She got up to measure the width and the length, putting one foot in front of the other and counting.

Over and over again she had to rein in her tendency toward cliché, had to squelch her inclinations toward ruffles and canopy beds and miniature rocking chairs with dolls piled in them. She didn't want to wind up with a cloying fantasy of a girl's room, a room that an actual girl, a flesh-and-blood person, especially one exhausted from a recent solo ocean crossing not to mention the succession of hardships that had come before that, would almost certainly feel overwhelmed by, would, Sylvia thought, feel flat and sad and small in the way people do when they're thrust into hackneyed and bloodless constructs that have precious little to do with lived life.

After a good bit of sketching and coffee drinking and poring over her notes and gazing out the window in a kind of stupor, Sylvia determined that she wanted a room that was welcoming, yes, that suggested permanence and the possibility of letting one's guard down (how vigilant this girl must be, she thought, how watchful) but that had, most important, a degree of neutrality, sufficient open space, a measure of the blank slate, room enough for the particular identity of its occupant to manifest.

She painted the walls and ceiling a soft white, white with a faint pinkish undertone, a blush. She bought a rug with small red and indigo flowers and green leaves against a beige background. A single bed, remembering how as a child she'd liked a tight fit. A double dresser, plenty of drawers and all of them low to the ground. A big, round borderless mirror, a perfect circle, hung so that an eight-year-old could see herself in it. A child's desk, a blotter and pencil cup, two brass lamps, a set of bookends, a small pitcher that sat inside a small basin for the mantel, a bookshelf painted to pick up the purple-blue flowers in the rug.

She went to a toy store and, remembering the joy of being let loose in such a place when she was small, not feeling the joy, exactly, but remembering, feeling the ghost of her old response— Look at all this stuff! Let me at it!—had to rein in her desire to buy and buy and buy, fill the bloody room with toys. See? You're welcome here, you're wanted. Look what all I got for you. How can you help but be happy here? She settled, finally, on a set of jacks in a nice leather pouch with a drawstring (she had herself been a passionate and agile jacks player) and a beautiful if somber doll in a navy blue coat with brass buttons.

There, she thought, looking around the room after she'd put sheets on the bed and daisies in the pitcher on the mantel. She hoped she hadn't been too restrained, hoped the final effect was soothing and not stark. Anyway, it's done and with no time to spare, she thought. This time tomorrow Maura will be here.

chapter 38

She was summoned not from the refectory but from French class. Uncle Joseph sat far forward on the sofa in the visitors' parlor, hat in one hand, car keys in the other.

"Hello, Maura. How big you've gotten. You've grown six inches since I saw you last."

"Your uncle's come to take you home," Sister said. "There's been an accident, I'm afraid. Your aunt Sarah—"

"Sadie, she was always Sadie."

"Right. Your aunt Sadie's had a terrible accident. She's passed on. She's no longer with us."

"Aunt Sadie?"

"Dead, I'm afraid," Joseph said.

"God rest her soul."

Maura recognized the car as she got into it. It was the one she'd wet herself in the night Agnes died. Afraid Joseph was going to mention the incident, tell her he hadn't forgotten what she'd done, she began to prepare a defense. I was younger then. I'd never do anything like that now.

"Your auntie Bell is waiting, of course. She's eager to see you again."

Maura turned to Joseph, flat-eyed.

"It's been a terrible loss for her. She and Sadie lived together all their lives. We're all counting on you to look after her. She'll need looking after now, won't she?"

"How long till I go back to school?"

"Ah, right. School."

"How long?"

"We'll see about that. Not straightaway, anyway. You shouldn't be thinking of school just now, Maura. You're needed at home."

The bloody dog nearly exploded. Was stationed at the window when Joseph pulled up in front of Sadie's house. Jumped into the air, all four paws off the ground. Yipped. Ran out of the room and straight back in again as if Maura's presence was too intense a pleasure to be borne without breaks.

Bell took Maura to Sadie's grave. The headstone hadn't been placed yet. They stood before a patch of fresh dirt. "I miss her something awful," Bell said. Maura, embarrassed, looked at her shoes, made her eyes wide. "God knows she was difficult, a difficult woman to be sure, but it's nothing compared to living alone."

The circumstances of Sadie's death were titillating. The death of somebody Maura had known well (she thought) but hadn't loved excited her, conferred a certain status, a certain sophistication. She was a person to whom things happened. Around whom things happened. She was intrigued by the suddenness of it. Sadie hadn't been sick. Had gone to bed as she always did. Got up in the night. Tripped. And died.

The staircase was suddenly so much more than a means of getting from one floor to another. It was a setting in its own right now, a moody and awesome one. Rex wouldn't go near it. The second floor was forever after off limits to Rex. He didn't wait outside Maura's bedroom door the way he used to. He caught up with her in the kitchen and said good night there as well. "You going up?" his expression seemed to say. "I'll see you tomorrow then, first thing." Maura walked up and down the stairs, scaring herself (it was here, it happened right here), noting scratches and splintery patches and convincing herself that they hadn't been there before. She imagined telling certain girls at school the story. They would be scared, spooked, and she, worldly, knowing, would explain that things like old ladies falling down stairs in the middle of the night and breaking their

necks happen all the time in the real world of adults coming
and going.

"I've good news for you," Bell said.

Maura slid onto a kitchen chair, scratched Rex where he liked
to be scratched, a spot just above his tail. She expected to be
told when she'd be taken back to school. Tomorrow? The day
after?

"Your father's sent word, finally. A telegram, too. Never one
to do things by halves, your father. Good news. You're going to
live with him from now on. You're going back to America. You'll
have to make the crossing all by yourself, mind, but you're a big
girl now, aren't you? You're not afraid."

All thoughts of Cavan evaporated. The memories very nearly
did. Cavan ceased to exist as far as Maura was concerned.
"When?"

"You're in such a hurry to leave us, are you? Do you hear
that, Rexie? She can't wait to be gone."

"When?"

"Soon enough. You're not afraid then? You're not afraid of
making the crossing all by yourself?"

They could have given her a rowboat and two oars, pointed
vaguely in the direction of America, and she'd have been off.
And might have made it, too. If desire was what it took. If will.
If longing.

Nobody bothered to mention, then or later, that Edward had
remarried. Bringing up the existence of the current wife, it was
feared, might invite talk of the former one. And nobody wanted
that, God knows, especially since Maura seemed to have gotten
over all *that* (the death of her mother) so nicely. Children
bounce back, don't they? They don't know half of what goes on
around them and remember even less. And lucky they are, too.
I wish I didn't remember so much. It's not our place anyway.
Not our responsibility. Edward should be the one to tell Maura
about . . . What's her name? Sylvia. Sylvia, right. Jewish. Divorced. Jesus, Mary, and Joseph. Sadie wasn't surprised, I'll tell
you. When the news came. Sadie said he'd landed with his ass
in a tub of butter. Mr. Heartbroken. Mr. Carrying On.

chapter 39

She has a second-class cabin all to herself. Two beds, a tiny bathroom that seems to have been designed with a child in mind, a narrow table, and two chairs. Every morning the ship's nanny, a blowsy woman, well past fifty, comes and gets her for breakfast or sends one of the other two unescorted minors, black-haired brothers, eleven and thirteen, who are resentful of even Mrs. Cunningham's vague authority and utterly uninterested in Maura. Every evening after dinner and whatever entertainment is on the roster for children, a puppet show, a sing-along (the brothers roll their dark eyes, the brothers are disdainful), she's deposited back at her cabin, told to lock the door, and sleep tight. He's waiting for me, she thinks, falling asleep at night. He's waiting, waking up in the morning.

"One day less than when you asked me yesterday, Maura. There's puzzles and things in the box there, see it? Pick one and sit yourself down and play nice, will you? Go on."

chapter 40

Sylvia's breathing is rapid and shallow. Her hands and feet are cold. Cold feet, she thinks, where the expression comes from, what people mean when they say so-and-so's got cold feet. She feels the way she felt dressing for her weddings. Something momentous is happening, is underway, something life-altering, the air is charged with it, electric, there's a buzz in her ears, she keeps wanting to stop and look in the mirror, look herself in the eye and say, Today's the day. She knows that when she looks back a year from now, ten years, twenty, there will be the time before this day and the time after it, this morning will happen only once and it's happening now, but still the tasks of dressing must be completed, stockings put on one at a time, seams straightened, lipstick applied, lipstick blotted. She's glad to be busy but still there's something incongruous about doing what she does every day, dressing, one button, another, and still another, on a day that for better or worse will be absolutely unlike any other.

She laid out her clothes the night before because she knew she'd have to get up at the crack of dawn, that's how Edward phrased it and so how Sylvia did, too, now, and because she hadn't been sleepy and because, after putting daisies in the small white pitcher and making up the bed she'd wanted to get something else ready, to go on getting ready for Maura's arrival.

A periwinkle-blue suit, dull and delicious raw silk, a cream-colored blouse, crisp cotton, neutral stockings, black shoes and bag. She wants to look nice, nice the way children use that word, nice, the polar opposite of mean. Is she nice or mean? Everybody is one or the other. She wants to look bright, optimistic, pretty but not distant, like a nice teacher or soon-to-be favorite aunt, the new wife of a favorite uncle, aunt so-and-so is nice, the new teacher, nice or mean? Nice, definitely nice from the looks of her. Setting out underpants and bra and girdle, she wondered how much attention eight-year-olds pay to the way somebody is dressed. Do they notice? Do they care? Some do, I guess. Depends on the girl. I probably did. Yep, I'm sure I did.

Edward is pacing from kitchen and coffeepot to front porch and back again, smoking. He checks his watch, checks it again. He walks down to the driveway. Gravel crunches underfoot; the air is cold and there's a pungency, a bite, that suggests the day will be clear when it breaks. He starts the car so the engine will be good and warm, pulls the hand brake too hard because he's got more energy than he can gracefully expend, gets out and opens the trunk to make sure it's empty, none of Sylvia's redecorating stuff left behind, so there'll be plenty of room for Maura's suitcases or trunk. Which will she have, he wonders, suitcases or a trunk? He hopes that Bell has seen to it that Maura is properly outfitted for the trip and wishes he'd thought to send along specific instructions to that effect, fifty dollars and specific instructions, he should have sent. A milk truck passes and something about the slumpy look of it makes Edward envision a porter carrying a couple of beat-up suitcases. (Bell would know she'd never see the ones she sent again and so would be unlikely to offer up her best. Maura would get what Bell was willing to part with.) Edward imagines Sylvia taking note, Sylvia frowning, then chastises himself for being superficial, thinks he ought not to be worrying about the quality and condition of luggage on a day like today.

Edward appears to have lost sight entirely of the fact that until very recently he was dead set against Maura's coming. This morning, nervous, eager, dressed way before time, he might be mistaken for one of those noble immigrants who come over alone and work tirelessly and live spartanly and save assiduously until they have money enough finally, oh happy day, to bring over loved ones left behind. In fact, Edward has all but mistaken himself for that sort of immigrant. Edward is under the impression, more or less, that it had been his intention all along to bring Maura over once he got settled. A broad and open-ended phrase, that one, once he got settled, the sort of phrase Edward could work with. And working he was. And working he had been. An argument could be made, an argument had been made, on a foggy plane, in a flinching and squirming dimension, that Edward had been about the business of getting settled right along, sure he had. All notions of exile, of grudges and nihilism had been . . . forgotten. They were of no use to Edward anymore, so he forgot them. Now that he's settled he's sent for Maura as he had every intention of doing sooner or later, he hadn't had a specific time frame in mind, true, but certainly he'd known the day would come when he'd be reunited with his daughter and it had. It has. The day has come, the day is here.

Edward is not acting this morning. He is not putting on a show. The version of himself he is now aligned with, the identity he has opted for, the Edward he now understands himself to be—I couldn't very well leave her over there forever, she's my daughter, she belongs with me (no mention of nuns or orphanages now, all that gone in the general bluntening)—had been present in his consciousness right along. Elements of it had been anyway. (He'd had memories. Pangs. Constrictions of one kind and another. Clutches.) They'd merely been out of favor. Cultivate certain strains. Suppress others. The Edward not taken. The Edward not been.

Until now.

Now that he's settled he's sent for her. And there's a hunger in his blood this morning. He badly wants to see his child again. To collect her. To claim her. To bring her back to the house where he lives. Being Edward, being eminently adaptable, setting up shop wherever he finds himself, getting down to the business of being where he is, he feels, even, a degree of eagerness to show off his circumstances. Settled? Is he ever! Settled and how! Bounding up the porch steps, he hears Sadie's voice in his head. Sadie talking not to him but about him. Done all right for himself, Sadie says. Landed with his ass in a tub of butter, he has.

"You'll want to bundle up. It'll be cold on the dock. Windy as hell."

Sylvia nods, puts on her coat, reaches for her scarf, hat, and gloves.

It's just getting light as Sylvia and Edward make their way out of Paterson. The earliness of the hour heightens the sense of occasion, of portent. No ordinary outing commences at dawn. They are up and fully dressed, up and out and driving in the first light. They don't speak. They are wide awake.

Before long they come to Edward's traffic circle, which lies halfway between Paterson and New York. Edward and Sylvia enter, lean right and then left, at once resisting and giving over to the gravitational pull. There's just one other car going round and at some distance, too, so the way through is easy, smooth and graceful, nearly balletic. Sylvia thinks she ought to say something, compliment Edward on the success of his design, but she is tongue-tied. Talking would require considerable effort. She'd have to get up and over the hump of her nervousness. She puts a gloved hand on the back of Edward's neck and says nothing.

Going over the George Washington Bridge, Edward points in the direction the liner will come. "This way, through the Narrows and in." The sun is up now. The Hudson is wide and gleaming.

In the vicinity of the pier, Edward loses his bearings. It's an aggressively ugly district, especially at daybreak, meat-packing plants and warehouses, cobbled streets devoid of charm. It occurs to Edward that he's always been on foot here, that he's never had to concern himself with parking a car—that, in fact, he's never met an incoming ship, has always been the one coming in or going out. Losing his way unnerves him, shames him, because he wants to be in charge today, wants to be Sylvia's guide to the waterfront. She may be more familiar with every other neighborhood in Manhattan, with Paterson, with all of America for that matter, but this, the docks, the farthest reaches of the West Side, this is Edward's turf, or it should be. He makes up his mind to head straight back to the waterfront, get within view and earshot of the river, before he drifts any farther east. He'll locate Pier 86—A sign, please God, a nice clear sign, too much to ask?—and then concern himself only with finding a place to park.

There is, it turns out, a parking lot intended especially for people dropping off or picking up passengers. Edward comes on it just as he is beginning to detect Sylvia's doubt, Sylvia's distrust of his navigational skills, and he's grateful, leaning back in his seat, taking one hand off the wheel, eased, confident, as if he knew exactly where he was going all along. He parks and gets a ticket from the attendant and is in charge again. He offers Sylvia his arm and she takes it.

The terminal is enormous, a cavern, damp and drafty, dimly lit. There are rows of metal benches on which a hundred or so people sit and shiver. The floor is dirty, cigarette butts and squashed paper cups, sheets of newspaper blowing. The whole production seems intent on reminding visitors that the waterfront is first and foremost a place of business, a worksite. Passengers and those coming to see them off or meet them will know that though their reasons for coming may be lighthearted, a vacation, a trip abroad, or heart-wrenching or warming, a reunion, a farewell, the waterfront is about engines and cargo and oil, longshoremen, handtrucks, dollies, wooden packing crates. Bring your flowers, your ridiculous fruit baskets, your champagne, what have you. But for God's sake stay out of the way of the work and the men who are doing it. Watch where you sit. Not there. You can't sit *there*. Heads up, be-hind, coming through.

Edward is glad for the meanness of the place, the grit and the grey. He hopes that Sylvia is appalled or at least sobered. He has some sense, a vague hope, that she's seeing how hard his life has been. The terminal and environs seem a manifestation of the many hardships he's suffered. He feels the need of understanding, of forgiveness. Two years nearly since he's set eyes on the small girl they're about to have in their midst. Not a figment any longer, not a child in conversation or declarations or letters anymore, but a child in fact, a child in flesh, a living, breathing girl with blinking eyes and suitcases who will, he

fears, reactivate Sylvia's disapproval, disappointment, her inclination to accuse, lay blame. Two years, a long time to be
sure, but she was well cared for ... with family and all. Look
around. Doesn't all this argue against too harsh judgments? Look
around you and see how it was.

Sylvia, for her part, is thinking only that the terminal seems
an unfortunate setting for what's about to take place, father and
daughter reunion, her own first glimpse of Maura, the girl she
will raise, will help raise, from eight to eighteen or thereabouts,
the girl she will take care of however the girl will let herself be
taken care of—I can be patient longer than you can be sullen,
Sylvia thinks. Her first look at Maura to happen here? Then,
crossing her arms against the cold and damp, she decides that
this setting may be absolutely appropriate for what is about to
begin, keep everybody's feet, especially hers, on the ground, remind them all, not let them forget should they be tempted to,
that the way forward from here, from this piece of ground, this
particular plot of damp cement, from the moment that's almost
upon them, is unlikely to be clear and straight and easy. (Suppose my mother had died and my father remarried?) There will
be rough patches, adjustments by the dozens, missteps, mistakes the nature of which cannot be anticipated. She thinks of
the room she's prepared, of the big, round borderless mirror and
the set of jacks in the leather pouch and the hothouse daisies.

And they wait.

Straining to understand staticky announcements over the
loudspeaker. Asking other outsiders, other civilians, how long
they've been waiting, if they've got any new information about
when the ship's due. At one point, fed up, Edward goes off to
find out how much longer and comes back looking sheepish so
that Sylvia knows he's been spoken to sharply, embarrassed.

"She'll put in in another half hour or so, they say."

His use of the seamen's term, put in, is, Sylvia knows, his response to having been barked at, his attempt to regain his dignity, his authority, and she understands that he's terrified and
wishes she knew how to tell him that whatever happens now,
whoever this child is they've come to meet, to collect, whatever
the atmosphere generated among them, she will not turn against

him. What she required of him he's done, he's here. Whatever happens now, however things go, they'll get through, they'll manage.

They hear a ship's whistle, a bellow. "Here she comes," half a dozen people say, getting to their feet. "Here she comes." Everybody spills out of the terminal and onto the dock. And there she is, moving slowly toward them, stately, mammoth, white. There are hundreds of people on deck waving. A little girl could get lost, Edward thinks, a little girl could get trampled so easily in the crush and the noise.

Here she comes.

With the help of three tugs, the liner edges her way to the dock. Men shout commands and warnings, easy, easy, ea-sy! Longshoremen suck their teeth and spit. Finally, finally the ship is in, the anchor dropped.

A wide gangplank is lowered, an awning set rapidly in place. The way is cleared for the first-class passengers and out they come in fur coats and long gloves and, good lord, Sylvia thinks, top hats. No sooner are they on solid ground than they are whisked away by limousines and private cars and taxis. Second class now, businessmen and families, groups of women.

Sylvia searches for little girls and spots several but none is alone. Every girl who walks over the arch is clearly part of a family, every girl belongs to a cluster of children and adults. So many little girls and none of them unattached, none alone. And then, a jolt—*Is that her?*—a ways off yet but coming on, a girl— *Eight? Is that what eight looks like?*—holding the hand of a steward in a dress uniform. Reluctantly, it seems to Sylvia. Sylvia sees prudence in the rigid curve of the girl's arm, awkwardness, circumspection. A girl holding the hand of a near stranger who's been given temporary authority and who boorishly assumes a child will happily hold the hand of any adult. Brown hat and coat, tan leggings, an unmistakably Irish face, unsmiling, blank the way children's faces go in the midst of adult hubbub, a sweet little face, Sylvia thinks, and her composure begins to slip, a face that resembles Edward's. Sylvia waits for a mother or father or sibling to appear and disqualify this candidate. None does. It's her. It's got to be her.

"I think I see— Is that her over there?"

"Maura!" Edward shouts, and then again, louder, *"Maura!"*

Maura flinches and turns in Edward's direction. Her eyes dart from one face in the crowd to another.

Edward is waiting to be recognized. Edward is beaming.

Sylvia steps back to give father and daughter a degree of privacy. Wait, she tells herself. Wait and watch. This you have to see. This you'll want to remember in all its particulars.

And then the blankness reasserts itself in Maura's face. She thinks she's made a mistake, thinks she didn't hear what she thought she heard. She's embarrassed, rattled. She stares straight ahead and begins to formulate a plan, what she'll do if he doesn't show, if it turns out he isn't here and isn't coming. She will get her suitcase, she will find a policeman.

"Maura! Maura!" Edward is yelling at the top of his lungs now. He's waving both hands in the air. "Oh, for God's sake, Maura, here!"

Maura scans the crowd and this time spots Edward. She grins, turns and says, "That's my father," to the steward who peers into the crowd, waves, gives a jaunty two-fingered salute, lets go of Maura's hand. Maura released, Maura free to go, is Maura suddenly reluctant. She knows well how to anticipate joyous reunions but hasn't a clue how to participate in one. Seeing Edward in the flesh and hearing him call her name, she's not able to trust the version of this moment she's imagined hundreds of times since Bell told her it was in the works. She doesn't know what's true now, what's real and what isn't. She doesn't know what's about to happen to her or what she can reasonably expect to happen in the coming hours, days, weeks. She wants, for a moment, to turn around and run back to the ship. She walks slowly and steadily toward Edward. What else can she do?

Look at her, he thinks watching her come. Look at her.

He cannot imagine how he's done without looking at her for so long. My baby, my little girl. He goes down on one knee to encourage, to reassure. He wishes she'd run to him. He'd go and scoop her up in his arms if she didn't look so frightened, if it wasn't so apparent that his scooping her up would scare the daylights out of her.

When she's close enough, when he can restrain himself no longer, he pulls her to him.

Maura allows herself to be hugged, hard, and hugs back after a second or two but only because she thinks she's obliged to return so ardent an embrace. The smell of her father's neck is intensely familiar and stirring, cigarette smoke, shaving soap, starched cotton. She inhales deeply, shudders, leans her weight against Edward but keeps her eyes open.

She spots Sylvia, then, over Edward's shoulder, Sylvia standing some ten or fifteen feet away, Sylvia wiping her eyes with a handkerchief.

Maura lifts her head like a deer or a rabbit. Who's that? Who's that lady?

Sylvia, smiling unsteadily, handkerchief balled hard in one hand, takes a tentative step in Maura's direction.

Maura's finely honed instincts tell her that the lady with the red hair matters. The lady with the red hair will have to be contended with, will figure significantly in what happens from here. The lady with the red hair has power.

Sylvia and Maura consider each other for a moment—Sylvia has never felt so thoroughly scrutinized—and then Maura squirms out of Edward's embrace.

Sylvia screws up her courage, takes another few steps toward Maura, leans in, and says the words she settled on, once and for all, finally, while she was putting new sheets on the new bed.

"Hello, Maura." Slowly. Softly. Distinctly. "And welcome. I'm so glad you're here."

Maura goes on staring, blinking in the bright morning sun. She says nothing.

Still kneeling, Edward brushes the hair off Maura's forehead, puts an arm around her. He quakes to feel how small she is. How impossibly narrow the span of her shoulders seems. What absolute, heartbreaking vulnerability is expressed there.

"What a big girl you are," he says, "to make the crossing all by yourself. What a big brave girl you are. It's a long way to come, a long time out on the big ocean, isn't it? You start to think you'll never see dry land again after a while, don't you? I always do, I know, but you, you managed beautifully. You were a big brave girl and you managed beautifully. Look at you."

Maura looks into her father's eyes briefly. "They had puzzles," she says. "And a puppet show. There was ice cream after dinner every night."

"Ice cream every night, was there? Well, there you are. What kind did you have? Strawberry, I'll bet. Strawberry's your favorite, I know. Strawberry ice cream every night after dinner. You had a grand time, I think, crossing all by yourself like a grown-up lady."

"Give me the keys and the ticket, Edward," Sylvia says gently but firmly. "I'll get the car and come back."

Edward hears the pedagogical note in Sylvia's voice and is glad for it. He knows he needs all the help he can get just now. He's grateful for whatever guidance is out there. And he trusts Sylvia wholeheartedly in this regard. If Sylvia thinks he and Maura should be alone for a few minutes . . . All the same the prospect of being alone with Maura terrifies him. He's been rattling on, he knows. He doesn't want to rattle on any more. He doesn't know how to stop, though. He doesn't know what to put in the place of the rattling on. He pulls keys and ticket from his trouser pocket, surrenders them.

He watches Sylvia go, then eyes the crush of people at the baggage claim and decides to wait until the crowd thins out before attempting to retrieve Maura's suitcase. Even in his panic he knows that negotiating the crowd and the harried baggage handlers with Maura now would be exactly the wrong thing to do. The connection between him and Maura is not sturdy enough yet—it barely exists, really, it's just a fog of good intentions and anxiety—to be subjected to the rigors of suitcase retrieval.

"Suppose we find a place to sit down," he says and his nervousness eases a bit. He takes Maura's hand—it is limp and damp, and it is impossibly small. Together they go off in search of a bench.

They sit side by side, silently watching the frenetic activity going on all around. They watch it dissipate. How quickly the crowd disperses. The diminution is apparent from one minute to the next. The spectacle has something of a clock ticking about it to Edward, something of a deadline fast approaching. For a brief moment he considers going after the suitcase, but he's certain that if he does, he'll have squandered an opportunity. If he moves off the bench now, an opportunity will be lost to him forever.

He puts his hand on the nape of Maura's neck and, with considerable trepidation, kisses the top of her head. Her hair smells loamy, as it always did, exactly as it always did. The dense and delicious smell of a little girl, authentic, subtle, complex, earthy.

"I ought not to have left you behind," Edward says.

Maura lowers her head, widens her eyes.

"For what it's worth I want you to know that I'm sorry about it. These last couple of years, Maura . . . I can't even imagine how hard they've been on you."

"It's okay."

"No, it's not. I'm your father. Your place was with me."

Edward closes his eyes and feels the tension drain from his body. He doesn't care how long it takes Sylvia to return with the car. There's no hurry now. He's happy to sit on a bench with his hand on the nape of his daughter's neck and the smell of the Hudson River in his nostrils. "Your place was with me," he says again. In the silence that follows Maura begins slowly, slowly, to nod her head.